THE SILENCE OF DECEIT
THE DECEIT TRILOGY

JILLIAN EAGAN

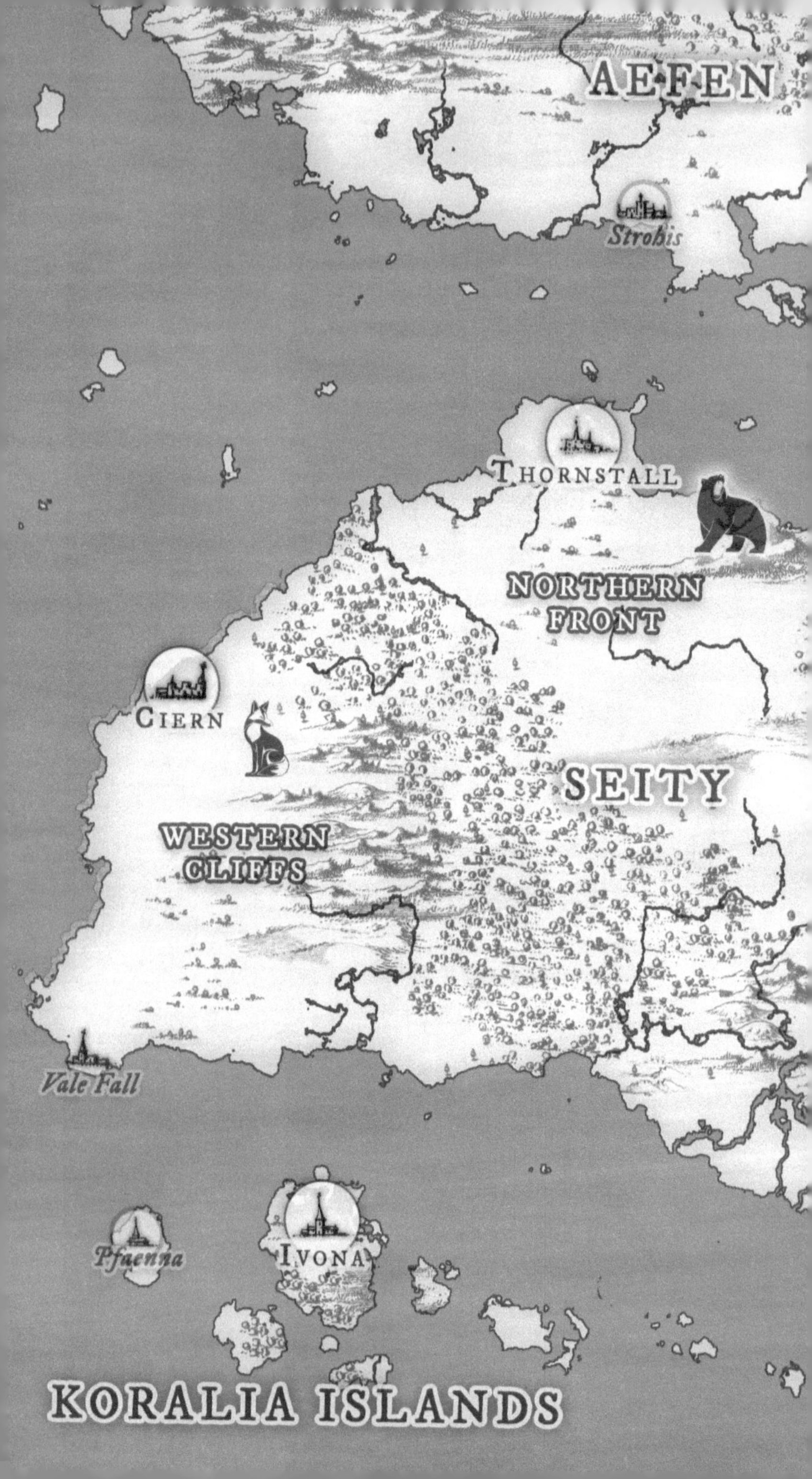

AEFEN
Strobis
THORNSTALL
NORTHERN FRONT
SEITY
CIERN
WESTERN CLIFFS
Vale Fall
Pfaenna
IVONA
KORALIA ISLANDS

Pagme
Karga
Eastern Hills
Avorae
Outer Territories
Saryir
Cross Row
Belris

PROLOGUE

"*Y*ou called for me, my lord?" Ever since Anselm could hold his head up, he made sure to bow in the presence of his father. After sixteen years, it had become an instinct.

Eldon stood at the window in the tallest tower of the manor. It had the best view of Cross Row's domain, but the stretch of land was never enough for him. "Who is the biggest threat to my rule?"

Anselm stopped at the center of the room, a sparsely furnished area he escaped to when he wanted to be alone. But it became cramped when someone else shared the space with him, especially Eldon. His father had always intimidated him, like any good ruler ought to.

"I'm not sure I understand," Anselm admitted, and concealed his trembling fingers behind his back.

"You are my heir; you should be able to answer such a question."

Anselm racked his brain for a suitable response. Independent nations were none of their concern. The Outer Territories were too fragmented and contained behind the mountains. Pirates were only a threat on the ocean, and their strength was limited.

All that was left was their homeland of Seity. As he thought about the lords in the north, west, and east, Anselm's mouth dried. Walls had isolated the families from one another, keeping them secure in the corners of Seity they ruled.

But the fragile peace that had held for hundreds of years was silently fraying.

Eldon didn't wait long for Anselm to respond. He turned and circled the tower's perimeter toward a map hanging on the wall across from the window. Cross Row was proudly labeled in gold, spanning across the southern coast. "A child is ruling the Western Cliffs, and the Northern Front is weaker than ever. Who does that leave?"

Anselm knew the answer to that one—the bane of his father's existence. "Taran Weller."

"His family's magic is a threat; our people fear it. Tell me, my dear boy." Eldon placed himself in front of Anselm and rested a hand on his shoulder. "Do you know of Taran's daughter and her powers?"

"Only rumors."

Eldon made a noise of acknowledgment. "Weller magic is volatile and ruled by strong emotion. My father always said it would be the ruination of order as we know it. However, if the Weller girl's magic can be contained, she might be the key."

Anselm was afraid to ask the question he already knew the answer to. But staying quiet would only anger his father. "The key to what?"

His father merely patted his shoulder and circumvented the issue. "Your brothers will never know what it means to be lord. You are blessed to rule Cross Row; it's in your blood. You are everything our ancestors desired for Seity's future. I vow that when you become lord, you'll hold power from the Western Cape to the Eastern Mountains. Consider it my gift to you."

A shiver racked Anselm, but he attempted to cover it with another bob of his head. "You have a plan, then? To target the Wellers?"

"Indeed, I do." Eldon started for the stairs but left his son with one more thought. "Once the Wellers are gone then who will stand in my way?" As he left, he passed by a gold flag bearing their family's crest.

Radille ent audrita

Swift and bold. Words Anselm's ancestors lived by. Words his father lived by. They were as destructive as they were concise.

A sliver of sun caught the window, the light rippling through the room like fire. Anselm's stomach dropped as he swallowed his father's plan.

Eldon did not speak without action behind his words; Anselm knew that for certain. Which only meant one thing: War was inevitable. Seity would burn.

CHAPTER 1- THE LADY

If Rosalie Yorke hadn't been forced to leave her home, then she wouldn't have been stuck in the stagecoach. And if she wasn't stuck in the stagecoach, she wouldn't have pricked herself with the needle. But when the stagecoach's wheel dipped low, her hand twitched and the needle stabbed her index finger a second time.

"*Vellah.* Not again," she muttered and fumbled for the handkerchief already spotted with blood.

"Did you forget to pack a thimble?" Silence asked.

If Rosalie had to be in that stagecoach, then she was at least glad her best friend was with her.

She gave a half smile, half grimace as she applied pressure to the prick point. "I knew I forgot something." Rosalie looked over her shoulder at the luggage strapped to the coach. Their entire lives were packed up, a pitiful solace as they were transported miles away from the only home they'd known. Rosalie had wasted no space, stuffing clothing, perfumes, and books into trunks. But there was no thimble among the usual creature comforts she craved.

Rosalie let the handkerchief fall into her lap and picked

up the needle again, the only suitable weapon a noblewoman should hold.

"Want me to try?" Silence offered.

"No, I'll manage."

Replacing her family's crest on her shawl was a tedious one. Silence had always been handier with a needle, but Rosalie's stubbornness was unmatched.

Now that she was eighteen, Rosalie needed to be independent and live up to her title as Lady Yorke—the title she had held since birth.

Rosalie scrunched up her face with concentration and set about fighting the royal blue thread into submission. She could feel Silence's eyes on her, but Rosalie was not ready to admit defeat yet. The tangle of thread distracted her from the snarl of thoughts in her head.

Thoughts of the coach wheels spinning, taking her farther from Ciern. Thoughts of the war bearing down on them. Thoughts of her brothers on the front lines.

Silence reached over to steady Rosalie's hands as she yanked at the thread. "Careful, you'll pull the fabric."

Rosalie sighed and relinquished the needle. "It looks a mess. I don't understand; Edme taught us both. Why does your work always look so much cleaner?"

"Because you don't practice enough." Silence slipped the shawl from Rosalie's lap and set about fixing the mistakes.

Silence had been ten when her mother, Edme, was hired by the Yorkes to work in the kitchens. Until that point, Rosalie's only companions had been her older brothers. Growing up in the lord's manor was a lonely existence. That was why she had been so excited to cross paths with Silence.

Rosalie had escaped one of her nurses and wandered to the kitchens. There, she'd met a girl with hair in tight curls and a warm smile. Silence had always been gentle and compassionate even from a young age.

Her soft demeanor was something Rosalie had been unfamiliar with. She latched on to Silence, and the two were inseparable from that point on. Rosalie, two years behind, watched Silence gracefully grow into herself. She had inherited her patience for braiding her hair from Edme and her russet skin from her late father.

"Practicing is boring." Rosalie propped her chin up with her hand. She watched Silence's purposeful hands unravel her mess.

Silence chuckled. "Then you can't complain about not being perfect."

Rosalie puffed up her cheeks and blew out a long breath. Her shoulders hunched forward as she enjoyed Silence's company. Silence, who never corrected her posture or told her to be quiet.

Her father... well, that was a different story.

Rosalie shifted to open the window. She poked her head out to see her father riding on horseback alongside the military escorts.

He'd been out there for miles, even though Rosalie had voiced her concern about the matter. War never left anyone's mind; there were threats everywhere.

But Basil Yorke either didn't hear his daughter's concerns or intentionally ignored them. He *had* ignored her worries back in Ciern when he announced Rosalie would be moved to the southern coast. He said only two sentences to her.

"You'll be safer there. You may return when I have sorted out this mess."

Basil hadn't allowed Rosalie to say another word about the matter. But she was confused. The war in Seity was not a simple skirmish that would be finished in a week—the violence was entering its twentieth year.

Safe places were becoming rare in Seity. War had infiltrated all four corners of the country, seeping deep into the population like venom. Yet Rosalie believed with all her heart that her family's home in the Western Cliffs' capital was secure enough. The Ciern manor had stood for generations, ever since the Yorkes first laid claim in the west. Rosalie never imagined she would leave its walls.

But there was no arguing with Basil Yorke.

By the time Rosalie shut the window, Silence was making swift progress with the shawl. She reached forward to run her hands over the soft hem. The shade of blue was like a soothing balm—a connection to her family and her ancestors.

"I can hear your thoughts from over here," Silence murmured. "What's on your mind?"

"How long do you think we'll be gone?" Rosalie asked.

Silence's brow creased, but she kept her dark brown eyes fixed on the needle. "I'm not sure. I asked around the manor, but no one had a definitive answer."

A vacant feeling filled Rosalie's chest, and her heart thudded painfully.

"All that matters to me is that I'm with you." Silence tied off the thread and cut it with her teeth. She leaned forward to drape the shawl over Rosalie's shoulders. "I was worried you'd have to go alone."

Rosalie wrinkled her nose. "As if I'd leave without you."

Silence merely smiled. They both knew that Rosalie never raised a fuss with her father. It was lucky they were allowed to remain friends in the first place. All those years ago, Basil had attempted to keep the two apart. He said he would rather Rosalie be friendless than have a friend below her station. As a headstrong little girl, Rosalie hadn't agreed and continued to follow Silence around like a shadow. Eventually, Basil had given up on keeping his daughter away from the girl with the curious name. It was so long ago that Rosalie wasn't sure why he had changed his mind.

She swallowed and straightened the shawl. Her fingers ran across the crest covering her heart. It was just how her mother once wore it.

"They might regret it," Silence said with an indifferent shrug. A glint of mischief crossed her face.

"Oh?"

"Without much supervision, there are a lot of rules we could break."

The dread building in Rosalie's stomach lessened. As much as she feared being away from home, she enjoyed getting into trouble with Silence. Over the years, several of Rosalie's nurses and tutors had resigned because of their antics. The girls were careful never to attract the attention of Lord Yorke, though. If Basil caught wind of their hijinks, the fun would end.

But now he would be far away in Ciern.

Rosalie grinned. "We could get away with sliding down the banister."

"Unlike last time."

She burst into laughter at the memory of when she was twelve and got it into her head that sliding down the stair banister was a good idea. It had ended with Rosalie and Silence landing none too gracefully at the bottom of the stairs, right at the feet of Basil's most sour-faced advisor.

"The look on Pierrick's face."

Silence snorted. "He looked like a wet cat."

"When *doesn't* he look like a wet cat?"

They laughed, but when the coach began to slow, their mirth was cut short. They went quiet as the door swung open.

Basil Yorke stepped inside and sat next to Rosalie. Without a word to her or Silence, he picked up some papers he had left on the seat.

The hush lasted, and neither Rosalie nor Silence dared

speak in his presence. As lord, Basil was the highest power in the Western Cliffs. He commanded unwavering respect from everyone, especially his children.

Rosalie once heard that the only person who had ever made Basil smile was his wife. Since her death eighteen years earlier, he'd maintained a stern expression. His hair was starting to gray, and disappointment was etched into his cobalt eyes.

Rosalie loved him dearly.

"Father," she spoke up tentatively, "I brought some books along with me. I thought I could read more about our history." Her voice faltered when Basil didn't even look up at her. Despite his indifference, she pressed on. "I figured I could be of more use regarding the war if I understood it better."

"How would you be of use in war?" he asked.

Rosalie looked at Silence, but her friend was just as timid around Basil as everyone else was. "I just thought it would be a good time to start assuming more responsibilities."

"You're in no condition to take on any responsibilities."

"I haven't had a fit in three months," Rosalie said. There were many consequences to her illness. She had suffered the condition since birth, but the pain and treatment from others never got easier. "I thought it was a good sign—"

"Rosalie, I've had it with your insolence," Basil interrupted with a sharp look over the papers. "All you must do in this life is listen and obey. It's simple, and you should be grateful you don't carry the burdens your brothers and I do."

Sheepishly, Rosalie bowed her head. Her eyes found the bag resting by her feet. One of the books poked out as if jeering at her. Her bookmark was already resting among the pages filled with Seity's complicated trade relations. Whenever she read the boring paragraphs, she imagined herself impressing her father with her newfound knowledge.

Basil let out a frustrated sigh as he flicked through

another pile of papers. "I don't know why you have to question every little thing I say." Although his eyes weren't on his daughter, he kept speaking. "Rosalie, understand that this is your place in life. You are not meant to have power over anything. You must live with the circumstances you were born into."

Rosalie knew when a conversation with her father was over, so she dropped the subject to spare herself further embarrassment. Across the way, Silence snuck her a sympathetic look.

Rosalie turned her head to meet her reflection in the window. A fragile girl peered back at her. A girl who yearned to be strong. An ill girl with hair the color of ash and a gaunt face. There was no sight of the fire burning inside her.

Beyond her reflection, the road turned, and the rocky coastline came into view.

* * *

VALE FALL SAT on top of a hill overlooking the ocean. Everything was gray—the gravel pathways, the stone manor, the waves on the horizon. Even the grass looked sickly. The estate had been named after the eldest daughter of the founding Yorkes. It had been in the family for decades, serving as a summer getaway.

In the early weeks of spring, it looked desolate. The estate was a sprawling mass with enough room for the Yorke family and their staff. It looked weary sitting on the parched lawns. The old structure had been neglected for years; all the money used to maintain the property had been funneled into the war efforts.

Once the violence began, the Yorkes had stopped visiting Vale Fall. So, it was Rosalie's first time seeing it.

Rosalie and Silence stepped out of the stagecoach after

Basil. They stayed close to each other as they surveyed their new temporary home. Neither of them had seen much outside the manor, let alone so far outside Ciern.

Something strange stuck out to Rosalie. "Father, are there no guards?" She'd grown up in a tightly secure world and was accustomed to stone-faced men guarding every entrance.

"What did I just say about questioning me?" Basil's long strides kept him ahead of the girls.

"I'm sorry, I just wanted to make sure we are safe here," she explained. "Being so close to the water, aren't we susceptible to pirate attacks?"

"Pirates?" Basil echoed as they neared the front doors.

"Emery said…"

The lord sighed heavily. "Your brother was telling tales. You're perfectly safe here; I've told you that countless times. There will be men on guard, they're just not from our military."

She looked to Silence, who shrugged.

"Who are they?" Though it risked further irritating him, Rosalie was curious.

"It doesn't matter. Just don't bother them; they're not here to keep you company."

When they stopped at the large double doors, Rosalie could tell her father didn't want to go inside. "Thank you for bringing us," she said, not wanting to say goodbye. She tilted toward him, wondering if he might grant her a hug before he left.

"Don't slouch, Rosalie. Just because you're not at home doesn't mean you can tarnish the Yorke name." Basil held himself tall over her.

Her heart felt like it had been pierced as she straightened her spine. "Sorry, Father."

Tender goodbyes were not Basil's specialty. Yet, Rosalie

could recall he'd been misty-eyed when her brothers left to fight in the war. But she wasn't going to war—she was fleeing it.

Basil gave her a lingering look but returned to the stagecoach without another word. Rosalie watched until Silence put a hand on her shoulder and turned her attention away.

One of the soldier escorts hustled over with his arms full of the girls' luggage. "Can I bring these upstairs for you, my lady?" He was even younger than Rosalie. Any boy over fifteen was recruited for military service in the Western Cliffs to fill the constant need for manpower.

"Yes, thank you." Rosalie and Silence followed him inside. Posted near the doors stood two men. They didn't wear her family's color or crest, but they were armed with long rifles and unforgiving glares. She didn't relax until she scurried past them.

The young soldier didn't lag for a second even as the luggage banged against his legs and made his arms tremble with strain. He appeared eager to please a member of the Yorke family, like most Westerners were.

"Excuse me," Rosalie spoke up. "Would you happen to know where these guards are from?"

"They're mercenaries, Lady Yorke, from outside Seity. My superior assured me that they won't bother you."

Rosalie frowned. Strangers were not warmly welcomed in the Western Cliffs. Two decades of war had made the people paranoid. Rosalie's brothers had always urged her to only trust their own people.

"That seems strange, doesn't it?" Rosalie asked in a quieter voice.

"Maybe there aren't enough soldiers to spare," Silence posited.

By Basil's instruction, no one was to discuss the war with Rosalie. It was like she was kept in a soundproof glass dome.

Silence bent the rules, however, and had confided in Rosalie about what she'd overheard. It provided a thin thread of insight into the struggle Rosalie's brothers were caught in the middle of.

"Maybe."

They passed through the foyer. A large tapestry hung on the right wall. The colors were faded, no longer the royal blue hue that the Yorkes were so proud of. Still, the design was highly intricate, depicting the family's crest—an orange fox posed beneath two dueling swords. The same one she wore over her heart.

Their motto was carefully woven at the top.

Devoanst iv nen Svel

Devotion above all else.

They were familiar words, but for the first time, they offered no comfort as she climbed the stairs. The soldier led them to the bedroom, setting down the luggage and leaving with a customary bow of the head toward Rosalie.

Silence skirted around the mountain of luggage to open the door. Inside was a chamber with two beds, solid furniture made of dark wood, and an impressive fireplace. Touches of blue marked the room—one of the few consistencies between Vale Fall and the manor in Ciern.

"We're much closer to the ocean," Silence said, shedding her traveling cloak and going to stand by a large set of windows.

Rosalie went to join her, taking in the view of the coast. There was a small spit of beach, although it consisted of more stones than sand. Farther down the hill, to the right, was a set of docks. They paled in comparison to Ciern's bustling port—a place Rosalie had only seen from the manor windows.

"It would be nicer if it was warmer. Why couldn't my father have waited for the summer to send us?"

"Well—" Silence shrugged, "—I don't think war waits for good weather."

"Hmm." Rosalie watched the tide lap at the rocks. "I've heard it's always warm on the Koralia Islands. Maybe we could swim there."

Silence laughed and nudged her. "It's too far. Wouldn't you rather take a ship?"

"I think I'd get seasick on a ship." Rosalie turned away from the windows and circled the barren bedroom.

"So, we'll make the most of our time here, then," Silence concluded with more optimism than Rosalie had. "Did you happen to notice the stairs in the main foyer?" She cocked an eyebrow.

"I did. Pierrick be damned, we're going to slide down that banister before nightfall."

CHAPTER 2- THE CAPTAIN

Crowe clutched his side, letting out a frustrated hiss of pain. Once he was certain he and his crew were out of trouble, he collapsed onto the deck and let his head fall back with a thump. He didn't care if he was being dramatic—outrunning a Durane naval ship was stressful. Outrunning a Durane naval ship at the crack of dawn after falling over a carelessly placed net and nearly caving in his ribs? Well, that was just unfair.

"Are you alright, Captain?" Kennedy cast a long shadow over Crowe.

"M'fine, just trying to catch my breath." Crowe knew his crew had seen him trip and fall. The embarrassment had spurred him to lead a quick evasion rather than linger and make another blunder. Being such a young captain was a constant battle of trying to prove himself. "There's no sight of them, right?"

The quartermaster shook his head. "They stopped pursuing. They must've thought we were scared off."

With a grimace, Crowe banged his fist against the deck. "They didn't scare me off. I just don't have a death wish."

"It was a wise choice, Captain."

Intent to continue wallowing, Crowe threw an arm over his face. The ache in his side was worse because it wasn't a battle wound, it was an embarrassing slip. His ego would be bruised all day. "*Vellah*. Those bastards followed us from Cilisca, I know they did," Crowe growled.

"I saw them there too," Kennedy agreed. "I wonder why they came after us. We didn't raise our flag while we were there. I thought we kept a low profile."

Crowe gritted his teeth and sat up. "We did. Someone set them on us." Pushing through the pangs shooting down his side, he got to his feet. "And I'd bet a lot of money I know who did it. They thought I wouldn't notice their flag in port. But I saw them." He could never ignore that stupid flag with the stupid beaver stitched on it. Only one man would be cocky enough to fly such a moronic flag.

His quartermaster looked uneasy. Crowe had many enemies, but few drove him to such rage as Rydlan did. "But we agreed we were going to ignore him and his men, right?"

"My patience has run out." Crowe dismissed the concern. "I was gracious to leave it be. I was being the bigger man. But if Rydlan wants to play games with me, so be it." He was tired of that swindler thinking he controlled the ocean. He had pushed Crowe around one too many times.

Kennedy knew as well as anyone on the crew that it was hard to talk Crowe down from a plan. Especially if it was a plan involving retribution. "Well, while we were in Cilisca I heard a rumor that a ship of raiders was headed to the Western Cliffs. The southernmost tip—it would be an easy place to blindside them. If they're going where I think they are, there's a cove that's easy to trap ships in."

The good news almost mended Crowe's ribs. "That's an excellent idea, Kennedy." He grasped onto the promise of revenge and would keep a tight-knuckled hold of it until the score was settled. He didn't believe in the old adage of an eye for an eye. If he was hit, he would hit back harder. He had narrowly avoided trouble with the warship, but when he came across the raiders, they wouldn't be so lucky.

"Set a course for Seity," Crowe commanded.

"Aye, Captain."

Now it was time to save face. Crowe crouched down to pick up the nets he'd tripped over. "Whoever left out these nets, you're scraping the hull until nightfall!"

CHAPTER 3- THE LADY

It took some cajoling, but eventually Rosalie convinced Silence to brave the chilly gusts and take a walk on the beach. They made their way down the steep hill, huddling close to each other to bear the strong winds.

Tall seagrass guarded the beach, where dark, cold waves met the stone-riddled sand. Close to the water, the air felt different. There was a heaviness to it, carrying salt across the coastline.

Although Ciern was on the coast of the Western Cliffs, Rosalie had never touched the ocean before. She hadn't been close enough to see the white-capped waves stirring and feel the spray on her face. The ocean didn't feel angry, even as it thrashed about with a roaring surf. No, it was demanding attention.

"I feel dizzy looking at it," Silence said in awe. "It's hard to imagine how big the world is."

Rosalie scanned the horizon in disbelief. Seeing the world stretch on for miles and miles made her want to shrink into herself. Her father had warned her how unprepared she was to face the outside world. She trusted him to know what she was capable of.

To her left, Silence reached down to take off her boots.

"What are you doing?"

"We didn't come all this way to stare. Don't you want to feel how cold it is?"

Never one to pass up a challenge, Rosalie fumbled with her laces. Her bare feet sank into the cold sand as she hurried to meet Silence at the edge of the water. She grabbed her hand, and together they waded a few steps.

They shrieked as the ice-cold water washed over them. Rosalie's feet became so numb that she couldn't feel the stones digging into her skin.

Silence jumped back, pulling Rosalie with her. "What a terrible idea!" she said, laughing. "I didn't think water could *be* that cold."

They made a beeline for their boots. "I suppose we're not swimming to the Koralia Islands."

Silence plopped onto the sand and tugged on her stockings. "Definitely not."

Rosalie sat close to her friend and felt warmth return to her toes. She pressed her hands between her knees to ward off the chill. "Emerson said my mother loved the beach."

Another gust of wind tried to sweep Rosalie up in its arms. Down the shoreline, she imagined her mother walking toward them. She could only visualize the portrait of Emelia Yorke hanging in Basil's study. Her willowy frame, blond hair, and enchanting green eyes conveyed sadness. Emerson said the artist had made a grave mistake: their mother was much livelier in person. Someone beloved by her people and adored by her husband.

Silence bumped her shoulder against Rosalie's. Until the two met, Rosalie had felt like the only person in the world who hadn't been blessed to meet Emelia. Everyone had a story about her, and their eyes would shine with happiness and grief as they recounted the late lady's presence.

But Silence hadn't met her either. The two of them could only watch as everyone in the Western Cliffs kept an eighteen-year mournful vigil.

The grief dredged up Rosalie's stubborn fear. "I think it's a bad idea we're here."

"My mother said it would be safer here. Your father knows what he's doing."

Rosalie leaned forward and touched her chin to her knees. "I'm being kept away from Ciern. When Emerson becomes lord, I want to support him. I can't do that if I don't know how anything works! I'll be useless."

A schism between Rosalie and her brothers had formed when they left for battle. But at one time, it had just been the four of them. Emerson and Emery accepted Silence as a second sister. The three youngest were rambunctious, and as a future ruler, Emerson did his best to keep them in line. But he couldn't help but join in when Emery spun stories about savage ten-foot monsters that roamed the Eastern Mountains and bloodthirsty pirates who prowled the coasts for maidens and gold.

Rosalie would give anything to go back to the idyllic bubble they once lived in.

"You're not useless," Silence chided as she helped Rosalie to her feet. "You'll find your way; it just might take time. I wish you weren't so hard on yourself."

It was a nice sentiment, but Rosalie knew no other way to be. She strove to reach great heights if it meant finally impressing her father. If only he gave her a chance.

* * *

THE NEXT MORNING, storm clouds rolled in and kept the girls inside. After breakfast, Silence returned to the bedroom to unpack her things.

Rosalie was hesitant to do the same. It was unsettling to wake up in an unfamiliar place when she was used to her routine in Ciern. So, she took to wandering the first floor of the estate to elude her worries.

She turned down a hallway lined with windows. Dark clouds loomed overhead, and heavy raindrops rattled the panes. She shuddered and pulled her shawl tighter around her body.

Emerson and Emery had described the estate as a magical place. They recounted sumptuous feasts on warm summer nights. Their parents sat side by side at the head of the table, surrounded by important dignitaries. Emerson reminisced how their mother could make even the most stern-faced military men laugh.

Now that Emelia was gone, the place felt empty.

At the end of the hall was a door left ajar. Tempted to explore, Rosalie passed the windows to peek past the door. The sight of bookshelves coaxed her inside. By the looks of it, Basil must have used the room as a study. It was similar to his office in Ciern, albeit smaller.

She crossed the dusty rug and let her gaze wander over the abandoned books. The titles aligned with the interests of a lord, tedious reports of terrain, and eye-blurring military diagrams.

A piece of paper jutting from the shelf caught her interest, and Rosalie tugged it free. After moving aside an oil lamp, she unfolded it over the desk. It was a map of Seity. Ciern was the most familiar dot, and she could trace the route they'd taken to Vale Fall on the southernmost tip of the Western Cliffs.

Although it was the farthest she'd traveled, it was merely

an inch on the map. Her finger ventured up to the Northern Front and its capital, Thornstall, where Jonas Gunn sat as lord. She crossed diagonally over the river that bisected the country. To the right of the delta was Belris, the capital of Cross Row. A den of traitors.

Her finger hesitated as she looked farther east. The map must have been made before the war because the Eastern Hills were marked independent. The capital city, Avorae, sat at the foot of the mountains.

She drew a circle around the place where the Wellers' line ended. Their bloody fate was a cautionary tale to noble-born children. No one was invincible. Not even the family who possessed magical abilities.

Rosalie would have liked to see the unique powers passed down through the Weller bloodline. But magic had died with them after the family was slaughtered by the Duranes.

She withdrew her hand and tugged her thoughts away from the war's onset. She folded the map but lingered around the desk. Her hand dropped to the drawers, and she wondered if her father had left anything behind that he might want returned.

However, each one was empty, and the top one was locked. She wriggled the drawer back and forth, but it remained steadfast.

A clap of thunder rattled her bones. Rosalie pulled her hand away as if she'd been burned by the gold handle. She held the hand to her chest and steadied her heart. "No more snooping," she whispered before hurrying out of the room.

* * *

ROSALIE STAYED ABSOLUTELY STILL under the blankets. She listened for Silence's soft breathing and the ticking of the clock. But neither sound comforted her.

Her fear of nighttime coincided with her fear of death. The dual phobias had held her in a stranglehold ever since she learned death was permanent. Doctors harped for years that night was the most dangerous time for Rosalie. Born with weak lungs and an even weaker heart, if she had a fit in her sleep she could suffocate.

The distress plagued Rosalie with incurable insomnia. As a child, she would sneak into Emerson's or Emery's room. It comforted her to have someone near; the thought of dying alone was too much for her young mind to bear.

After a bout of pneumonia that nearly killed her at sixteen, Rosalie could not sleep alone again. But her brothers were off to fight by then. So, Silence stepped in and slept in Rosalie's room to ease her anxieties. It helped Rosalie feel tethered to the living world, at least for another night.

The clock downstairs in the foyer chimed, and Rosalie counted the hours.

Midnight.

The rest of the day had been monotonous. She and Silence played chess, had tea, read, and ate dinner. The sun never broke through the clouds, so day blended seamlessly into night.

Silence retired to bed early, but Rosalie stayed awake. Sleep refused to come, too weak against her loud thoughts.

The locked drawer haunted her.

Unsure why, Rosalie couldn't shake the feeling that the drawer was hiding something. She just needed to see that it was empty, and she could put her ruminating—and maybe herself— to bed.

Moving as silently as she could, Rosalie donned her slippers and retrieved a box of matches off the mantel.

Vale Fall was eerily quiet as Rosalie reached the staircase. There were no guards doing their hourly rounds like in Ciern—no nearby city noise either. The loudest sounds were the ocean surf and her slippers padding across the stone floor. She retraced her steps down the hall, passing the pitch-black windows.

She groped her way through the dark, doing her best not to jump at every shadow. She located the lamp and lit a match. The flame wobbled from her trembling hands. There was a scant amount of oil left, but it would do.

"Father's not here," she whispered over and over as she tugged at the drawer. "He's miles away." The sturdy lock held firm against her. It spurred her stubbornness into action.

Rummaging around, she found a letter opener and wedged it through the narrow opening. Determination gave her the strength to jimmy the opener against the lock. The mechanisms popped and the drawer surrendered, clicking open.

Rosalie's chest tightened when she found it wasn't empty as she suspected.

A stack of letters, all correspondence from high-ranking military officers, filled the drawer. Rosalie rifled through them, unsure why Basil would leave them behind.

One weathered parchment was dated February 1840.

My lord,

We have intercepted messages from Eldon Durane to one of his generals. Our intel about Constance Weller was correct; she was kept alive up until recently. The letter detailed her death by poisoning. Also in the letter, Eldon expressed fear someone in his employ has escaped with a child. I have reason to believe that this child is of Weller descent. It may be that Constance had

a child we were unaware of. According to the
letter, they were smuggled out of Cross Row, but
their whereabouts are unknown. I have no leads
on who freed the child. Given the circumstances,
I can only speculate what power the child holds.
I will continue to search for more information.
  -Major General Vidal

Suddenly, the lamp burned out and left Rosalie in darkness. She stuffed the letter back into the drawer and forced it shut. With her heart racing, she staggered back and ran into something firm.

She clapped a hand over her mouth to muffle her shriek. Blood rushed through her ears, and she stayed frozen in place. She reached back to find she had merely run into the bookcase behind her.

The Wellers had all died at the same time. Their entire family was eradicated. That was the story. Those were the facts. No one ever said otherwise.

Yet doubt trickled in. Could there be a surviving Weller? Could it be they had escaped their family's grim fate at the hands of the Duranes? Or was it misguided hope?

Rosalie couldn't imagine what it would mean if a Weller had survived. Despite the confusion, one thing was clear—whoever this supposed child was—Eldon hadn't wanted them to escape.

CHAPTER 4- THE CAPTAIN

Crowe hummed an old tune from his homeland as his ship turned toward the mouth of the bay. Far ahead, across the wine-colored water, a large sloop was slinking toward the coastline. So, his patience *would* be rewarded.

He eyed his target through a scope, using the last dregs of sunset to survey the landscape. He had no fears or reservations, only a healthy appetite for payback. Turning back wasn't even a thought in his mind. The ocean was unforgiving to those who hesitated.

"What business do the raiders have here? I thought they were congregating around the Row these days," Kennedy wondered aloud. As quartermaster, he held the task of being the most rational aboard. When things appeared even marginally amiss, he noticed.

"I couldn't tell you."

Out of all the scum on the ocean, the raiders were the worst. Their leader, Rydlan, had tried to get him killed more than once. He thought the *Deceit*'s captain was an easy target given his age, but Crowe would show Rydlan how wrong he was.

He trained the scope on the land. There was no town in sight, only a large estate atop a hill. A few lanterns dotted the space. "Looks like a private home."

"Yes, my thoughts exactly," Kennedy said. "The area's not well-populated."

Crowe chewed on the odd information before lowering the scope. "I don't suppose it matters what they're here for. It only matters what *we're* here for. Come morning, they won't know what hit them."

Kennedy made a vague noise of agreement. "I think that's Kelan's ship; I recognize the figurehead."

"Even better." Crowe had experienced more than enough run-ins with the mouthy raider. He was going to target whichever raider ship he could find first. Now he could settle two scores at once.

"What if they aren't carrying much gold? You know Rydlan keeps the lion's share on his vessel."

Crowe looked up at the first stars blinking in the purple twilight. Sunrise couldn't come soon enough. "Revenge is always worth my time."

"And we're sure this isn't a trap?"

"Please, raiders can't even spell the word, let alone set one," the captain scoffed. "In and out, Kennedy, mark my words."

CHAPTER 5- THE LADY

osalie's fingers would not stop trembling. The knitting needles in her hand clicked incessantly against each other, absorbing her tremors. With each loop of the yarn, another question knocked against her brain and rattled her.

A missing Weller could change the trajectory of the war if they were found. Not only because of their birthright claim to the Eastern Hills but also because of their magic. Eldon Durane had attacked the Wellers because their magic was his biggest hurdle to conquering Seity. If magic still existed, it could be the greatest threat to Eldon's rule. And if Rosalie possessed all this information, didn't that make her useful?

She dropped another stitch and mumbled a curse under her breath. *"Vellah."*

Silence must've heard, because she stifled a laugh. "Rose, what are you making?" she asked when she peeked up from her work.

"Uh." Rosalie lifted what she had done so far. It was just rows and rows of uneven and dropped stitches. "I suppose it could be a blanket if you're not too concerned with being completely covered."

Silence shook her head in amusement. "Then it's a job well done."

The door to the parlor opened, and the mercenary entered. He did not bow his head to Rosalie, but he did speak her title—perhaps he hadn't bothered to learn her given name. "Lady Yorke, a ship has docked in the bay. The captain has requested your presence."

"Oh." Rosalie set her needles aside and stood. "Very well." It sounded more interesting than knitting. Besides, she took any opportunity to have a shred of Yorke family duty.

"What kind of ship?" Silence rose as well. Her nose was scrunched, a good tell that she sensed something strange.

"A merchant's ship. They have not yet said where they're traveling from," the mercenary answered.

"I thought incoming ships were being handled by your men," Silence said with suspicion lacing her voice.

"They asked for an audience with Lady Yorke," the mercenary replied, maintaining his stoic demeanor.

"Well." Rosalie smiled to quell Silence's concern. "The sun is shining. We shouldn't be cooped up inside all day." She linked arms with Silence and coaxed her to the door. "If you ask me, a little adventure to the docks will be fun."

* * *

From her bedroom in Ciern, Rosalie used to watch ships sail in and out of port. From so far, they looked like soap bars bobbing in a bathtub. But up close, they were sights to behold.

"Goodness," Silence said in disbelief as they descended the hill, "are merchant ships usually that big?"

"I'm not sure." Rosalie took in the massive vessel. Its off-white sails were rigged to masts that stretched to the sky. The hull needed a good cleaning, and the mermaid figurehead was missing a nose and a chunk of her hand. With the low wind, it was difficult to see what was stitched on the flag, but oddly enough Rosalie thought she could pick out a beaver's tail.

"I can't imagine what they want to speak to you about."

Rosalie couldn't come up with a guess either. No one had ever called upon her for any house business. It left her feeling unprepared. "I hope they won't think me rude if I don't know how to properly address a ship captain."

An ear-piercing explosion cracked across the landscape. The sound ricocheted through Rosalie, making her teeth chatter. Shouting filled the air as men dropped from the ship. In a blur, they stormed the shore, brandishing weapons. Their steel glinted in the sun.

Silence's hand clamped around Rosalie's wrist and yanked her back to the direction of the estate. But in her fear, Rosalie's muscles locked up and she fell forward. Her chest seized up and dark blobs crowded her vision.

Before Silence could help her to her feet, someone grabbed hold of Rosalie's waist. She screamed as a burlap sack was shoved over her head. Panic overwhelmed Rosalie and all she could think of was keeping her hand in Silence's. She fought to hold on as she was hauled off her feet, but Silence's fingers were slipping away.

"No!" she shrieked when her sweaty hand lost her grip. No, she couldn't go. She couldn't be separated from Silence.

"Let me go!" Rosalie thrashed against her captor. The burlap scratched her skin.

The man cursed when she landed a wild kick to his stomach. "Quit your fighting, girl!" he barked.

The world swung underneath Rosalie, and she couldn't tell which way was up. Finally, she was roughly deposited on the ground. The wood below her creaked as it swayed. A ship — she was on the ship, and there was no telling where Silence was.

Before she could think to run, her hands were bound together in front of her. The rope squeezed her wrists. Her body ached from being yanked around. Her throat was raw from screaming.

Was she going to die? Was Silence okay?

Footsteps approached, and the light shifted through the coarse material blinding her. The stench of sour ale and tobacco insulted her nostrils.

A low chuckled sounded in front of her. "Welcome aboard, Lady Yorke."

CHAPTER 6- THE CAPTAIN

When dawn broke, the ocean was calm and visibility was clear. It made a fine morning for revenge.

Crowe breathed in the salt air as he stood on the forecastle deck. "There's nothing better than this, is there, Upton?"

The bosun standing beside him chortled. "S'pose not, Cap'n. Setting traps for raiders never gets old."

"No, it does not."

A sharp and girlish scream echoed across the bay. Crowe frowned at the odd disruption and reached for his scope. The raider ship was moored at the docks, but a commotion stirred on land. Crowe couldn't make out the figures from so far away. "They must be carrying out a job for Rydlan," the captain mused.

Upton hobbled closer to the bowsprit. "I'll be honest, Cap'n, I think we should steer clear of Seity waters after this," he said. "S'been some strange rumors swirling 'bout. Think war's gotten to those people. Heard 'em saying all sorts of crazy things at port."

Crowe cocked an eyebrow. "Well, seeing as you believe in sirens, what you heard must've been outlandish. What were they talking about?"

The older man hunched his shoulders and shook his head. "Oh, Cap'n, I don't dare talk 'bout those things," he said in a low voice.

Upton's superstition was nothing new. However, most of the time it was lighthearted and just a good bit of fun.

"Well, I don't think anyone but me is listening," Crowe said, "so you might as well say it. I'm sure I'll hear it eventually."

After taking a nervous glance behind him, Upton pursed his lips. "Wellers, Cap'n. I've heard more talk 'bout the Wellers recently than I have in twenty years." His voice trembled with his spooked demeanor. "I don't like it, Cap'n. That name's cursed and something bad's gonna happen. We'd best be far away from this place when it does."

The name sent a chill down Crowe's spine. He hadn't heard anyone talk about the extinct family in a long time either. Some things were better left unsaid. Still, rumors would not deter him from his plan. He'd existed so long without interference from Seity's sordid past—and present.

Across the water, the raiders' ship set sail and headed right for them. Crowe shed his coat and rested a hand on the hilt of his saber. "Seity's already at war, Upton, I doubt things can get any worse there."

CHAPTER 7- THE LADY

When the bag was snatched away from her head, Rosalie flinched. She blinked a few times to adjust to the sunlight. She was sitting up against the mast of the mysterious ship with her hands bound in front of her. A crew of men stood around, each one looking more menacing than the last, with a profuse number of weapons strapped to them. Their arms were covered in tattoos and scars, marks of men who did not earn an honest living. This was not a merchant's vessel.

A wiry-looking man with cropped hair and sun-damaged skin knelt in front of Rosalie. With the wide berth everyone was giving him, he emanated authority. "You put up a bit of a fight there," he said with a smug grin. "For someone so weak, I didn't think you had it in you. Your friend went a bit more nicely. Seems she knows when she's beat."

She turned her head to see Silence sitting against the mast of the ship next to her. Her hands were also bound, and her brown eyes were wide with fear. For a moment, Rosalie was filled with relief. But a horrible thought struck her: Now they were both doomed.

"I'm sure you want to know what's going on," the man continued. "You'll learn in due time. If you're quiet and don't make a fuss, our trip will go a lot faster."

The pain in Rosalie's chest was so severe, she couldn't manage to talk. Helpless, she began to weep.

"Oh, Lady Yorke, no need for tears," he said, and stood. "I thought you Yorkes were supposed to be brave." He walked away with a snide chuckle. Then, he clapped his hands. "Oi! Get a move on. We're on a deadline! Lady Yorke has an important meeting to get to," he shouted to the crew.

"Are you hurt?" Silence whispered to her once the crew dispersed.

"No," Rosalie answered without thinking. Her pulse raced, and she could only feel the stabbing pain in her chest and the tears staining her cheeks. "What do we do? Who are these men?"

"I have no idea." Silence's quivering voice only made Rosalie feel worse. Her friend had always been a strong and patient person. If she was rattled, it meant they were in dire trouble.

Rosalie shied away from the leering glances of men passing by. The ominous threat of a meeting swirled around her head. "What could they want from us? Are they going to kill us?"

"We just have to stay calm. I'm sure we'll figure this out. Try to breathe."

They were out in the ocean on an unknown ship. Neither of them could swim, and even if they could, there was no telling how far from land they were.

"If they're after me, I could try to get you off the ship," Rosalie said in a hushed voice. It would ease her conscience to know she saved her friend. Rosalie wasn't long for this world, but Silence had a full life ahead of her. If one of them deserved to live, it was Silence. "Maybe they'll listen to me."

Silence closed her eyes, and her forehead creased with thought. "I don't know if it's a good idea to reason with them. It might make things worse. They don't seem like the rational type."

Rosalie craned her neck to look over the side of the ship, but she couldn't see how far they were from Seity. Before she could formulate any sort of plan, another explosion erupted across the water.

"Captain, off the port bow. It's the *Deceit!*" a voice high above them shouted.

The alert sent the crew into a frenzy. Orders were shouted and weapons were drawn. Below, Rosalie heard loud noises like metal shifting and heavy weights dropping.

The captain looked irate as he crossed the deck toward the girls. He made quick work of obscuring their vision again. When he was closer, he muttered what sounded like a prayer under his breath.

"See me through this. I ain't dying today. Not at the hands of that monster."

Rosalie tensed up. What sort of monster would *this* man be afraid of?

* * *

EVERY EXPLOSION and gunshot made Rosalie flinch. With her eyes covered, she wouldn't see any bullets aimed at her. All she could do was hold her breath and wait for stray ammunition to pierce her skin.

When the cannons fired, the entire ship shuddered, and the sound drowned out the men's riotous shouts. The ship they were so afraid of must've been closing in fast.

Then the sounds of explosions ceased. A heavy clunk on the deck made Rosalie's heart skip a beat. Maybe it was over?

Rosalie was yanked to her feet. By the familiar stench

wafting nearby, it was the ship's captain holding her by the arm. Something cold and metallic pressed against her temple.

"Not another step, Crowe!" the captain warned. "This is Rydlan's ransom, and he'd sooner see her dead than let you touch the reward money."

"A ransom, aye?" Someone with an unfamiliar accent spoke up. The deck creaked under footsteps. "I'm not here for any ransom. I'm here to settle a score."

Rosalie was stuck in the middle between two scoundrels, but she didn't know who to fear more. Her legs trembled and tears streamed down her cheeks.

"I had a close call with a Durane ship the other day, and I know Rydlan was behind it. So, I'm here to remind him why he better think twice before doing that again."

"You're getting real cocky, Crowe," the captain snarled. "Rydlan had to put you in your place."

"He and I had an understanding. I don't interfere with his dealings, and he doesn't interfere with mine," the stranger said. "But he crossed a line, and I won't tolerate it."

The hand around Rosalie's arm tightened, and her knees buckled from the pain. She wanted to shout for mercy but couldn't find her voice.

"Rydlan has no allegiance to you; his fleet outnumbers you by dozens," the captain said.

"Right, and he'll be down one more ship once I'm through with you."

Rosalie couldn't follow the conversation. Without warning, she'd been thrown into the dark underworld that encircled Seity. Her fate hung in the balance, mixed in with the bad blood between the men.

"Please," she gasped through her tears. "I just want to go home."

Neither man acknowledged her cries.

"Tell you what. I'll spare your life, Kelan." The man named Crowe spoke with a teasing lilt in his voice. "Once I take everything of value off this ship, I'll let you go. You can run back to Rydlan. Tell him that if he ever sics the Duranes on me again, I'll burn every ship in his fleet."

"Nice try. But I'm not surrendering to anyone, let alone a Territory rat like you."

A deadly quiet overtook the ship. Rosalie could feel the rage coming from the faceless voice. "Say that again, I dare you."

"I said I would never surrender to a Territory rat. I'd sooner—"

A gunshot rang out, and a bullet grazed past Rosalie. The hand holding her in place went slack before falling away. She screamed and pitched forward. Her body was so numb with shock she couldn't hold herself up.

Fortunately, or unfortunately, someone caught her and threw her over their shoulder. The deck erupted into chaos once more, but it quickly faded away as Rosalie was carried off into the blind oblivion.

"Silence! Where are you?" she cried.

She heard no response over the shouts.

CHAPTER 8- THE CAPTAIN

After both women were shut away in Crowe's personal quarters, he strode across the deck. The blond one's screams were still ringing in his ears. It was a worse noise than cannon fire, and now he had a headache growing. He wondered if it would be too much to ask for an hour of peace and quiet. But even as he entertained the idea, he knew it was a lot to ask for on the ocean.

Kennedy was waiting for him by the mast. The quarter-master looked like he was trying to conceal his nerves. He folded his hands together until his knuckles were strained from the tension, and his jaw was taut. "Captain, what are we going to do with women on board?"

"One fire at a time, please," Crowe muttered. He wasn't sure what he had anticipated finding on Kelan's ship, but he certainly hadn't expected two kidnapped women. It didn't disrupt his plan, but it sure complicated it.

"Captain," Kennedy implored. "Maybe you should reconsider getting involved in this. We don't know what's going on."

"If I can spoil one of Rydlan's jobs, then I'm happy," he

replied. "Now, if you would, I have unfinished business to attend to." He skirted around Kennedy and boarded the raider ship again.

Such battles were never too difficult, because raiders were brainless. In fact, Crowe would hesitate to call it a battle. Perhaps a better label would be target practice. Once their captain was maimed, they reacted as a headless chicken would. They were loud and jerked around but were easy to quash.

Kelan was still alive but the amount of blood pooling underneath him determined his time was short. He pressed a hand to the wound over his heart and spluttered out a wet cough.

Crowe approached, removing another loaded flintlock pistol from his belt. "I gave you a fair chance. You and I both know it didn't have to end this way."

"You've made a huge mistake." Kelan heaved out the words as if each syllable drove the bullet deeper.

"I've made a mistake? I'm not the one bleeding out."

"You have no idea what you're walking into."

The mystery was wearing thin for Crowe. He tilted his head to the side. "You gave up information about a ransom. So, don't you worry about me. Worry about Rydlan; he's next on my list."

Kelan let out a spiteful laugh between labored breaths. "You're a fool." A dribble of blood-coated saliva streaked down his chin. "The Yorke's ransom is nothing compared to the other one."

Recognition rang like a bell in Crowe's head. The Yorke? Had he disrupted a noble kidnapping? He tried to conceal his grimace. Just his luck. Kennedy needed to be right about everything, didn't he?

"Any other, more coherent, last words?" Crowe didn't

have time for the ramblings of a dying man. Everything he needed from Kelan, he'd already taken.

The raider's face was drained of color, but he gave Crowe a wicked smile. "May the Duranes grant you a more painful death than mine."

"I wouldn't hold your breath," Crowe responded, and put a bullet right between Kelan's eyes.

CHAPTER 9- THE LADY

Rosalie counted her breaths to make sure she was still alive. It was all she could be certain of. She didn't know where she was, who had taken her, or when she would be rescued.

If she ever would be saved.

She was terrified to move even though the burlap scratched her nose. After an agonizing wait in the darkness, Rosalie dared to speak. "Silence?" she whispered.

"I'm here," Silence replied with a gasp of relief. "I thought you had been shot!"

Some of the tension in Rosalie's muscles eased. Silence was alive, and they were still together. "I'm not convinced this isn't just a terrible nightmare."

"I hope we wake up soon, then."

The muted air around them was eerie. There was no breeze, but the floor below them rocked. Rosalie wondered if they were on a different ship, because she couldn't hear any violence nearby.

With no knowledge of what was going on, Rosalie didn't know the odds of escaping. The worst-case scenario loomed, and fear squeezed her around the torso. "Silence," she whispered. "If anything happens …"

The door swung open with a creak, interrupting Rosalie. The bag was tugged from her face, and she cowered away from the stranger in front of her.

"Thank you for not screaming again," said a familiar voice. "You nearly blew out my ears the first time."

So, this was the man Kelan called Crowe. His accent was unlike anything she had heard before. His skin was a deep olive tone and his hair a thick wave of black. He wore an eyepatch, but his uncovered eye was a stormy gray. Although he spoke with authority, he had an unmistakable youthfulness to his features.

Her eyes continued to adjust to the light, but she was grateful to see Silence sitting next to her in what looked like the cabin of the ship's captain.

"Are you here to rescue us?" Rosalie asked, trying to suss out what sort of ship they'd been swept away to.

"Rescue you?" He stepped back and cast aside the burlap bags. "I'm not in the business of rescuing people. Although, I suppose it's an act of grace that I got you away from those raiders. Few ships are as terrible as theirs. You can thank me now or later, whichever you please."

"Thank you?" An acidic taste formed in Rosalie's mouth at his brash attitude. She would've thought he would have some sympathy for the horrors they'd gone through. Some of the horrors *he'd* inflicted. "What was your reason for taking us?" She stood up, though her legs still felt like jelly.

Crowe eyed her before pointing to the chair behind her. "Sit."

Her teeth ground together as he spoke to her with such discourtesy. She made no attempt to move. "No, thank you. I'll stand."

He took a step toward her and rested a hand on the gun at his hip. "I wasn't asking."

"Rosalie," Silence whispered, urging her to comply.

She pursed her lips together, glaring at the man before slowly lowering back into the chair. Her blood boiled when he gave her a smug look.

"Wasn't that easy?" Crowe asked in a simpering tone.

Rosalie grabbed a handful of her skirts and squeezed. She decided it was in her best interest to keep her mouth shut even though she wanted to scream.

"I'd like to welcome you aboard the *Deceit*," he said. He spoke the ship's name like it was his firstborn child. "My name's Captain Crowe and I'm in charge of this vessel and crew. If you want to stay alive, you'll listen to every word I say."

Rosalie restrained her surprise. He looked barely older than she was. How was he the captain of anything?

Her eyes scanned the area for any clues as to what sort of mad crew would put this man in charge. A small sleeping area was built under a window, and the rest of the space was a study of sorts. The room was cozy, but the displayed wealth drew Rosalie's attention. Bits of gold winked at her from the impressive desk, but there were more subtle markers of luxury that she knew by sight. A handwoven rug sat beneath a solid carved desk. A wool coat dyed an expensive midnight blue with brass buttons was slung over a leather chair.

Then silver caught her eye. Knives, curved blades, and pistols.

"You're a pirate," she blurted. Bitter hilarity almost forced a laugh out of her. All her anxieties were not as unfounded as her father thought.

"Yes, Lady Yorke, this is a pirate ship. Is that a problem?" He tilted his chin down toward her.

Rosalie bristled under his gaze. "You know who I am?"

"A person is easy to identify by the family crest they wear." He gestured to her shawl as he leaned up against the desk.

"But you're not from Seity. How would you recognize the crest at all?"

Kelan had disparaged the Territories when confronting Crowe. Rosalie could only guess the captain was from the land on the other side of the Eastern Mountains.

"Your father's war has far-reaching consequences. The Outer Lands have no choice but to be familiar with your politics." His eyes narrowed slightly, and he gave her a bitter smile. "I bet that makes you feel special."

Rosalie sucked in an indignant breath. The raiders had shaken her to the core. Crowe was no less scary, but his cocky manner was blood-boiling.

"My father's war?" she snapped in disbelief. "My family is fighting hard against the Duranes to stop their campaign of terror. My family started nothing, so perhaps you're not as smart as you think."

"Rosalie," Silence hissed—perhaps to get her to stop goading a seafaring bandit.

The backhanded remark appeared to amuse Crowe rather than anger him. "Believe what you'd like. But this ship doesn't operate under Seity law."

Rosalie's fingers tightened around her skirts again. "What do you want from us?"

Crowe ran a hand through his dark, wavy hair. "The raiders didn't just stumble upon you. They were sent there for a reason. Seems Eldon Durane wants to use you as bait to dangle in front of your father."

Rosalie's red-hot anger froze into panic. She wouldn't put it past the Duranes to have her kidnapped. She was a piece of the Yorke dynasty and any piece that was removed weakened the family. If Eldon wanted to twist Basil's arm, then Rosalie was a good target.

She had to get home. She refused to be the reason her father surrendered.

"So." Rosalie let out a slow breath. "You plan to hand us over to the Duranes for money."

"Wouldn't dream of it, Lady Yorke," he replied. "The *Deceit* is loyal to one Seity family. Fortunately for you, it's not the Duranes. Unfortunately for you, it's not your family either."

Rosalie blinked. That left only one family. "What does Jonas Gunn have to do with pirates?" she asked. Although Rosalie had never met him personally, the Northern lord didn't seem like the type to ally with sea bandits.

Crowe clicked his tongue. "Wrong again."

Bewildered, Rosalie looked to Silence. But she didn't move a muscle; her eyes were staring off into space as if she'd gone into shock.

"The Wellers… You've pledged loyalty to a family that doesn't exist anymore?" Rosalie questioned. Even if a Weller child survived, there was no ruling family to pledge loyalty to. Besides, Crowe couldn't have been more than an infant when the Wellers were killed.

"What I do on my ship doesn't concern you."

"It *does* because I'm sitting on your ship!" Rosalie snapped. "If you have no plans to hand me over to the Duranes, then let us go."

Crowe's stare was unwavering. The quiet unnerved Rosalie, and she slunk low in her seat.

"I don't do anything for free, Lady Yorke." He spoke in a measured voice. "Your father will have to pay for your return."

Rosalie's jaw tightened. She didn't want her family to relinquish a single gold piece to this man. But she saw no other way out. "Very well," she said through clenched teeth. "Then you may let my friend go."

Crowe glanced at Silence as if he'd forgotten she was there. "Yes, the quiet one. I bet she wouldn't be so quiet if I let her go. She'd run right to your father, and then he'd send his naval fleet after my ship."

"That would be what you deserve," Rosalie snarled.

He let out an amused hum and pushed away from the desk. He directed his focus to Silence. "You look petrified. Did I scare you that bad?"

"No, I know your ship's name, that's all," she responded with her dark eyes fixed to the floor.

Rosalie paused and wondered how her friend knew the name of a pirate ship. Perhaps it had been some story Emery told them, one that Rosalie forgot.

"Do you?" Crowe looked both impressed and proud. It seemed he held his reputation only second to his beloved ship. "I thought for sure Seity had forgotten the name. You're all too busy killing each other; you haven't given us scoundrels enough to do. War is a noble's game; pirating is for rule breakers."

"At least you're honest with yourself," Rosalie spat, trying to draw his attention away from Silence. Although she was terrified, she had to play her cards right and get Silence off the ship. It was their only hope of survival.

The captain let out a low laugh. "Lady Yorke, I think you'll find that the men who pretend to be something they're not are the most dangerous. Believe me, nobles are just scoundrels in disguise." He tilted back against the desk's edge again. "Tell me, how does your father see himself? A savior of the people? A fair leader? A defender of the peace?"

"My father is a good man."

He only let out a brief exhale of amusement. "I'm sure you think so."

Rosalie seethed. How dare this man speak about things he knew nothing about? It was laughable to hear a pirate captain speak about morality. "If you let my friend go free, I will ensure you receive a fair sum."

Crowe didn't take the bait. He rubbed a hand over his chin as he glanced between them. "Tell me, how did you two meet? I didn't think ladies had friends, only underlings."

Silence lifted her gaze and said, "My friendship with Rosalie is none of your concern."

Before Crowe could respond, someone pounded at the door and shouted, "Captain!"

Crowe frowned and strode across the room. He snatched a cutlass resting by the door and left without another snarky remark.

Rosalie was just as quick to act. As soon as the door slammed shut, she was on her feet. Her mind whirred as she located a small blade on the captain's cluttered desk.

"What are you doing?" Silence asked in a hushed voice.

She didn't answer immediately, focusing first on cutting away Silence's restraints. Once she was free, Rosalie handed her the blade next. "I'm the one they want, right? They're trying to force my father's hand."

Silence took a moment to steady her shaking hands before sawing at the ropes around Rosalie's wrists. "I think this is more complicated than either of us know. It might be best to just stay quiet and hope we're rescued soon."

"No one knows we're out here." Rosalie rubbed at her sore wrists. "It might take days for my father to find out, and who knows where we'll be then? How can we trust that this pirate won't hand us over to the Duranes if they offer a high enough price?"

Urgency took control. They weren't that far from the coastline yet; Rosalie could still see the bay through the windows. But that could soon change with the wind. The farther they sailed into the open ocean, the less likely it was they would be found.

"There are smaller boats, right? In case the crew has to abandon ship?"

Silence blinked rapidly, maybe trying her best to keep up with Rosalie's reasoning. "I'm not entirely sure. I would assume." Then her eyes lit up. "Yes, actually, I saw one on the other ship. It was attached to the side."

Rosalie pursed her lips and gathered as much courage as she could. With a cushy life in the manor, her survival instinct had never had a reason to form. She could only hope sheer will would equip her to escape.

"We need to make a run for it while that poor excuse for a man is distracted."

"Are you sure?" Silence rubbed the rope marks on her wrist. "It sounds dangerous."

"No more dangerous than staying here." Rosalie went to the door and cracked it open. The deck outside was abuzz with activity. From where she stood, she couldn't see any small boats, but she did spot two sets of ropes lashed to the side of the ship.

"Rose ..." Silence whispered.

But Rosalie was already hiking up her skirts. She nudged the door open and ran faster than she ever had before. The world was a blur around her. Shadows of men passed by, but she didn't slow.

With her goal a pinpoint in her vision, she didn't see a hand reach out. She was yanked back by her wrist. As if time had slowed, Rosalie watched a bullet zip past her face and embed itself in the mast.

Out of breath, she looked back to see Crowe's stern look. Just beyond him, Silence stood with her mouth open in frozen distress.

Another explosion rocked the ship, but Crowe didn't

flinch. He was too busy glaring at Rosalie. "Are you trying to get yourself killed?" he demanded.

She yanked her arm from his grip. "You want me dead anyway, so why do you care?" As strong as she tried to be, she was shaking. Her only plan had been thwarted. The vastness of the ocean made her dizzy, each wave taking her farther from home.

"You think I want you dead? You're worth more to me alive." He herded her toward Silence who still looked petrified.

In her periphery, Rosalie saw the raiders' ship quickly approaching. "They're coming back?"

Crowe rolled his eyes. "It's astounding how shrill you can be. You're going to start attracting whales." He didn't give her the chance to refute him. "Yes, they're coming back, and I suspect it's because of the high price on your head."

"I'm not a commodity."

"You're the most expensive thing on the ocean right now, Lady Yorke."

With the assurance that Crowe wanted her alive, Rosalie didn't hesitate to stand her ground. "I won't be sold to anyone. And I refuse to let you make money off my existence!"

Each passing second drilled more agitation into Crowe's expression. "How about a thank you for just saving your life? How about a thank you for stepping in when you were days away from being in the hands of the Duranes?"

"Yes, thank you, I'm *thrilled* to be on a pirate ship," she bit back.

Crowe stepped toward her. As tall as she tried to make herself, he still towered over her. "Pirates have codes, Lady Yorke. Raiders don't."

She tilted her chin up to glare at him. "I don't care. I've

had enough of men on ships. I just want you to take us home!"

He didn't jump into action at her order. Rosalie's cheeks flushed red under his glare.

"Tell me," Crowe said, "are you standing on my ship right now? Because you're mouthing off like you own this vessel and I assure you, you don't." He put both hands on her shoulders and moved her out of his way. "I don't have time to argue with a princess."

"I'm *not* a princess!"

"Call yourself whatever you like. But unless you want the next bullet to hit you, I suggest you go back inside," Crowe called over his shoulder.

Rosalie was shaking with anger as Silence corralled her back inside. She was barely cognizant of the door closing behind them.

"Rose?" Silence's voice echoed in her head.

Rosalie knew what was coming. After a sprint and a tirade, she had worked herself into a frenzy. An invisible dagger hit its mark, unlike the bullet she narrowly avoided. It drove into her heart and brought her to her knees. She hunched over and fought against the fit.

Her fists clenched over her head. Weak. She was so weak. She couldn't fight against her kidnappers, couldn't fight her way to freedom, and couldn't fight her own body.

"Breathe." Silence's voice broke through the ringing in Rosalie's ears.

Rosalie sucked in a breath just as a cannon fired.

CHAPTER 10- THE CAPTAIN

"Something's wrong. Raiders usually know when they're beaten," Crowe muttered to his quartermaster. He'd had brushes with the likes of Kelan before. Raiders were like vultures; they swooped in to feast on weaker ships and took flight when a stronger ship sailed in. The only nice thing he could say about raiders was they knew when to surrender.

So why weren't they backing down? Crowe had killed their captain, and anyone with common sense would know they stood no chance against the *Deceit*.

"If the Duranes contracted Rydlan to kidnap her, I'd suspect there is a good deal of gold involved," Kennedy guessed.

Since he became captain three years ago, Crowe had made it a point to avoid the mangled web of war. The *Deceit* had a history with Seity, but Crowe hesitated to carry that burden when he was still inexperienced. Nevertheless, things happened for a reason. Lady Yorke had been practically dropped into his hands, so he was going to make the best out of the situation. It had to be a sign he was ready to take on bigger foes.

"Well, I can spin this into a new deal with Lord Yorke." Despite the impending battle, he smiled. He was captain; he was allowed to gloat as their enemies advanced. "Imagine our luck. I came looking for revenge, and I'll leave with gold."

Kennedy made a less than confident noise. "Captain, you heard what Kelan said about another ransom, right?"

"For all we know he was trying to bait me into keeping him alive. I don't trust raiders, not even their last words are truthful."

"Understood," Kennedy said. "As requested, we removed any papers from the ship. I left them in your office."

"I'm sure we'll find correspondence with Rydlan in there. Maybe we'll find out how much the Duranes were willing to pay for the Yorke." Crowe grimaced. The leader of the raiders never failed to give him a headache. Rydlan's reckoning was long overdue. "Mark my words, before this year is done, I'm going to put a bullet through that man's head."

"I wouldn't blame you, Captain," the quartermaster concurred, clearly unbothered by the violent threat. "I've never understood his motives before, but lately his movements have been erratic."

They were within firing distance, so Crowe readied himself for round two. "He can do what he likes in Seity. Upton's right—that place is nothing but trouble—that's why we don't get involved."

"But…"

Crowe knew his hypocrisy was glaring, but good captains didn't second-guess themselves. Even if he had a gnawing feeling that he'd made a grave mistake. "Trust me, this will be worth the pain. But I've got a plan in place, so we don't even have to go near that war-torn country."

Kennedy nodded. "I trust your judgment, Captain. What are your orders?"

The foolish raiders were not turning away. He had let them live so that they would report back to Rydlan that the *Deceit* was out for blood. Oh well, Crowe would have to deliver the news himself.

"They've had their act of mercy. If they didn't want to take my gracious offer, that's fine. Sink their ship. We're not taking prisoners today."

After narrowly avoiding a full-blown fit, Rosalie remained curled up on the floor. She covered her ears to block out the battle raging outside. With every shaky breath, she hoped again it was all a nightmare. She would open her eyes to find they were at Vale Fall and the raiders and Crowe were nothing more than cruel figments of her imagination.

Silence sat next to her, her arm firmly wrapped around Rosalie's shoulders, her cheek was pressed close to Silence's thigh. They were stuck there with nowhere to run to and no one to call for.

Rosalie squeezed her eyes closed. Although she was trying to stay calm to avoid a fit, anger seeped through her. It was both terrifying and humiliating to be an object being bartered over.

To make things worse, Silence would suffer by no fault of her own. Rosalie would never have predicted their friendship would lead to trouble. Apart from the mischief they liked to cause every so often, their lives didn't have an impact on the world. Their routine was so simple. They always took care of each other, but now Rosalie's existence was harming Silence.

Rosalie's thoughts were so loud, she didn't realize the world had gone quiet until Silence shifted. Withdrawing her arm, Silence got to her feet. Rosalie lifted her head and watched her cautiously inch toward the window.

Silence made a small sound of shock and Rosalie hurried to her feet. Once at the window, she saw the raiders' ship sinking. The men she had been terrified of were reduced to rats, helplessly jumping ship and plunging into the ocean. Rosalie didn't count herself lucky to be on the *Deceit*, but at least she wasn't drowning alongside her kidnappers.

The two watched in horror; neither of them had ever seen such violence. Yet Rosalie didn't dare to look away. As she stared at the devastation Crowe had caused, she noticed the wreckage was getting smaller. As was Seity.

Rosalie's mouth felt tacky, and all hope fell flat at her feet. "Sie… are we ever going to get home?"

The brief quiet filled Rosalie with more dread. Not even Silence could comfort her as she said, "I don't know."

The odds weren't in their favor; Rosalie knew that. They'd been raised in the center of civility. Their hands were soft, and their instincts were not built for seafaring. It was a grim reality.

But in Rosalie's opinion, the worst part was the biggest obstacle between them and home. One insufferable pirate.

CHAPTER 12 - THE CAPTAIN

Crowe was a little hoarse from shouting orders, and his headache hadn't dissipated, but overall, he was pleased. With the threat neutralized, he could wrap his head around the *Deceit*'s new additions.

A shooting pain behind his eyes made him groan. He needed advice.

With a huff, Crowe walked across the deck toward Upton, who was whittling away at a hunk of driftwood. It was an impressive feat for someone with only one hand.

The bosun had been a pirate longer than anyone could even guess. He'd been a part of the *Deceit*'s crew ever since the ship's maiden voyage. She wasn't his first ship, but she must have been his favorite because he never abandoned her for another.

Upton was a good mentor, even if his only education was that of an old sailor who'd spent more years on the ocean than on land.

"I might've made a mistake," Crowe admitted in a low voice. He couldn't show doubt to his crew—not even Kennedy. But no one was more loyal than Upton.

"I'll say, 's bad luck having women on the ship, Cap'n. The faster we get those lasses off the ship, the better. We're tempting fate, lad." Upton often slipped in and out of addressing Crowe as a captain and as the lanky kid he once was.

Crowe sighed and pinched the bridge of his nose to quell the migraine. He decided to ignore Upton's long list of superstitions. "This isn't something I can do quickly. If I slip up, I'll have a naval ship on my tail." He dropped his hand from his face. "I thought I knew what I was doing. I should've left them with the raiders."

Upton snorted. "You hear yourself? You wouldn't have left them with those bastards even if you had a gun to your head. You're too much like Braxton. Got soft hearts. Hearts soaked in seawater, but still soft."

Crowe absorbed the compliment. Everything he did was to make their old captain proud, even if he was gone. "Is that why he pledged loyalty to the Wellers? A soft heart?"

"He always cared for the innocents." Upton shrugged and continued shaving off pieces of wood with a blade cleverly fixed to his thumb like an extension of the finger. "Collected you lot like a buncha stray pups."

It was true—Braxton maintained a crew of refugees, runaways, and lost souls. The *Deceit* was a haven for those who didn't fit on land. But he didn't stop at the ocean; he'd risked everything to save as many Easterners as he could when the Duranes attacked. Crowe wasn't yet alive then, but he'd heard the story enough times to retell it word for word.

Braxton's pledge of loyalty was solely symbolic, because there were no more Wellers to be loyal to.

"If it were him," Upton continued, "he wouldn't think twice 'bout taking those ladies aboard."

Crowe grunted in disapproval. "Yeah, and he'd bring

them home? Send them off with a hot lunch and a bottle of aged whiskey?"

Upton chuckled and shrugged. Instead of answering, he turned his attention toward the cabin door. "What do you make of the lady's friend?"

"Don't know," Crowe admitted. "I can't get a read on her. She's said no more than a few words in front of me." He rubbed his cheek. "Why would the raiders kidnap her too?"

"They probably bungled the kidnapping 'n' had to take her with 'em." Upton thought out loud. "Raiders aren't the brightest, aye?"

"Yeah." Still, the whole matter stank of something foul.

"Here." Upton pressed something into Crowe's hand. "Something for a job well done. I hope it reminds you who you are. Who *he* saw you as." He poked a finger at Crowe's chest.

Crowe uncurled his fingers and smiled faintly at the small carved crow. "Thanks, Upton." He tucked the token into his pocket and begrudgingly headed back to his quarters. As much as he wanted to, he couldn't avoid Lady Yorke forever.

When he opened the door, he found the girls standing at the window. They turned to gawk at him. He figured his display of destroying the raiders' ship had proved he wasn't one to mess with. Maybe then a certain noblewoman would stop mouthing off.

The hope was short-lived because the Yorke turned to square off with him. Rosalie—that's what the dark-haired girl had called her. Who *she* was remained to be seen. But Crowe was intent on finding out who was traveling with a Seity lady.

"Seasick, Lady Yorke?"

Her eyes narrowed, and she put her hands on her hips. Wait. Weren't their hands bound? Crowe walked toward his desk and saw cut ropes next to a pocketknife. He grimaced. So, they were a little more resourceful than he anticipated.

"Are you going to kill us?" Rosalie was trembling, but it looked as if she was trying to hide it.

"No, I plan to keep you alive until one of your father's naval ships passes by." Crowe swept the knife into a drawer and made a mental note to clear the room of weapons. He didn't want Rosalie to stick a knife in his shoulder. She seemed more than angry enough to do so.

"If you intend to extort my father for money, he's in Ciern."

Idly, Crowe wondered if all nobility were this unbearable. He supposed it made them suitable opponents in war. Stubbornness mixed with a superiority complex made a formidable foe. But on a ship, it was akin to torture. "If I bring you to Ciern, I'll sail into a port full of naval ships. I'm sure all their guns would be pointed right at my head. A plan like that doesn't benefit me, does it?"

"But—"

"Nonnegotiable. I may be a pirate, but I pick my battles. I'm not going to tempt a naval fleet without good cause." He eyed her. "And you are not a good cause."

Her lips puckered, and Crowe could've laughed at how easy it was to rile her up. Interestingly, her companion remained stone-faced. She was damn good at acting invisible.

"Your title means nothing out here," Crowe stated, and rested his palms on his desk. "I'm not here to cater to you or your family. A family who has done nothing but cause chaos. Make no mistake—I hate the Duranes, but that doesn't mean I'm fond of your father either."

Rosalie didn't say another word, and Crowe wondered which of his words magically silenced her.

"You." He turned his attention to Rosalie's companion.

Her brown eyes looked at him with trepidation. "My name is Silence," she said, sounding far less abrasive than the Yorke.

"Well, you certainly live up to the name." He didn't have a problem with her yet, but she was loyal to Rosalie. He moved to the door and pushed it open. "Would you join me outside, Silence?"

She glanced at Rosalie before standing. Without a fuss, she followed his request and passed by him.

Crowe gave her a nod, but when Rosalie tried to follow, he blocked her path. "Didn't call for you, did I, Lady Yorke?"

Rosalie bumped into him, startled by his refusal. "Pardon?"

"Right, I'll spell it out for you." Crowe faced her. "This is my ship. I get to say where you can and cannot go. I know back home you're used to waltzing through any door you please, but you're not home, are you?"

She peered up at him. "Silence is my friend."

"That's all well and good, but remember what I said about your title. It's useless here." He saw a myriad of emotions pass over her face, her lips struggling to form words. It was satisfying to see someone of noble blood be reminded they didn't own the world. "Welcome to reality," he said, and went to close the door on her.

But it wouldn't be so easy to get rid of her. She acted fast and wedged her foot in the doorway. "I don't trust you to be alone with her. Anything you can say in front of Silence, you can say in front of me."

If she wasn't getting under his skin so much, Crowe would've been impressed by her tenacity.

"Captain, if I may?" From behind him, Silence began to speak. It was a good tactic to address him properly, but he didn't appreciate the pushback. "Rosalie is fragile. Her illness—"

His nerves were wearing thin at having the two badger him from either side of the door. He turned to face Silence, still barring Rosalie from sneaking by him. "With all due respect, she's been a thorn in my side since she boarded this ship. Thorns aren't fragile."

"If I'm a thorn in your side, then bring us home and be done with this!" Rosalie shouted.

Several crew members turned their heads. It was certainly the loudest she'd been so far, which was saying something. Slowly, Crowe turned back around with an eyebrow raised. There was no subduing this noblewoman; she was like a whirlpool churning ships into bits and pieces and tearing sailors limb from limb.

"You've got a lot of anger in you for such a small thing," he remarked.

Her eyes flashed at the comment on her stature. "Small? How dare—"

"I'll dare to do whatever I want on my ship," he interrupted. "You know the plan, you know the rules, so you can sit still and wait patiently for a naval ship."

Rosalie's face twisted up into a spiteful scowl. "I hope they sink your precious ship when they find me."

Crowe's headache raged even fiercer. Yes, there was a chance he'd be tangled in battle with a Yorke ship. Having Lady Yorke on board was worse than any other contraband. Nevertheless, his odds on the ocean were better than on land. Without a word, he knocked Rosalie's foot out of the way and closed the door.

From inside Crowe could still hear Rosalie stewing and muttering what he assumed weren't glowing words about him under her breath. He couldn't help but smirk slightly before turning around.

Silence was standing a few feet behind him. She looked like a rabbit facing a hungry coyote. He could sympathize with her. She was collateral damage in Seity's pitiful struggle over land.

"How long have you been in the Western Cliffs?" Crowe asked, keeping a hand on the door handle so Rosalie couldn't leave.

"My whole life," Silence replied, her eyes darting around the ship as if she expected to be attacked from all sides.

"Do you work for the Yorkes?"

She shook her head. "No, my mother does. Rosalie and I are friends. I've lived in the manor for ten years."

At least Silence was talking, but none of the information clued Crowe into who she was. "Hmm." Hundreds of questions flitted through his mind. Pointed questions to pry information from her. But as he looked at her, he wondered if it mattered.

She didn't look like a spy—didn't look like some mastermind behind some twisted plot. She was just a young woman too far from home.

Crowe sighed. "I don't suppose you have any magic trick to getting Lady Yorke to settle down?"

The corner of Silence's lips turned up in a weak attempt at a smile. "She's willful." The dash of amusement waned. "However, I'm afraid she's not safe out here."

"I'd say so; the Duranes have a new strategy it seems." Crowe noticed the subtle twitch of Silence's eye when he spoke the name that haunted the country. "I doubt they'll stop after one attempt. Her father might need to lock her in a tower to keep her safe." He paused, reading Silence's expression. "I'm kidding. Sort of." He muttered the last two words under his breath.

"Is there any way we can make this go faster?"

The captain frowned. There was a great deal of urgency in her begging. No doubt she wanted to return home, but she clearly cared for Rosalie's well-being too. "I can't conjure up a Yorke naval ship. It might take time before we come across one. And I won't tolerate any tricks. I'll sooner cut my losses before I let her father put a cannonball through the hull. My ship is worth more than she is."

Rosalie likely would have disagreed. Loudly. But Silence pressed on in a tactful manner. "Her father is focused on the war. I don't believe he would want to waste manpower on getting revenge." Her words were laced with fear. "I'm sure he wants her home safe."

"Unfortunately, trusting a stranger's word can lead to death out here," Crowe replied. "And I don't trust nobility, no matter how well I know them."

"Please," she implored again. "Rosalie is very sick. We can't wait out on the ocean for weeks."

Crowe rolled up his shirt sleeves. "I've found the sea air can be very helpful. Now, I've work to do before the sun sets."

CHAPTER 13- THE LADY

Rosalie landed a hard kick to the doorframe. First Crowe had the gall to order her around, and then he had the audacity to call her short? For good measure, she kicked the door again, marring it with a scuff mark. Good, the damned pirate would remember her long after she got off his stupid ship.

Her heart sank. *Would* she ever get home? Did anyone know she and Silence had vanished? She couldn't be certain the mercenaries had seen the ordeal, and if they had, would they go to Basil? Would they admit to him they'd let his daughter get kidnapped?

She scrubbed her hands over her face to fend off tears. A distraction—she needed a distraction. She paced the captain's office, stopping by a shelf with books shoved into any available space. She frowned. Out of all the people in the world, she thought a pirate would be the least likely to read. But the books were worn with the affection of an avid reader. Bindings of the spines were frayed and corners were torn. The titles boasted an array of different languages, not just the common tongue.

"A pirate who reads," she scoffed, and turned her attention to Crowe's desk. He wasn't the tidiest person, but Rosalie supposed that could be expected from a rogue. He displayed his wealth above everything else; a gold-plated compass rested next to a heavy paperweight with a silver coin encased in the glass.

She noticed that the weight was sitting upon a stack of papers. Glancing behind her to make sure the door remained closed, Rosalie pulled the papers out. Buried under ship logs, she discovered a brief, handwritten note.

> Kelan,
>
> The fawn wears blue, not red. You'll find the kit in the farthest point of the southwest. Let nothing stand in your way or else you'll answer to the boar.
>
> —R

Rosalie mouthed the words a couple of times. They sounded foreign, hidden behind layers of secret meanings. But she recognized the name Kelan as the raider who had kidnapped her and Silence.

The kit. That was her; Rosalie knew that for certain. She was the youngest of the family and would represent a young fox like the one on their crest.

The boar... that was Eldon.

The fawn? If she followed the note's encryption, it didn't make sense. None of the families had deer on their crests.

She read the note again, and her mouth went dry. Crowe was right—the raiders were working as liaisons for the Duranes. That only meant one thing—the kidnapping attempt was just the start of it. There was a plot to finish off the Yorke line. Not on the front lines, but discreetly in the shadows.

Her brothers and father were in danger. Yet she couldn't warn them until she returned to land. Even then, she couldn't make sense of the first sentence. If she couldn't decode it, then how could she know what the threat was?

Was there a spy? Had Eldon planted men at Vale Fall to ensure Rosalie was kidnapped? The fawn must have been a spy, wearing the Yorkes' blue.

The door swung open, and Rosalie stuffed the letter into her pocket. She turned to see that only Silence had returned.

"He didn't hurt you, right?"

Silence shook her head. She didn't appear as scared as before, but she didn't look happy either. "No, I tried to reason with him, but he's set on his plan. I'm afraid all we can do is wait."

Defeat weighed on Rosalie like lead lining her skirts. Her hand dropped to her side and the paper in her pocket crinkled. What if she couldn't warn her family in time?

* * *

THE CAPTAIN reluctantly gave the two women his quarters for the night while he slept outside with his crew. Rosalie was pleased Crowe had taken the path of least resistance. She was fed up with arguing with him, but if he had made her sleep outside, she would've made her displeasure clear.

She was lying on the floor next to Silence. Crowe's sleeping area looked comfortable, but it made Rosalie's skin crawl to think about sharing a bed with him even if he wasn't there. Instead, she and Silence made a comfortable nest out of furs they found in the cabin. Rosalie ran her fingers through the soft gray fur she rested her head on. It probably came from an animal she'd never heard of before.

Setting aside her hatred for a second, Rosalie considered how free Crowe was. He had probably been all over the world—beyond Seity, beyond the Outer Territories, beyond the Koralia Islands. What lay beyond that, Rosalie didn't know. The Yorkes didn't concern themselves with anything past their trading routes, thus Basil's maps ended at the edge of the Islands.

In the darkness, Rosalie felt her frustration dissolve into grief. "Sie, I'm so sorry," she whispered. Tears formed in her eyes, and her throat felt thick. "It's not fair you were caught up in this."

"It's not your fault," Silence replied gently. "I guess it just proves what everyone always says."

"What's that?"

"We have to do everything together."

Rosalie giggled tearfully and wiped her cheeks. "Like getting kidnapped by pirates."

"Kidnapped *twice* by two different ships on the same day. That must be some sort of record."

Rosalie hiccupped and pressed her hands close to her chest. Undoubtedly, there was darkness in the world—her entire life had been plagued by war. But there were still flickers of light.

CHAPTER 14- THE CAPTAIN

Crowe wasn't entirely pleased that he was sleeping on the deck instead of his bed. But if he had made Rosalie and Silence sleep outside, he was sure he never would've heard the end of it. Despite her stature and frail appearance, Rosalie Yorke sure could complain.

Too exhausted to go toe-to-toe with the lady again, he would tolerate the arrangement. The ransom money he planned to demand from her father would make the sacrifice worth it.

Crowe was awake, sitting up against the foremast. His crew was scattered around the deck, some asleep and some merely resting. It had been years since Crowe had slept outside, and although he'd given up his nice warm room to a bratty lady, he did like sleeping under the stars.

"Captain?" Ori, the youngest of the crew, approached.

"Whatever Upton told you about women and bad luck is nothing but superstition," Crowe prefaced. "The ship's not going to sink because there are women aboard."

"No, I know." The boy was just shy of sixteen and had

been a part of the crew for a little over a year. Though Crowe hadn't had much say in the matter. Not long after sailing away from the country of Aefen, they'd discovered the boy stowed away like a kitten belowdecks.

"I was wondering if we're going to Strohis after we get the ransom money." Ori sat down and crossed his legs.

"Think we're going to the Islands first. Kennedy wants to see his beloved. I can't bear separating them for much longer," he said as he pretended to get choked up.

The quartermaster was sprawled out on the deck, his head propped up on his coat. "His parents want him married to someone else," Kennedy said, and stared up at the stars overhead, never one to feed into Crowe's dramatic side.

"Well, they might think twice if you show up with a large dowry, aye?" Crowe reached over to jostle Kennedy's shoulder. "What did he say to you last? He said he's never loved anyone like he loves you. Said he would be lost when you left for sea again."

"Captain, please," Kennedy pleaded sheepishly.

Crowe grinned but let him be. "After that, we'll go to Strohis," he reassured Ori. "Just in time for your mother to tear me to shreds."

The boy smiled. "She likes you—honest, she does. You know she's hard with everyone."

"Especially pirates." Crowe cocked an eyebrow at the boy's cheeky grin. "You know, one of these days, I'm going to leave you there. I'm going to drop you off on your mother's doorstep and sail off without you." He said those exact words to Ori a handful of times every week, but they both knew it was an empty threat. "Now go check on Danny in the crow's nest. That better not be his snoring that I hear."

"Aye, Captain." Ori stood up and went to climb the ratlines.

"Kids." Crowe rolled his eyes and rested his head back.

"You were like that not so long ago," Kennedy reminded him. "You used to run circles around Braxton."

Crowe snorted and rubbed his weary eyes. It certainly had been easier to be a rambunctious teenager with a blade in hand and the world at his fingertips. "I'm sure I did."

"Wonder what he'd think about us now," Kennedy mused.

"I think he'd slap us both upside the head." Crowe closed his eyes. "But we're not doing anything he wouldn't do himself." He smiled at a recollection that passed his thoughts. "Remember the trouble we got into? With Della and Xavier?"

"Which time?"

"I suppose there were plenty of times. But I was thinking of when Della was caught counting cards in Dhael."

Kennedy groaned at the memory as if it caused him pain. "You were counting cards alongside her! You nearly got Xavier and me stabbed."

Crowe grinned. There was something special about nighttime. Titles and roles were cast away so long as the ocean was calm and they were far from enemies. Kennedy eased up a bit, and Crowe didn't bother with asking for respect. It was how things had been when Braxton occupied the captain's cabin.

"Braxton made us clean every inch of the ship. But Della got away with it. That girl never got in trouble." Crowe opened his eyes and traced lines through the constellations, navigating the sky. It was always good to be reassured of where they were on the ocean.

"He was harder on you because he saw your potential." Kennedy yawned and closed his eyes. "We all did."

Crowe wanted to disagree but let the quartermaster drift off. He looked around the deck at his sleeping crew and wondered if Braxton had ever doubted himself. Because despite a few years of leading, Crowe truly didn't know if he was capable of the burden.

Well, perhaps a sizeable ransom would reassure him he was doing the right thing.

CHAPTER 15- THE LADY

Rosalie couldn't remember the last time she'd slept through the night. So, it was a shock to open her eyes to sunlight. Groggy with sleep, she pressed a hand to the floor and heaved herself up. She yawned and rubbed her eyes, feeling the good night's sleep sink deep into her bones.

By the looks of it, Silence wasn't as lucky. She was sitting up with her back against Crowe's desk. Her knees were pulled to her chest, and her head drooped a bit. Her eyes were bloodshot, and Rosalie wondered if she had gotten even a minute of sleep.

"Did you get any rest at all?"

Silence's eyes turned to her. She gave a weak smile and a shrug to go with it. "I suppose I'm not used to sleeping on a ship."

"Did anyone come for us?"

Silence shook her head. "I haven't been outside yet, and I haven't seen the captain."

"Well." Rosalie stood and stretched her arms overhead. "Maybe our gracious *host* wised up overnight and has decided to bring us back. I'm going to go talk to him."

"Wouldn't you like to stay here where it's quiet? It sounds hectic out there."

Indeed, various clunks and shouts could be heard through the door. But it sounded friendly compared to the sounds of battle the day before.

Rosalie attempted to fix her hair, but it was tangled beyond help from her heavy sleep. No matter, she wasn't there to impress anyone. "Now that the excitement has died down, I'm sure Crowe and I can have a cordial conversation. Surely even pirates have a sliver of civility." She straightened her skirt and marched out to the deck.

Immediately, Rosalie caught the curious glances of the crew members, and it drained her confidence. She wasn't used to being around strangers, let alone uncouth strangers holding her captive.

"What are you doing out here?"

Rosalie spun around to see where Crowe's voice was coming from. Finally, she looked up and saw him standing at the wheel of the ship. He didn't strike as impressive a figure in plain trousers and a white shirt with the sleeves rolled up. But he still bore the pretentious airs of a cocky pirate captain.

"I just woke up," she said.

He gave her a funny look. "You've been sleeping this whole time? It's nearly ten."

"Well, I had a long day of being kidnapped," she snapped. "It was exhausting if you can believe it." Even though she had resolved herself to have restraint, the very sight of him annoyed her. Taking a deep breath, she climbed the stairs to join him on the upper deck. Next to him was a tall, dark-haired man writing in a ledger.

"I thought I made it clear that you didn't have free rein over the ship," Crowe said, though he didn't move to grab her.

Rosalie would give him credit where it was due. In the past day, she'd been grabbed and thrown around enough for one lifetime.

"Well, the door was unlocked, so nothing was stopping me."

Even with his eyepatch, he could still give her a withering glare. "I'm stopping you. My words as captain are forbidding you to wander around wherever you please," he asserted. "I thought nobles liked to follow rules."

"I came to speak to you about your plan. I think you ought to reconsider."

"I *ought* to?" Crowe let out a sharp laugh. "Kennedy, make a note that Seity nobles are as bold as they are delusional."

The man next to him glanced up at the captain but continued jotting down notes in the book without question.

"Delusional?" Rosalie tried to bite her tongue, but the smug look on the captain's face made it impossible to have the civil discussion she'd hoped for. "What's delusional is waiting around for a particular ship to show up. I think we both know how massive the ocean is."

"Lady Yorke, naval ships are extremely common out here. I think you've failed to consider the war that's going on in your country."

Her face felt like it was going red with fury. "How long is this going to take?"

"As long as it takes." He gave her a confident side glance. "When it comes to a hundred thousand gold, I'm an extremely patient man."

Rosalie's eyes bugged. "A hundred thousand—are you mad? What makes you think you deserve even close to that amount?"

He cocked an eyebrow at her. "You think you're worth less?"

Her cheeks burned when she realized that by insulting

him, she'd inexplicably insulted herself. "I just don't think a criminal should dictate what he's owed."

"Returning nobles isn't cheap. Keep it up, Lady Yorke, and I'll add a hefty fee."

She dug her fingernails into her palms. "For what?" she hissed.

"For your whining," he answered, looking down at her with amused disdain. "Kennedy, what phase is the moon in?"

"Waning crescent, sir," the man answered without hesitation.

"Ah, then Lady Yorke's behavior can't be blamed on a full moon. This is just how she always is."

Rosalie wrapped her fingers around her skirt and tightened her grip. He harped so much about her title being useless, but he had no problem using it to taunt her. "And what's your excuse for your behavior?" Rosalie retorted, raising her voice. "Kennedy, is there anything in that logbook of yours that explains your captain's absolute lack of decency around women? If there isn't, then you should make a note of that."

The quiet man blinked skeptically when she addressed him by name. His pen hovered and his eyes flicked to Crowe.

The captain pointed a finger at her. "No, no, you don't get to order my crew around."

"Then don't try to boss me around either," Rosalie hissed. "It's bad enough that you've denied my request to let Silence go."

Crowe just scoffed. "Why is it that your companion acts like she's been raised as a lady all her life and you act like you've been raised by feral wolves?"

Rosalie scowled but knew arguing further would only prove his point. So, she squared her shoulders and resumed her goal of asserting herself as a polite, well-mannered young woman. "Fine, we'll see how your harebrained plan pans out." Though she tried to maintain a composed conversation, anger bled through when she saw Crowe smirking at her. "Good day," she said through clenched teeth and stomped back down the stairs.

"You forgot to curtsy!" the captain called after her.

Her fists tightened and she fought every urge to look back. Instead, she closed herself back into the captain's quarters.

Silence appeared to have heard most of the loud conversation as she gave her a sympathetic smile. "So, how did that go?"

Rosalie balled up her shawl in her hands and pressed her face into the fabric to hold back every curse word she knew.

* * *

AFTER SULKING INSIDE FOR AN HOUR, Rosalie was sitting with her arms crossed over her chest. She had tried the knob and to her frustration found it was now locked.

"You were out like a light last night. You were even talking in your sleep," Silence said.

Rosalie lifted her head. "Was I?"

"Something about a fawn." Silence stood up from her watch at the window. "Weird dream?"

In all her fury toward Crowe, Rosalie had forgotten about the letter. She stood, shaking out the pins and needles in her legs. "Does this mean anything to you?" She pulled the piece of paper from her skirt pocket and showed it to Silence.

"Where did you get this?" she asked in a quiet voice.

"On Crowe's desk. I think he found it on the raiders' ship," Rosalie said. She wouldn't apologize for taking something that wasn't hers. If Crowe had a problem with it, he would brand himself a hypocrite.

Her friend looked alarmed that Rosalie had gone through

Crowe's things, but she paused to read the letter instead of admonishing her. Her eyes ran back and forth a couple of times. Her lips parted, but she didn't speak for a long while.

"Silence?"

"It doesn't mean anything to me." She shook her head adamantly and dropped the letter as if it had caught on fire.

Rosalie wasn't sure what to make of her reaction. She stooped down to collect the letter. "I thought maybe I was the kit and the Duranes were the boar. Because of our crests... But I don't know about the rest." She gave the paper another puzzled look.

"It doesn't matter because we're not on the raiders' ship anymore," Silence said and retreated. "Whatever plot they had is over."

"But if it's a plot against my family, shouldn't I figure out what it all means?" Rosalie pressed. "Silence, I think this is bigger than either of us know and—"

"Which is why we shouldn't get involved," Silence interrupted. She took a deep breath and touched Rosalie's arm to turn her away from the desk. "We'll get home, and everything will return to normal. We just have to be patient."

Rosalie bit her tongue to keep from arguing further. She wanted to agree that whatever plot the Duranes were brewing was far beyond what they could handle alone. But she knew her father needed to know so *he* could handle it. And perhaps then Basil would see her value.

"Okay," she whispered. But she had no intention of letting it go.

CHAPTER 16- THE CAPTAIN

"*R*ight, c'mon. Bets in, bets in. No, I ain't taking that as payment." Upton swiped Danny's attempt at a bet, a poorly disguised paste gem, off the table. "D'you think I'm dim, lad? I've been playing this game longer than you've been alive!"

Belowdecks in the galley, the crew were playing their biweekly card game. No one wanted to play more often than that because the chances of winning were slim. Kennedy and Upton were seasoned players with lengthy win streaks.

Crowe had learned a long time ago not to bet, but others in the crew hadn't wised up. Still, he liked spending time with them, so he pulled up a chair.

"You sure you don't wanna play, Cap'n?" Upton goaded as Kennedy shuffled the flimsy cards with practiced agility. "A good game'll sharpen that mind of yours. You need it too; that lady is giving you the run 'round."

The crew all chattered their jeering agreements.

Crowe just rolled his eyes. "Anyone who wants to take my place dealing with her, be my guest."

"Danny will!" One of the men clapped the boy on the back. "He's been moon-eyed over her."

The comment pricked at Crowe. It made him pause, unsure of what the emotion was. Crowe wasn't blind, he saw why she caught the eye of others. Her blond hair and fragile form were obvious indicators of her Western lineage. But those features were like the bright colors of a poisonous fish. Getting involved with a Westerner, and a noble one at that, would only lead to misfortune.

The boy sank low in his seat and tried to cover his embarrassment with his hand of cards. "That's not true."

"I wouldn't dare give him a punishment that terrible. Five minutes alone with her and Danny would throw himself overboard," Crowe muttered. "Silence is far less of a pain."

"Silence?" Upton's eyebrow lifted. "The other lass, you mean? What kinda name is that?"

Crowe shrugged. "Not sure; I've never heard it before."

Upton tapped his cards against the table with a strange yet inquisitive look. It was the thoughtful intelligence that manifested when he was a few drinks in. "I remember Braxton talking 'bout the Duranes."

The crew around the table looked uncomfortable at the mention of the deceased captain and the family who killed him.

"Used to be they named their daughters like that after different traits. What was Eldon's sister's name... er... Prudence, I think."

Crowe furrowed his brow. "Well, she's not a Durane. Besides, what kind of trait is silence?"

Upton took a swig from the bottle of rum they passed around. "Dunno. Are you playing or what?"

"No, I'm not a fool."

They all booed him, hubris leading them to believe they'd be lucky that night.

The bosun gave Crowe a wicked smile across the table. "His head's in the clouds for the Yorke. Are you hoping she'll fall for a rogue?"

It earned him a rowdy bout of laughter. They were too drunk to care if their captain took offense. And Crowe was too bored to mind. Come morning they'd regret it when he had them scrub the ship while hungover.

He crossed his arms over his chest. "I think that would happen when the sun starts rising in the west."

"Ah, he's too proud to admit that he likes when she argues with him."

He groaned. He'd hoped to have a night free from Rosalie, even in discussion. "Right." He stood up and slapped a hand on the table. "Have fun losing your coin."

The crew called after him, trying to coax him back, but he needed to be alone. He climbed up to the deck and found solace in the open space.

Up in the crow's nest, he saw Ori keeping a lookout. As a boy, it had been Crowe's job to sit up there for hours and scan the horizon. He seldom complained because he'd loved the freedom he felt up above the ship. It was the closest he got to flying.

As Crowe looked up, a fat raindrop plopped onto his forehead. It came on without warning, peppering the deck with heavy thuds. "Ori, rain's coming, get on down!" he called.

The boy quickly descended the ratlines and jumped the last two feet. "Can I play cards with them, Captain?"

Everything Crowe learned was from experience, not lectures. So, he reached into his pocket and handed him two coins. "Here, when you lose, you'll see that you need to be smart with what you bet money on."

Ori grinned. "I might win, Captain."

"Go on," he urged as the rain worsened. He pulled his coat

over his head and went to his quarters. Damn rain, he was going to sleep in his own bed.

Silence and Rosalie were asleep on the floor, so Crowe did his best not to make a sound. A strong wave of exhaustion hit him, and he only had the energy to shed his damp coat.

He collapsed in the berth. As he drifted off, he heard Braxton's warning voice.

You bet your own life before the life of your crew.

CHAPTER 17 - THE LADY

The lulling waves coaxed Rosalie into another night of deep slumber. It was odd that the only time she'd gotten a good night's sleep was as a hostage on a ship.

A dark morning marked the third day. Blearily, Rosalie sat up with her mind in a sleepy haze. She felt as if she'd slept ten hours straight, so why was it dark? She twisted around to find Silence but jolted when, instead, she saw Crowe sitting at his desk.

"Morning," he greeted tersely.

Rosalie opened her mouth to ask what he was doing in the room while they were sleeping, but a loud clap of thunder interrupted her.

The captain pointed at the window with a pen. "There's a storm passing over us."

Behind him, Silence was again sitting near the window. A crack of lightning lit up her face. For a fleeting moment, panic flashed across her dark eyes. No doubt she was worried about weathering a storm out on the ocean.

"How long will it last?" Rosalie asked.

"I appreciate that you think I'm smart enough to know

the will of a storm, Lady Yorke," he replied glibly. "But the wind is low, so I wouldn't hold your breath. Trust me, I'm not looking forward to being stuck in here with you either."

Rosalie sucked her lower lip between her teeth. She redirected her rage toward her tangled hair, all while keeping unpleasant thoughts to herself.

* * *

HOURS later the rain still hadn't let up. The thick sheet of rain and occasional rumble of thunder made the quarters feel cramped. The three of them remained stuck together, much to Rosalie's dismay.

She thought it wise to watch what she said in front of the pirate, so she avoided conversation. But the quiet picked away at her sanity. Unable to sit still, Rosalie paced while Silence watched the storm from the window.

The third time Rosalie passed Crowe's desk, he slammed his book down. "You're doing my head in with that pacing."

Rosalie stopped moving but didn't sit. "I'm bored."

"I don't care," he replied, and picked up his book again.

She huffed a sigh and remained planted in place. Her eyes studied the book in his hand. "So, those books aren't just for decoration. You *can* read."

Crowe didn't look up from the pages but responded, nonetheless. "Didn't anyone teach you not to bother someone who's reading?"

Rosalie pressed her tongue against her teeth. Emerson had always told her to be the better person. They had noble blood, so they needed to take the high road. But Crowe made it impossible when he set bait for her anger to snap at. To him it seemed it was just a game to pass the time. Driving a nobleborn to take the low road.

"Bothering a reader is a greater misdeed than kidnapping?" She could see she was pestering him enough that his eyes kept going over the same page. Fine—two could play the game.

"I'm not debating morality with a member of a warmongering family."

Another jab at her family made her blood spike. "If you want me to be quiet, you could offer something to occupy my time." Her eyes went to the bookshelf. A nice book would help her mind escape for an hour or so.

"I'm not in the business of entertaining the likes of you, Lady Yorke," he said when he spotted her eyeing the shelf. "So, don't get it into your head that you're going to touch any of those books. Some of them are first editions."

Rosalie crossed her arms over her chest and started to pace again. "That's a shame; I'd be terribly upset if anyone stole my first editions."

"Rose, please..." Silence begged. She stood up, perhaps sensing that the argument would continue to escalate.

But it was too late. Rosalie had hit the right nerve, and Crowe snapped the book shut. "Didn't I tell you to stop pacing?"

"You can't—"

He interrupted her, "It's my ship. If I tell someone aboard to jump, they ask me, 'How high, Captain?'" He stood and rested his hands on his desk, looking poised for a fight.

She laughed scathingly. "And you accuse us nobility of being despots! You're the tyrant of your ship!"

"I've earned my place, Lady Yorke. I worked hard to gain respect. You were born into your title without any say from the people your father rules over. If my crew doesn't like me, they can vote me out and chuck me overboard. Your people don't have the same luxury. I'm certain if they did, they'd waste no time trying to get rid of a whiny princess like you."

Rosalie clenched her teeth and hissed, "I told you, I'm *not* a princess!"

"Are you still talking?"

His blasé words grated through her. "So long as I'm here against my will, you won't have a second of peace."

"That was obvious from the second you opened your mouth," he replied. "I'm starting to think the Duranes kidnapped you to use you as a torture device. You could irritate their prisoners to death."

"You think you're so clever—"

From the corner, Silence cleared her throat. Both Rosalie and Crowe turned their heads. "I think the rain has stopped," she informed them.

It was quiet; the usual sounds of waves settled back in. Glints of sunlight broke through the clouds and filtered through the window.

"Excellent. I thought I was going to have to jump out of a window to get away from her." Crowe stood up and let the door slam behind him.

Rosalie couldn't help but be annoyed that he'd gotten the last word in—again.

"I've never heard you talk to someone like that," Silence said. "I'm not sure if I should be proud or terrified that you're willing to talk back to a pirate."

"What else am I meant to do? I know he's not going to kill me, so what's the worst he can do?" She looked out at the choppy ocean. She hoped somewhere in the near distance a ship bearing her family's flag was sailing toward them.

Truthfully, she wasn't sure why she dared talk to Crowe in such a manner. She would never dare speak that way to her father.

"Besides," Rosalie continued, and wandered past the bookshelf again. "He doesn't look much older than us. Where does he get the nerve to talk down at us like we're children?"

Silence made a noise of intrigue. "He does seem young to be a captain."

Rosalie paused when she saw the door had been left ajar in Crowe's hasty exit. She quickly made her way over.

"Rosalie?"

But she waved a hand to reassure Silence. She nudged the door open more and saw Crowe's men returning to the water-slogged deck. A young boy cheerfully whistled as he mopped away the puddles.

One crew member was sitting beside the door, sharpening a blade as he idly hummed the same tune as the boy. Between notes, he added a few words.

"*Chase a fawn 'cross the land. All the magic in her hand. Dashed in red and gold. Think of all she holds.*"

Overwhelmed with interest, Rosalie threw the door open and stepped out. "That song, what does it mean?" she asked in a hushed voice so Silence wouldn't overhear.

The burly man was caught off guard when she jumped out at him. "Er… dunno. Someone who used to sail with us sang it."

"Was he from Seity?" Rosalie's heart raced as she desperately tried to trace the thread.

"Yeah, from the Eastern Hills."

"Lady Yorke!" Crowe shouted from the opposite side of the deck.

But she was too caught up in her newfound information to care. "The Eastern Hills?" she whispered. She tried to picture the Weller crest, but she drew a blank. Not even a hint of an image conjured in her mind.

Before she could ask anything else, Crowe grabbed Rosalie by the wrist. "You astound me with your persistence," he growled.

Rosalie yanked her arm away. "Do *not* touch me!" she

snapped. But when she looked up at him, her breath caught in her throat.

She hadn't seen the captain so close before. Only then could she see how his dark hair was disheveled in only a way a rogue would wear it. He also bore a small scar under his right eye, another telltale sign of his unscrupulous profession. All of his traits were warning signs of danger. So why was Rosalie's heart racing?

He reached over her head to push open the door. "Inside," he ordered.

"I'm going," she hissed. "But not because you told me to." Breaking the trance, he'd caught her in, she turned and went back inside as he slammed the door.

CHAPTER 18 - THE LADY

*L*ife on a ship was not what Rosalie expected, but she had no prior information to draw from. There were enough provisions that everyone ate, although the food was terrible. Everything was salted to the point where it all tasted the same. She almost chipped a tooth biting into a biscuit. But since she had assumed she would starve, it was tolerable.

Rosalie spent most of the time sitting near the door, listening to Crowe's crew work. They laughed a lot. Their familiarity with each other was evident in their voices. To an outsider, they sounded like family.

It didn't offer comfort; it only incited jealousy and anger. How could these men act so casually as they held her and Silence hostage?

Despite Silence's reassurances, Rosalie was growing increasingly frustrated with Crowe's harebrained plan. She and Silence watched the horizon for ships, hoping to one day see a familiar blue flag against the clear sky.

Rosalie felt like a caged animal. She had managed to slip out of their prison a few more times, but Crowe always caught her. Closed inside, Rosalie was haunted by the strange information she'd learned. How were the Eastern Hills involved in this plot against her family? What game was Eldon Durane playing?

The stress and confusion weakened her body, but her anger kept her animated. As much as Silence tried to keep her distracted, it did no good. She was just as consumed by her thoughts as Rosalie was. Yet Silence didn't voice her concerns and said very little.

At midmorning on day six, Rosalie spotted a ship heading in their direction. Every ship had brought a burst of hope, and this one was no different. She jumped to her feet and rushed for the door. It was unlocked, so she slipped out before Silence could react.

The crewmember who was supposed to be keeping guard had dozed off, yet Rosalie didn't make it very far before Crowe's arm hooked around hers. He yanked her to a halt.

"I don't know how many times I have to have this conversation with you." Unlike the other times, he sounded tired of her games. Maybe she was finally wearing him down. If she pushed hard enough, maybe he'd let them go.

She pulled away from him. "As many times as I've told you to keep your hands to yourself."

"Don't flatter yourself; I have no interest in touching you. I'm also never in the mood for your antics, especially not right now. Inside."

"There's a ship."

Crowe glanced over his shoulder. "Yes, Lady Yorke, that's a ship. Ships sail on the ocean."

His patronizing tone threatened to ignite Rosalie's ire, but she took a steady breath to stave it off. "It could be a part of my father's navy."

"I wonder what that's like, having a father with a navy at his fingertips." His eyes scanned her with a faint smile. When she gave him a scowl, his smirk deepened. "That's a small sloop, not suited for a navy. The design on the hull is common on a Territory ship. Now quit bothering me." He pointed toward the doorway, where Silence was standing and looking confused.

When he started to walk away, she followed. "That's where you're from, isn't it? The Outer Territories?" she called after him.

He let out a huff of a laugh. "You Westerners draw the Territories on your maps? I thought you'd forgotten about everything past the mountains."

"Well, it's where Seity folk came from."

"Centuries ago." His eyes narrowed. "You have no idea what it's like there now."

Rosalie couldn't argue with that. She didn't know much about the land beyond the Eastern Hills. Her father had said it was a good example of why nobility needed to be in power. After the monarchy dissolved in the Outer Territories—the monarchy Rosalie's ancestors fled from—the land had broken up into regional rule. There was no war, but according to Basil, the divisions ran deep.

"We have parts of it on our maps." She started to feel a bit uneasy under his scrutinizing gaze. "But I didn't think Seity had much effect on any place beyond the mountains. The Territories were left to their own devices; we have nothing to do with them."

Crowe's face clouded over. "I think you'll find that whatever you were taught is wrong," he said sternly. "Now get off my deck."

"Can you let Silence and me outside? We both need fresh air, and we're cramped in there. I'm not going to disrupt your crew; I just want to have some space."

"What you want really isn't an issue of mine, is it?" he

retorted. When she opened her mouth, he held up a hand to stop her. "That was a rhetorical question."

"If you allow Silence and me a little more freedom, I promise I'll make it worth your time." Rosalie caught onto the fact that the pirate wouldn't do anything unless money was offered.

Crowe rolled his eyes. "I know you don't control the purse strings."

"I can pay you upfront." She reached back to undo the clasp of her necklace and dangled it from her fingers. "It's pure sapphire."

Eyeing her suspiciously, he stepped closer and took the stone in his hand. He turned it over and made a soft noise of interest. When he held it up to the sunlight he asked, "You're so desperate for a little bit of freedom that you'd hand this over?"

"It has no sentimental value," she replied. The necklace had been a gift from a nameless ambassador trying to impress the Yorke family. "It's nothing but a cold, hard rock, much like your heart."

He snorted at her insult. "Alright, Lady Yorke, you have yourself a deal," he agreed. "You and your friend can have time on the deck. But if you interrupt my crew's work, the offer is rescinded, and I keep the gem."

Her eyes narrowed at the stipulations he added, but she knew she would take whatever she could get. "Fine."

"Pleasure doing business with you." He pocketed the sapphire and again went to pass by her.

"How old are you?" Rosalie piped up again.

In the back of her head, her father's voice scolded her for asking so many questions. She couldn't help it. There was something odd about the captain. He looked younger than Rosalie's brothers, yet he carried himself as if he'd lived three lifetimes over. She hated to admit it, but he had a sharp wit about him and surely knew what he was doing if he was still alive on an intact ship.

He paused and glanced over his shoulder. "Why are you so intent on asking me personal questions?"

When she met his gaze, she suddenly became shy under his scrutiny. It wasn't fear, it was… she couldn't say for sure.

"I told you, I'm bored. I suppose you lawless types are interesting." It was the closest she'd come to complimenting him.

Surprisingly, he didn't take the bait. "Well, my life is not entertainment for nobility to enjoy. I'm busy."

For a second, she swore she saw a flash of humanity behind his eyes. Or maybe her time on the ocean was unraveling her brain.

* * *

LATER THAT NIGHT, Rosalie was frustrated beyond belief. Back in Crowe's quarters, she had been trying for five minutes to undo the braids in her hair. She'd needed to make do without the luxuries she was used to. A ship full of men had no use for the things women required, and Rosalie's long hair was not cooperating with the sea winds. Her braid had to be done up tighter to keep her hair from getting tangled. It took nearly half an hour to get them in and out. Just another thing that wasn't working out as planned.

"Why do you think Crowe hates me so much?"

Silence's brow arched in confusion. "Why are you so worried about that?"

Rosalie pursed her lips. Being disliked was a long-standing fear she held on to. She wanted to be liked by everyone she met just as her mother had been. Rosalie wasn't keen on making friends with Crowe, but deep-rooted anxiety still gnawed at her insides when she thought of his contempt for her. "I just want to know why."

"I don't think pirates are supposed to like the people they kidnap."

Rosalie tugged her hair out of its tight plait. "You should've heard the ridiculous sum Crowe wants. I would've thought they'd be grateful."

Silence laughed. "Rosalie, you can't expect everyone to like you. There are people you won't get along with, and that's okay."

Wincing at the pins tearing out of her hair, Rosalie huffed. "Father says a leader needs to be respected by everyone."

"In an ideal world, maybe," Silence agreed, and helped gather the hairpins into a neat pile. "But we both know the world is not ideal—especially right now."

"I know," Rosalie lied. Aside from her illness, she had been spared the hardships of life. She'd never gone hungry or slept without a roof overhead. With such little experience, how was she meant to be everything she'd hoped to be as a lady? All she had credit for was thwarting death so many times. It had nothing to do with skill or tenacity. It was just luck.

CHAPTER 19- THE CAPTAIN

There had been a time when life on the *Deceit* was a lot simpler for Crowe. As Braxton's newest recruit, he knew his place and what was expected of him. He'd been just a young, headstrong teenager and spent his days learning to fight and sail.

Braxton's crew had accepted him because his life story wasn't much different from their own. They were drifters, misfits, and lonely souls. The *Deceit* had become his home, and her crew his family. Untying himself from the burden of land had been a freeing experience. He never once doubted where he wanted to be.

But his confidence had been shaken when tragedy found him on the ocean. Losing Braxton was like losing his parents all over again.

In the wake of his untimely death, Crowe had been shocked to learn Braxton wanted him to captain the *Deceit*. The other crew members voted him in, and he'd found himself in command. Only seventeen, he wasn't sure how he was going to manage. Suddenly, he was Captain Crowe, and he was responsible for everyone on board. It was a burden he never expected. Territory boys like himself didn't occupy leadership positions. They worked themselves to death under the thumb of an unforgiving boss.

But sometimes not being the one who made the hard decisions was easier.

"Thought she'd be bossier." Danny was fixing a loose deadeye, bolting it back into its place.

Crowe didn't like to micromanage his crew, but he hovered around Danny to appear busy. It was the best way to avoid conversation with their kidnapped guests. He didn't want them to question what he was up to that day. If he was being fair and honest, he was up to no good. But for a pirate, that was expected.

"She is bossy," Crowe said.

"Not toward us, just you, Captain."

He rolled his eyes. "Fantastic."

Danny smiled. "Just thought princesses were supposed to be bossy." He fiddled with the rigging to test if the mechanism was secure.

"Well, she's not a princess. Seity's got its unique way of doing things, complicated as it is." He was aware of how strict Seity was with all their titles and decorum. Calling Rosalie a princess was just a way to get under her skin. At one point Braxton had spelled out how each family had different guidelines for succession. Crowe had deemed it useless information, so he didn't remember how the Yorkes passed on their titles.

"Her family rules over their people, right? Doesn't that make her a princess?"

"I guess it's a matter of word choice."

Upton swooped in with the same fear he'd been harping about all week. "Princess or not, she's bad luck. They both are, being women 'n all." He dropped a heavy sack of provisions onto the deck.

"Della was on this ship for years and you never had an issue with her," Crowe reminded him, referencing the only woman who'd ever been a part of the *Deceit*'s crew.

"Eh—" the bosun hesitated, "—Della's different."

"Whatever you say."

Danny snuck a look over to where Silence and Rosalie were. "I didn't notice how sick Rosalie looks."

Crowe recalled what Silence had said to him days ago. It had been something he'd overlooked as he adamantly tried to ignore Rosalie's sharp green eyes. But in the light of day, it was apparent she was unwell.

"I'm sure she'll survive until we get our money." He looked out on the horizon. "Just wish someone would come looking for her already," he muttered.

The absence of naval vessels was noticeable. Nearly everyone on the crew had mentioned how strange it was because of how close they were to Seity's coast. Only a few weeks earlier, the *Deceit* had to be vigilant to avoid run-ins with warships, ducking in and out of their paths. Suddenly, it seemed the navy's presence had vanished overnight. It left Crowe with an eerie feeling.

"Gonna send some money back to my mum. She'll be thrilled," Danny said.

"Yeah, then you'll have to explain where you got it from." Crowe clapped Danny on the back. "Lowly sailors don't earn the kind of money that pirates do."

"You'll be telling Mummy you're a pirate?" Upton cackled. "Go on, lad, get back to work."

Danny's cheeks turned red, but he smiled and hurried belowdecks.

Crowe leaned against the side of the ship, crossing his arms over his chest. Again, he glanced at Rosalie and Silence. He thought it amusing that Upton feared the young women. But after squaring off with Rosalie enough times, Crowe was starting to see the merit of the bosun's argument. Some women were forces to be reckoned with.

"If they end up cursing us with their feminine ways, Upton, I'll give you my share of the ransom."

The old salt looked impressed with the prospect of a higher reward. "Hope you're ready to pay up then, Cap'n." Upton heaved the sack back over his shoulder and ambled on his way. "If we don't capsize first."

Crowe chuckled until Kennedy came up behind him. "What did you see?" he asked.

"It's a fast brigantine, but it looks undermanned. I'd estimate it has a crew of about seventy men."

With no one on board watching, Crowe ascended the stairs to the quarterdeck. He took out his spyglass to view a ship approaching from behind. A ship that Rosalie, thankfully, hadn't noticed yet. "Has it flown a flag?" he asked.

"No, Captain, but I have reason to believe it's a merchant from Strohis."

"Looks like they're coming from the Islands; could be a good haul."

"I worry that this will draw attention to our ship," Kennedy said when Crowe lowered the scope from his eye. "We're drifting close to Durane territory."

It was dangerous, but Crowe was bored. He was sick of waiting around. "The ocean's been quiet; I doubt anyone will notice. Besides, I haven't lifted the *Deceit*'s flag in days. Can't let the ocean think we've gone soft, aye?" He clapped Kennedy on the back. "Let's slow a bit, let them pass us, then we'll get down to business."

"What about…" Kennedy jerked his head to where Silence and Rosalie stood on the main deck.

Rosalie made a noise of surprise and pointed out a large fish fin poking out of the waves. She jostled Silence in excitement.

Crowe turned away. "Alert everyone except them. Maybe Lady Yorke will see that I'm not someone to be questioned," he said, feeling confident with himself.

"Why does it matter what she thinks?"

It wasn't rare for his quartermaster to question him. Kennedy was as rational and bright as he was quiet and unassuming. He was good at reining in Crowe who was keen on maintaining the *Deceit*'s fierce reputation throughout the seas.

"I didn't—I don't care what she thinks." Crowe was a bit caught off guard. Did he care too much about what a lady thought about him? True, Rosalie had occupied a great deal of his thoughts, but only because she never ceased badgering him. He swore she would start pestering him in his dreams soon enough. "What I care about is this ship's reputation. Think of the stories she'll tell about the *Deceit*. It's always good to sow a bit of fear on land."

But the quartermaster didn't look convinced, expressing his disagreement through his silence.

Crowe frowned and adjusted the collar of his coat. "Just keep a lookout and tell me when they're close."

CHAPTER 20- THE LADY

It was no surprise that a pirate ship held a crew of colorful people. With access to the deck, Rosalie was curious to meet the men who willingly sailed with Crowe. However, though she tried to be nice, most of the crew hadn't shown interest in engaging with her or Silence.

The one-handed man named Upton didn't speak to them. Whenever they were near, he muttered something about bad luck and averted his eyes as he hobbled away.

Kennedy, who was the captain's second-in-command, was a man of very few words. But he would give her a polite nod if he noticed her.

The two youngest crew members, Ori and Danny, were the friendliest. They were fascinated by the company they had on board. When Crowe wasn't around, they bombarded Rosalie with questions about being a lady. In return, they regaled her and Silence with seafaring tales.

"You should've seen it, Lady Yorke—biggest creature I've ever seen in the water." Ori was replacing a nail in the deck as he talked to Rosalie.

She had wandered outside while Silence rested inside the cabin. Happy to be distracted, Rosalie perched herself on top of a barrel to talk to Ori. "What was it?" she asked, her interest piqued.

"Had to be a whale; don't know what else it could be."

"It wasn't a whale." Crowe stood at the side of the deck watching the horizon through a scope.

Rosalie frowned at his sudden interruption. She didn't think he'd been eavesdropping. "Then what was it?"

The captain pocketed the spyglass and turned to face them. "It was an orca," he said, and took a few steps toward them. "What did I tell you about distracting my crew?"

She crossed one leg over the other and held herself tall. "Ori can work while he talks," she argued.

Crowe's fear tactics had waned as they had begrudgingly reached a stalemate. Crowe needed Rosalie to collect a ransom, and Rosalie needed him if she wanted to stay alive on the ocean.

"And he can also work without talking to you," Crowe replied.

"I'm done, Captain." Ori stood up with a proud smile. "I think you're right 'bout it being an orca. Whales aren't colored black and white like that."

"Right, go to the galley and help Tucker." The captain nodded to shoo off the boy.

Ori gave Rosalie a lighthearted smile before taking his orders with stride. He left the captain and lady alone, taking with him any warmth. All that remained was an icy tension harbored between the two.

"He's just a boy; you should be easier on him," Rosalie said.

"I don't need your opinions on how I run my ship, Lady Yorke. I had it tougher than him when I joined."

It was a mere sliver of information that he offered, but Rosalie was curious as to how a boy from the Outer Territories had become a pirate captain. So again, she asked, "How old were you?"

"Old enough," he said, and retreated to his original spot by the ship's railing.

Rosalie hopped off the barrel. She went to stand next to him, disregarding his rigid tone. "Fifteen? Sixteen?"

"Why are you out here? I know we had an agreement, but don't ladies prefer being indoors?"

"Not me. Besides, Silence is resting. I think she's feeling a little nauseous from the waves."

He made a huff of amusement. "I thought you'd be the one to get seasick." He pulled out his spyglass again.

"Me?"

"Silence said you were sick."

Rosalie wrapped her arms around herself. "I've been sick my whole life." It drew a subtle side-glance from Crowe. A lengthy pause sat between them before she pivoted his attention. "Tell me how old you were when you became a pirate. I'll keep asking until you tell me."

He sighed and lowered the scope. "Fine, but I'm only answering so you'll drop the matter. I was about to turn fourteen."

Rosalie thought back to when she was that age. She had slept with a cloth doll to cope with her fear of nighttime. She couldn't imagine leaving home, let alone joining a pirate crew. Perhaps that's why Crowe seemed so adept at survival and Rosalie didn't.

She didn't like Crowe. But he was compelling in the same way destructive forces of nature were. Maybe that was why she continued to badger him with questions. Or maybe she just wanted to be the thorn in his side.

"If what Ori saw was an orca, then do you ever see whales?"

"Very often. There are dolphins farther south as well. Orcas are a type of dolphin."

Rosalie shifted her weight between her feet. She silently noted how she had become accustomed to the sway of the *Deceit* underneath her. "I wouldn't risk running into a Durane warship to see a dolphin."

"Wouldn't consider Durane territory the south. If you're looking at a map, I'd call it east—southeast if I'm being generous. I thought you said they put the Territories on your maps. Or are you so single-focused?"

She frowned. "I had a good education."

"You had a Western education," he corrected.

Although it was aggravating, Rosalie had to concede that he was right. "It's hard to think of other places when we've lived in chaos for so long," she said in a small voice.

"Of course; you have to sort out the winner of the war before turning to other places to conquer."

Rosalie got a bad taste in her mouth, and she once again regretted engaging with him. "Another great conversation," she muttered, and went to leave.

"Where did you learn about whales?" he asked before she got too far. "Thought you knew nothing about the ocean."

She halted in her steps. "They draw them on maps," she explained, skeptical as to why the pirate had changed his tune. "I've always wanted to see one up close because they seem big."

"Aye, they're massive beasts. Could probably capsize a smaller vessel if they wanted. What do you think, Lady Yorke? Would you prefer a whale or a Durane?"

Her face twisted in disapproval. "What sort of question is that?"

The captain shrugged with an aloof smile. "Something to consider," he said as he walked away.

Rosalie scowled as she watched him leave. The tails of his long coat rippled with the wind. As he moved across the deck, his crew greeted him with nods or friendly words. It was baffling. What did they see in him that she didn't?

CHAPTER 21- THE CAPTAIN

Crowe found Silence in her usual spot, sitting on the sill of the window in his quarters. He let out a slow sigh, wondering when he was going to get some time alone. At least Silence was easier to get along with.

"Was Rosalie with you?" she asked when he stepped inside. She appeared to have just woken from a nap, with a fur draped over her shoulders.

"She's out on the deck, bothering my crew as we speak," he huffed, and collapsed into the nearest chair.

Rosalie Yorke was by far the most aggravating yet engaging person he'd ever had the misfortune of coming across. By some feat, she'd dredged up more information about his past than some of his crew knew. It would have been simpler if she was a snobby, whiny lady whom he could disregard without a thought. But there was something about her that made Crowe susceptible to telling her more about himself than most people knew. It would be impressive if it wasn't so infuriating.

"Could I ask you a question?" Silence hesitated as she spoke.

"I guess it has become my job to answer questions." He rubbed his temples, and for the first time in his life, he prayed for a warship to find him.

"Can you tell me about your previous captain?"

Crowe sat up a bit. While Rosalie wouldn't let him forget who she was, Silence's identity remained a mystery. She had slipped out of his mind while Rosalie tormented him. It was no mistake; Silence's presence was crafted to be overlooked. And he wondered if Rosalie was in on it, concealing her friend with nonstop banter. But now one question had sparked his interest again, and Rosalie wasn't there to distract him.

"If you tell me how you learned of the *Deceit*, I'd be happy to oblige," he negotiated.

Silence smoothed her hands over her skirt, her head bowed slightly. "My mother told me. She was near the border between the south and west when the Duranes attacked. Everyone talked about the ship that came to save Easterners. She heard rumors about the ship's captain, but the details were murky. Everyone had a different story about him."

The answer was less than satisfactory. But he had promised an answer in return.

"Braxton was a high-ranking officer in the Duranes' navy. They called him Braxton the Banished because he defected. When he heard about the planned attack on Avorae, he left his post. He commandeered this ship and went inland to smuggle Easterners out. He never forgave himself for failing to save the Weller family."

Silence's eyes were big as she listened. Her fingers wove together as if she were collecting all the information in her palms.

The captain took a deep breath. It was both a privilege and a burden to speak about Braxton. He was proud to boast the man's accomplishments, but then Crowe was reminded how much he missed him.

"He was a good man and an excellent captain, no matter what anyone else says." He took great care to not let Braxton's name be vilified by history's reshaping dialogue. "He was like a father to me—took me in and showed me how to fend for myself."

"If he survived the attack on the Eastern Hills, then how did you become captain?"

Crowe knew it was Silence's way of asking whether Braxton was still alive. Pirates had a shorter than average life expectancy. It was rare for them to retire back to land—either because they were killed before they had the chance or because they didn't want to leave their home amid the waves. Braxton never would have left the *Deceit*.

"I became captain after he was killed by Eldon's sons."

"His sons?"

Crowe didn't like being emotional in the company of people he didn't know well. He crossed his arms over his chest and turned his head to look out the window. "There was a long grudge against Braxton for defecting to save Easterners. He was hunted for almost two decades; they never gave up the chase. One day, we were accosted by the *Lord's Dagger*, the Duranes' own ship."

If he closed his eyes, his mind would revisit the memory. The ocean outside the window was placid, but it had been wrathful on that fateful day.

"They ambushed us. The youngest, Lowell, killed Braxton. I tried to avenge his death, but I was too green. He would've killed me too if Upton hadn't stepped in. Upton lost his hand, and I almost bled out." He turned his attention back to Silence.

Silence was frozen in place as she whispered, "That sounds terrifying."

"They might call themselves honorable, nobleborn gentlemen but that's not what I saw. They're nothing but a bunch of scoundrels," Crowe said.

Silence swallowed. "I'm sorry about Braxton. It sounds like he meant a lot to you."

A faint knock on the door halted the conversation. Crowe was surprised to find he was disappointed at the interruption. Silence lent a sympathetic ear.

Kennedy stepped inside. "Captain." His eyes flicked to Silence.

Crowe could read his quartermaster's face well. He had to because Kennedy said so little. "Is everyone prepared?"

"Yes, sir."

He stood up and shed his coat. He wanted to shake the memory of Braxton's death. "Excellent timing."

Silence looked confused, her eyes darting between the two men. "What's going on?"

"Just a quick detour. Nothing you or Lady Yorke need to concern yourselves with. I'd urge you to both stay out of the way unless you want to stand in the line of fire."

"Line of fire?" Silence hurried after him.

Crowe was pleased to see that his crew was prepared to close in on their prey. Rosalie backed away from the side of the ship. He had to give the two women credit, they caught onto things quickly. But they needed to realize life on the ocean wasn't all stories and intrigue.

"Captain!" Ori shouted from the crow's nest. "There's a naval ship off the starboard quarter!"

Crowe's thoughts stuttered to a halt. "No," he whispered under his breath. He'd been so certain they were in the clear. When had a warship snuck up on them? "Any sight of their flag?" he yelled up to the boy.

"Not yet, sir!"

Crowe looked at Kennedy. There was a chance that it was

a Yorke vessel. But based on the direction it was coming from, he couldn't be sure. Looting near a naval ship was a risky move, but pirates weren't meant to live on the safe side.

"This won't take long." Crowe decided despite the quartermaster's wordless doubt. "We can lose the warship quickly."

Rosalie stormed over with the same pout she sported whenever Crowe displeased her. "What if that's my family's ship coming to rescue me?"

"Could be, or it could be a Durane ship. Won't know until we know. Until then, I've other business to attend to; step aside." He slipped by her. "Upton, raise the flag, let our guests know who we are."

"Aye, Cap'n!" Upton gleefully went to task.

Crowe watched the black flag lifting into the air. He smiled, proud to see the banner bearing two crossed swords behind a bleeding heart. It was a sight that struck fear in even the most experienced seafarers.

"You're purposefully putting us into battle?" Rosalie gawked at him.

He was almost impressed by how well she could kill the mood of looting. "I'm doing my job, so go back inside. If you interfere, I can't guarantee that you won't be killed."

"You are meant to be keeping us alive! Do you want the ransom or not?"

"I'll get your ransom," he huffed.

"Not if I'm dead!"

The very idea felt like a slap. Innocent people dead on his ship, because of him. Crowe shook his head. No one was dying on his watch. "I'm not providing you with a service, Lady Yorke. Now get out of my way."

* * *

As EXPECTED, the merchant ship had raised the white banner. Most ships did when they saw the *Deceit*'s flag because her reputation preceded her, and few were willing to test her prowess. Crowe appreciated a challenge, but they were running on borrowed time, so he was grateful for the surrender.

As Crowe was preparing to dispatch his men, a rifle shot rang out and the bullet barely missed his shoulder.

"*Vellah!*" Crowe ducked and drew a pistol from his belt. "That's a funny way to surrender," he said through gritted teeth, and cautiously rose to his feet, ready to return fire.

"You're not stealing anything else from me, Crowe!" the merchant yelled.

Crowe squinted, unable to see if he recognized the man. "Should I know this ship?"

Kennedy grimaced. "It sounds like the captain we attacked a few weeks ago. The fur trader."

"Ah, yes." Crowe's memory was jogged. Once they had looted the ship, the merchant swore he'd get revenge. Crowe had ignored the threat because he'd heard it so many times that the words lost their meaning. "I'm sure he thought it was clever to pretend to surrender. Such a coward's move."

If things didn't start going his way soon, he'd start believing in Upton's superstition about women.

"Kennedy, inform the captain that if he doesn't surrender as he so indicated, I'll go over there, take everything of value, and sink his ship. And make it quick."

"Aye, Captain."

Pressure pushed against the back of Crowe's neck. He climbed to the helm and watched the horizon. A large warship trailed in the distance. There was no mistaking it, her bow was pointed right at the *Deceit*, stalking her from afar. To his dismay, he had a sinking feeling they had a Durane ship on their tail.

Nervously, he looked back to where Kennedy was boarding the merchant vessel. There was shouting and he saw the glint of steel being crossed. With one more apprehensive look, Crowe hurried to aid his crew.

CHAPTER 22 - THE LADY

The second Rosalie stepped inside the cabin, she lost feeling in her legs. She had avoided a fit days ago, but this time she was too late. The last thing she felt was Silence's arm straining to support her.

She fell like a dead weight. A buzzing sound like a swarm of angry wasps flooded her ears, drowning out Silence's words. In the brief seconds of consciousness she had left, she cursed her illness and her lack of control. If she wasn't incapacitated, she would have screamed.

Darkness enveloped her as she fell victim to her own body.

* * *

ROSALIE COULD GO weeks without a fit, or she could suffer multiple a day. It was a fickle enemy that governed her life. But after almost every fit, she woke to Silence's voice.

"Rose?"

When she opened her eyes, Silence's fear-stricken face was hovering over her. Rosalie groaned and waited until the ringing in her ears died down. She lifted a limp hand to her forehead to wipe away the sweat trickling down her forehead.

"That was a long one," Silence whispered. "You need a doctor; I'm worried about your heart."

At the mention of a doctor, Rosalie grimaced. She'd seen plenty over her lifetime, and yet she was still burdened by illness. When the tingling in her limbs faded, anger burbled up to fill its place. She rolled onto her side and hauled herself to her feet.

"Wait, where are you going? Please, you need to rest," Silence urged.

But Rosalie couldn't be rational. Her mind was nothing but a soup of emotions, and she had a bone to pick with a certain pirate. She was unsteady as she shoved open the door with her shoulder, her arms still numb.

Crowe was the picture of smugness as he stood on the deck, a chest teeming with gold at his feet. In the distance, the merchant ship was making a hasty escape.

She shouted at the top of her lungs, "You could've had us killed!"

Silence swooped in to put herself between the captain and the lady. "Please, don't engage with her. Her heart is very weak; she just had a fit."

Crowe folded his arms; his eyes wouldn't meet Rosalie's. "We're not out of danger yet."

"What do you mean?" Silence asked.

"We've got a Durane naval ship coming for us. They'll catch up to us by nightfall."

Rosalie's knees buckled, and her heart thudded painfully in her chest. "Your greed has led them right to us."

Silence didn't move, standing firm in front of Rosalie as if to block her barbs. "We can't outrun them?"

"They've targeted us," Crowe replied honestly. "Even if we run, they'll follow. Warships are like bloodhounds."

It was difficult, but Rosalie steadied her breath to avoid another fit. It helped that Crowe wasn't taunting her. In her dizzy state, she realized he was scared. He wore no smirk and continued glancing over his shoulder. Good—he was the one who had gotten them tied up in this mess, he ought to be nervous. "Then you'll do everything to hide us if they come aboard," she said, and left no room for compromise.

"Duranes have a habit of tearing ships apart looking for contraband," he said.

"I'm sure you have hiding spots for contraband. You can hide us there."

The captain skirted around Silence and stood in front of Rosalie, looking down at her. But he didn't speak.

Hiding her labored breathing to appear stronger, Rosalie wouldn't be intimidated. Not even as his stare sparked some strange feeling in the pit of her stomach. "If the Duranes find me, what will happen to your plan then? They'll take us and probably punish you for intervening with the raiders. If you're lucky to escape with your life, you'll have a damaged ship and not a single coin from my father."

He glared at her for another tense second. "Belowdecks," he clipped. "I'll do what I can to distract them while you two hide."

CHAPTER 23 - THE CAPTAIN

Dusk fell, and Crowe tried to conceal the tension he felt in his neck and shoulders. He held his hands behind his back, watching the four Cross Row naval officers row from their ship to the *Deceit*.

"That's a big ship, Captain," Ori whispered.

Indeed, Crowe saw dozens of Durane soldiers milling around the warship's deck. "That's why we have to compose ourselves," he replied. "Any misstep and we'll have a battle on our hands. Take Upton's gun from him; he's quick on the trigger."

"Aye, Captain." Ori nodded, giving the enemy ship one more nervous look.

Kennedy lowered a ladder to the naval officers.

Crowe braced himself for the start of a dangerous game. He had to be quick on his feet yet calm. He would have to bite his tongue and play nice with the enemy. Pirates and military didn't mix well, but in such a scenario, he couldn't be a pirate.

So, as the men began to board, Crowe went to greet them.

"Captain Adana. Welcome aboard," he said with a feigned smile.

The officer removed his gloves and seemed averse to the ship he stepped foot on. "Commander Bourne," he said, reciprocating the introduction. "I'm not familiar with this vessel." He wasted no time with further pleasantries. His spine was straight, and his hands were folded behind his back. He and his fellow officers looked around the deck with a similar air of distaste. "You're not flying any colors; who are you loyal to?"

"We're from outside Seity," Crowe said. "Not loyal to any of the families—strictly neutral."

"There are sanctions on these waters. Foreign ships cannot sail through without express permission from Eldon Durane. I'll have to inspect your vessel before you can be on your way."

Nothing was worse than allowing soldiers to rummage about. It made Crowe itch to bend to authority. But he'd do it to save his skin. "Inspect for what?"

"Contraband. Ship logs. If I find you're in contact with other armies, we'll have a problem, won't we?"

"I suppose, but we've had no dealings with Seity. Just sailing through. I'd no idea about any sanctions." Crowe wanted to point out that no one, not even Eldon Durane, ruled over the ocean.

Bourne narrowed his eyes. "If you have nothing to hide, there won't be a problem. Let's start with what you have in the hold."

"Of course." Crowe led the officers down into the depths of the ship. "Navies don't normally take an interest in what we have on board. But I'm in a good mood, so I'll let you do your inspection."

"Your cooperation is most generous, Captain," Bourne replied icily.

"Can I ask what you're searching for? I'm sure Seity has a different definition of contraband, aye? What one thinks is a sin, the other thinks is a gift to mankind."

The commander continued inspecting the hold. "I'm sure word has gotten around that Lady Yorke of the Western Cliffs has gone missing."

Crowe didn't let the information cause a reaction. But it was telling. By now, Rydlan must've known his plan was dead in the water along with Kelan. He couldn't be certain if the raiders' leader knew it was the *Deceit* who interfered.

No matter who knew what, the plan had been foiled, and it wouldn't be long before the Duranes set out for blood.

"Yorke… Yorke… Oh yes, I caught wind of it last we were at port," he answered. "Thought it might be worth it to keep an eye out for her if she fetched a good reward. But we don't spend enough time on land to go looking for people."

Over the years, Crowe had learned how to lie his way out of trouble. Braxton had taught him how to glean information while not giving up any of his own knowledge.

"Has anyone claimed the money yet?"

"No," Commander Bourne reported. "Rumor is she was kidnapped. There was an attack off the western coast." He paced around, eyeing every inch and looking behind crates and barrels. "Witnesses said they saw a vessel exchanging fire with a raider ship. You wouldn't happen to know anything about that, would you?"

Crowe let out a casual scoff. "If I kidnapped her, I would be off spending the gold." He chuckled as if he and the officer were old friends.

Bourne didn't look amused. "I suppose." He studied Crowe, no doubt trying to detect if he was lying. He made a noise of distaste and walked another circle around the perimeter. "Anyway, we're more interested in the location of her companion."

A cold feeling overcame Crowe. "Her companion?"

"A dark-haired girl who never leaves her side. We're offering a hefty sum for anyone who delivers her to Lord Durane."

So that was why the raiders had kidnapped Silence too. The Duranes had placed a price on her head as well. But why?

"So, Lady Yorke isn't the target?" It was a risky question to ask, but Crowe needed answers.

Commander Bourne paused his inspection to pivot back. "If Lady Yorke ends up dead, it's no problem of mine. But while she's alive she will not be permitted to return to Ciern."

The plot was getting more convoluted by the minute. "Huh. Well, I haven't seen anyone of that description. It's bad luck to have a woman on board anyway; the money wouldn't be worth the risk. Kennedy, you didn't catch sight of a dark-haired girl while we were at port?"

Artfully, the quartermaster had positioned himself over the hatch that led below the galley. His foot covered the latch. "No, Captain. There were so many people, I didn't pay anyone any mind."

"Too many people at port to question if any of them are wanted."

Bourne's eyes narrowed when Crowe dared to crack another joke.

Crowe hid his growing dread. Some officers could be disarmed by breezy sailor talk, but Bourne seemed too high in the ranks to be swayed.

"Where are you from, Captain?"

Crowe considered lying but he had a feeling it would make things worse. "The Territories."

The officer's cold look twisted into something more sinister. "Ah, yes. Just beyond the mountains. Not so far, wouldn't you say?"

"It feels far enough away on the ocean."

"Yes, but not so far for armies."

Crowe understood the veiled threat. "Seity wants the Territories, then?" He tried to sound nonchalant, but his blood boiled.

The deck creaked as Bourne crowded into Crowe's space. "Lord Durane will do what he thinks is fit," Bourne replied. "Men of your… birth needn't worry."

Crowe gritted his teeth. He'd been talked down to more times than he cared to count. Usually, he responded swiftly, but if he drew a weapon, Bourne wouldn't hesitate to retaliate. However, Crowe couldn't bite his tongue. "Eldon Durane might find it difficult to subdue Territory men like me."

For an older officer, Bourne moved remarkably fast. He used his forearm to pin Crowe against a supporting beam. There was a corresponding rustle, and Crowe knew his crew was ready to attack. But he held up a hand to stop them. One slip of the tongue wasn't going to sink their ship.

"That's a lot of talk for a merchant," Bourne hissed, not releasing his hold. "Are you sure you're not loyal to any family?"

Crowe looked the man dead in the eyes. "Positive."

A few more tense moments passed before Bourne eased up. "Very well. Where is your vessel heading now?"

"The Islands," Crowe answered. "Going to stock up on rations."

"I see." There was a tense pause. "Well, it's obvious you haven't come across who we're looking for. I appreciate your candor, Captain."

"The pleasure's all mine." Crowe was eager to get the man out of the hold. He kept talking, distracting him as best as he could. "Good luck with your war. Can't say I'm jealous; must be difficult, aye?" As they returned upstairs to the main deck, he rambled on to hurry the man along.

But the commander was attentive and stopped in his tracks when he saw a hairpin lying on the deck. Crowe's heart leaped to his throat as the officer stooped down to pick up the object. "I thought you didn't have women on board," he said in a frosty voice.

"Oh, that's just a token from home." Crowe plucked the pin from the man's hand before he could inspect it further. "Poor Leyla would be heartbroken if you lost this." He pushed the sapphire-tipped object toward Kennedy.

He didn't blink an eye, always in sync. "Thank you, Captain. She told me to keep it safe. Must've slipped away," he said, and pocketed it without hesitation.

Commander Bourne eyed them both, and Crowe feared a little hairpin would be their undoing. But he gave a curt nod. "I'll advise you again of the sanctions, Captain. You should be on your way, and stay out of these waters. The next time you're spotted out here, there will be consequences."

Crowe stifled a sigh of relief. "We'll start our course for the Islands immediately. Won't see us around these parts again," he replied, an obedient tone plastered over the disdain he buried.

After one more sweeping glance over the crew, the officer nodded to his counterparts, and they returned to their ship.

As they rowed away, Crowe stood frozen on the deck. Once he dropped the mask, the information hit him like a well-aimed boulder.

"Captain, I'm not sure I understand," Kennedy said, and pulled the hairpin from his pocket. "I thought Lady Yorke was the only target."

"As did I. But it seems like the Duranes are keener to find Silence." Crowe's mind was whirring with any possible explanation as to why Eldon Durane would be interested in Silence. "They've got some questions to answer."

CHAPTER 24 - THE LADY

From her hiding spot among the discarded barrel pieces and ropes in the storage, Rosalie felt like she'd been hit in the gut. Her mind was running wild, swooping and circling like the gulls that fished from the air.

What did the Duranes want with Silence? Rosalie cautioned herself to not relax even as the voices left the hold. She'd been positive she was the target and Silence was collateral damage. But how did they even know about her? Edme and Silence had lived a quiet, unassuming life in the Yorke manor for a decade.

In the dim light passing through the slats above them, Rosalie couldn't make out Silence's expression. But she could feel her trembling. Certain they would sort out the misunderstanding, Rosalie reached for Silence.

Footsteps creaked overhead and Rosalie tensed up, wrapping herself tighter around Silence's arm.

"Just me," Crowe assured them before he opened the hatch. He offered a hand to help Silence out of the hold first.

"They're gone?" Rosalie asked, reluctantly taking his hand next.

"Yes, but we were nearly caught by a hairpin someone left out on the deck," he replied, his words sharpened for a fight.

"Oh, so this is my fault?" Rosalie scoffed and followed him back up to the main deck. The stress was weighing down on her, and she felt like a wounded animal, persisting despite it all. Her skin was warm, and she was starting to lose track of what to focus on. Everything seemed to blur together. "Not the fact that you needed to loot someone in front of a warship to feed your own ego?"

"I'm not apologizing for how I run my ship," he asserted. "But you two have a lot of explaining to do."

"What do you mean?" Rosalie snarled. "There's nothing to explain. We know just as much as you do—perhaps even less."

"You both heard what that man said. He was looking for her too." Crowe pointed at Silence.

Rosalie placed herself between them, determined to defend her friend. "Then they're mistaken because she has nothing to do with any of this!"

"Men like that don't make mistakes, Lady Yorke. They know who they're hunting down and why," Crowe retorted. "Now, she has to tell me why the Duranes are after her."

"She doesn't know!" Rosalie yelled. "Silence is innocent, and I don't appreciate you accusing her of anything." She was overheated and assumed it was the anger she always felt in the captain's presence. But the deck below felt like it was falling out from under her feet. She wasn't aware she was swaying until she felt Silence's hand on her shoulder. Her firm touch held Rosalie steady.

"What's the matter with you?" Crowe's nose wrinkled.

"I felt how warm she was when she was next to me down below. She's not well." Silence's voice sounded miles away. "Sometimes when she has fits it's an indication that she's caught a fever."

"M'fine," Rosalie slurred.

Crowe stepped toward her and pressed the back of his hand to her forehead. "You're right—she's burning up."

With a limp hand, Rosalie batted him away. "Ge'off."

But Crowe ignored her protests and scooped her up in his arms. "Follow me; I have a few tricks to break a fever."

Rosalie snorted in delirious amusement when her stomach swooped from the change in altitude. Her pulse pounded in her ears, and a cold sweat started to chill her to the bone. She wasn't sure if she even made it to the captain's office because the world started to fade away.

But three words followed her into the darkness.

Fawn in blue.

CHAPTER 25 - THE CAPTAIN

None of it made sense. The Duranes were after Silence, and Crowe had felt genuine panic when Rosalie went limp in his arms. He couldn't decide which was more puzzling.

After the chaos, a strange lull had taken hold of the ship as Rosalie recovered. Around midnight—thanks to a cold cloth—her fever broke, but she remained unconscious.

Crowe stepped into the cabin to check on Silence, who had watched over Rosalie all evening. "How is she?"

It didn't matter how loud they talked; Rosalie seemed to be in another plane of existence as she rode out the fever.

"She'll be okay." Silence looked down at her friend curled up under a bundle of furs. "The fever broke, thanks to your help."

Crowe didn't dwell on the praise; he would've done the same for anyone on his ship. "Does this happen a lot?"

Rosalie had taken ill so rapidly, it caught him off guard. So much so that he had entirely forgotten what they had been arguing about when she passed out. He knew she was fragile, but it was worse than he'd expected.

Silence nodded with a grave expression. "It's a miracle she's lived this long. I've known her since we were just children, and there have been many times that I thought we were going to lose her to a fit or an infection. But she never gave up."

Crowe thrummed his fingers on his desk. "That must have been difficult." The words sounded strange to him. He rarely had any sympathy for anyone outside his crew. Sympathy was a sign of weakness, and those who were weak were taken advantage of.

"For so long, I thought she would be cured. I thought someday we'd find the one doctor who could help her, but I don't think it'll ever happen. All we can do is hope that she can keep fighting." Silence reached down and adjusted the cloth resting on Rosalie's pale forehead.

He didn't want to pity Rosalie. She had known nothing but luxury. A warm bed, a roof over her head, expensive clothing, and servants. He'd seen many men become more wicked the wealthier they got. Crowe had never wanted that path for himself. What mattered to him was the ocean, his crew, his ship, and the thrill of adventure. He couldn't say for sure what mattered to Rosalie aside from Silence. All the things she possessed were hollow and were worth little when everything eventually turned to ash.

"She used to talk about traveling across the ocean," Silence added. "I'm sure this isn't what she thought it would be, but I think she likes it more than she anticipated."

He smiled slightly to himself. He knew all too well what that was like. The ocean's pull was too strong to ignore. He couldn't go far on land without hearing the waves calling to him. If he could have one wish, he wanted to die on his ship and be buried at sea.

"Well, I suppose we can agree on one thing, then. The world isn't complete without the ocean."

Silence looked up with kind eyes. "You're passionate about your crew, and she's passionate about her family. You two might have more in common than you think."

"I've found that pirates and ladies mix as well as oil and water."

She made a noise that neither agreed nor disagreed. "I've never seen anyone encourage her to stand up for herself like you have."

"Encourage?' His eyebrow rose. "I assure you, I'm not encouraging anything."

With a faint smile, Silence just shrugged. "You do in your own way."

The room went quiet. Crowe inhaled and steeled himself for the inevitable. He couldn't ignore the trouble he'd brought onto his ship.

"So, you have a history with the Duranes?"

Silence flinched but shook her head. "No. As I said, I've lived at the Yorke manor for ten years. Before that, I lived with my mother in the heart of Ciern. I've seen just as little of the world as Rosalie has."

It didn't allay Crowe's suspicions. "But they know you exist. I've never known the Duranes to care about anyone they haven't crossed paths with before."

Despite his bluntness, Silence didn't crack. She pursed her lips and continued fussing with the cloth on Rosalie's face. "I don't know what to tell you; I'm sorry."

She was lying. From day one, he'd seen how she hid her secrets. He didn't think she was malicious—rather, she was trying to survive. He frowned and wondered if Rosalie knew. She had been so rabid trying to defend Silence from accusations. Still, Rosalie didn't seem to know much about many things.

"You don't think she deserves to know?" Crowe nodded to Rosalie.

Silence took a slow breath. "I know you were insistent upon your plan to wait," she said. "But I think it might be better if you brought us back to land. You can collect your ransom there with no threat to your life. It would be better for everyone."

Crowe's mouth went dry, and he understood what Silence was saying even if she didn't speak the words. Out in the ocean, his ship and crew were at risk because of the company he had on board. What they witnessed the previous night was just a taste of what was to come if Rosalie and Silence stayed.

"I suppose if I knew what we were dealing with, I'd be better prepared." But he glanced at Rosalie, her face ashen as she recovered. Even without the Duranes on their tail, there was no denying Rosalie was in rough shape. Time was not their ally.

"I'm sorry," Silence echoed herself. "There's nothing I can tell you."

Silence didn't have to tell him the truth, but he wasn't going to pretend to believe her lies.

"Then we're left in the same spot as before."

Silence stood up and avoided looking at him. "Would you mind watching her for a moment? I need some fresh air."

"Sure," he answered. "I'll stay with her."

Silence thanked him and stepped outside onto the deck.

Crowe wandered over to his bookshelf and idly scanned the titles. He had to conjure up a new plan, and fast. But his brain was moving slowly, and he was desperate for a break.

He sighed and ran his fingers over the spines of the books. He had read every single one, some more than once. His eyes landed on one of his favorite stories. It was a book Braxton had given to him as a boy. After Kennedy had painstakingly taken the time to teach a younger Crowe how to read, he devoured books faster than Braxton could supply them.

But one had always been his favorite. The story of a boy who sailed every sea in the world, fighting sea creatures and finding sunken treasure.

Rosalie let out a quiet noise and stirred. Crowe looked over his shoulder to see if she was waking up. But she turned over and went still again. He paused, waiting for her shoulders to move so he knew she was breathing.

The fragility of life was not lost on him. At fifteen, he'd watched a storm sweep a crewmate off the deck. The ocean had swallowed him whole and left no trace that he'd ever existed.

It seemed life kept trying to sweep Rosalie into the depths. But she kept clawing her way back onto the ship.

Crowe pulled his favorite book off the shelf. The pages were worn from years of being reread. It was a treasured possession—even more valuable than gold. He rounded his desk and stooped low to place the book next to Rosalie.

A captain needed to know when to cut his losses. With no answers, no naval ships, and a sick lady, the losses were building. His previous plan had run its course, and he found himself in dangerous waters. It was time to rid himself of the burden of Seity's most wanted.

CHAPTER 26- THE LADY

Something was digging into Rosalie's hand. The sharp pressure spread across her body, shaking off the numbness. When she opened her eyes, all she could see were fuzzy blobs of color. So, it was daytime. Hadn't it been nighttime when she fainted?

As her vision cleared, she saw her hand resting on a book, part of her palm resting on the corner. She pulled her hand away to see the faint indent it had left in her skin.

Her thoughts were slower than her body as she sat up. The book at her side was worn, and the title's gold letters were faded.

The Twelve Adventures of Bedros the Brave

Her fingers grazed the spine and went to open it. But she wondered if Crowe was taunting her with a book from the collection he'd banned her from touching.

Forgetting the book, she placed her hand over her heart to feel it pulsing rhythmically. Rosalie wasn't sure if she'd suffered another fit. All she could recall was hiding with Silence in the belly of the ship. Dread bloomed across

Rosalie's chest when she remembered what the military officer had said.

Before Rosalie could make any sense of it, the door opened, and Silence stepped inside. "Oh, thank goodness," she said breathlessly, and hurried over. "How are you feeling?" She lifted a hand to Rosalie's forehead and cheeks.

"Confused."

Silence lowered to the floor beside her. "You had a fever. After your fit, I realized—"

"No, not that." Rosalie wasn't concerned with what had knocked her out. "I'm confused about what I heard."

For ten years, their friendship had been as honest as they came. Her father and brothers had kept things from her on the basis that she didn't need to know the plight of war. But Silence had never withheld anything from Rosalie. They were honest with each other even when they'd bickered over petty things.

But since leaving Vale Fall, something had shifted. Silence pursed her lips and looked away. "I wish I could tell you what that was about." She patted Rosalie's hand with a faint smile.

The door swung open again, interrupting the conversation. Crowe went to step inside but stopped in his tracks when his eyes landed on Rosalie. "Oh, you're awake. Good, uh..." He cleared his throat. "About time."

Rosalie raised an eyebrow. Since when had he ever been relieved to see her?

"You left your book lying around." She picked it up and held it out to him. "Don't want to lose one of your precious first editions."

"I didn't—I left that for you to read." He didn't move from the doorway to take it from her.

"You said—"

"I know what I said. But that's not a first edition, and I

was being generous. Don't get used to it," he said, and backed out of the cabin.

Rosalie lowered the book but didn't release her grip. "Every time I think I have him figured out," she muttered.

Silence didn't seem to hear her as she stifled a yawn. "I was up all night, so I'm going to take a nap."

"Thank you for keeping me safe." All the doubt in the world couldn't put a wedge between her and Silence. "I wish I could do something for you in return."

"I don't need anything in return because I know you'd do the same for me." She squeezed Rosalie's shoulder before heading over to the pile of furs.

Rosalie's legs were shaky as she stood and left the cabin. After a night of suffering a fever, the ocean air felt incredible on her skin.

She found Crowe watching Danny spar with another crew member. She stood next to the captain and pressed the book to her chest.

They watched the duel side by side without saying a word. It was fun to watch two experienced fighters without the threat of harm. It almost looked like a dance—an art of quick steps and clever maneuvers. Out of nowhere, she felt a burning passion to wield a blade. The thought had never crossed her mind before. Before, she had only wanted to take on the role of a lady who didn't need any weapons aside from wit and charm.

But seeing the sabers glint in the sunlight sparked a deep desire. Maybe she'd spent too much time among pirates.

"Can I help you?" Crowe broke her fixation.

"What's the book about?"

"I suppose the point of reading books is to find out what they're about," he replied without looking at her.

"What changed your mind?"

"Nothing changed my mind. It's an act of grace; savor it, because that's the only book you're getting."

Although he was back to acting prickly, the gesture of giving her a book said more than his words did. "Why did you pick this one? Is it your least favorite?"

"On the contrary," he said, still avoiding eye contact. "It's my favorite, so I'd prefer nothing happen to it."

She made a noise of interest but didn't say anything else. The captain had lent her a book—not just any book, but his favorite one. It was hard to unravel, but in a way, she felt like she had won at least one round of bickering.

In her victory, she threw Crowe a smirk. But it faded when she saw the late morning sun beaming down on him. His eye color warmed, and the wave of his dark hair caught every ray and rustled a bit in the wind.

At the worst possible moment, he looked her way. When their eyes met, he looked… nervous? "Why are you looking at me like that?"

"Huh?" she blurted with too much gusto. "Why are *you* looking at *me*?" When his eyebrow quirked up, she shuffled backward. "Thanks for the book." She ducked her head and made a quick escape to hide her blush.

CHAPTER 27- THE CAPTAIN

"How easy would it be to track down a Seity army squadron?"

When Kennedy's pen stilled, Crowe knew he'd caught the quartermaster off guard with the question. Both he and Crowe were in the galley going over the records of rations. They were meant to be in Ivona by now, but their detour was eating away at their reserves. All the careful planning back in Cilisca had been picked apart.

They'd been working out a plan to maintain the ship as best they could. Well, Kennedy worked out a plan. Crowe was distracted.

Silence's warning had weighed on him all night. Having Rosalie on board was a threat he could account for. He knew her enemies and knew her allies. But Silence remained an enigma, and he couldn't predict what danger her presence might attract.

"I suppose it depends on why you need an army squadron, Captain."

Crowe didn't want to raise alarm on his ship. But he needed to carry out his next steps with precision. "The

Durane ship was a close call; I'm not sure we can stay in one place for much longer."

"So, you want to bring them to land? Yet you still want Rosalie's father to pay for her return."

"Exactly." Crowe could always count on his quartermaster to understand his plans, no matter how convoluted they might be.

Kennedy closed the ledger, further displaying his unease. "Battles on land aren't exactly our specialty, Captain. I can't imagine a military officer giving us the time of day to explain ourselves."

"It'd be a delicate operation," he admitted. "But I'm not going to Ciern's port to be ambushed." Crowe knew diverting to another plan meant he was admitting his first plan was flawed. He imagined how Rosalie would taunt him. His crew might see him as weak.

Kennedy appeared to mull over the details. "Maybe if she wrote a letter and gave some type of evidence that she's on the *Deceit*. That way, we wouldn't be shot on sight."

Crowe clapped the quartermaster on the shoulder. "There's a bay on the border of the Row and the Cliffs. It's a safe place for the ship, and the land will be crawling with Yorke soldiers." His mind was made up. He wondered if he could spin it in a way that made it clear he wasn't changing his mind because of Rosalie Yorke's bidding.

"Captain, I trust your judgment, but if this goes poorly, if we don't receive money…"

"Your concerns are noted, but I have a good feeling about this, so let's set a course."

CHAPTER 28 - THE LADY

The cycle of recovery was familiar to Rosalie. If she overexerted herself too soon, she fell back into the pit of pain. However, maintaining her composure was difficult aboard the *Deceit*.

Doubt flew at her from all sides. Crowe seemed so certain Silence was keeping secrets about the Duranes. He had refused to listen to Rosalie, who knew her friend had no dealings outside the manor. She'd lived a sheltered life just like Rosalie.

Once Rosalie told her father about Eldon Durane's plot, everything would be settled. He would take care of any threat.

Basil often warned his daughter to keep her questions to herself. Even if Rosalie decoded the letter, she wouldn't know what to do with the information. She was too fragile and too inexperienced. For her, everything felt out of reach.

To keep herself away from unanswered questions, she dove into the book Crowe had lent her. It helped to spend the afternoon with her mind in another world.

It wasn't until she noticed movement in her periphery

that she lowered the book to glance out the window. To her surprise, the *Deceit* was moving at a fast clip through the waves.

Shocked, she set the book down and hurried outside. The sails were rigged, and Upton was barking out orders. A strong gust of wind rushed forward, making her braid swing and her skirts rustle. It felt like it was beckoning her to dance.

"Ah, Lady Yorke, no doubt you're here to tell me I'm doing something wrong," Crowe called out, disrupting her serenity. He stood near the mast with Silence at his side.

"I suppose it depends on where you're taking us now."

"He's bringing us to land," Silence said with a smile on her face.

Relief washed over Rosalie. She was flooded with the desire to step foot on land again, eat a hot meal, and take a long bath. "It seems you've finally come to your senses, then," she said to Crowe.

"My decision had nothing to do with your input," he responded. "We're doing this my way, so don't look so smug."

But Rosalie still took it as a victory, so she gloated a bit.

Crowe rolled his eyes. "It'll take a few days until we're there." He walked past the two of them.

"But Ciern is—"

"Didn't say I was taking you to Ciern, did I, Lady Yorke?" he called over his shoulder.

Her satisfied smirk morphed into a scowl. "So, it'll take even longer? If we aren't going to Ciern, then where is he bringing us?" Rosalie asked Silence.

"Somewhere neutral. He wants your father's army to deliver a ransom first. I'm sure from there, the men can escort us back to Ciern. The end's in sight." Silence seemed more hopeful about it, even though the plan sounded unnecessarily difficult to Rosalie.

At first, it was a relief to hear. But Rosalie had a nagging feeling that even when they got back to land, the end of this mystery would remain far out of reach.

* * *

A FEW DAYS. Rosalie could survive a few more days. Perhaps she should've paced herself with Crowe's book; she worried she would finish it long before her time on board the *Deceit* was up. But she couldn't help herself; sitting on the deck with the book resting against her knees, she kept turning the page. The adventure captivated her. Strangely, it made her feel more excited to be out on the ocean like Bedros. With the salty wind in her hair, she could imagine herself living out his thrilling escapades.

"Going to join you for a bit."

Rosalie looked up from the pages to see Crowe approaching. The late afternoon sun framed his tall figure. With his hair askew and his sleeves rolled up, he looked in need of a break.

"Okay…" Warily, she moved to the side to allow him to sit. It seemed when the plan changed, so did their dynamic. Suddenly, Crowe was much more tolerant of her presence.

It didn't help that Rosalie couldn't decipher her own feelings about the pirate. As a person, she wasn't fond of him. He was smug and aloof, with questionable morals. But whenever he was near, she felt captivated by him in the worst ways.

Crowe let out a long sigh as he sat down. He bent one knee and let the other leg stretch out.

Rosalie pretended to keep reading. "Nothing to say? What? Are you tired of mocking me?"

He tipped his head back. "Yes, you exhaust me."

A laugh bubbled in her throat, but she shoved it down. She ought to be mad at him for endangering their lives the other day. But the book maintained the provisional peace, as if the pages themselves were a temporary ceasefire.

Rosalie knew they only had to tolerate each other for another couple of days. And in the precarious calmness, she supposed it didn't hurt to make idle conversation. "Can I ask you a question?"

"You told me you would continue asking me the same question until I answered. So, I've learned that I can't stop you."

"Your eyepatch. How did you—I mean, has it been a long time since you lost your eye?" Her face reddened, and she tried to rescind her awkward words. "I apologize; that wasn't polite of me to ask."

Crowe looked delighted at the question, which Rosalie found strange. "I'll tell you how I lost my eye; it's a fascinating story." He leaned forward, resting an arm on his knee. "It was only a year ago; the *Deceit* was under attack. We'd looted a privateer ship and kidnapped their doctor on board. Very helpful for a ship, a surgeon is. You see, when you need a limb cut off, you want a man with a trained hand. Otherwise, you'd have Upton's shaky hand trying to saw through the bone."

Rosalie let out a squeak of discomfort at the thought.

"Exactly." He chuckled. "Of course, our foes would not let us get away without a fight. The captain boarded our ship, and I had to fight for my life."

She was rapt with attention. He spun the story like he was reading one of Bedros's adventures off the page.

"I made it out alive, but not unscathed. The privateer stuck me right in the eye and ripped it out of the socket. I tried to find it once the battle was won, but it was probably lost to the sea. A fitting burial for it, I like to think." Without warning, he flipped up the eyepatch.

Rosalie jolted in surprise and went to look away. But a

macabre curiosity goaded her to peek. To her surprise and annoyance, he had tricked her.

Crowe had two perfectly intact eyes.

"Fooled you, didn't I?" He let the eyepatch stay flipped up over his forehead.

"You could've just told me the truth," she mumbled, annoyed that she had been so gullible. She thought having two brothers would've made her wise to such tricks.

"It was too tempting to pass up the opportunity."

Rosalie frowned, but her curiosity persisted. "Then why wear it? Just to fool people? To make yourself look intimidating?"

"No, and no. The patch isn't meant to cover a gouged-out eye. I suppose it could if needed, but that's not why it was created." He slipped off the patch to show her. "If a battle goes under the deck, a pirate needs to see so he can duel his opponent. Your enemy won't give you time to acclimate to the darkness." He reached over to let his hand hover an inch from Rosalie's right eye. "If you keep one eye covered, it's already adjusted to lack of light. Once you go under the deck to fight, you simply switch—" he shifted his hand to her left eye, "—so you're prepared to fight immediately."

Though she didn't want to credit pirates with their ingenuity, Rosalie couldn't help but be impressed. She also couldn't help but notice how close he was sitting. "That's brilliant," she breathed.

"Aye, pirates are brilliant in their own ways."

For the first time, he looked at her without the patch. His gray eyes held the same power as the ocean. They shifted with his emotion, and as he looked at her, they gleamed with a hint of playfulness.

Rosalie made sure she didn't stare. Especially when she wondered if she had ever seen such a beautiful person before. Her cheeks flushed, and she scolded herself. There was no way she could think he was good-looking or charming—not after all the grief he had caused her.

She pointedly looked away, and a glint across the deck drew her attention. A few tarnished bronze hilts poked out from a box lashed to the mainmast. "What are those?"

"Sparring sabers," he responded. "Nothing for a lady to wield."

Again, the desire to hold a weapon seized control over her. "Then what *am* I meant to wield? What if another Durane ship apprehends us?"

He shrugged as if it wasn't a scenario he bothered to anticipate. "Even if you had the finest blade, you wouldn't stand a chance."

Rosalie marked her page in the book and placed it on Crowe's lap. "Well, Silence says in order to get good at something, you need to practice." She stood and headed to the box.

"It takes years to master, not hours." Crowe was fast on her heels. "Besides, you think I'd let you brandish a weapon on my ship?"

"What harm could I possibly be if it takes years to master?"

"Rosalie, I mean it."

"Oh, no more *Lady Yorke*?" she taunted, and withdrew one of the dulled sabers. "Come now, Captain, surely you can't be afraid of me."

He stood in place with the book in his hand. His eyes raked over her, and he cleared his throat. "What I'm afraid of is you were on your deathbed last night. Do you think Silence would take kindly to me if I let you around a weapon?" He set the book down and looked ready to intervene.

But Rosalie didn't give him the chance, turning away to test the weight of the blade. It was deceptively light and easy to maneuver. She looked over her shoulder to see Crowe still staring at her. She couldn't quite decipher his expression. The way his gray eyes watched with intensity, how his lips parted ever so slightly.

She shook her braid off her shoulder and cleared her throat. "I'm bored, and I'd like you to teach me how to wield a saber."

He scoffed and broke his gaze. "You're always bored, and I'm beginning to think it's just a game for you. You asked for a book; I gave you a book. You're going to keep asking for things, and before I know it, you'll want to steer my ship and run her aground."

When he turned his head, Rosalie saw the natural sharpness of his jaw. The rogue thought struck her. Disgruntled, she raised the saber.

"Uh… what's going on?" Silence was frozen in mid-step on her way out of the cabin.

It must've been a sight to see Rosalie flaunting steel in front of the captain. "Crowe is being most uncooperative."

Silence blinked. "So, you're trying to stage a mutiny?"

Crowe barked out a laugh. Apparently, something about Rosalie attempting to steal power from him was amusing. Nevertheless, he implored Silence, "Will you please tell her she's in no condition to fight me? Healthy, well-trained men three times her size are in no condition to fight me."

With the threat of a mutiny quelled, Silence shrugged with an easygoing smile. "Rose bounces back remarkably fast. And you know how stubborn she can be." She took a seat, looking the part of an eager spectator.

"What in the world do they teach you Seity girls? That weapons are fun toys?" he huffed before pulling a saber from the box. "Fine; it won't take long for you to regret this. I'll even let you have the first move."

Now that she'd been invited to fight the man who had teased her for days on end, Rosalie lunged. Without even moving his feet, he deflected the blow and twisted the saber right out of her hand.

She watched her weapon clatter to the deck in disbelief. "How did you…"

"Six years of training, love. Now, are we done?"

The nickname tore through Rosalie. Her heart fluttered, and her mind wrinkled. She was breathless for a moment, suspended in his careless slip of the tongue.

"No," she replied, and bent down to retrieve her saber. Concentrating, she tried to approach him from his non-dominant side.

It was no good; the captain moved with such sharp but fluid movements. It was as if he could anticipate her every move. Untrained and weakened from years kept at rest, Rosalie struggled to keep up. Yet her frustration fueled her, and she refused to back down.

Love. How dare he tease her with such pet names?

After the fourth time he disarmed her, a cold sweat formed on her brow. Nevertheless, she stooped to pick up the blade.

"You haven't given up yet?" Crowe taunted.

"Not a chance." Before he could respond, she attacked. Faking a swing, she used the ploy to step closer toward him. She thought he wouldn't be able to defend himself if she was closer. But Rosalie was blindsided in an instant. He grabbed her wrist to stop her attack. His strong hand kept her in place as he brought his blade within inches of her side.

Breathing hard, Rosalie opened her mouth to say something but found herself transfixed by his eyes—the very epitome of a stormy sky—flashing with mischief and intrigue. His height was more pronounced up close, and she had to tilt her chin. Her lips parted, and goose bumps raised on her arms.

Crowe broke the spell and drew his weapon back. "Are

we done here?" He took his time uncurling his fingers from around her wrist. It felt like the imprint of his fingertips had burned her skin. The pressure and warmth lingered.

"*Vellah*," she grumbled under her breath. "You haven't taught me anything. Except that you're infuriating, but I already knew that."

He went to return his weapon to the box. "I never once said I was going to teach you anything."

Her exhaustion would not let him have the last laugh. Rosalie raised her blade and pressed the dulled tip between his shoulders. "Then perhaps I'm here to teach you to never turn your back on your opponent."

"Interesting move, Lady Yorke." He turned. "But I'd still have the upper hand over you."

So, they were back to Lady Yorke again.

"No, you'd be dead."

"Trust me, I wouldn't."

Her grip on the blade tightened. "If this was sharpened—"

"You would've sliced off one of your fingers by now." He stepped toward her and plucked the saber out of her hand. "I could fight you blindfolded with one hand tied behind my back."

Rosalie rolled her eyes. "Your confidence astounds me."

He just gave her a sweeping bow and a mocking wink. "Then I've proved my point." And without another word, he strode past her.

Rosalie huffed and looked to Silence, who had watched the entire exchange. Her friend smiled and gave a little clap. "I thought you did pretty well."

"For someone who's sick," Rosalie muttered, and went over to her.

"I was going to side with him on asking you to rest. But I saw it in your eyes."

"Saw what?"

Silence's nose crinkled with thought. "I'm not sure how to describe it. It was just… different. How do you feel?"

It was a question Rosalie had been asked thousands of times in her life. It served to remind her she was always teetering on a delicate balance of survival. Still, it had been nice to feel like she could fight, even if Crowe was patronizing her. For once, she felt in control of herself. But a little stint with a sword hadn't cured her desire, it had only inflamed it.

"Fine," Rosalie replied. "I feel perfectly fine."

CHAPTER 29- THE LADY

According to Kennedy, they were two days away from Seity. Forty-eight hours, give or take, until Rosalie and Silence would stand on dry land again. Rosalie's hope was revived, but it left a hollow feeling in her chest.

In the darkness of night, a curious question popped into her head. Where would the *Deceit* go next? As Silence slept soundly next to her, Rosalie mentally scolded herself. She shouldn't bother with the dealings of pirates.

She tried to close her eyes, but for the first time on the ship, sleep eluded her. With a quiet sigh, she got up and snuck out of the room. She found the deck empty aside from Crowe.

The moon hung overhead, barely illuminating his figure. His back was turned to her, and he had a small cutlass in hand. With graceful, quick motions, he fought an invisible enemy. It had been a blur when she sparred with him, but from a distance, he made swordplay look like a delicate art.

She stepped closer, and the deck creaked under her. She paused in place and stifled a curse under her breath.

Crowe stopped and lowered his weapon. "I know you're

there," he said before turning. His face reflected mild surprise. "Oh, I thought you were Ori."

"Where is your crew?"

He sheathed the cutlass. "They're belowdecks playing cards." As if on cue, a rousing cheer sounded from under their feet.

"Why aren't you playing?"

"Because Kennedy is too smart and Upton cheats by counting cards. It's a rigged game from the start." He took a seat on the stairs leading up to the quarterdeck.

Rosalie cautiously moved toward him, trying to determine if he was offering an invitation to stay. "He counts cards? How do you know that?"

"Because he taught me how." He flashed her a grin.

Her muscles relaxed, and she sat on the step next to him. "I can see how your charm keeps you alive."

"Do my ears deceive me, or was that a compliment?" he asked in faux shock.

"No. It's merely an observation. I'm not here to compliment pirates." She lifted her gaze to the stars decorating the night sky. She remembered Emery telling her how sailors used stars to navigate the ocean.

Crowe didn't respond for a long while, and when Rosalie glanced over, she caught him staring. Quickly, he cleared his throat and averted his eyes. "Aye, I suppose you're just here to drive me mad."

"It was your decision to hold us for a ransom," she reminded him.

"Not many options when there's a good deal of gold up for grabs."

"Is that all you really care about? Gold?"

He let out a terse laugh. "That's easy for you to ask; you've never known what it's like to be poor."

"You don't have to have money to know there's more to

life than being wealthy," she argued. "There're more important things to care about."

"I care about a lot of things. I care about my crew and the *Deceit*. And to keep all this running smoothly—" he gestured to the ship around them, "—we need money."

Rosalie had never gone without when it came to the necessities of life. She'd known security and never suffered through what others did. Still, she disagreed with how Crowe earned a living. "And this sum you plan to demand from my father—will it be enough for you to quit?" she asked, suspending her criticism for a moment.

"Quit?" He raised an eyebrow. "Pirates don't quit. We're killed or imprisoned. Growing old is a luxury most can't afford."

A chill went down Rosalie's spine. "And you're okay with that?"

He gave an unbothered shrug. "I like my life out here. Best to live the life you have for as long as you have it."

Rosalie chewed on the inside of her cheek. Old age was a luxury to her too. Many doctors had given her estimates on how long she would live. Some she had outgrown; some still loomed. No amount of money could buy her more time.

"Do you know how to throw a proper punch?" Crowe asked when the air between them went stale.

"Pardon?"

"I was watching you fight and you're not… great."

"Thanks," she deadpanned.

"It was the first time you picked up a blade. I warned that you weren't going to be good." He paused for a moment. "But you have some fight in you. I mean, I already knew that. Most girls your size wouldn't pick fights with pirates."

Her eyes narrowed. "I told you to stop calling me short."

He snickered. "Would you rather I lie?" When she just

scoffed in response, he continued. "Look, you said it yourself: You just need practice."

Rosalie sat up a bit straighter. "You think? Most people say I'm too sick to do anything."

"Well, you've been battling your illness, so I figure that makes you something of a fighter." He shrugged, apparently not concerned whether he was complimenting her or not.

It was praise she had never heard before. Rosalie had always assumed her life was nothing more than a mistake or a string of failures. People pitied her and thought death was a kindness to take her pain away.

"I'm still not capable of—"

"You've got high expectations for yourself, don't you?" he interrupted.

"As a lady—"

"What does being a lady have to do with anything? Why do you care so much about what people expect?"

She blinked, taken aback at his direct challenge. "Upholding those expectations is important to my family."

Once the words hit the salty air, they rang false. Her father expected two things from her—to stay quiet and respectful. She hadn't been allowed to attend important dinners and knew very little about the state of their land. She had never shared the responsibilities her mother once bore.

"And you like people telling you what to do? Since I've known you, you've been pretty averse to it."

"I wouldn't expect a pirate to understand what it means to follow rules."

Beside her, Crowe yawned and leaned back on his elbows. "Why can't *you* just quit? Say you're done and toss the title?"

Such an idea had never crossed Rosalie's mind. She had presumed she would live and die within the walls of the

Yorke manor. Inside, it was safe and she wouldn't have to brave the world. A world she would never get to explore.

"Pirates don't quit. Well, neither do nobles." Rosalie had never heard of any heir relinquishing their claim to a title.

Gunn, Durane, Yorke—and at one point, Weller—children knew where their fates lay. The expectations of a leader were injected into the bloodstream at the moment of birth.

Rosalie clasped her hands together. "I owe my family my loyalty."

"Why?"

Leave it to the pirate to ask the hardest questions because he wasn't bound by the usual decorum. Nothing was standing in his way to challenge her beliefs. In fact, it seemed like he enjoyed the pastime. "Because of what my existence means."

"Ah, because you're very important."

For the first time, Rosalie knew Crowe wasn't intentionally trying to hurt her feelings. From the outside, her title commanded respect. But most people didn't know her true role in the family. A placeholder and nothing else.

"My mother wanted to name me Emeline," Rosalie blurted.

Crowe raised an eyebrow, seemingly confused as to how the conversation had diverted course so drastically. "So, why is your name Rosalie?"

She tried to shake off the chill from the night air. "I was born much earlier than expected, and my mother didn't survive the delivery." She couldn't speak above a whisper. "The midwife didn't think I would last the night."

"I can imagine your father was happy you survived," Crowe said, his voice softer than she'd ever heard. "I'm sure it's always good to have an abundance of heirs." His reasoning was sound, but the truth lay miles away.

"No, he wasn't happy."

"No?"

"He loved my mother very much."

Rosalie had been conditioned to defend Basil. Anyone who criticized the lord criticized the Western Cliffs. She corrected anyone who would dare suggest her father was wrong. It was easier to ignore the rift her birth had caused and pretend nothing was wrong. It fueled her hope that she could eventually win Basil's affection.

"They had been friends since childhood; sometimes she was all he had. The life of an heir is often lonely, and she filled the void."

Her brothers had told her the romantic story of their parents many times. As a girl, Rosalie wanted what her parents had. As she matured, the hope of romance slipped away. Who would want a bride who was on death's doorstep?

Crowe's brow wrinkled with distaste. He'd voiced his opinions about Basil plenty of times, but that night he kept the rest of his criticisms to himself. "Then what does that have to do with your name?"

"It's a tradition in the Western Cliffs to name noble children after their mothers. Her name was Emelia, so they named my eldest brother Emerson. Then Emery came along. I would be Emeline, per my mother's wishes. But after she died, my father thought I didn't deserve to bear a resemblance to her name. So, instead, he named me Rosalie."

She smoothed down her skirt and tried to ignore the trembling in her hands. It was dangerous territory to venture into. The painful truths her family chose not to speak aloud.

"I know my title is something my father had no control over. It's Western tradition that the eldest woman is named Lady Yorke. I won't lie and say I'm important. My existence is a reminder of my mother's death. I at least owe it to my family to be a good daughter."

Crowe straightened up from his lounged position. "You

know your mother's death was not your fault, right?" His voice was strangely void of the usual taunts and sarcasm he seemed to like using around her. It made her feel vulnerable —in a way, she wished he was still teasing her.

"If I hadn't been born, she would still be alive," Rosalie replied. It was something she had parroted to herself for years but never spoken out loud.

The captain tipped forward, searching for her gaze. "How could you have intended for that to happen?"

Rosalie felt uneasy. "What happened is done. You must understand though, my father loved my mother more than life itself." She sighed and shivered when an icy breeze rustled through her hair. Desperate to stitch up the wound that she had reopened, she faked a smile. "That's why I can't quit." But even as she tried to explain herself, the words sounded distorted and hollow.

Crowe ran a hand through his hair, the black locks rippling through his fingers like the ocean waves at night. He tilted back again and sighed. It was different from the annoyed sighs he uttered when she pestered him. Instead, it sounded like he had set down something heavy.

"My mother named me Reis after an old folk hero from the Territories," he said. "Some heroic type that defended the poor. I always thought it was sort of ironic. Or maybe she knew I was born with rebellious blood."

Rosalie did a double take. She hadn't considered his fore-name before. He concealed himself under the image of a ruthless pirate captain and Crowe was a suitable moniker.

"So, Crowe is merely an alias?" she asked.

The corner of his lips tugged up. "When I was fourteen, Braxton told me to take on a nickname. A name people would whisper in fear. Reis Adana doesn't quite strike fear into the hearts of men."

"Reis Adana." She tested the name out loud. It was beautiful, the syllables lilting up and down like a bird's song.

As she spoke his name, Reis swallowed and ruffled a hand through his hair again. "It sounds nice when you— I mean— I don't think I've heard someone with your accent say it before," he stammered like a schoolboy.

Rosalie felt light—airy even—as if she'd held her breath until her vision spotted. "So how did Reis Adana from the Outer Territories become a pirate?"

His eyes lingered on her. Unlike before, he obliged without protesting. "When I was thirteen, I decided there wasn't much for me at home. I made no money working on the docks. I'd hear about all the riches pirates came across, so I packed up everything and joined the *Deceit*. Braxton took me under his wing and taught me everything I know. I never looked back."

"Don't you have family back in the Territories?"

Reis shook his head. "My parents died when I was young. My sister raised me until I was old enough to work. After she got married, she and her husband left to find a better place to live. I didn't want to go inland, so I made my own way in the world."

"You seem happy though."

"Aye, best decision a man like me could make. Don't have anyone telling me what to do. Not until you came aboard, that is."

She caught a glimpse of his sly smile and rolled her eyes.

They sat in a quiet lull. Reis appeared comfortable next to her with his hand resting lazily on his knee and his shoulders relaxed. So close, she could catch the aroma of sea salt clinging to his clothes. He embodied every characteristic of the ocean. From the storm in his eyes, to the wave of his hair, to the persistence of his nature. The ocean was ancient and eternal, like the wisdom Reis held in his eyes. Yet it was fresh and always changing anew. Rosalie finally saw the youthful-ness cracking through his façade.

Rosalie didn't want to think fondly of the man who was holding her in exchange for money. But there was something different about him, as if he lived two separate parts of an identity. The pirate captain who had to survive and the young boy from the Outer Territories who craved adventure and freedom.

Suddenly, Reis slapped his knee and stood up. "C'mon, show me a good punch, then." He faced her with his hips squared.

Amused at his insistence, Rosalie stayed seated. "My brothers taught me how to punch. Why does it matter?"

"You're in the middle of a war." He held a palm up in front of him. "Knowing how to punch might protect you."

"And you care?"

He gave her a wry smile. "Indulge me."

Begrudgingly, she stood up and walked over. She formed a fist and swung a punch into his palm. It connected with a satisfying smack.

"Not the worst I've ever seen," the captain said.

"Oh please. You can't tell me that didn't hurt even in the slightest?"

He rested his hands on his hips and tilted his head to the side. "Let's just say it was the best punch I've ever seen a lady throw."

"Is that so, Reis?" she challenged.

"Yes, that's right. Now, if you'll excuse me, I want to make sure no knives have been drawn over the card game. Good night, Rosie."

"Rosie?" she squeaked in shock.

He just laughed as he descended to the galley.

As their conversation echoed in her head, Rosalie

wondered if she was in a fever dream. Maybe she had never woken.

Dazed, she stepped to the side of the ship and watched the water slosh against the hull. Belowdecks, there was a loud collective jeer and muffled chatter. It was too real to deny.

Everything she said, the words were out there in the wind instead of being lodged under her heart. Reis was the first person she'd opened up to about her mother in a long time.

Yet Rosalie didn't regret telling him. It was like confessing everything to the open sea. Letting it absorb her heartache and releasing it into the sky. Despite it all, Rosalie had found some semblance of peace on the ocean.

CHAPTER 30- THE CAPTAIN

After watching Upton swindle the crew out of their last coin, Reis tried to sleep. But the conversation with Rosalie haunted him.

He climbed up to the crow's nest and watched the sky begin to pale with the rising sun. He felt younger up there, shedding his responsibilities high above the sails.

Only Upton and Kennedy knew his name. The rest of the crew had met him after he assumed his alias. He recalled the day when Braxton had implored him to take on a nickname.

Reis had been hiding in the crow's nest. What he had been upset about, he couldn't recall. But he could remember Braxton yelling up to him.

If you stay up there long enough, the gulls will start to see you as one of their own. I'd prefer you spend time around crows; they're much smarter.

The memory still brought a smile to Reis's face. A flitting thought passed by as he wondered if he should tell Rosalie the story.

His smile was dashed when he remembered his place. He

wasn't holding Rosalie on his ship because they were friends or because he was the hero his mother had named him after. He was after gold. There would always be a divide between them.

So why did she feel so close? Why had his heart skipped a beat when she spoke his given name?

Maybe it'd been a mistake being honest with her. He shouldn't have been swayed by her sad story. Even if it did solidify what Reis already thought about Basil Yorke. The lord was irredeemable and deserved to pay a hefty price.

Reis yawned, and his eyes ached with exhaustion. As the sun broke over the horizon, he saw how close Seity was. A twinge of doubt stabbed at his gut.

He could see a trap coming from miles away. And as the sun illuminated the coast, he anticipated that someone was lying in wait. Who was the intended target?

He couldn't be certain, but it was too late to turn back.

* * *

REIS DOZED off for a couple of hours in the crow's nest. When he stirred, the bay was visible. It had been one of Braxton's favorite places to smuggle contraband into Seity. Reis hadn't been there in years in his effort to avoid the war's mess.

It gave him a headache to know his efforts had failed. He was headed right for the country that was too dangerous for his liking. A country where he would leave Rosalie and Silence.

With a gruff grunt, he climbed down to the deck. Reis felt out of place among his crew as they worked in sync. He rubbed his hands over his face. There was a job to finish. Once Rosalie Yorke was off his ship, he hoped she would cease tormenting him.

Reis walked to the bow, where he found Silence. Her chin was resting on her arms as she observed Seity.

"We'll arrive in two hours," he said.

She hummed in acknowledgment but didn't respond.

"You seem worried."

"Seity can be dangerous," she whispered just above the sound of the surf.

"Can't imagine living there," he concurred. "Are you sure you want to go back? Isn't it dangerous to have the attention of lords? If you wanted, I could drop you off somewhere safer. The Islands are nice."

Silence lowered her gaze and fussed with the necklace around her neck. "I can't leave my home behind, and I can't leave Rosalie either."

"Well, I can appreciate the loyalty. I just hope you know what you're getting into." Whatever Silence had done to attract the attention of the Duranes, the end result would not be good.

"Morning, Rosalie!" Danny piped up.

Reis looked over his shoulder to see Rosalie crossing the deck. He was surprised that she appeared to have a pep in her step and some color in her cheeks. "Looks like the princess slept in again. Why am I not surprised?"

Her pout was bright in the morning sun. "*I'm* surprised we haven't arrived yet."

"That's a funny way to say, 'good morning.'"

She sighed and quipped back, "Good morning, when will we arrive?"

"We'll arrive when we arrive." In the light of day, their usual banter rekindled. But before Reis could write the previous night off as a fluke, he noticed a softness to her voice.

"That doesn't inspire confidence, Captain."

He fought off a smile. "I'm *confident* we'll arrive when we're meant to; is that better?"

Silence stepped in. "Can I ask what the plan will be when we get there?"

"Lady Yorke needs to write a letter directing her father where to send money. There's parchment and ink in my office. I'll read the note before it's sent, so don't think you can pull any tricks."

Rosalie lifted an eyebrow. "Are you afraid I'll slander your good name?"

"It wouldn't surprise me. You're not the first person to speak poorly about me, and you won't be the last."

Her eyes landed on his for a moment. It was as if she was searching for something. When it appeared she found nothing, she made her way back to the cabin.

"She'll be okay once she's home," Silence said unprompted.

"Again," he replied in a terse voice, "that's no concern of mine."

But the lie tasted sour on his tongue.

CHAPTER 31- THE LADY

Esteemed officer of the Yorke army,

By now I am sure my father has reported my and Silence's disappearance. We are alive and have avoided being captured by the Duranes. Please send word to my father that an exchange must be arranged for one hundred thousand gold. Should my brothers' squadron be nearby, alert them as well. Leave the men who delivered this message unharmed. They will lead you to my location.

Rosalie Yorke, the First of Her Name,
Lady of the Western Cliffs

Before Rosalie could seal the letter with her signet, Reis snorted at her lengthy signature. Then the letter had been sent with Kennedy and Mendon, the burliest man of the *Deceit*'s crew. An hour after they left, it began to rain. It rained every day they waited in the cove.

Silence, Reis, and Rosalie stayed in the captain's quarters most of the time to keep out of the downpour. For the first few days, the mood had remained civil. Rosalie and Reis had held their tongues and avoided falling into a bout of bickering. Yet when the conversation touched on Seity, things began to unravel.

"Father has always talked about Jonas Gunn losing his power soon. He was so young when he became lord."

Silence frowned and nodded. Her focus was split between the conversation and the frayed edge of her skirt. She carefully pulled loose threads as she tried to salvage the hem. "Emerson told me he was fifteen."

"Goodness," Rosalie whispered. She stole a glance at Reis across the desk. But he had no comment about the Northern Front's leader. He'd been quiet for most of the conversation, hiding behind a book. She picked up a gold compass sitting on the desk. Without looking up, Reis reached over and plucked it from her hands. His finger brushed against hers.

Rosalie ignored the slight touch and said, "I suppose we can be grateful the North is weakened. Maybe when the main aggressors are dealt with, the North and West can find peace."

"We can only hope," Silence agreed.

Reis snorted.

"Do you have something to add?" Rosalie asked tersely.

"No, by all means, go on about your fairy tales." He waved her on, but the curve of his lips taunted her.

She pressed her tongue to the roof of her mouth to resist fighting with him. But they'd been stuck in the cramped space for days, and he was testing her patience as per usual. "My father is fighting to free Seity from the Duranes. Our disagreement with the Northern Front was a consequence of the war's start."

"Tell me, when the Duranes launched their attack on the Eastern Hills, where was your father?" Reis questioned. "Because Braxton was there, and he saw no Western aid."

Rosalie swallowed hard. She didn't know much about the beginning of the war. She'd been led to believe her father had declared war in response to the Wellers' demise. "I'm sure he needed to organize his military. It takes time to cross the country."

"I think we can agree that Eldon Durane began the war," Silence said. "But everyone has an opinion about what happened afterward."

Reis abandoned his book on the desk. "Do you know much about Eldon's sons?"

"Not very much, no," Silence answered. Rosalie shook her head too.

"They're nasty creatures."

Rosalie hugged herself close, fending off the chill going down her spine. Hardly anyone spoke the names of Eldon's sons, as if uttering them would bring bad luck. In Eldon's older age, his two heirs stood at the forefront of the battle for Seity. Lowell and Fineas cast a dark shadow over the country.

"They made sure I would never forget meeting them." Reis lifted his shirt. Spanning from his hip and lashing across his abdominal muscles was a scar. It was healed but looked jagged and angry as if the wound persisted because the memory was still so raw.

"You've met them?" Rosalie asked.

Reis tucked in his shirt again. "Years ago, yes."

"What makes them so vicious? How does someone become that kind of person?"

Reis didn't appear hung up on the question of morality.

"Their father is the product of a long line of power-hungry men. History tells us they were all the same and they will remain so until their luck runs out. It'd be nice to see their downfall."

Rosalie frowned. "What about their mother? You're telling me they're evil for no reason?"

"I think she passed away before the war," Silence said.

Rosalie felt the pieces fitting together, and it revealed a grim picture. "Then Lowell and Fineas were young when they lost her. They only had Eldon to guide them, and that's probably how they lost empathy."

Reis's hand formed a fist on the desk. "Don't humanize them. We've all been through suffering and loss, and we didn't turn into monsters. Those two were born that way. I'm sure Eldon made them worse, but they're Duranes all the same."

"No one is born evil."

"I have evidence to beg to differ," the captain responded coldly. "I know what evil is; I've looked it right in the eyes."

"Losing family is enough of a reason to turn bad. Family is everything."

"Then how can you explain generations of their behavior? Maybe you're right about blood, but that only perpetuates the vileness. I wonder what that means for you, Lady Yorke."

An acidic taste burned her mouth when he spoke her last name with such vitriol. "My father is a good man. And I know everyone is born with humanity in them, even the Duranes."

"You're wrong. You should learn that now so you don't trust someone who will show you what true evil is." Reis stood up and left the cabin.

Silence's posture sagged. She rested a hand on her collarbone and wrapped a finger around the chain of her necklace.

"He lost a lot to the Duranes. Many people have. Sometimes there's no room for forgiveness."

Resentment surged through Rosalie. Without a word, she stood and stormed out. The sky pelted heavy raindrops at her as she sloshed her way across the deck. "Don't walk away thinking you have the moral high ground over me!" she shouted to catch Reis's attention as he stalked toward the bowsprit.

He faced her as if he had expected her to follow. "I'm pointing out the obvious. Don't pretend you're a benevolent person because you're foolish enough to think they're anything but monsters."

"Circumstances happen. It changes a person!" She raised her voice over his. The rain drenched them, but she was too worked up to feel the icy chill lifting goosebumps on her arms.

"Does it even matter? They do bad things, Rosalie. That's all we need to know about them."

"And what about you?"

He threw his hands up. His ivory shirt stuck to his wet skin, but he didn't appear bothered. "What about me?"

"What will people see when you return me to land and demand a ransom? Do you think they'll see a well-meaning pirate who wants to provide for his crew? Or will they see a monster who holds ladies hostage for a high price?"

Reis pursed his lips and crossed the deck until he was within inches of her. "I'll write my own narrative, love; don't worry about me."

"You think?" she challenged. "Will the world even listen to what you have to say after you run with the money?"

The rain plastered Reis's hair to his forehead, and he pushed it back with a rough swipe of a hand. "You were just a quick errand. I don't need a single coin from your family."

Rosalie laughed in disbelief. "Is that what you're telling

yourself now? Suddenly you're too good for Yorke gold? I don't think you could refuse—what was it, a hundred thousand gold?"

His eyes darkened. "You don't think?"

"I'd like to see you try!"

His jaw was tight as he stared down at her. "You'll see; I'll drop you off on that beach and walk away. Don't need your father's money."

The ferocity in his voice made him sound believable, but it didn't make him any less smug. Frustrated by his change in tune, Rosalie was overcome with an emotion that seemed right in her face yet unattainable. She couldn't place the feeling, couldn't sort it into any category. All she knew was that her blood raced, and she had to do something.

By the time she acted, it was too late to turn back. She reached up blindly and pulled his face to hers, kissing him with abandon.

She expected Reis to push her away, but to her surprise, he grabbed her by the waist and pulled her flush to him. His mouth was insistent on hers, a mix of intensity and heat with an afterthought of gentleness.

Rosalie had never kissed anyone before. It was far from the chaste peck on the lips from a kind gentleman she'd always daydreamed about. It was untamed, and she couldn't get close enough to him. A tangled mess of emotions flooded through her. She wanted to hate him, but she would hate him more if he let go of her.

In her frustration, she lightly bit his lower lip. Reis hissed and put a hand on her cheek. "Easy, Rosie," he said in a low voice.

The second they parted, the rain's chill caught up to Rosalie. Reis's arm loosened around her waist, and she dropped her hands to her sides.

Reis stared at her with the same nervous look she'd seen

once before. Wordlessly, he tilted toward her again, but she cleared her throat and ducked her head. "I probably look like a wet cat." Her anger had been sufficiently doused by the rain.

"Going out in the rain wasn't my brightest idea." He shivered. "We should get back inside."

Every muscle in Rosalie's body urged her to kiss him again. She needed to feel that rush again. She craved his touch. But she kept her hands to herself as they walked back. Rosalie's skirts dragged through the puddles. When they crossed the deck, Reis opened the door for her. She quietly thanked him.

Silence hadn't left her seat, but she had a small, palm-sized book in her hand. When she heard them return, she placed it on the chair underneath her thigh. "You two look freezing, but I can't say I'm surprised."

Rosalie worried Silence could somehow sense that she had kissed Reis. Silence knew her better than anyone and could pick up on even the slightest of differences. And after her first kiss, Rosalie was certain she looked different. So, she let out a vague noise of amusement to try and seem as normal as possible.

Then Reis was in front of Rosalie again. At a respectful distance, however. He cleared his throat and offered her a woven blanket. Before she took it, she needed to know one thing.

"Did you mean what you said?" she asked quietly. "About the gold?"

Reis pushed back his wet hair. "Yeah, I did."

The change of tune made Rosalie's heart unexpectedly swell. But as her lips tingled, she knew she could not kiss him again. When she went to take the blanket, their hands brushed, and Rosalie felt like she couldn't breathe all over again.

CHAPTER 32 - THE CAPTAIN

*R*osalie Yorke had kissed him. She had yelled at him and then kissed him.

Both facts trailed after Reis as he paced the main deck. The rain had let up by morning, but his shirt was still damp from standing out in the torrential downpour the day before. The day he had kissed Rosalie.

He wanted to forget it ever happened, and yet he wanted to relive the moment a hundred times over. It was everything he craved and nothing he ever knew he needed. He wanted to keep her at arm's length but was desperate to feel her close again.

It was no time to be indecisive, and yet circumstances were tearing him apart piece by piece. How could he have allowed himself to be so vulnerable? How could he have let Rosalie goad him into saying he didn't need her father's money? Of course he needed it. His crew needed to be paid, and once he had the money in hand Reis looked forward to spending a couple of carefree weeks on the Islands.

Without a certain noblewoman.

She'd done it. She had successfully invaded his thoughts

so deeply that he couldn't imagine life without her. He had no clue how she'd done it but hoped the feeling would wear off soon.

Reis stopped at the front of the bow and let his head hang. He didn't even want to see Rosalie again. One look from those green eyes, and she would ruin him.

"Captain!"

He lifted his head to see Kennedy and Mendon crossing the beach. Following close behind was a small group of men dressed in blue uniforms.

At the lead were two blond men who looked eerily familiar. Their striking green eyes were the same shade that Reis was sure would haunt him for the rest of his days.

"Oh," Reis whispered when he realized why. They were Rosalie's brothers. "Just my luck," he muttered before turning to call, "We've got company!"

Seconds later, Rosalie came running with Silence at her heels. Her eyes lit up when she saw who was waiting on the beach. "Emerson! Emery!" she cried.

The older one's lips were pursed, and he rested a hand on the sword at his hip. The other smiled and waved to his sister.

Reis swallowed when the eldest locked eyes with him. The look he gave Reis was deadlier than some glares he'd gotten from his worst enemies. "*Vellah*," he muttered under his breath.

Silence hugged Rosalie close. "Didn't I tell you we'd all be together soon? Can you believe it?"

Rosalie agreed, "It's been so long."

"Alright, hurry up." Reis ushered the two of them toward the rope ladder. "I don't want them to open fire on my ship because you two are taking too long to show up."

Kennedy rowed the dinghy up to the side of the ship. Reis hesitated. He eyed the tree line but saw no movement. Only six men, including Rosalie's brothers, stood on the beach. He'd been certain the letter would prompt a full squadron. Maybe even more than one. Surely, a kidnapped lady would raise the alarm, right? Unless Rosalie's brothers thought a pirate ship wasn't a formidable foe.

So, the *Deceit* wasn't worth the Yorkes' time? Reis scoffed, and his apprehension mutated into contempt. They would soon see it was a mistake to underestimate him.

He reached deep into his pocket to retrieve his eyepatch. It had been days since he'd worn it. He wasn't sure why, but there was something about the way Rosalie looked into both of his eyes that compelled him to keep it off. But the time for such foolishness was over. His fingers were steady as he tied the patch back in place. It was time for Captain Crowe to get what he was due.

CHAPTER 33 - THE LADY

After Reis climbed down to the small boat, they rowed to the beach. Overwhelmed with joy, Rosalie jumped out a foot from shore and waded through the water. It had been over six months since she'd seen Emery and two years since she'd seen Emerson. Rosalie couldn't even remember the last time the four of them were all together. Emerson looked much older and took after their father more than when she'd last seen him. Emery had matured too but he still retained some of the same carefree airs he had before.

She couldn't run fast enough into their awaiting arms.

"There you two are." Emerson sighed in relief and checked her and Silence over. "Are you hurt?"

"No, we—" But before Rosalie could finish, Emerson fixed his attention over her shoulder. Emery drew her and Silence closer to him as Emerson strode toward Reis.

He drew his sword and pointed it at the captain. "Give me one good reason I shouldn't cut you down where you stand."

Reis held his hands up. "I could give you several, but if you're only asking for one…"

Emerson's grip on his blade tightened and his eyes narrowed. "Don't play games with me, pirate. I know your ship, and I know what kind of lowlifes sail on it."

"Emerson, stop," Rosalie urged. She had wanted to enjoy returning to land, not have it descend into violence. Besides, after what had happened the day before, her feelings about Reis were properly jumbled. She didn't know where his fate should lie.

"Stay out of this." Her brother hushed her.

"If she wants to explain, you should let her." Reis cleared his throat. "I'm sure you won't believe a word a lowlife pirate has to say." He fidgeted at the end of the sword.

"He delivered us here safely," Rosalie said firmly. "There's no need to get violent. Silence and I have been caught up in enough violence for a lifetime. Please just let it be."

"Rosalie, he's been holding you hostage!" Emery said as if she could forget.

"The Duranes were looking for us, and he hid us. At least he had the decency to do that."

"No doubt to save himself!" her brother argued.

"Wait." Emerson held up a hand to hush his siblings. "You said the Duranes were looking for you?" he demanded, and turned his attention back to Reis. "Explain."

The captain raised a brow. Perhaps he hadn't expected the Yorke heir to address him again. "I didn't take them from the coast. I intercepted a raiders' ship that did. I know the raiders well enough to presume they're working for the Duranes. It was confirmed when we were inspected by a Southern warship."

"So, the Duranes plotted to have her kidnapped," Emerson concluded.

Rosalie subtly glanced at Silence, but her friend didn't speak up. She stared at the sand as if she were trying to count every grain. "A few things need to be straightened out," Rosalie said tactfully. "But I think—"

"You are going back to Ciern at once," Emerson interrupted. "I can't keep track of you two. The war is escalating. You need to be in the manor, where you can be kept safe."

It was what Rosalie had said from the beginning. If they'd never left the capital, nothing bad would have happened. She never would've met Reis. The fleeting thought whizzed by her and threatened to do more damage if she ruminated on it.

"It would be best to return home," Silence agreed.

Emerson finally lowered his sword but didn't relax his glare at Reis. Rosalie's brother ran a hand through his honey-colored hair as he returned his weapon to its sheath. He frowned and kept his strict military stance. "You'll be safe with a soldier escort. It'll only be a couple days' journey back home."

With medals pinned to his navy coat and a gun holstered opposite his blade, Rosalie hardly recognized the boy she'd grown up with. She briefly tried to recall when she had last seen him smile.

Reis drew their attention again. "Before you leave, there's the matter of payment."

A cold chill went over Rosalie, although the wind was low on the coast. She was convinced he had given up on collecting money from her family. But the truth twisted like a cord around her neck.

He had lied.

Emerson's jaw tightened, and his hand went back to the hilt at his side. "What did you just say to me, *pirate?*"

Reis stood his ground. "We can all be reasonable about it. Your family doesn't do anything unless it benefits you. My ship operates the same way. And as it stands, my crew far outnumbers you."

Rosalie felt frozen in place, unable to process his words. Had she been that blind to trust him? Had she been foolish enough to fall for a single kiss? A kiss that had probably meant nothing to the pirate.

"Are you threatening me?" Emerson gave Reis a stormy look.

"Merely stating facts," Reis replied. "You'll know when it turns into a threat."

"You're lucky I didn't kill you the second you stepped off your ship. Now you're trying to extort me?"

Reis crossed his arms over his chest. "I'm not extorting anyone. It's a fair exchange. I disrupted the Duranes' plot and kept Rosalie and Silence alive. Sort of felt like I was doing your job. Figure I ought to be compensated."

Emerson's face clouded over with rage. "I expected such insolence from a pirate."

"If you expected this, then you brought the gold."

Rosalie's knees wobbled. This was everything Reis had planned from the beginning. He'd warned her. He'd spelled it out for her. Reis was an act, a disguise to make him appear trustworthy. Crowe was who he truly was, who he showed her he was. Yet she had still fallen for his charm.

Emery's eyes flicked to the *Deceit* moored in the cove. Rosalie glanced over her shoulder and saw the crew watching. All of them stood at the ready with weapons aimed toward the beach.

"I'll pay you," Emerson said through clenched teeth. "So long as I never see your face or your ship near Seity again. If I do, I won't show you the same mercy."

"The *Deceit* will stay far away from your country. I've had my fill of your war."

Emerson's face twisted into a snarl. "Emery, go get the money. Silence, Rosalie, come with me."

Emery gave Rosalie a half-hearted smile before returning to where the soldiers were keeping watch.

Reis lifted a hand as a signal, and Rosalie watched his crew lower their weapons. That's when she noticed Reis had donned his eyepatch before disembarking. He'd slipped back to his old ways. Or maybe he hadn't changed at all, and Rosalie deluded herself into believing there was something under his mask. No, he *was* his mask.

Reis didn't move to follow Emery to collect the money. He buried his hands in his pockets. "Understand that—"

"Understand what?" she snapped. "You told me— Forget it." She shook her head, frustrated with her naivety. "I have nothing else to say to you."

"This was always the plan," he said. "I told you I have to make sacrifices for my crew."

"Sacrifices," she spat. "Just go; I can't even look at you." Hatred coursed through her veins. She hated him for fooling her, hated herself for being duped, and hated her heart for feeling an ounce of sympathy for him.

"Rosalie, come along," Emerson urged.

"You should be careful," Reis warned, his gaze fixed on Rosalie. "Things aren't right in Seity. You need to double-check who you can trust."

Trust? Rosalie wanted to scream. All at once, she was reminded of what had divided them to begin with. Her father was good. He protected the innocent, and soon enough he would put an end to Eldon Durane's tyranny. Her family were the only ones she could trust. The sentiment already etched into her bones was sharpened by Reis's lies.

"I think the only people who should be careful are your crew. They're fools to trust a man like you to lead them. You'll only bring them ruin," she said as Silence looped an arm around hers.

Reis didn't react. She was used to him matching her anger

to get the last word as they traded barbs. His silence was unnerving. He seemed like he was trying to say something—something too risky to say out loud. His eyes were like marble, still and impervious against the harshness of the world.

"Rose," Silence prompted softly, and tugged Rosalie a few steps back.

But Reis wasn't done reeling her in. Slowly, he unsheathed his cutlass and held the hilt toward her. "Take this."

Rosalie looked at the weapon and then back to him. Her stomach lurched as she felt the overwhelming urge to hit him, and yet she mourned that flash of time when she'd thought he was decent. "I don't want it."

"You're not out of danger. You'd be wise to arm yourself."

Something about the two simple phrases cast an eerie shroud over her. Hesitantly, Rosalie took the blade, sensing Silence and Emerson's eyes on her. Without another word, Rosalie turned away from Reis.

He could have the final word. She didn't want to see the *Deceit* again. She didn't want to feel the yearning pull of the ocean. He got what he'd wanted from the start. It was time for her to get what she wanted—safety at home.

She stumbled up the beach, diverging from Silence and Emerson. She clutched the cutlass but let it drag a line through the sand behind her. Her lungs felt like they had been pierced a hundred times over.

When she reached a steep incline leading to the tree line, a young soldier came to her aid. "Are you alright, Lady Yorke?" He offered a hand to stabilize her.

Instead, she held out the cutlass. "Could you find me something to carry this in?"

"Yes, my lady." He bowed his head and hurried off.

Once she stepped away from the cove, she needed to put

on a brave face and return to the life she had been stolen from. She breathed deeply to steady her pulse. Curling over her knees, she allowed herself a minute to cry. But when the seconds ran out, she reminded herself that Reis's actions proved one thing: Ladies could not trust pirates.

CHAPTER 34 - THE LADY

Dark clouds had rolled in, but it was hard to see the sky through the dense tree canopy. They had traveled five miles into the thick forest that spanned the western section of Seity. It was abundant with wildlife, herds of wild turkeys, and small rodents skittering through the undergrowth.

The animals seemed used to humans passing through. The Yorke and Gunn armies frequently used the woods to travel in stealth.

Although it would be dangerous to stop, Emerson had wanted Rosalie to rest. But she'd urged everyone to keep moving. Eventually, they had talked her into mounting Emery's horse to get her off her feet.

The mare quietly plodded along, and Rosalie kept her gaze ahead. But anxious movement to the left caught her attention. As Silence walked, she fussed with the pockets of her skirt. She wore a nervous frown, and she glanced behind her a few times.

Before Rosalie could ask what was wrong, Emery asked,

"How was sailing with pirates, then? I can't even begin to imagine what it was like."

"It was interesting, to say the least," Silence admitted. "I suppose for more reasons than one."

Rosalie's chest ached. "I don't want to talk about it," she muttered, and nudged her heels into the horse's side, urging her farther down the path. She continued ahead until she reached Emerson at the front of the group.

He acknowledged her with a brief glance. "Father wrote to me about your disappearance. He was distraught. I'm sure he'll be overjoyed when you return." It seemed her brother was ready to put the past behind them. Talk of pirates would fade away, and Rosalie would go back to the person her family knew.

Quiet and obedient.

"I've missed home." Even Rosalie could hear how hollow her voice was. She couldn't convince herself that things would ever be the same again. But she yearned for the status quo, even if she had a cutlass strapped to her hip. "It will be nice to see him again."

Up ahead, a doe jumped into the path. A fawn followed, and they both stared at the approaching group. The fawn's legs wobbled as it turned to face them. Quickly, the mother coaxed her baby along to avoid the soldiers.

Rosalie's right hand let go of the reins to adjust the sword now hanging at her hip. She felt in her pocket for the note. Faint recognition battered at her skull. The truth was at her fingertips. She just needed to clear away the fog.

Fawn in blue.

* * *

THEY TRAVELED another day until they were back in familiar territory. Vale Fall was a day's walk away. From there, a stagecoach would bring Silence and Rosalie to Ciern. On her feet again, Rosalie was pleased things were going smoothly. Aboard the *Deceit*, everything that could've gone wrong had gone wrong. Back on land, she could bask in order and civility.

But she soon had to swallow her words when they reached a small clearing and found a large armed battalion waiting for them.

Seeing the gold flags emblazoned with boars, Rosalie's gait faltered to a stop. She looked behind them and saw soldiers appearing from the forest's shadows. The circle closed, and they were surrounded by rifles pointed at them. Steel sliced through the air as swords were drawn.

The air shifted to a winter chill as a man stepped toward them. Lowell Durane's eyes had a shadow cast over them, and with a single look, he had control of everyone in sight. He wasn't tall, but his stance made him appear intimidating. He stood with such authority, the very trees seemed to bow to his will.

Rosalie's stomach dropped. Instinct told her to run, but her legs wouldn't work. Instead, she reached out to grab Silence's arm. Her friend looked like she had gone catatonic.

Observing his prey, the youngest Durane heir spoke with sickening glee. "Perfectly punctual. Our sources were well-informed."

Emerson drew his gun and placed himself in front of Silence and Rosalie. "Stand down."

They were far outmatched. The grim reality settled in, and Rosalie wondered if death came without warning. For so long, she had thought her illness would steal her away in the night. She would have no way of knowing when it would happen. To die in the middle of the morning, out in the forest, seemed surreal.

"I'm here on orders of my father. I've been authorized to

leave you and your siblings alive if you relinquish the girl." He pointed lazily at Silence. "Consider it my father's last act of kindness for the Yorkes."

"What do you want with Silence?" Emerson demanded. Even in the face of such danger, his voice was strong.

A grin spread across Lowell's face, and he began to circle them like a shark. "And here I thought Yorkes were supposed to be smart. Tell me, Lady Yorke," he addressed her in a mocking tone, "did the raiders say anything about your friend?"

Rosalie's lower lip trembled as she remembered that fateful day. She thought back to the letter in her pocket. The raiders had known who Silence was. They'd known something Rosalie didn't.

She looked to her right. Silence hadn't moved, and yet everything had changed. Her expression was in such a state of shock that it was unreadable. She was wearing Emery's coat. She'd worn the shade of blue before, fitting in with Rosalie and her brothers. She had always fit in so well. But it was not the color she was born to.

Red.

"They didn't tell you, then." Lowell gleaned the answer from the dead air. "I thought for sure they would fold the second they were accosted. Perhaps they aren't as spineless as I presumed." He shifted from Rosalie to face Silence. With a quick movement, he snatched her locket, yanking hard to break the chain from her neck.

Silence yelped and lurched forward. "No!"

Lowell held up the broken necklace, dangling it in front of her. "*Tor honar ig vareur*, the crest of the deer. The Wellers, a family of cowards."

Rosalie's breath stuck in her throat, her lungs withering away until she felt sick. All this time Silence had been living under the Yorke crest to disguise her identity.

"It seems at least one of you has figured it out." Lowell smirked. "Silence Weller, heir to the Eastern Hills. The last blotch on my family's history. I'm sure after all this time you thought you had vanished from our sights. But my father never forgot. He would not rest until you were found."

"You're lying…" Rosalie accused in a trembling voice.

"You can deny it all you'd like. But you know the truth," Lowell said, cocking his head in a derisive manner. "Constance Weller corrupted my brother, and your friend is the mistake they created together. But soon enough my father will correct that mistake. You might believe she's brave and noble for being a Weller—the poor martyrs of your history books. But don't forget, dear niece, you have Durane blood too."

Rosalie staggered backward a few steps and ran into the end of a rifle. Her pulse set off at a rapid pace and she couldn't catch her breath between blows. "I don't understand…"

"I'm sorry." Tears welled in Silence's eyes, and her voice trembled. "I wanted to tell you, but—"

"Enough," Lowell interrupted. "What is it going to be, Emerson? Will you risk the lives of your siblings for her?"

Emery and Emerson looked at each other, and Rosalie knew exactly what they were thinking. Silence had become like family to them over the years, but Basil's rule overshadowed everything. Blood was blood.

Like most of Seity, Lowell must have known this well. "I've heard Yorkes are so loyal to their own."

After a long pause, Emerson said, "You'll leave us alive?"

"No!" Rosalie was indignant that her brother would even entertain the idea. After years of friendship, Silence was being treated like she was a bargaining tool. Her grip on Silence's arm tightened, unwilling to separate from her.

"I promise on my family's honor," Lowell replied, the corner of his lips turning up into a mocking sneer.

"Your family has no honor!" Rosalie refuted. "Emerson, please, don't do this. You can't trust him!"

Her brother appeared unmoved. "Rose, I have no choice. My first concern is you; don't make this harder than it already is."

Rosalie's vision narrowed to pinpoints, and her breath sounded too loud in her ears. She had survived so long, much longer than anyone expected. But where was the end? What had kept her alive all this time?

"You'll never get away with this." The words forced their way out of Rosalie's mouth, and all at once, she knew her purpose. She might not have known who her best friend was, but she vowed to protect her.

"Let me go," Silence whispered as she pried Rosalie's fingers off her arm. "I promise it'll be okay."

"What? No! I won't let them take you. I won't—" Rosalie's breath shortened. Her heart thumped irregularly, and vertigo made her vision blur.

Silence leaned in slightly to whisper, "Listen to me. I accidentally left a diary on the *Deceit*. Somehow you need to find it. It will explain everything."

"I don't understand. Please, we can figure out another way." Rosalie was hyperventilating, and the ground spun under her feet.

"Don't worry yourself too much, Lady Yorke; your poor heart can't take it," Lowell ridiculed. "I was told how fragile you were; best to not waste your breath. You don't have many to spare." His eyes had her in a hold as if he were strangling her. When he smiled at her, she saw the face of death.

The misty, murky being that had lurked over her from birth—finally, Rosalie could stare it down. Like she'd planned, she would not go without a fight. Her stomach roiled with anger.

Silence stepped away before Rosalie could grab hold of her again. "If you promise to leave them alive, I'll go with you without a fight."

"Of course." A faint smirk lingered on Lowell's face, and he held out a hand to her. "You're just in time to see a new chapter in Cross Row."

Death would claim Rosalie one day, and she would gladly go if it meant defending Silence. Without thinking, she drew Reis's blade and pushed past Emerson. "You're not taking her." Her arm shook as she maintained her stance. If her brothers weren't going to fight, she would.

Lowell laughed at her attempt to be brave. "You learned a lot from those ship rats, didn't you?"

"Rosalie!" Emerson grabbed her upper arms and wrenched her backward.

"You've terrorized this land long enough. I will make sure everyone in your family pays!" she shouted.

"I'll be waiting for the day. But I wouldn't worry about my family, Lady Yorke. I'd worry about your own." Lowell's face darkened, and the sick amusement disappeared from his face. "Now scurry home. You children are in over your heads. Interfere with the boar again, and you'll pay."

Emerson twisted Rosalie's wrist to make her drop the cutlass. She yelped in pain and folded helplessly against his strength.

"There's nothing else we can do," her brother said in a defeated voice.

"No!" she screamed as Silence was swallowed by the gold banners. Her body finally gave out on her. Her throat constricted as she went limp in Emerson's hold. The world whirled, and her eyesight was muddled.

"Breathe, Rose." Emerson lowered her to the ground. "Just breathe."

But she couldn't breathe. There was no hope left.

CHAPTER 35- THE CAPTAIN

Reis had been lying face down in his berth for hours even after the sun rose. His body felt weighed down as he grappled with his emotions. Even though a day had passed, Rosalie's look of betrayal continued to haunt him. Why did it hurt so much? Why did he feel so lonely without her on board? Magic was dead, but it felt like Rosalie Yorke had managed to cast some spell on him.

To wallow in his complicated feelings alone, Reis had expressly banned anyone from entering. By noon, the rule was broken.

The door creaked open, and sure footsteps crossed the cabin floor. The bed dipped as someone sat by Reis's feet.

"You haven't eaten since yesterday morning," Kennedy noted.

"I'm not hungry," Reis said into his pillow.

Kennedy didn't move.

The captain groaned and sat up. "If I eat, will you leave?"

The quartermaster didn't answer—merely handed him a small bag. Reis peeked inside and found a handful of pink jelly candies dusted in sugar. He stared at them for a long while. As a child, his family could never afford such a luxury, but they still reminded him of home.

"Did you get them from Cilisca?"

"I saved you the last bag."

Reis plucked out two candies and offered one to his quartermaster. They sat together, two Territory boys born in poverty, savoring something they never thought they'd have.

The rosewater melted in his mouth, but it finished with a sting. Like a thorn. He couldn't stop thinking about her. She'd taken up so much of his day for almost two weeks. It was too quiet now, and he hated how he yearned to see her pout one more time—to hear her snappy retorts.

No, he had to move on. She was gone.

"How is morale?"

"Well, no one is happy you turned down the Yorkes' gold," Kennedy said with plain honesty. "But it's been smoothed over."

Reis swallowed the candy. "How?"

"Upton threatened to bash in anyone's skull who suggested mutiny."

He couldn't find a trace of humor to laugh. "I deserve it. I can't believe I let this happen. She just—"

Kennedy interrupted before Reis could get too deep into his wallowing. "You seemed more like yourself when she was around. When you became captain, you turned so serious. I don't know, it was nice seeing you banter with someone again."

Maybe that was why he'd told Emerson Yorke to keep his gold. Reis had been so certain to make a point—to make Seity nobles realize he was not a pirate to mess around with. But standing on that beach, Reis hadn't been able to do it. He couldn't interpret the shredding sensation of guilt that had prompted him to turn away from the money.

Reis put his head in his hands. "You're not helping." He'd

stayed inside to place distance between him and Seity. He wanted to get far enough away so that he couldn't turn back.

Luckily, Kennedy didn't linger on the subject. "We need supplies. We won't make it to Ivona. There's a fishing village not too far from here. It's Yorke territory, but I don't think we'll be noticed if we're quick."

The crew was already disgruntled that they'd spent days waiting for a windfall that would never come. Reis couldn't make them survive on scant rations on their way to the Islands. "Alright, we'll stop there. Then I want to get away from this place."

CHAPTER 36- THE LADY

Mud and dew seeped into Rosalie's skirt. She was numb to the chill creeping in.

"How could we have not known?" Emerson asked, his agitation growing. "She lied to us for years."

Rosalie held a hand over her heart, trying to stay calm even as her world was falling apart. Although she knew the truth, her knee jerk reaction to defend Silence kicked in. "He was lying."

"I didn't hear her denying it!" Emerson snapped.

Emery came over to kneel by Rosalie. He touched her shoulder and gave her a sympathetic look. "I think we have to accept the truth. Silence is not who we thought she was."

"I know who she is; she's my best friend! My best friend who you two let fall into the enemy's hands!" Rosalie shook him away. She refused to believe Silence had Durane blood.

Both Yorke sons went silent.

Rosalie wasn't done. "We're going to trust that monster? In what world would Constance Weller fall in love with a Durane? It doesn't even make sense. Eldon only has two sons; the timeline doesn't add up."

"Three," Emerson said. "He had three. Anselm passed away not too long after the war started."

Another wave of nausea passed through Rosalie. Silence was the missing Weller. She had Durane blood, and she'd evaded Eldon's grasp for twenty years.

"How long after the war started did he die?' Rosalie asked.

Her brother shot her an exasperated look. "How am I supposed to know? I didn't even know there *was* a missing Weller!"

Rosalie's eyes narrowed in confusion. "But Father knew."

"No, he didn't."

She got to her feet. "Yes, he did. I found a letter in Vale Fall from Major General Vidal. He told Father about Constance Weller and her missing child. He wasn't the only one who knew either." She pulled the letter from her pocket. "This was sent to the raider who kidnapped us. Eldon knows who she is."

Emerson took the weathered paper and scanned the short note. His fingers trembled as he folded it on the creases. "Father did not know about Constance."

"I know he did!"

"Rosalie, you have no idea what you're talking about. You—"

"I know what I'm talking about!" she shouted. "I've been on the frontlines of this for days!"

Her brother matched her anger without hesitation. "I've been on the frontlines of this war for *years*! You haven't seen the things I've seen, Rosalie. You haven't had men die in your arms. Do *not* lecture me about war."

Emery stepped in between the two of them. "The Duranes want us to tear each other apart. If we're divided, we have nothing."

Rosalie clenched her jaw as she forced her tired body to stay upright. "Someone told the Duranes we were here; they were lying in wait. Lowell said he had an informant. Who would've known where we would be?"

"Very few people," Emerson said, the anger in his voice dying out. "I wrote to Father saying that we were going closer to the Cross Row border to search for you. It had to have been the pirate. It was a mistake to let him leave with his life."

Rosalie felt like she was going to throw up. She knew her father would never work with the Duranes. He would never betray his children. That only meant one thing: Crowe had been playing both sides all along. After all the times he had lamented the Duranes' terror, he was lying. He lied about everything. It was yet another stab to her heart.

"What do we do? We can't let Silence die." Rosalie's own voice sounded so distant it didn't feel attached to her body.

"You need to go back to Ciern. It's too dangerous out here for you," Emerson said. "Father can keep you safe in the manor."

"Don't you think we should go after them?" Rosalie was frantic. With every passing second, Silence was getting farther away. And Rosalie had wasted precious seconds arguing with her brothers. "If we go now—"

Emerson interrupted her before the thought could spiral into a plan. "Rose, the best thing we can do for Silence is form a strong squadron to rescue her. Emery and I will go. I'll delay my travels to the Northern Front, but you're going home immediately."

"The Front? Why were you planning to go north?"

Emerson swallowed and fidgeted with the lapel of his coat. "Father asked me to begin a dialogue with Jonas Gunn. We're working out a treaty."

Rosalie had a hard time wrapping her head around the idea. "A treaty? And this was Father's idea?" The lords of the families did not stay in contact with one another. Diplomacy was a relic of the past.

"Yes," Emerson confirmed. "If we can create a united front, then we might have a chance in this war. But that will have to wait for now. My men will take you back to Ciern, and you can tell Father what happened to Silence. He may be able to send reinforcements."

She wrung her hands together. The plan made her nervous, but what else could she do? "Please do everything you can to find her."

Emerson looked solemn as he nodded. "There's no telling what she means for the survival of Seity. This war is about to change, but I'm not sure how the tide will turn."

When her brothers turned to consult with the men, Rosalie located Silence's locket in the mud. She wiped it clean and held it up to the light. The etched stag glinted in a stray sunbeam. She could not translate the Weller motto.

Tor honar ig vareur

* * *

"WE CAN STOP HERE if you're hungry, my lady," the younger soldier said. He was the same one who had attended to her days before on the beach. They'd walked for miles before they reached a small fishing village wedged between the forest and coastline.

Rosalie felt like a ghost as she found herself among crowds of people. Losing Silence hadn't quite hit her yet. Her mind comforted her by conjuring up false hope that at any second, her friend would appear at her side. It was all she could do to stop herself from spiraling into a panic.

"It's a few more hours to Vale Fall. A stagecoach will be waiting for us there."

Her brothers trusted the two soldiers to deliver Rosalie to

Ciern, but there was something odd about their demeanor. Not only had they said very little, but they also kept looking at Rosalie in disbelief.

She paid them no mind. Her thoughts were fixed on Silence and how Reis had given up their location. If Rosalie ever came face to face with the pirate again, she was certain she would hit him.

The grief laced with anger took up so much room, she hadn't had the chance to dwell on Silence's parting words about a diary.

Everything felt so far out of reach, and it made her feel helpless. She couldn't wait to be back home where she belonged. She couldn't wait until she was reunited with her friend. They had survived their kidnapping; this could not be the end. Rosalie would see Silence again, and their lives would go back to normal. Whatever normal would look like after everything they had been through.

Tears blurred her vision, and she wiped them away. She needed to compose herself before arriving at Ciern. She didn't want to greet her father looking like the journey had broken her. She didn't want to become an even worse disappointment to her family.

The seaside settlement was extremely crowded for such a small space. The docks attracted many ships, and their crews milled around. Rosalie's stomach churned when she passed a crate of headless fish.

Soon, she found herself caught up in a wave of men speaking in a rapid tongue she couldn't recognize. She lost track of the soldiers, and her heart squeezed with panic. When she turned in a circle to see where they went, she caught sight of a familiar one-handed man ambling by.

Upton entered a pub along with a few other crew members Rosalie recognized.

Her heart raced as she turned to see the *Deceit* docked on

a nearby slip. Reis must have come right here to sell her and Silence out.

Abandoning the soldiers, Rosalie hurried down the docks.

From below, she couldn't hear any movement on the deck. It seemed the crew was off spending her family's gold in the pub. She wanted to ignore the ship, but if there was something on board that belonged to Silence, she needed to retrieve it.

Rosalie climbed back up onto the deck she'd thought she would never see again. She crossed the space where she'd first held a saber. Passed by the stairs where she'd told Reis about her mother. Her rage bubbled; she loathed everything about the ship around her. How stupid she had been to get swept away by the ocean's allure.

She entered the captain's cabin. It held Crowe's woodsy ocean scent that she'd grown accustomed to. Trying her best to ignore all the captain's familiar things strewn about, Rosalie hunted around the desk for the diary. Out of the corner of her eye, she saw something poking from under the chair. Relieved, she went to retrieve it.

As she grabbed it, the door swung shut.

"Looking for something?"

Rosalie spun around with a gasp. Crowe was leaning up against the wall closest to the door. He took a few steps toward her.

For a moment, they stared at each other. But Rosalie's shock transformed into anger, and she slapped him. "You dirty swindler! I should've known you'd do something like this. The money wasn't enough, was it? You had to get something from the Duranes too! After all those lies about upholding loyalty to the Wellers, I was such an idiot to believe you!"

His brow furrowed. "What in the world are you talking about?"

"You sold out Silence!" Rosalie shouted, her voice already hoarse from the tears she'd shed. "Did you know this whole time who she was? Did the Duranes pay you more than my brothers did? Are you happy with yourself? They're going to kill her, and it's your fault!"

"Rosalie, I have no idea what you're on about!" he yelled over her ranting. "What do you mean, I knew who Silence was?"

"You can lie, but I know you knew. The raiders probably told you." She could hardly get a breath in between her venomous words. "*Vellah,* I never should've trusted you. I should've known better. You're a filthy, no good, lying, stealing pirate!" Rosalie went to hit him again, but he was more prepared the second time around.

Crowe grabbed her wrists. "What happened?"

Despite the pain in her chest, Rosalie didn't back down, trying to wrench away from him. "The Duranes blindsided us; they took Silence! I know you did it. And if it wasn't you, then it was someone on this stupid ship."

His eyes flashed with concern and disapproval. "Don't insult my character or my crew, Rosalie. I'd never help the Duranes even if I had a gun to my head. And whether you believe me or not, I don't know Silence's identity. I tried asking her, but she wouldn't tell me."

She couldn't trust him. She couldn't fall victim to his lies again. "You lied to that officer from the Duranes' ship."

"To keep you and Silence alive."

"But it proves that lying comes so naturally to you."

To her confusion, not a shred of guilt appeared on Crowe's face. His eyes didn't even shift from hers. "I didn't lie to you about anything."

"Don't patronize me," she snarled over the waves beating

against the piles of the pier. "You lied to me about refusing my family's money, but you took it anyway!"

His voice raised over hers. "Do I need to spell it out for you? I didn't collude with the Duranes!"

Before she could help herself, she blurted out, "She's the missing Weller!"

Crowe went mute, and his hands slipped from Rosalie's wrists. "Silence is… How is that possible?"

Tears sprung to Rosalie's eyes. Her knees knocked together, and it took her last dregs of strength to stay standing. After everything Crowe had done, she hated crying in front of him. But the emotional toll was too painful to hold inside. "I don't know. I still haven't put it all together. All I know is it's true. Lowell Durane said something about his brother. Anselm? I didn't even know about him."

Crowe's face darkened at the mention of Eldon's son. "You saw Lowell? He took Silence?"

She wiped her tears and nodded. "I tried to fight for her, but I didn't know what else to do. I wasn't strong enough."

"Why did you come back here?"

"I was going home. But Silence told me that she left this on your ship," Rosalie said, and held up the diary.

He studied the book. It seemed like he hadn't noticed it was there. "What is it?"

"I don't know! I don't know anything, Reis!" Her throat constricted. She'd tried to bury his name, but it was impossible to deny there was more to Crowe. Despite that, Rosalie knew she had to keep her distance.

"This entire time, I've been lied to. If Silence had told me, maybe I would have been able to protect her!" Rosalie's body began to give out, and she slumped into the chair closest to the desk. The diary slipped from her hands.

Reis picked it up and read aloud, "*Constance Weller, 1838.* Well, there's your answer."

Rosalie's head jerked up in surprise. "It's Constance's diary? From when she was imprisoned?"

"Seems like it. Here, look." He pointed out a page. "Anselm."

Rosalie pressed the heels of her palms against her eyes. "She's the daughter of Constance Weller and Anselm Durane."

"I'd like to say stranger things have happened, but I'm drawing a blank," Reis replied, and set the book on her lap. "What are you going to do?"

"Do I look like a military general to you?"

"Hmm, there are the pleasant noble manners I've missed so much."

Fury tore through Rosalie as she got back to her feet. She charged at him, making him stumble back in surprise. "The only friend I've ever had in this entire world is being led to her death, and you have the gall to joke?"

"Sorry," he replied in a clipped voice. "But you're the one who snuck onto my ship."

She gritted her teeth and turned away from him. "You're unbelievable. You said your lousy ship was only loyal to one family in Seity."

"Lousy?" he grumbled in offense. "That pledge of loyalty was made at the start of the war, and it wasn't made by me."

"Oh, so you respect loyalty when it's convenient for you. Suddenly you care about technicalities because you're too scared to go up against the Duranes! I should expect nothing less from a pirate who lied to me."

Reis looked more agitated the harder she pressed. "You want to have this conversation right now? Fine, I risked my life, the lives of my crew, and my ship to save you. And I did it all for nothing. So go on, love, tell me what a wicked man I am."

"*All for nothing?* I was there when you demanded the

money, Reis! You threatened my brothers after they were willing to let you leave without punishment."

He huffed out a sigh and ran a hand over his face. "Ask your brother; I didn't take a single coin."

Her racing thoughts came to a sharp halt. "What?"

"It doesn't matter anymore."

It was like untangling a snarl of yarn; she couldn't keep track of all the knots and threads. "I don't…"

"Breathe; you're going to pass out."

The dash of care unraveled her. She began to cry, and her words came out like a flood. "Eldon could kill her the second she arrives in Cross Row. I don't know what to do. I don't know if my brothers can find her. I don't know if my father can send help in time."

"Then it sounds like you have to go find her yourself."

Go out on her own? Of course she wanted to take charge and become the lady she always thought she could be. But she would only do so with her father's blessing.

"I can't."

Reis looked unconvinced. "Can't or won't? Because you have a knack for being unbearably stubborn when you set your mind on something."

Rosalie realized there was nothing she wouldn't do for Silence. There was nothing she wouldn't sacrifice. If Rosalie had to lay down her life, she would without hesitating. She swallowed and looked up at him. If she had a well-skilled pirate ship on her side, the odds would be better. "Is that your way of offering your help?"

He tilted his head to the side and pushed his hair out of his eyes. "If you don't trust me, then I don't think it would do us much good to team up."

"She is a Weller; your ship swore loyalty to her," she replied. "Doesn't that mean you'd do anything to save her?

Even if it means teaming up with someone you can't stand? Because that's what I'm doing by asking for your help."

Reis didn't speak for a moment. He drew in a long breath, wincing as if it physically pained him. "Stay here and don't make me regret this, Lady Yorke."

After he left, she huffed and sat down. Around her, the ship creaked as it bobbed in the gentle waves. Outside, she could hear the everyday noise from the village's docks. Against all reason, she was back on the *Deceit*—not as a kidnapped victim but as a willing passenger.

She sniffled and dabbed the angry tears from her eyes. With a shaky hand, she picked up the diary. When she opened it to the first page, something fell out. Rosalie stooped down to recover a small piece of wood. Mountains were carved into one side.

Rosalie held the trinket in her palm, unsure of what it was. Warmth emanated from the unassuming oval like it was pulsing with life.

CHAPTER 37- THE LADY

September 1st, 1838

My days are numbered. It almost seems foolish to keep a record that no one will ever see. But I suppose I can use this journal to keep calm and make my final mark on the world.

The Duranes have killed my entire family. I feel numb as I write this, and I wish it was not true. But I witnessed it with my own eyes. Those monsters did not even give my father a chance to say goodbye to me or my mother.

Truthfully, I believed I was next. Slated to be beheaded in front of my family's home. But after my mother was murdered, I was bound and blindfolded.

My captors brought me to Belris and locked me in the Durane manor's dungeon. My heart is heavy to know I will never see my family or my homeland again. I still do not know what Eldon has planned for me. He and his family must be wise to my power because I have heard nothing. They all speak about inane things in their lives as if they did not commit genocide. How coldhearted they are to be so unbothered.

With my final breath, I will curse their family.

Days have passed, and the dungeon has had a shocking arrival. Anselm Durane.

At first, I believed he was here to kill me. But, to my surprise, he was placed in the cell across from mine. He was wounded, and I could not make sense of it. He was silent and didn't move for a long while. I thought for a moment he had perished.

Eventually, a guard came to his aid; they seemed familiar with each other. They whispered to each other, apparently oblivious to who I am and thinking I would be unable to hear them. Anselm said he had called back his troops from attacking Avorae. He directly defied his father's orders and it landed him in prison.

I sat with the knowledge that Anselm was a traitor to his family. I was skeptical, wondering if it was a trap. Still, his injuries look ghastly. I wonder who dared attack him.

Yesterday, he sat up and finally noticed me. Neither of us said anything because we were meant to be enemies.

Yet today, he made a peace offering. The guard Anselm was familiar with, Brice, brought me extra blankets, a diary to write in, and the locket that was stolen from me.

I dared to exchange a few brief words with Anselm. I am not ashamed to admit that I was hostile. I do not think I should be expected to behave any other way toward him. His father has destroyed the Eastern Hills, and now I am forced to live with the loss of everything I once held dear.

Anselm took the verbal attacks without flinching. All he said was he wished his father was dead too. I am unsure if I can trust him. I do not even know why he refused to attack Avorae.

I will keep listening; surely someone in the manor or indeed Belris will slip up and give me a clue as to what my fate will be. For now, I will again wish for a more useful ability. I should like the power to stop hearts or tear down buildings. I remember how Father used to tell me my ability of hearing was a gift. But I have yet to see any validity to this.

I should not speak ill of him.

I miss him and my mother terribly.

* * *

FOR AS LONG AS Rosalie had known Silence, she'd assumed her quiet and composed demeanor was the mark of a self-assured person. When every little thing upset Rosalie, Silence had been a calming force in her life. Someone who had made her feel less alone and treated her like a person with value and not just a dispensable Yorke heir.

Now Rosalie wondered if it had been a strategy to stay out of focus, to avoid being found out. There had been no secrets between them, or so Rosalie thought.

After ten years of being oblivious, she held an entire diary full of secrets that Silence had kept.

Rosalie curled up on the windowsill of Reis's quarters. She watched the *Deceit* detach itself from land. Reis was on the main deck, informing the crew of the change of plans.

After reading Constance's first entry, Rosalie felt heartbroken. Although confused and upset, what bothered her most was that Silence carried the burden of her family history for years. As friends, Rosalie and Silence had shared each other's hurts so that they could try to make life a little easier.

Now she knew their mothers had both died before Rosalie and Silence were able to comprehend such a loss. She didn't know why Silence didn't trust her enough to share the grief.

Rosalie wondered if her concept of trust had been wrong without her even knowing. She'd trusted Silence, who kept the very core of who she was a secret. She'd trusted Reis briefly and came to regret it. Rosalie wasn't sure how the events had unfolded, but Constance Weller had trusted a Durane enough that they had a child together.

Feeling alone in the quiet lull of the ship, Rosalie ran her fingers down the spine of the small diary. She held the locket and wood carving in her lap. She had no guess as to what it was for. But she could feel its energy—it was no ordinary token. She hadn't even broached the subject of the Wellers' powers. Silence had never displayed any sort of extraordinary abilities.

Rosalie's shoulders sagged. How could she have not known?

The door opened, and Kennedy entered. But he hesitated when he saw her. "Oh, Rosalie. Sorry, I didn't know you were in here."

He went to leave, but Rosalie stood up. She gathered the locket and token and put them in her pocket. "Can I ask you something?"

The quartermaster paused. "I suppose."

Rosalie held Constance's diary close to her chest. It was difficult to confront, but she needed to know what it meant to trust someone who had slighted her. "Did Reis take the money from my family?"

"No," he answered in his usual concise manner.

"Why not?"

Kennedy shrugged. "He didn't tell me why. He's a lot like Braxton. He's got a good sense of what's right and wrong. Suppose it just didn't feel right to him."

"Braxton?"

"Our old captain."

"Oh, I see." Rosalie realized it was probably Braxton who had pledged loyalty to the Wellers. So maybe he had a moral compass—something he might've passed to Reis. She blinked and noticed that Kennedy had slipped away while she lost herself in her thoughts.

The door didn't shut all the way. From out on the deck, she heard a familiar song being sung.

"Dashed in red and gold, think of all she holds."

Silence's very existence disrupted Seity. Born with the blood of two families, she revived the Wellers' claim to the Eastern Hills. Everyone in Seity seemed to think the Wellers' magic had gone extinct. But for twenty years, those powers had been lying under the surface. Waiting.

CHAPTER 38- THE CAPTAIN

The mood aboard the *Deceit* was strange. Some crew members were disgruntled; others were worried about what lay ahead. Not to mention, Rosalie and Reis were walking on eggshells around each other.

He had a hard time looking at her. The accusations she'd hurled at him were deserved. It did a number on the guilt that was already festering inside him.

Maybe the mood was because of his bad decisions. Decisions that managed to alienate both Rosalie and his crew. If Reis could go back and do it over again, would he change his mind?

Reis stood in front of his bookshelf. As he feigned interested in the books, he let his mind wander. All the while, he felt Rosalie's presence sitting at the desk behind him.

The world wasn't black and white. There were plenty of gray areas, and as a pirate Reis had found a comfortable place in them. He was in a gray area with Rosalie as well, but it wasn't comfortable. She'd driven him to the brink of madness but kept a tight hold on him. There was no name for it, as far as he was concerned. She'd possessed his every thought and haunted his dreams. The feeling had snuck up on him, apprehending him before he had time to draw his weapon.

"Tell me your plan." Rosalie's voice pulled him out of his web of thoughts. "I can't imagine you're going to go storming into Cross Row with just your crew."

Of course she would ask him to plan. She had known him as the captain who made plans. But Reis had no strategy when it came to the Duranes. Sure, he could elude their navy time and time again. But to face them head-on? It sounded like a death sentence, yet such danger called for risky plans.

"The men who kidnapped you from the coast were raiders."

"I remember."

Reis turned to face her. "They all answer to one man, Rydlan. He was an old confidante of Braxton's. We had a falling out a couple years ago when I wouldn't follow his orders. He wants his personal armada, but the *Deceit* isn't a naval ship, and she never will be as long as I'm her captain."

"He sounds dangerous."

Reis grimaced, thinking about the times he'd had to cross paths with the man and his fleet of scavengers. "He is. But he has eyes everywhere in Cross Row. The Duranes trust him, but he can be bought off for some information. If anyone knows what Eldon is planning, it'll be Rydlan. I'll get him to tell us what he knows, and we'll plan from there."

Rosalie shut her eyes and sank deeper into her seat.

Since she'd been back on board, Reis had been careful not to bring up Silence. He hated seeing the agony cross Rosalie's face. It didn't help that Reis was still struggling to come to terms with the news himself. It made sense, but it seemed so unbelievable that his mind couldn't connect the two identities. How could Silence have hidden who she was for so long? Surely Rosalie would have noticed if Silence had presented Weller magic, right?

The odds were stacked against them. Reis could only hope Rydlan's information would give them an edge over the Duranes.

"Okay," Rosalie said, and stood up. "Excuse me."

Reis couldn't get in another word before she took her leave. He sighed and slumped into his desk chair. He picked up his gun and began to clean it, desperate for a tedious distraction. Even with Rosalie onboard again, the ship still felt quiet. Gone were the days of her feisty bickering.

Reis wasn't sure how long he'd been lost in his thoughts when the door opened again. Kennedy stepped inside. "Captain?"

He sighed but didn't look up. "Yes?"

"You're making an unpopular decision."

"That doesn't surprise me."

"The very fact that you're planning on meeting with Rydlan after he sent his men after us—"

Reis slammed down the unloaded pistol on the desk in front of him. "What choice do I have? No one else has the information I need."

Kennedy didn't flinch at the sudden movement. "It was bad enough that you refused the ransom money."

Reis could appreciate that his men were unhappy. "I'll make up for it later."

"Captain, the crew fear you're going to insert this ship in the war," Kennedy said. "Once you engage with the Duranes, they'll take it as a threat and target us."

"They've targeted this ship for years. You were there. The *Deceit* has more than enough reason to go after the Duranes after what they did to Braxton." Reis could hold on to grudges, but he'd held the grudges from a distance. Nothing would bring Reis greater joy than to plunge a blade through at least one of the Duranes' chests. But to maintain the safety of his crew and his ship, he had let it be a wild fantasy. Now he might have an opportunity to act on his hatred.

"Then that's your stance? Are you enlisting your crew for battle?"

Reis crossed his arms over his chest. He turned his head to look out the port window. In the three years he'd been captain, he'd often taken the easy way out. Life on the open sea was hard enough, so what was the point of chasing after the Duranes? What was the point in fulfilling an old loyalty to a family everyone had thought was erased from existence?

Now things were different. Reis couldn't turn away from the fight and couldn't ignore Braxton's voice in the back of his head.

A good captain doesn't yield because the fight looks too difficult. A good captain measures the risks and rewards.

"Braxton declared this ship's loyalty to the Wellers. Silence Weller may be the only one left, but that doesn't mean we aren't loyal."

"I know, but..." Kennedy's sentence died out before he could finish. Perhaps not even the quartermaster could argue against the wishes of their dead captain. "Most of your men weren't here when Braxton made that decision."

Reis wasn't going to argue semantics. The plan was set. His mind was made up. "Where's Rosalie?"

Kennedy let out a small sigh, surely not pleased about the change in topic. "I think she asked Ori how to climb to the crow's nest."

"You're kidding, right?" He stood and pushed past his quartermaster to step out onto the deck. Some of his crew were peering up at the sails. "Rosalie?" He walked over to the mast and saw a glimpse of blue skirt hanging over the edge of the crow's nest. But she didn't move to look down at him. "Rosalie!"

When he got no reply, he turned around to shoot Ori a deadly look. "What made you think this was a good idea?"

The young deckhand's face paled. "Captain, she just asked how we got up there; I didn't think she'd start climbing."

Reis closed his eyes and pinched the bridge of his nose. Behind him, he could hear Kennedy and Upton having a terse discussion.

"Did you talk to him?"

"He got distracted by this."

"The lads don't want to go into battle," Upton said.

Reis's last nerve was frayed. He whipped around and pointed a finger at the bosun. "You think I'm happy about this? You think I'm pleased that the Duranes have wreaked havoc on all our lives? You may think this has nothing to do with you, but you're mistaken. The ship you're standing on is an ally of the Weller family and an enemy of the Duranes; it's that simple."

Upton's gaze went downward. It didn't matter how long it had been; loyalty didn't expire on the sea.

"If they win this war, they'll be looking for more people to subdue. Anyone who doesn't fit will be their next targets. Look at us, aye, you think we fit their worldview?" The deck around him was silent as Reis went on his tirade. "They look at places like the Islands and the Territories and see land inhabited by people they believe are inferior to them. They see no issue with taking what's not theirs and killing anyone who stands in their way. So, whoever wants to abandon this ship, I won't beg you to stay. But I'll not have any more discussion of insubordination. Get back to work." He turned around and stormed back to his quarters.

"Captain, what about Rosalie?" Ori jogged a few steps to catch up. "Do you want me to help her climb down?"

"Let her be. I'm done arguing for the day," he said, and slammed the door shut.

CHAPTER 39- THE LADY

*M*ay 10*th*, 1839

Brice kept lookout so I could spend last night with Anselm. I cannot say for sure how I feel about him. Love does not feel like a strong enough word.

Admittedly, I am scared about how I feel. Am I being naïve? Anselm told me that we are one and the same. We were both once heirs, and now everything has been taken from us. He spoke about what could be if we left Seity.

The Eastern Hills are lost, although it pains me to say so. I have no one left. All I have is myself, and if I so chose, I would have Anselm too.

He talks about the Outer Territories. Somewhere far beyond the mountains where no one would be able to find us. I want to run away with him. I want to give every part of myself to him. But I fear I cannot give him my trust, even if we are both imprisoned.

Though he is a Durane, he is boyish and charming. He makes me laugh even when I fear my fate. When he held me this morning, I felt safe. Strange to think I could ever feel safe in the arms of the enemy. But is he my enemy? I have heard Eldon speak of his son. He considers Anselm an enemy after refusing to kill Easterners.

Although I do not know if that automatically makes Anselm my ally.

Anselm wanted to know more about my magic. He knows I can hear every word everyone says in the manor if I choose. He asked what I had heard his father say. I told him the truth. Eldon declared Anselm dead, killed in battle.

Anselm was quiet for the rest of the day. I tried comforting him, but we were separated when Brice was relieved of his duties.

I wish Mother was here to talk to me. Luckily, I have made friends with Edme, a Westerner and another captive of the Duranes. She has been here for two years. She told me rumors of the day Avorae was attacked. There was a group of men helping Easterners flee. Edme said she heard they were pirates. I cannot imagine that pirates would be more helpful than our fellow noble families. But I pray it is true. Perhaps many survived.

It is nice to have Edme's company, although our conversations often veer off toward fantasizing about escaping. Maybe there is a way out.

* * *

THROUGH SHEER DETERMINATION, Rosalie had climbed her way to the crow's nest. She'd ignored Ori's nervous caution and fought through the pain in her chest to reach the top. She had spent most of the morning there, marveling at the stunning cobalt ocean. Seity was a sliver on the horizon as they sailed deeper into enemy waters.

She'd heard Reis's impassioned speech to his crew. It did not rekindle her trust, but at least he was willing to risk everything to rescue Silence. For the time being, they were on the same page.

Sailing on the *Deceit* was fitting because she felt adrift, completely lost in the tide of her emotions. Rosalie became nauseous when she thought about Silence. Tears welled up in her eyes, and she wanted to scream into the open sky.

It wasn't over. Rosalie would save Silence even if she had to face Eldon Durane himself.

The hours wore on, and Rosalie's cheeks turned pink from the sun. Needing a respite, she carefully lowered herself down to the deck.

Reis was waiting, but she brushed past him. He sighed when her shoulder grazed his. "Rosie…"

"Don't call me that." She didn't care if he was trying to ease the tension between them. She wanted to cling to her anger and let it drive them apart. It was best to keep him at a distance.

"What can I do? You won't listen when I tell you I've done nothing to harm you or Silence."

"An innocent pirate." Rosalie stopped but didn't face him. "Those words contradict each other, don't you think?"

"Rosalie, I didn't take the ransom, and I didn't conspire with the Duranes. I might not be innocent in many respects, but I'm not taking the blame for things I didn't do."

She braced against the honesty in his voice. It had to be an act. Everything he did was a performance. Perhaps he didn't conspire with the Duranes, but it didn't explain what she knew. "My brother said two people knew where we would be. My father and you. Maybe there's another explanation, but forgive me for being skeptical."

Reis didn't speak, but Rosalie felt the words he wanted to say. Odd, he never had an issue openly maligning Basil before.

"The only thing I've had in life is family. If I can't trust them, I can't trust anything," she said.

"None of my crew are blood, but I trust them with my life."

Her nose wrinkled, and she wanted to swat away any defense he had. "You wouldn't understand."

He barked out a laugh of disbelief. "You don't think I understand loyalty? I've been double-crossed more times than you can count. But I don't doubt the loyalty of my crew."

"Why do you want to win back my trust so badly? You were more than happy to get rid of me!"

Again, he went quiet. He didn't have to say anything; Rosalie could read his face.

"Get your blade."

"What?"

Without answering, she went to the box by the mainmast.

Reis followed and took the sparring saber she offered him. He turned it in his hand. "You really want to do this again?"

Rosalie's frustration coated her pain in armor. She rushed forward, and Reis barely blocked her blow in time. He eyed her as he doubled back to get his bearings. Although he looked reluctant, he squared his shoulders and indulged her. Unlike the first time they had crossed swords, his movements were slower and more forgiving.

Rosalie didn't want him to go easy. A need for destruction spurred her on. "You made a fool out of me. I never should have believed you when you said you wouldn't take the money."

Reis grunted when she managed to whack him in the side with the flat edge of the blade. "I *didn't* take it."

"But you were going to!" She didn't let up even as she talked in a ragged voice. "I'm sure you think it's fun to kiss women right before you betray them. It's all just a game to you, isn't it?"

"Is that what this is about?" He blocked another lunge. He

closed in, their sabers clashed together, their faces inches away from one another. "You kissed me first."

"You're right; I don't know what came over me. I was so stupid to believe you cared," she snapped through gritted teeth, and shoved him away with all her might.

Reis shifted his weight to his back foot. "I never said I didn't care about you."

She didn't give him a moment to catch his breath. With all the energy she had left, she stepped back into the spar. "Don't even say that."

"I'm not going to lie to you."

Sweat beaded on Rosalie's forehead, and tears distorted her vision. "I don't believe you!"

"You don't have to. All I can do is show you. Words are worthless; I know that." He lowered his weapon.

Her breathing was off kilter as she stared, waiting for Reis to retaliate. When he didn't, she hit the hilt of his cutlass and made him drop it. Her hand trembled as she pointed her blade at his chest. She had to keep him at a distance.

But the dull blade did not deter him. He moved it aside and stepped toward her. His eyes searched hers as he took her face in his hands. Despite the callouses on his fingertips, his touch was gentle and sent shivers down Rosalie's spine.

"Reis…"

He kissed her.

Grief and affection flooded Rosalie's veins. She dropped the sparring saber and wrapped her arms around his neck. It felt natural to knot her fingers in his hair and taste the salty ocean air on his lips. When he pressed a hand to her lower back to hold her close, she could have wept from how protected she felt.

Reis pulled away, and she let out a small noise of protest.

"Sorry," he whispered. "I know this isn't the time. Sometimes with you, I just feel…"

Cold reality crashed over Rosalie, and she withdrew her arms. "Don't say anything you don't mean."

He nodded absentmindedly. His lips were a thin line, as if sealing his mouth to keep words inside.

Suddenly, Rosalie became painfully aware that they weren't alone on the deck. A handful of crew members were doing everything to avoid looking at the captain and lady. Even Ori had his head tilted up to look directly at the clouds.

"I can see you're all listening. If you can listen, you can work. Get to it!" Reis scolded the crew. Then he bent his head and muttered, "Tomorrow isn't going to be fun."

* * *

THE SUN ROSE on another day separated from Silence. Before she opened her eyes, Rosalie held on tight to what little hope she had left.

But Lowell's words to Silence kept echoing in the air.

You're just in time to see a new chapter in Cross Row.

Rosalie couldn't make sense of the statement. In an attempt to escape Lowell's haunting voice, she stumbled outside. She clutched her shawl around herself and tried to shake off the exhaustion.

Reis stood by the bow of the ship. His hands were folded behind his back as his trained eyes scanned the hazy horizon.

Rosalie cleared her throat so she wouldn't scare him when she stepped beside him. He gave her a nod. Again, neither of them acknowledged the kiss. She was too scared to admit how safe she'd felt in his arms. Rosalie had been wrapped in conflict because of the betrayal and trust that flooded through her when she looked at Reis. Knowing she couldn't be distracted during Reis's plan, she decided to set all her turmoil aside for the time being.

"How do you know he'll be here?" Rosalie asked.

"He's easy to find if you know his patterns. I swear he can smell a deal from miles away." Reis revealed a sizable bag of gold pieces from inside his coat. They went quiet for another moment before Reis broke the peace again. "Who taught you Territory curses?"

"Pardon?" Rosalie raised an eyebrow.

A small smile tugged at his lips. "The day you came back aboard—you said *vellah*. I never thought I'd hear a lady drop a curse like that."

Her cheeks warmed. "I must've learned it from my brothers or Silence. I don't know where they learned it from. I didn't mean to offend you."

"Didn't offend me." He chuckled. "Just makes you fit in a bit more around here."

Rosalie's heart skipped a beat, and she had a hard time deciphering the emotions flitting across her. To refocus her thoughts, she turned her attention back to the issue at hand. "Can you trust Rydlan?" Trust remained a sensitive subject, but Rosalie didn't want to walk into another trap set by the Duranes.

"No," he answered without hesitation. "But it would be worse to go blind into Cross Row. Rydlan's a coward and only picks on people smaller than him. The worst he could do is talk."

Like a knife, Rydlan's ship sliced through the fog. It was a loud display of the man's wealth. The large frigate had the same ebony accents Kelan's ship had. The ship that was sitting on the sea floor because of Reis.

Reis gently touched her arm. "I…" He quickly withdrew his hand. "Sorry, I should prepare to meet him."

"I'm going with you," Rosalie said.

He opened his mouth to argue but perhaps realized it was a losing argument. Or at least one that would eat up time they didn't have.

"Fine, but let me do the talking."

* * *

REIS'S DESCRIPTION of Rydlan wasn't too far off. Even to Rosalie, he looked like a coward. The man awaited their arrival on his ship's main deck. A mousy-looking fellow who had a crooked air about him, he would've been unassuming had Rosalie not known his reputation beforehand. His hair was graying, but he emanated a boisterous energy.

"Look at him, all grown up and the captain of the most feared pirate ship on the seas." Rydlan smiled toothily and clapped Reis on the back. "And Rosalie Yorke, no doubt."

Her eyes shifted subtly over to Reis. It all seemed a bit strange. Reis had disrupted Kelan's attempt to deliver Rosalie and Silence to the Duranes. Now Rydlan—who stood to make a lot of money from the Duranes—was acting as if they were all old friends coming to visit for a spell. Perhaps if there was a large deal on the table, past transgressions could be swept under the rug.

"Come in, come in." He ushered them into his quarters. It was similar to Reis's, just more cluttered and with no book-shelves.

Rosalie noticed gold and silver objects strewn about. Fist-fuls of jewels had been deposited here and there, like ripe fruit waiting for anyone to take. As if Rydlan was tempting someone to steal so he could make an example out of them.

The most concerning was a sizable pile of military-issued weapons. Some bore the Yorke crest; others bore the Gunn crest. But a certain boar was noticeably absent.

Reis pulled out a chair for Rosalie before sitting as well.

"I thought you had given up on me entirely. I haven't heard from you since our little disagreement." Rydlan's brow creased. "Don't trust an old man anymore?"

"Braxton may have trusted you, but I don't," Reis replied coldly. "You've caused more than enough trouble for me."

The man clicked his tongue in disapproval as he lounged back in the ornate leather chair. "Well, I was willing to overlook what happened on the western coast. I thought you were coming to bury the hatchet."

"No, I still have a score to settle with you."

Rydlan laughed throatily, not at all perturbed. "You've gained a quick wit, my boy. Nevertheless, I'll clear the slate." His hand swept through the air with a grand flourish. "A fresh start."

Reis remained emotionless, and Rosalie could feel how tense he was next to her. She wanted to reach over and take his hands in hers. But she kept her fingers laced together on her lap.

"Can we skip the act? I'm looking for information on Silence Weller's whereabouts," Reis said.

The older man tilted his head to the side and bridged his fingers against his chin. "That name has become louder among the whispers. What a truly enticing story. Eldon has big plans for her, of course; we all know his end goal. He wants the last two families out of his way." He glanced at Rosalie out of the corner of his eye, his lips curling into a sneer.

Cold sweat stuck to her palms as Rosalie tried to maintain her composure. She didn't want to give the man the satisfaction of seeing her afraid. He'd terrorized her enough already.

Reis stepped in as if to divert Rydlan's attention away from her. "You knew about her reward; that's why you sent men to the Cliffs to begin with. Lowell Durane captured her. Now has she arrived in Belris yet?"

A flash of anger crossed Rydlan's eyes, but he maintained a calm manner. "The girl is alive. Lowell will deliver her to

Eldon any day now. I wouldn't worry yourself too much; she won't die when she enters Cross Row."

"What do you mean?" Rosalie couldn't bite her tongue.

Rydlan looked delighted when she'd spoken up. "Well, Lady Yorke, I'm sure you're aware those with Weller blood hold special abilities. Eldon has known of Silence's power since she was born. How do you think he picked which Weller to kill and which to keep alive?"

A chill went down Rosalie's spine, and she couldn't find the words to answer the question.

"Constance Weller could hear a pin drop from miles away. A useful tool in war—one Eldon sought to exploit. But unfortunately, she met Anselm Durane and the rest is history. Constance was too dangerous to keep alive because of her *entanglement* with Anselm. But she produced what could be Eldon's most powerful weapon." He paused for a moment as if to study Rosalie's reaction. "Did you know, Lady Yorke, that Wellers cannot use their powers on someone they're blood-related to?"

Rosalie swallowed hard. She wasn't sure even Silence knew that fact. Nervously, she side-eyed Reis, but his face was like stone. Dread filled her to the brim as she came to understand what this meant.

Rydlan folded his hands together. "This was never an issue between the Duranes and the Wellers before since they were never kin. But now? Well, let's just say it's both a blessing and a curse for the Duranes."

Reis seemed to have caught onto what the man was implying. "That's all we needed." He pulled out the gold and set it down on the desk with a heavy thunk.

"You think you can penetrate Belris's border? My boy, you're sorely mistaken. You'll be shot before you get the chance."

Reis hesitated. The corner of his lip twitched and his eyes darted around the room. "Then your information is useless."

He reached toward the gold, but Rydlan held out a hand. "Don't give up so soon. I'll tell you what—since we've let bygones be bygones, I'm in a generous mood."

Rosalie sensed a shift in the air, and she felt the urge to flee for the door.

But Reis stood his ground. "I'm listening."

"Your ship will stick out in Belris's port. If you had an escort—say someone who has a good rapport with the Duranes—you could slip right under their watchful gaze."

"You think I'm stupid enough to trust you," Reis deadpanned.

Rydlan leaned forward. "I think you're desperate." When Reis didn't respond, the man sighed and slumped back. "You said you have a score to settle with me. Consider it settled if I help you with this."

Doubt burned under Rosalie's skin, but she didn't dare speak.

"What's stopping you from double-crossing me?"

Rydlan pointed lazily to the port window. "I know you still have that old bosun on board. Ask him if I ever double-crossed Braxton. We might have our skirmishes, but a deal's a deal."

Rosalie's heart was beating so heavily she feared they could hear.

"Fine," Reis said after some thought. "But if you make one misstep, I'll kill you."

Rydlan held his hands up. "Precisely why I never double-crossed Braxton."

"Then we have a deal."

"We'll have a deal when you offer more sufficient payment." Rydlan picked at the gold with an unimpressed frown.

"I'll double it. Half now, half when the job's complete."

"I'll take the girl."

Reis's expression was so cold, it felt as if the temperature of the room plummeted. "What did you just say to me?"

Rydlan, with two ruby-adorned fingers, pointed at Rosalie. She tensed up. No, she'd had enough of being someone's prisoner.

"The Yorke—she's worth more than a pitiful handful of gold. I'd go after the Weller's ransom, but it seems that offer has already expired."

Reis reacted faster than lightning. He slammed his hand down on the desk so hard, the gold coins rattled. "You lost the ransom—your raiders were all too easy to intercept. I'd tell you to take it up with them, but they're all dead. You'll take what I'm offering, and you'll shut your mouth about ever seeing her."

A faint smile formed on Rydlan's lips. "Oh, Reis," he said in a simpering tone. "Look at you getting involved in Seity *politics*. How disappointed Braxton would be with you. How much could that ransom have given you and your crew? Yet you've thrown it all away, and for what? We both know her time in this world is short."

A flash of anger coursed through Rosalie, mixing fluidly with her fear. But Reis beat her to the punch.

Literally.

In a blink, Reis lunged across the desk to grab Rydlan by the shirt collar. He punched the man so hard, Rosalie swore she heard something crack.

Rydlan cursed and clutched his jaw. "Stupid boy, you've gone and broken one of my teeth!" he snarled.

Reis didn't let go of his shirt. "Apologize."

Rosalie scooted back, the chair legs grinding across the floor. She reached for Reis, but part of her *wanted* Rydlan to rescind his words.

"Fine, fine!" Rydlan looked like a puppy caught by the scruff of its neck. His face started to turn red. "I take it back! I'm sorry!"

"You'll accept double that payment to escort us into Belris," Reis hissed, and yanked the shirt to give Rydlan a good dose of whiplash.

"Triple and I'll forget I ever saw the girl."

Reis relinquished his hold. "Fine."

Rydlan reached for a handkerchief and dabbed his face. "You've gone and let love rot your brain, then, aye?"

The word *love* hummed around Rosalie's head like a fly. She was too stunned to make any sense of it.

Reis stood, offering a hand to Rosalie. "I'll bring the rest of the gold," he said to Rydlan. "After this, I don't ever want to see your face again."

Rydlan rubbed his jaw. "I suspect that won't be an issue. Always a pleasure doing business with you, old friend."

CHAPTER 40- THE LADY

August 17th, 1839
    Anselm was brought upstairs to speak with his father. I was so nervous, especially since I was hoping to tell him the news this morning. Brice tried to assure me that Eldon would never kill his son. Duranes do not spill each other's blood, he said. But they would imprison each other.

    It felt like days until Anselm was returned. He was hurt, but alive. I told him that I am with child. There is no denying it anymore—I am showing, and Edme is convinced. Since she is a trained midwife, I trust her opinion entirely. And she believes I am going to have a girl.

    Anselm looked a little faint when I told him the news. But he assured me he was happy. I suppose his fear comes from what our child means to Seity. She is both a Weller and a Durane. Our houses have never mixed before, so my daughter sets a precedent. Already she is special.

    Anselm and I discussed names. I have to admit he seemed a little apprehensive to know our child would possess a power. He let me know that in the South, it is tradition to name female heirs after a desired trait to inspire their future. I think I will decide what to name her when I finally see her.

My desire to escape grows more urgent now that I know I will have a daughter to look after. When I first arrived here, I resigned myself to the inevitable. But I refuse to let anyone harm my child. My strength to fight has been rekindled.

RYDLAN'S SHIP led the *Deceit* through the sparse fog. Rosalie watched by the bowsprit. Her worry would not rest. She'd seen pure deception in the man's eyes, but what other choice did they have? Rydlan had been right; if they tried approaching Belris's wall from the outside, they would be killed on sight.

But they could access the wall from the inside.

It was risky, but Emerson and Emery could not save Silence on their own. They needed backup, and they needed the information Rosalie now possessed.

Doubt darkened Rosalie's thoughts. They were courting death with little certainty. She wondered if she had made a mistake turning away from Ciern.

Constance's diary entry swirled in her head. She had been so hopeful she would have a life with Anselm and their daughter. Where did hope get women? The question gave Rosalie a headache as she went to discard her shawl in Reis's quarters.

He was sitting at his desk but turned toward the window. It appeared his mind was in as much turmoil as hers was.

"What are you thinking about?" she asked, and placed Constance's diary on the desk.

Reis blinked a few times as he acknowledged her presence. "I'm thinking about how Braxton died. I'm wondering if I'm doomed to the same fate."

"You're a good fighter. I've seen what you're capable of."

"As much as I appreciate that, Rosie, pirates aren't mili-tary-trained."

The nickname slipped through—Rosalie captured it and held it close to her heart. "Would it help you to know that I have faith in you?" she asked. If they were headed into an unknown fate, she knew it was best she said everything that was on her mind before it was too late. Unfortunately, she couldn't find the words to accurately describe how she felt about Reis.

It wouldn't matter, because a shout from the deck inter-rupted them before he could answer. "Cap'n!"

Reis stood and hurried out of the cabin with Rosalie on his tail.

The fog had dissipated to reveal Belris and its port up ahead. She'd thought Cross Row would be unrecognizable, as if the Duranes' vileness would manipulate the architecture into something grotesque. But it was almost identical to Ciern's port.

Reis wasn't focused on what the city looked like. He swore under his breath as he ran to the port side. Rydlan's ship had veered away from Belris, slipping back to the open ocean like an eel slithering under a rock.

"Captain!" Danny called from the crow's nest. "Durane galleon on the starboard quarter!"

Rosalie rushed to the side and looked to the stern. A ship was sailing straight for them. Boars on gold fluttered in the wind and warned of death. Rosalie's face felt prickly as the rest of her body went numb.

They had been betrayed.

"Ready the cannons!" Reis shouted. He took Rosalie's hand. "Come with me," he urged, and attempted to bring her back inside. "I don't want you involved in this."

Coming to a halt, Rosalie refused to take another step. "That's not for you to decide. I'm going to fight for my friend."

"This is no place for someone like you." When she stopped following, he looked back at her. Regret was embedded into his face. "This is my mistake. I won't have you pay for it."

"You have no say in this. You can't tell me not to fight." She matched his stare and stood straighter. It reminded her of simpler times when Reis's biggest trouble was keeping her from wandering the ship.

Reis cursed under his breath. "Stubborn as ever. This is life or death we're talking about."

"Every day is life or death for me."

The crew was gearing up for battle around them. There was little time left. Rosalie knew things were unsaid, but it provided another incentive to stay alive.

"Now, go be a captain, and let me be a lady."

They were out of time.

"Right!" Reis turned toward the main deck. "No one does a thing without my instruction, is that clear?"

The *Deceit*'s crew all responded in unison. "Aye, Cap'n!"

* * *

IN BETWEEN SHOUTING ORDERS, Reis cursed Rydlan's name and promised to get his revenge. The *Deceit* couldn't run. The blindsiding tactic had boxed them in.

"They're making for a broadside," Upton barked.

Rosalie slipped through the activity on the deck. She used the starboard shroud to climb up so she could see what they were dealing with.

The warship was not the largest of its fleet. It was

marginally bigger than the *Deceit* with rows upon rows of cannons. It moved through the calm bay waters to become parallel to the *Deceit*.

Rosalie almost lost her grip on the rigging when she caught sight of a familiar head of braids. "Don't fire!" she cried. "Silence is onboard!"

Reis came up beside her and looked through his spyglass. "It's worse," he said. "Your brothers are with her."

"No…" Rosalie's voice wavered with panic.

"They must've intercepted your brothers at the wall." He backed up to shout to his crew, "Hold your fire!"

The galleon cut through the sea, settling into its planned formation. Once it was close enough, Rosalie could see Silence standing between Emery and Emerson. They were placed on the side facing the *Deceit*, acting as human shields.

The galleon stayed stationary alongside the *Deceit*. A quiet fell over both crews of the opposing ships as Lowell and his older brother Fineas came into view.

"I gave you all a chance to stay out of our way." Although his voice was full of venom, Lowell looked thrilled that the Yorkes had disobeyed him. Now he could carry out his threat.

"Reis," Rosalie urged.

"Wait," he said. "Just wait."

Lowell turned his attention to another victim. "Did you miss me, Crowe? I was almost certain I'd killed you the first time we met. But I got the job done with Braxton, didn't I?"

Rosalie was amazed by Reis's composure as Braxton's killer taunted him.

"A fantastic audience to show off our new addition." He smirked at Silence. "But I'm getting ahead of myself."

The Durane's crew placed a plank to connect the ships. Reis tensed up but still held firm.

Eldon Durane walked out onto the deck, and it felt like the ocean itself went hushed. He was older than expected; the myth of his brutality kept him eternal. He was not a particularly tall man, and his hair was gray. But his eyes were cold and unforgiving, a trait his sons inherited from him.

He walked with a limp, but the past injury didn't fool Rosalie. He held power that had been passed down for generations. The very sight of him was dangerous. Reis was right—these men were too evil to be seen as human.

"Rosalie Yorke, it is truly a miracle to see you alive. I'll admit, you're harder to kill than I expected." Through the cold demeanor, a cruel smile tugged at his lips. "Now, you have something that belongs to me."

Confusion dampened her anger for a moment. She had nothing that belonged to any Durane. She gritted her teeth and climbed her way onto the plank. "I will fight you until my dying breath. Silence will never be your victim."

"Rosalie." Reis attempted to pull her down.

No. Her friend was coming home, even if it killed Rosalie. Driven by blind rage, she began walking across the plank.

"No!" Reis lunged to grab her but missed by a mere inch, the fabric of her skirt slipping through his fingers.

"Rosalie, stop!" Emery yelled.

Eldon smiled as Rosalie advanced. "That's it. Hand over the talisman, and I may grant your beloved pirates a stay of execution."

Her heart was in her throat as she reached the halfway point. Her skirt fluttered against her ankles as the waves churned beneath her. *Talisman.* The word echoed around her in a daze.

"Don't give it to him," Silence begged.

"Be quiet," Eldon snarled.

Rosalie's mind went blank. She took the last few steps.

No miraculous plan pieced together. All she knew was she would not leave Silence behind again.

When her feet hit the deck, chaos erupted. Emerson attacked the closest soldier, elbowing him in the face. Emery fought his way to protect his sister. But the naval officers overpowered him, forcing him to the ground.

Eldon grabbed Rosalie by the upper arm and shoved her toward Lowell. "Take her and the girl below deck. Find the talisman."

"Let her go!" Silence yelled as Fineas wrestled her back. Lowell turned his attention to Rosalie.

Before he could get any closer, Reis jumped onto the ship's deck. He stepped in between Lowell and her.

"You're wasting your time, Captain. Go back to your ship; it's worth more than she is." Lowell stared right at Rosalie even as he spoke to Reis.

"Real men don't talk while fighting," Reis replied, then lunged.

Rosalie regained her composure and acted on adrenaline-fueled intuition. She threw Emery her cutlass and rushed to free Silence from Fineas's grasp.

"No, Rosalie, stay back!" Silence warned.

The air was thick with the clash of steel and yells from both crews. Rosalie was knocked off her feet. As the ship dipped with the waves, she slid farther away. She looked up and spotted her friend through the fray.

Silence stumbled to her knees, her weight throwing Fineas off balance. Her brown eyes were wide, and her lips parted. For a moment, the world went quiet. Rosalie fought her way back to her feet. She could not look away from Silence's panicked face.

Then, like an explosion, a sharp, ear-piercing noise filled the air. It was louder than thunder and echoed across the waves. Every man within a few feet collapsed, clutching their ears in agony. It seemed endless, the high-pitched shriek rattling the world.

An invisible force thrust out, pushing everything in its path away. The deck splintered and the ship pitched. Rosalie fell to the deck, and the world went black.

CHAPTER 41- THE CAPTAIN

Reis's vision blurred. His ears rang. It felt like the world had vanished from all around them. All he could sense was Rosalie's weight in his arms. His feet landed by instinct as he jumped the gap to make it back onto the *Deceit*. He didn't know who he'd left behind on the Duranes' ship.

For a split moment, she felt lifeless. Her body went limp, and just like the naval ship, his world shattered. The air was thick with gunpowder and his lungs felt blistered. He forced himself to breathe through it, fighting for any oxygen to survive.

Rosalie wasn't moving in his arms. He looked down, desperate to sense any life from her. He could've fallen to his knees in relief when he saw her chest move. But she was still unconscious. He lurched toward his quarters but remembered his place as captain. He needed to know his crew was safe.

With his ears still feeling like they were stuffed with cotton, he looked back. Chaos sprawled over the bay. His crew was a blur around the deck. He saw Upton shouting orders but couldn't hear what he was saying.

The Duranes' ship was in flames as the ocean dragged it down into its cold embrace. He couldn't see anyone on board. His stomach dropped.

The sails were rigged, and the *Deceit* made a hasty exit. Amid the fray, Reis caught sight of Rosalie's brothers. But someone was missing.

"No," he whispered just as his hearing returned.

* * *

WHEN REIS SET ROSALIE DOWN, her temple left a blotch of blood on his shirt. His hands trembled as he cleaned the cut.

"Rosie." He continued to call her name to wake her up. In between the repetition, he let the strange battle sink back into his thoughts. Rydlan had betrayed him. The entire Durane family was on that ship. Reis was so damn close to getting his revenge.

But that sound. It was like the world itself opened up and unleashed mayhem. Nothing on a ship could make such a noise. Frankly, he wasn't sure anything in nature was capable of it.

Minutes ticked away before Reis realized he hadn't checked to see if *he* was injured. His ribs felt alright; he didn't find any source of bleeding, and the only pain that registered was a nasty headache.

Exhausted, Reis slumped against his desk next to Rosalie. He kept his eyes on her to track every inhale and exhale she took. He took her hand in his and rested his fingers against her wrist. Every pulsing beat reassured him that she was okay.

This fiery spark couldn't be snuffed out—not so soon. She

had swept through his life, rearranged everything he knew, and did so with a goading smile. It was agonizing to think about the hole she would leave behind if she ever did leave him.

It felt like all Reis could do was wait for something else to pull them apart. It haunted him to wonder what it might be.

He sighed and said her name again. At least for now, she was here.

But Silence Weller was not, and he couldn't begin to face the fear and hopelessness her disappearance would cause. Reis wanted Rosalie to rest a little while longer. Because when she woke, she would be faced with one of her greatest nightmares.

CHAPTER 42 - THE LADY

Fear jolted Rosalie awake. Her body felt sluggish, but the instinct to flee urged her forward. Her palm pressed onto the floor, and she lifted herself into a sitting position.

Reis rocked forward to catch her before she fell over. "Steady, love. You're still recovering."

Her fingers wrapped around his, and the panic dwindled. She was safe. The *Deceit*'s subdued rocking reassured her.

"What happened?" she asked.

Reis shook his head in bewilderment. "I can't say for sure. It was unlike anything I've ever seen… or heard."

Brief flashes of memory came back in waves. "That noise. Where did it come from? Was it a cannon?"

"No, never heard a cannon make that sound in all my life. I can't say for sure, but I saw Silence standing there," he recounted in a daze. "She looked unaffected. I know it sounds impossible, but I think it came from her."

Rosalie put a hand to her mouth. Silence's calm demeanor wasn't just a personality trait. It was to conceal the magic she had inherited. "Then she does have a power."

Reis tilted back, sitting on his heels. His hand slipped away from Rosalie's. "But she can't control it."

"Maybe she can learn how to control it."

He pursed his lips and avoided her eyes. The air between them hung thick with tension.

"Wait... where is Silence?" Rosalie looked around. Her friend was always by her side when she came to.

He pinched the bridge of his nose and sighed. A spatter of red decorated his shirt. Rosalie couldn't distinguish if it was his blood or someone else's. "After the noise, the Duranes' ship started to go down. I grabbed you, but Silence was too far away, I lost sight of her. Your brothers were lucky to make it to the *Deceit* in one piece."

The dread was swift and debilitating as it plunged through Rosalie's heart. "No—Reis, tell me you're lying."

"I'm sorry," he said. "The Duranes must've escaped with her. They were close enough to port to abandon ship."

Rosalie brushed off his hand and scrambled to her feet. She dashed out of the cabin, rushing to the side of the ship. "Silence!" she shouted. The blue sky was clouded over. The sea stirred angrily, the choppy waves beating at the ship's hull. A few bits of debris bobbed in the ocean, severed pieces of the galleon destroyed by a single scream.

Some of the crew spared her regretful glances.

"Silence!" Rosalie cried again. Her breathing became rapid, and her head spun with anxiety. "They can provoke her power." She recalled what Rydlan had said. Constance had produced Eldon's greatest weapon. One that couldn't hurt him. "He's going to use her power to end the war."

Reis put his hands on her shoulders. "Breathe; I don't want you fainting."

Rosalie couldn't be placated. "How could this happen? How could I let her get taken again?"

"It's not over. We'll keep fighting."

But his words fell away. Rosalie collapsed to her knees and screamed. She did not tear the ship to shreds like Silence had. As she sobbed, she felt Reis's arms wrap around her.

Talisman.

Eldon's voice swirled like a tempest in Rosalie's head. She broke free from Reis and stumbled back inside. Her fingers tingled as she riffled around for Constance's diary. Tucked under the cover was the wooden token. She picked it up and felt it tremble like an egg about to hatch. Clutching it in her fist, she leafed through the entries until she found Silence's birthday written in the top right corner.

JANUARY 14TH, 1840

I gave birth to my daughter today. I remember Mother telling me how thrilled she was to first hold me. Now I know the joy she felt.

I cannot take my eyes off her. She is beautiful and everything I could have hoped for. When she took her first breath, she let out a scream that nearly deafened Edme and Brice.

Her power can be dangerous, but in a way, it makes me relieved. Should anything happen, I believe she could protect herself.

While she sleeps, I've been creating her talisman out of a piece of wood Anselm found for me. It is not my first choice. I would have rather made it from a rock from the mountains like my mother did for me. But it will channel her powers just as well.

Anselm and I decided to name her Silence. Not to keep her quiet when she wants to speak, but so that she might know the peace of silence. I want her to have a life outside of this war. War is so loud and destructive. I only want her to know serenity. In that peace, she will be able to express herself properly.

Anselm joked that we will need to find a farm big enough in the

Outer Territories. There she can use her gift whenever she wants without hurting anyone. To me, it sounds like a lovely existence.

It seems so far, but I cannot help but dream. Keeping Silence hidden in a prison is tearing me apart. I want her to be free.

We did not discuss her family name. But I will not have her bear the name of the man who murdered my family. She will always be a Weller.

Silence Weller.

If she stays in Seity—even in hiding—she will never know peace. She will always be targeted. She cannot protect herself against the Duranes if they are blood. Not without a Card.

Eldon had been right; Rosalie had the talisman. The wooden token could help Silence control her magic. But she zeroed in on one word. It was partially obscured by a blot of ink, but Rosalie could still decipher it.

Card?

What kind of card? One apparently so special Constance had capitalized it, and something that could allow Silence to use her magic against the Duranes.

She leafed through a few more pages for clarification but didn't find any more mention of the card. Where could it be? What did it look like?

"Rose?" There was a faint knock on the door, and Emery poked his head in. "Are you doing alright?"

She shut the diary and quickly stowed it, along with the talisman, in her pocket. "I'm managing," she answered, trying to keep her nerves at bay.

"Well, Emerson wants to see you." He gave her a half-hearted smile and offered his elbow to her.

Taking a deep breath, Rosalie walked out onto the deck with him. No longer was she surrounded only by pirates; she was among family. So, she squared her shoulders and held herself tall like a lady ought to. Even if her spine wanted to bow under the weight of her stress.

The sky remained cloudy as they sailed out of southern waters. Emerson waited by the foremast, watching the ocean with a stony expression.

Rosalie carried her guilt and apprehension across the deck. She was finally piecing together Silence's past, but it meant nothing if she couldn't save her. She just wanted to wake up from the nightmare and find herself back at home in Ciern. Life had been simpler there, even if she'd been unhappy. After years of wanting more responsibility, Rosalie was starting to see that the burden was too much to bear. Her father had been right: She would never be capable. No matter what she did, she was thwarted by someone stronger.

Her thoughts turned back to Constance's journal and the mysterious card. Well, maybe she didn't have to be stronger. Maybe she could just be smarter.

She and Emery reached Emerson. Their older brother was disheveled but still held his composure. "I suppose we can't doubt she's a Weller anymore."

Emery swallowed. "If they brought her back to Belris, we'll never be able to rescue her. No one has ever breached the city."

"But Eldon knows we would try," Emerson replied.

"He won't hide her away, and he won't kill her," Rosalie said. "He's going to use her as a weapon."

Emerson passed a hand over his face. Rosalie wondered what he and Emery had gone through when they'd been captured by the Duranes.

"Father needs to know what has happened. I don't know how we'll strategize against this development."

Rosalie took a deep breath. "I have something that might help us."

CHAPTER 43- THE CAPTAIN

*R*eis's ears had finally stopped ringing. But he kept his distance from the Yorkes, unsure if he wanted to hear what they were talking about. No doubt Emerson was eager to get Rosalie off the *Deceit*. The thought chipped another piece off Reis's heart.

"She looks like a lady next to them." Kennedy was sitting on the quarterdeck, mending a tear in the ship's flag. Now that the *Deceit* had to be a little more inconspicuous in the water, they couldn't fly their beloved banner.

"She's always been a lady." Reis leaned his arms against the railing overlooking the main deck as the Yorkes conferred with one another. From a distance, he noted how different yet similar the siblings were. Emerson's emotions were hard to detect behind the solemn mask he wore. The only thing that broke through was soft affection for his younger siblings. Emery was a bit more lighthearted and animated despite the war that loomed overhead. But all three of them resembled one another.

"You're happier when she's onboard," Kennedy said. It wasn't a question or even a theory. It was a fact.

Reis frowned. "I haven't changed at all," he argued. Even as he denied it, he couldn't take his eyes off Rosalie.

She looked a little disheveled from the skirmish, although it didn't make her any less beautiful. Her ashen hair was coming undone from her braid, but she hadn't bothered to fix it. She had a scrape across her cheek and a sizeable injury on her temple from when she'd collapsed.

He sighed and let his head hang. "I doubt she'll stay out here much longer. Her brothers will want her home where it's safer."

"Sounds like you're afraid of that."

"Well, that's where she belongs. That was the plan all along, and it still is." Reis lifted his head. "Besides, I'm not afraid of anything."

Kennedy just made a noise of vague disagreement.

"I'm not fond of this war, but I'm not afraid of it," Reis corrected him even though the quartermaster hadn't said anything.

Kennedy shrugged and jerked his head down toward the main deck. "That wasn't what I was talking about."

Reis glanced over his shoulder and locked eyes with Rosalie. She gave him a small smile. He swallowed and looked back to Kennedy.

The quartermaster held up the flag to inspect his work. "Do you know why Braxton used a bleeding heart on this?"

"It means death to anyone who would dare resist."

"To others, maybe. But to him, it was to represent the wife he lost." Kennedy stood and folded the flag with careful veneration. "You remember how he always said he would give anything to have just two more minutes with her."

Reis could still picture the pained look their former captain always got when discussing Naomi. "I remember."

"It seems you're wasting those precious minutes,"

Kennedy said. "Minutes you might want a few years from now."

"Reis?" Rosalie called.

He gave Kennedy a final look, lost in the mire of what his quartermaster was implying. Trying to put it aside, he descended the stairs to join the Yorkes.

Emerson stood ramrod straight as he faced the captain. "I thought I told you to stay out of Seity waters."

"Trust me, I tried." Reis tensed up but attempted to be diplomatic for Rosalie's sake.

"Nevertheless, I applaud your bravery in battle. My brother and I are grateful you were able to save Rosalie."

"Saved our hides too," Emery piped up with a lopsided smile.

Emerson did not smile. "Yes. That too."

Reis was surprised by the compliment even if it was said through clenched teeth. Surely it wasn't easy for a noble to admit a scoundrel was decent at his job.

"As a matter of principle, I wouldn't allow anything to happen to Rosalie." But something had almost happened to her. It'd been such a close call, and the recent memory already caused him distress.

"I see." Emerson frowned. "Then if you'd be so kind as to bring us to land, unless you're going to threaten me for another ransom that you don't plan on taking?"

Reis snorted at the jab. "Allow me to apologize. I'm sorry you felt so threatened."

The eldest Yorke subtly fumed in place. "You're testing your luck, pirate. I'll make sure you—"

"Let's stay on track, please," Rosalie interrupted.

Emerson exhaled. "Emery and I will try to determine where the Duranes fled to with Silence. It's too dangerous to go after her until we have proper reinforcements. Your ship will bring Rosalie to Ciern so she can inform our father of the matter."

Reis cocked an eyebrow. He had been certain Emerson was going to whisk Rosalie off the dangerous pirate ship. To know Reis would have a few more days with her was an instant relief.

Still, he didn't like being told what to do. "I don't take orders from you."

He could almost hear Emerson grinding his teeth. "If you're looking for money…"

Reis held up a hand. "I'm looking for nothing more than a bit of respect. You see, your sister has learned that the only Seity title that matters on this ship belongs to Silence Weller. Now, Rosalie has earned her place among us pirates. You two —" he eyed the Yorke brothers, "—have not."

Emerson paused a second, taking another slow breath through his nostrils. "Rosalie, I am going to have this pirate hung from his thumbs."

Reis didn't blink at the threat. "That's no way to ask me to sail to Ciern. You know, Rosie, I now see where you get your stubbornness from."

"Rosie?" Emerson stepped toward Reis with clenched fists. "How dare you address my sister in such a common way? She is the lady of the Western Cliffs, and you should refer to her as such!"

"Alright, that's enough." Rosalie stepped in between the two men. "Reis, would you please bring me to Ciern?"

The captain didn't recoil from Emerson's glare, maintaining his satisfied smirk. "See, that's how you ask nicely. You could learn a few things from her. Now, if you would stay out of my crew's way, I've got a lady to escort home."

CHAPTER 44 - THE LADY

The *Deceit* was starting to feel like a second home to Rosalie. She hadn't bothered to count the days she had spent on board. First out of spite and then out of comfort.

It'd been hard to say goodbye to her brothers when they'd disembarked. Emerson hadn't made it any easier when he told Reis he would gut the pirate like a fish if anything happened to Rosalie. But in the pit of her stomach, she'd felt secure and knew she would see her brothers again. The Yorkes were strong.

When the *Deceit* had set out into the open ocean again, she'd been wrapped in an unexpected layer of comfort. However, it'd been rattled when the ship's bow pointed west. Her idle time in the manor felt like a distant memory. Her mind hadn't accepted that she was going home. Rosalie's insides twisted with concern when she thought over everything she had to do.

First, she needed to tell her father everything and hope he didn't dismiss her. Second, she had to ask Edme what she knew about the card that Constance had written about. If

Rosalie possessed even a speck of luck left, the card would be at the manor.

When she found it… well, she hadn't planned that far ahead. Rosalie had learned that even the best laid plans were subject to attack.

"Hit the deck!" Danny hollered.

Before Rosalie could duck, she felt a hand grab her and tug her backward, out of the path of a swinging boom. Letting out a surprised exhale, she turned to see Reis giving Danny a stern glare.

"I should've been watching where I was going, sorry," she apologized.

"You have a lot on your mind. It's understandable." He dropped his hand from her arm.

She nervously avoided eye contact, rubbing her forearm where the pressure of his touch lingered. "Have you ever gone overboard? Bedros goes overboard, you know, in the book you gave me."

A familiar glint lit up Reis's eyes. "I like that part. He doesn't know how to swim, so he thinks he's done for. But his friends save him." He rolled up the sleeves of his shirt and looked to his right at the horizon. "I've never gone overboard. I can't swim, but I've never been too worried about it. Maybe because of the book. Figure there'll always be someone who will fish me out of the ocean."

She moved to the side of the ship to peer down. The ocean was murky, and there was no telling what was below the surface. The water slapped against the hull, the sunlight making the waves appear like sharp knives.

Reis stepped next to her.

"You said Duranes were born that way," Rosalie whispered. "But Silence shares their blood too."

"I suppose you're not meant to be anything you don't want to be. Duranes are the way they are because they don't want to change. Why would they? They're the most powerful family in Seity. Silence is different; she doesn't think in the same way the Duranes do. Can't say for certain, but she probably thinks more like a Weller."

"But you said circumstances don't matter. All that matters is the family you were born into," she reminded him.

"I can admit when I'm wrong. I was wrong about you."

Rosalie inched closer to him until their arms were touching. "I was wrong about you too. I was wrong about a lot of people. It's maddening because I don't know who else I'll be wrong about."

"Trust is a harsh lesson to learn," he said. "But I promise there are people you can rely on. The world isn't all good and it's not all bad, it's somewhere in the middle. We're just trying to survive. Sometimes you have to count on yourself to survive, and sometimes you can trust others to help you along."

Rosalie focused on the faint warmth and pressure from Reis's arm against hers. The sun's reflection on the water was almost blinding. "I can't swim either."

"One person can't do it all. That's why ships are run by different people with different roles." He paused for a moment before offering a bit of solace. "Kennedy can swim. So, I suppose if we both go overboard, he can rescue us."

She gave a faint smile in reply. Looking back over the edge, she remembered her frantic attempt to escape the ship. What if, in her mad rush for the lifeboat, she had gone overboard? Falling for a few moments before plunging into the depths. As the dark waves would swallow her up, she pictured opening her eyes in the stinging salt water. She wondered whose hand she would find as she reached out for help.

Moving her eyes from the horizon, she saw Reis's hand dangling by his side. She linked her pinkie finger with his. He responded by curling his, tugging gently like a fishhook to pull her hand closer.

Neither of them said a word.

* * *

CIERN'S PORT was bustling as usual. Rosalie watched as Reis concealed the *Deceit's* flag in a chest on the quarterdeck. His lips were pursed, and Rosalie could practically see the thoughts swirling around his head.

They were close enough to port to see the motto written on the blue flags flying above a few of the buildings. Ever since leaving Vale Fall, she'd pictured her triumphant return to Ciern. But as the *Deceit's* crew prepared to dock, Rosalie felt uneasy.

Reis stood up after locking the chest. "Devotion to what?"

Tilting her head to the side, she frowned. "Hmm?"

"Your family's motto." He pointed to the fox-covered banners undulating in the air. "'Devotion above all else'— devotion to what?"

"Family… At least that's how I always interpreted it."

"I suppose that's the problem with not being specific; everyone can make up their own meaning."

"I guess." She looked up past the port, atop the hill where most of Ciern sat. From a distance, she could see the towers of her family's manor. She could pick out her bedroom window. The one she used to look out of to catch sight of the ships coming in from the open ocean. Now she was on the opposite side.

"I'm going to stay here," Reis said, pulling Rosalie's attention away from the manor. "You'll come back when you find that card, right? I assume I'll bring you back to Emerson?"

Rosalie hesitated. "I suppose I need to ask my father what to do next."

"I thought you were going to take this on yourself. Once you find the card, you'll have everything Silence needs."

Being so close to Ciern felt like she was a piece of metal being drawn in by a magnet. She feared her instincts would tell her to stay put where it was safe. Besides, how could she be certain she could safely deliver the talisman and card to Silence? With her string of misfortune, it seemed unlikely.

She turned to face her home, doubt clouding her vision. "I don't know if I'm the one who can save her."

"I think you underestimate yourself, Rosie," he replied.

Tears stuck in her throat as she faced him again. "No one has ever called me that before."

He smiled wryly and the world seemed to become a bit clearer. "Your brother was about ready to tear me to pieces when I said it."

She let out a weak laugh. "For a long time, I liked when people called me by my title. I never held power, but at least I had the title. But now I just hate it. It reminds me of the person I'll never be."

"Do you even still want to be that person?"

She realized how familiar she was with the stormy gray nature of his eyes and the small scar on his cheek. Even if she could sink back into the oblivious daze of her old life, would she? Would she want to forget the way Reis made her feel? The aggravating, dizzying, whirlwind of emotions she couldn't sort out?

"I don't know." Her voice struggled to rise above a whisper. "I want to be there for Silence. She's always been there for me."

Reis nodded but didn't press the matter. He lifted a hand but pulled it back to rub at his neck. "I trust you'll make the right choice. Whatever you feel is best. I'll stay until you decide."

Rosalie smiled and tilted forward to kiss his cheek. When

she pulled back, she realized it was the first time she'd kissed him without feeling like her emotions were going to devour her. Instead, it was simple and felt natural.

It wasn't goodbye. Even if she didn't know what mayhem would bring them back together, she still counted on it.

CHAPTER 45 - THE LADY

osalie had to ask for directions from the port to the manor. The man she'd asked had given her a funny look as it seemed he'd recognized who she was by the crest she wore. But despite her title, Rosalie didn't know her way around Ciern, having spent most of her time behind the manor walls.

As she traveled up the steep road, Rosalie thought about how she had been to more places in a few weeks than in all her eighteen years. It was a miracle she'd survived it all. Yet as she approached the gates of the manor, it all felt wrong. Silence wasn't by her side, and Seity had sunk deeper into violent chaos.

"Lady Yorke?" The soldier standing at the manor wall gawked at her.

"Open the gate, please," she ordered in a firm voice. "I have business inside."

"Yes, my lady." He bowed his head.

The gate lifted, and Rosalie looked up at the high arched windows of the manor. As she made her way inside, anxiety strummed at her nerves. Maybe because she was aware of how things had changed. The young woman walking through the manor was certainly not the same person who had left for Vale Fall a few weeks earlier.

As Rosalie strode down the halls, guards and servants did double takes before correcting themselves, bowing their heads in her direction and uttering a shocked, "My lady."

She had assumed her father would keep her disappearance quiet. Basil wasn't one to publicize weaknesses in the family.

All the attention made Rosalie's dread deepen. The odd feeling persisted as she climbed to the third floor and turned the corner toward her father's study. Two guards stood in front of the grand doors, indicating that Basil was inside.

When Rosalie approached, both guards startled to attention. "Lady Yorke," both men said in unison as they bowed their heads.

"I'd like to speak with my father."

"My lady, Lord Yorke asked to not be disturbed at this time," the guard to the left informed her. "I apologize for—"

Rosalie rolled her eyes and pushed past them. She'd almost forgotten how tedious common courtesy was. Maybe the pirates *had* been a bad influence on her.

Basil's study hadn't ever changed in Rosalie's lifetime. She was so familiar with its contents, she'd become blind to them. All the books, the polished furniture, and the vase of fresh orchids, Emelia Yorke's favorite flowers.

As a little girl, Rosalie used to wander in when the doors weren't locked. Sometimes she would find Basil hunched over the war map, strategizing. Without fail, he would sigh and stand. Taking her little hand in his, he would walk her down the hall to her room.

"Do not disturb me again, Rosalie," he'd say sternly before shutting her bedroom door, leaving her in the dark.

But she would repeat the pattern the next night since it

was the only way she could get her father to pay her any mind.

As she grew older, she had shifted tactics. When she felt her insomnia take over, she'd still roam the manor's halls. Without fail, she would peek into his office when she inevitably passed by the double doors. She'd see her father, who often fell asleep at his desk. Part of her had yearned to wake him up and guide him to his room. Perhaps if she showed him care and concern, he would accept her.

For a moment, Rosalie felt like a little girl again standing in the doorway of her father's study. The sight of him sitting behind his desk was jarring. Especially since—through all her recent ordeals— she had feared she would never see him again.

"I said I didn't want to be disturbed." Basil glanced up from the work on his desk. His annoyance made a sharp shift to disbelief. He stood. "Rosalie. When did you return? I thought that—" He paused for another moment before approaching her. He rested his hands on her upper arms. "How fortunate that your brothers found you. I shouldn't have doubted that they would succeed."

She gave him a small smile. "I'm sorry, I was a little delayed. I was—"

"We don't have to discuss it." He cut her apology short and let his hands fall from her arms. "You're home now."

Rosalie wanted to be relieved, but there was still so much unresolved. "I don't know if you heard—"

He stepped back behind his desk and held up a hand. "I'm handling everything. None of this is your concern anymore." He was reverting to the man she had always known. The terse and dismissive father who kept Rosalie away from everything that mattered. It seemed his lukewarm welcome could only last so long.

"But Emerson wanted me to—"

"Rosalie," he interrupted. "I'm handling it. Your brothers are where they're meant to be, I'm sure. And you are home where you're meant to be. Leave the rest to me."

Despite his insistence, she wasn't certain he knew all the new developments. But he didn't appear to be in the mood to go over every little detail. Maybe she could try again after working on her second task.

"Is Edme downstairs?" she asked. "I need to ask her about something important."

"No, she took ill. She went to stay with her sister outside of the city."

Rosalie frowned as a little thought nudged for her attention. She wondered if Edme had become so distraught by Silence's disappearance that it had made her sick. Whatever the case, her absence left Rosalie at a disadvantage. How was she meant to find this card now?

"That's a shame."

"Yes. A shame," her father replied.

Rocking back and forth on her heels, Rosalie glanced at her mother's portrait. It hung on the wall to the right of Basil's desk, beside the window so the sunlight wouldn't fade the colors. Her father was determined to keep it well preserved, as it was the only portrait ever made of her.

Emelia stood within the gold frame as she had for years. Her stance was relaxed, her shoulders even, and her hands clasped in front of her. Her long blonde hair fell over her shoulders. A faint smile graced her face, but her green eyes held so much sadness. As if she'd known what was to come.

"I think I'm going to go to my room," Rosalie said in a faint voice.

Her father merely made a noise of acknowledgment and didn't look up.

Rosalie swallowed. It was starting to feel more like home, much to her dismay.

* * *

THE DOOR to Rosalie's bedroom creaked as she pushed it open. The room felt cold and the drapes had been drawn. She couldn't recall if she'd left them that way when she departed for Vale Fall.

She went to pull the curtains aside and stepped onto the balcony. The fresh breeze pushed past her, clearing away the stale air. She stood by the railing to see if she could spot the *Deceit*'s mast from afar.

Seeing the ship, even from a distance, made her feel a little more reassured. Reis was still there waiting for her like he promised. Comforted, she stepped back inside and closed the door behind her.

Without Edme's guidance, Rosalie wasn't sure where to start looking for the card. That was when she saw one of Silence's shawls hanging over the chair in front of the vanity. She must have forgotten it when they left for Vale Fall.

Fighting through the grief and exhaustion, Rosalie gathered up the wool shawl and hugged it close. She inhaled Silence's familiar floral perfume and pictured how the shawl would envelope Rosalie when they embraced. "I'll find you," she whispered, hoping somewhere out there, Silence knew she hadn't given up yet.

CHAPTER 46- THE CAPTAIN

After giving Rosalie his blade, Reis had to find a replacement. In his haste, he'd grabbed one that had been abandoned belowdecks. It'd done fine in a pinch, but it needed to be sharpened and polished—tasks Reis didn't have the energy for now that he was knee-deep in nobility clashes.

So, he pulled out a thin, long lockbox stowed under his berth. As he wiped the dust off the top, he took a deep breath. He'd been seventeen when he left it there. It'd been days since they'd buried Braxton at sea and a half hour after the crew had voted Reis in as captain. He'd walked around Braxton's cabin, refusing to believe the ship would ever be his. He hadn't believed he deserved any of it. Especially not what was in that box. So, he'd hid it from view and tried to forget it existed.

Until now.

Reis unlatched the lock and picked up Braxton's beloved cutlass. It was a work of art, with a curved blade and a silver hilt. On the inside of the grip, lined up to where the finger-tips touched, there was a name engraved.

Naomi.

Braxton's wife. He had explained it was the name he fought for. The blade would keep him safe so he might return to her.

Reis let the cutlass rest in his lap. He hadn't held it before. Upton had been the one who packed it away and hefted the box into Reis's arms. When Reis had taken it, Upton saluted and called him Captain for the first time.

As Reis ran his fingers against the flat side, he still didn't feel worthy. But if he was going to fight the Duranes, he needed a cutlass that had faced them before.

He needed Braxton by his side. But the world was cruel and would withhold what the soul needed most.

"Captain." Kennedy came through the open doorway after knocking on the door jamb. "You're going to want to see this."

Reis sighed. The old adage that a ship at port was at peace was a myth. He stood and sheathed Braxton's cutlass at his hip. He followed Kennedy to where a group of the crew was watching the docks.

"Are you trying to look suspicious?" Reis hissed. "Go make yourself busy with something else." When he shooed them off, they scattered like gulls.

Kennedy pointed out a ship a few slips away. A large green flag flew above it—the bear stitched into the crest was a rare sight on the ocean. The *Deceit* didn't encounter Gunn ships very often because their navy was smaller than the raider fleet.

"What are they doing here?" Reis asked with dread creeping up to his chest. His first thought was Rosalie.

"No one has stepped off the ship," Kennedy said. "There are Yorke soldiers everywhere, but they don't seem alarmed. If it's an attack, it's certainly a delayed one."

Reis ran a hand over his weary face. "Does anything

normal happen in Seity? Can there ever be a single day where nothing happens?"

"What should we do?"

Reis's head spun as he tried to sort through all the tangled lines of loyalty. "You all stay here; I have to warn Rosalie. If it is an attack she needs to know."

"And how do you think you're going to get inside? They're not going to let a pirate in just because you say you know her."

Reis hated walls. "Don't worry—I always find a way."

CHAPTER 47- THE LADY

Urgency held Rosalie by the nape of her neck. With every passing second, it squeezed tighter and tighter. Despite her panicked breaths, she hadn't stopped for a moment. She'd rummaged through Silence's room like a windstorm. The sun had faded away while she'd searched every piece of furniture, rifled through the drawers, and even rooted around for hidden compartments. Her hands had trembled as she fanned through every book Silence owned. Rosalie despaired. How was she meant to find something with no hint of its appearance?

Growing more frustrated, Rosalie looked behind her to see that the sun had disappeared. She stifled a yawn and rubbed her eyes. But she couldn't sleep—not until she found the card.

She got up from looking under the bed and wondered if she should find her father and attempt another conversation.

Rosalie shuffled toward the door and returned to her room to change into some fresh clothes. In her exhaustion, she reached for her neck to unclasp her necklace, but her fingertips only brushed skin. "Right," she whispered. She had given the necklace to Reis.

After emptying her pockets, she put the diary and talisman on her vanity. It was nice to don fresh clothes, but the relief didn't last long. She set her shawl over the bed and bent down to take off her boots. They had seen better days, and her father wouldn't appreciate if she tracked grime across the manor.

Her muscles were weak, and she couldn't muster the strength to stand again. She exhaled shakily and pressed her forehead to her knees.

"I don't want to fail you," she whimpered. "You never failed me."

Suddenly, the balcony doors shattered. Rosalie yelped and fell back as pieces of glass flew across the floor. To her horror, a shadowy figure stepped into the room. His head was covered by a cowl and a scarf. She could only see his eyes as they scanned the room. Lamplight cast an eerie glow over his blue irises when he trained his gaze at her. But his attention turned to the talisman in plain view.

Fear jolted Rosalie to stand. She rushed to the vanity as the man sprang into action. They reached it at the same time, Rosalie's hip jabbing into the furniture's sharp corner. The oil lamp was knocked over, which cast the room into darkness. The talisman skittered to the floor, and Rosalie dove toward it.

The intruder grabbed her ankle and yanked her back.

She twisted around and kicked at the disguised man. But he got the upper hand and wrestled her aside. She was shoved to the left, cutting her hand on the shards covering the floor.

The intruder swiped the talisman and turned to run out the destroyed doors.

"No!" Rosalie cried, and scrambled back to her feet.

Both she and the mysterious man stopped in place. Reis stood on the balcony railing. With a deadly look, he drew his cutlass. "Yield," he ordered as he dropped down.

The intruder said nothing and made a mad dash for the railing. Reis didn't hesitate, cutting his blade down to slash the man across the stomach.

The stranger grunted in pain and dropped the talisman to clutch his side.

Rosalie leaped forward to seize it. The intruder lunged—a hand covered in blood reaching toward her. Instinct took over and she jabbed her elbow out, colliding with the man's nose.

The scarf slipped, but he covered it with a hand while ducking Reis's second attack. The intruder retreated to the balcony and jumped over the balustrade. Just a shadow vanishing into the darkness.

She and Reis stared at each other in disbelief. Then he enveloped her in his arms as she let out a sigh of relief. She closed her eyes, leaning into his embrace. The talisman was clutched to her chest; she was afraid to release her grip.

Reis let go with a breath. He picked up the cutlass and wiped the blood from it. He looked back to the shattered doors with a murderous scowl.

"The Duranes must've sent someone to retrieve that." He nodded toward her clenched hand. "I'm sure Eldon needs it for whatever he's planning."

The darkness of Rosalie's room overwhelmed her. Her home was no longer safe. "Then we've been infiltrated by spies," she whispered. "I thought I was safe up here; I never thought someone could reach this room."

"Well, with a little skill you can get into any window."

Rosalie blinked, remembering that he'd appeared from nowhere too. "You climbed the wall? Why didn't you just go through the gate?"

"Pirates aren't usually welcomed inside—especially not into noble houses." He gave her a wry smile that quickly ebbed.

"Right..." She reached up to push hair out of her eyes. Her fingers dashed something warm and sticky across her forehead.

"You're bleeding." Reis stepped forward to help.

The pain hadn't reached her senses yet. It was overshadowed by humiliating shame. "Reis, I haven't found the card. I don't know what to do."

"One thing at a time." Reis picked up the lamp and relit it, casting shadows across the wall. He looked around the room and located the wash basin.

Rosalie watched him move around the space. She had only seen him navigate a pirate ship before. He didn't walk with the commanding nature he exhibited on the deck of the *Deceit*. His steps were more delicate, though he swayed a bit —accustomed to the rocking of the ship, not the steadiness of land.

After finding what he was looking for, Reis knelt in front of her to clean the blood away with great care.

The gash across her palm triggered a numb hopelessness across her. Even if this card was in the manor, it would take weeks to scour every nook and cranny. How could she help Silence now?

Reis inspected the cut, picking out a few shards of glass. "It's not too deep. Do you feel any more glass?"

She flexed her fingers and shook her head. "Why did you come?"

"A ship arrived in port," he said, and clasped the towel tight around her palm. His hands applied pressure and warmth to soak up the blood. "It's flying the Northern Front flag, so I came to warn you."

"Oh, right." She had nearly forgotten about the treaty

Emerson was tasked with negotiating. "I think that's a good thing. They should be here to create a truce with my father."

"Huh, I thought Seity lords didn't make compromises."

"Desperation can force one's hand."

Reis hummed in agreement. He kept the cloth firm against the wound, but his eyes raked over her arm. "Did you get into a scuffle? Where'd this one come from, aye?" His thumb traced a long but faint scar that ran down her inner forearm.

Rosalie shivered under his soft touch. "Oh, that was from years ago. I was trying to climb a tree in the courtyard, and it went poorly. And Silence…" Her voice trailed off as her throat thickened with tears. She bowed her head. "Reis, I failed her. Again."

"No, you didn't. We'll just have to find another way to save her."

A few teardrops landed on her lap, a stray one hitting Reis's hand. He cupped her face. "Rosie…"

His tender touch threatened to coax another wave of tears. Hastily, she wiped her cheeks and pulled back to stand. His fingertips grazed over her jawline as his hand slipped away.

"I need to find my father so he can greet the Northern dignitaries." She walked in a small circle as if to follow her spinning thoughts. "You stay here, and I'll come back to help you sneak out of here."

"Sneak out… Oh, because— Right." He smiled ruefully.

Rosalie was already on thin ice trying to talk about the war with Basil. Introducing the pirate who held her for ransom—a pirate she was now quite fond of—would not go over well. She kissed his cheek as a consolation. "I'll be right back," she promised, and hurried out of the room.

CHAPTER 48 - THE CAPTAIN

Reis couldn't follow Rosalie even if he wanted to. Judging by Emerson's contempt, Reis concluded Basil wouldn't be happy a pirate was in the manor. So, he stayed in her room to collect his thoughts.

It had scared him half to death to see a man shrouded in black climbing up to the balcony. Reis relied on his instincts, and he was glad he'd followed them without hesitation.

For now, the danger was subdued, but Reis stayed alert with one hand resting on Braxton's cutlass. He stepped over the glass and looked around Rosalie's chambers. It was by far the most luxurious room he'd seen. The canopy bed was more than triple the size of his berth. The ornate curtains had gotten mussed in the fight, and a splatter of the intruder's blood marred the blue fabric.

Seeing the life she was used to, Reis was baffled how Rosalie had survived on a ship without her perfume bottles and fine clothes. Reis almost laughed at himself when he wondered why she hadn't complained *more*.

But as he circled around the room, feeling out of place, there was a certain hollowness. Rosalie's bedroom felt like the world's finest prison cell. A place just comfortable enough to keep a young woman content and docile. A place to keep her away from the world without her being any wiser.

He frowned as he lifted his gaze to the vaulted ceilings. Every part of the manor stretched into any available space. Now that he'd seen the place up close, he had no idea how Rosalie expected to find anything in such a sprawling monster of a home. If one could even call it a home.

Reis stopped pacing and took in the muted atmosphere of the room. The air was dead quiet—far too quiet to be normal. He'd heard Rosalie's yell from outside. Surely, if a lady was heard screaming, a dozen guards would storm the room. But minutes ticked away, and no one came running.

The hair on the back of his neck stood up as he approached the door. He poked his head out into the hall. The place felt abandoned.

The silence was only broken when he heard someone running. Rosalie turned the corner, terror painted on her face. "Reis, my father is gone!"

Reis caught her by the arms as she nearly collided with him in panic. "Easy, love. What happened?"

Her breath was raspy as she hyperventilated. Her green eyes darted around. "The Duranes have spies here; they kidnapped him. I'm sure of it! This was their plot all along!"

Reis believed her, but where was the alarm? Why were there no soldiers running amok trying to find their lord? Where were the shouts and turmoil?

"You can't find him?"

"No! He's not in his study. I don't know what could've happened to him. He might be hurt. This is terrible. We have the Northern Front here to negotiate a treaty; we can't let this fall through." Her words were rapid fire, and Reis tried his best to get her to breathe before her heart gave out.

"You're the lady of this manor; you can speak to them about the treaty," he said over her fretful rambling.

"No, Reis, I—I can't—what could I possibly do? I have no experience at all!" she stammered. "Not to mention, every plan I have disintegrates. I can't accomplish anything that important."

"Rosalie, you talk circles around me. If you weren't trained in persistent conversation, then it must be something you were born with. If something happened to your father, then maybe the North can help."

"But what about the card? It might be the only thing that could help Silence defeat the Duranes."

"If what you're saying about spies is true, then it's not safe in the manor," he said. "We need to cut our losses. Silence will find another way."

She appeared poised to doubt him. But before she could open her mouth, voices were heard down the hall.

A rough voice called out, "Search every room."

Reis took Rosalie's hand. "We need to go. Do you know a way out? Something hidden maybe?"

Her face paled, but she nodded. She squeezed his hand, and they made a mad dash from her bedroom.

"That's her!"

Reis saw a figure in his periphery point their way. Rosalie led him to a staircase that swept down into a large, grand foyer. Instead of going out the large front doors, she directed him down another hallway.

Reis heard clattering movement behind them, and he rested his free hand on the hilt of his cutlass. He should have known he would find trouble in a nobleman's manor.

CHAPTER 49- THE LADY

Rosalie knew her time was fading. She wasn't sure when she had last slept, and her lungs strained with every labored breath. She worried a fit was imminent, but there was no time or space to rest.

The path to the kitchens was a familiar one. As a child, she would skip all the way there, joyful to see her best friend. But as Rosalie reached the stairs, she was only met with dread. No heat from the ovens wafted up the steps. No noise, no clatter of pans, no chatter between the cooks. She'd never heard it so quiet before.

Rosalie hustled as fast as she could down the stairs. Reis's hand kept her from tumbling down the rest of the way.

The rooms making up the kitchen beneath the manor were dark, and all the usual faces were nowhere to be seen. Rosalie weaved her way through the tables and stepped over a sack of flour that had been knocked on its side. It was as if everyone had vanished while Rosalie was upstairs.

She couldn't make sense of it but wondered if the manor had been evacuated without her knowing. If that was the case, then why hadn't anyone come for her? Her fearful thoughts kept pace with her legs.

When they passed the wine cellar and storage rooms, voices rang out at the top of the stairs. Rosalie had no interest in slowing to see who was after them.

At the end of the narrow hallway, she pushed open the door leading outside to the courtyard.

Clouds had rolled in to cover the moon, and it was hard to make out anything in the expansive garden. It didn't matter; Rosalie knew the area well enough that she could find her way blind.

"Aren't we closed in?" Reis asked.

"No, there's a way out." Rosalie continued through the stone paths lined with overgrown wisteria bushes and weeping willows.

Reis slowed and applied pressure to her hand. He pulled her close, bringing them behind an apple tree to melt into the darkness. "Stop to breathe," he whispered.

Reluctantly, she sucked in air. She rested a hand on the tree and tried to calm the wheezing rasp in her chest. She looked up at the leaves and remembered when Emerson used to hoist her onto his shoulders to pick fruit for Edme. She could still smell the cinnamon in the apple tarts baking in the oven.

Her inhalations grew shallow again, and her vision dotted. Things had been so simple back then. Rosalie's fingers dug into the bark as she fought back tears.

Reis wrapped an arm around her waist, silently comforting her.

The back gate creaked open, and her pulse spiked again. Rosalie grabbed Reis's wrist and backed up, looking for the exact place in the dark. Her skirt caught on the rosebushes that climbed up the courtyard wall. Exactly what she was looking for.

Rosalie guided Reis to drop to the ground and slip into the rosebush. The thorns pulled at her clothes and scraped her skin. She bit down on her lip to keep from yelping in pain.

"He said she'd still be here," one of the pursuers said in a gruff voice.

"She wasn't upstairs. Where else would she be hiding? She couldn't have left the manor without us knowing," the other replied.

Rosalie held her breath as she listened. These men were after her just like the masked intruder. It only confirmed her worst fears. Her father had been taken or killed. The Western Cliffs would certainly fall into the hands of the Duranes.

She carefully made her way farther into the bush, finding a small hollowed-out space. The brambles acted like a cage around them. She pressed a hand to the wall, searching for the gap, hoping it hadn't been patched up. Her heart skipped a beat when she felt the narrow opening in the wall.

It'd been there ever since Rosalie was little. Emerson had found it first. He and Emery would use the passage to sneak out of the manor without Basil knowing. Rosalie had been too scared to follow them out into the large capital city. But she remembered sitting behind the rosebushes with Silence, waiting for the boys to reappear through the gap in the wall.

"He'll have our heads if we let her get away again!" The voices drew closer.

Rosalie dared not breathe. She shut her eyes when she heard the footsteps stop right in front of the rosebush.

"She must still be inside. Go tell the others to tear this manor apart until we find her."

Through the darkness and thatch of branches, Rosalie could see movement. The voices faded and she allowed herself to exhale in relief.

"Follow me," she whispered to Reis, and sidled past the

brambles to the wall. She squeezed through the opening, the stone grating against her arms. Once on the other side, she turned to see Reis making himself as small as possible to pass through.

Over the wall, a loud bang echoed through the courtyard followed by a stampede of footsteps crowding into the garden. "Someone saw her enter the kitchens. She had to be out here. Find her!" a man barked.

Reis quickly threw the hood of Rosalie's shawl over her head. Neither of them spoke as they disappeared down the path to the port.

* * *

THE HARBOR WAS QUIETER than usual. A great deal of soldiers milled about, and most of the homes and businesses on the pier were closed—their windows dark. News about Basil must've spread quickly. She hoped her father's best men were already searching for him.

It felt like heavy stones were plummeting to Rosalie's stomach. The pillars holding up the life she once knew were crumbling. How much more could the Duranes take?

"It's all lost," she whispered.

Reis didn't look mournful over the city; he was too focused on Rosalie. "This is far from over. Don't give up now." He touched her shoulders to turn her toward him. His hands lifted to cradle her face.

She noticed something embedded in his skin. "Stay still." She carefully plucked the spiny barb from his arm and held it up for him to see. "Guess I'm not the only thorn in your side."

He smiled. "Thorn or not, you've got allies now." He directed her attention to the docks.

A sizable brigantine moored near the *Deceit* boasted its flag of a fighting bear and proud words.

Fêst e duthlig trich allit

Steady and diligent through all.

Rosalie wasn't sure what to feel as she read the Northern Front's motto. For her entire life, they'd been enemies. Although Jonas Gunn was not much of a threat to Basil, they were not allies.

She wanted to believe the tides were turning in their favor. "Did they send Jonas's advisors?"

"I'm not sure. What does a Northern lord look like?"

Men clad in green disembarked the ship, but one stood out. Jonas Gunn was tall and broad. He would cut an imposing figure if he didn't have such sad eyes. With his shoulders covered in the fur of a bear, he held himself like a lord but walked with hesitation in his step.

Rosalie straightened up and tried to look mildly presentable. She hoped Jonas would overlook her bloodied hand and rose-scratched arms. "Let me do the talking." She echoed the same instruction Reis had given her before meeting Rydlan.

"Aye, Lady Yorke," he said with a playful smile.

With Reis by her side, she approached their guests. "Lord Gunn," she greeted with a polite bow of the head.

Jonas peered down at her. "Lady Yorke, I presume?"

"Call me Rosalie, if you'd like."

The Northerner glanced at the man to his right who bore the airs of an advisor. Rosalie resisted the urge to wrinkle her nose. Advisors were insufferable.

"I expected Emerson to be the one to escort me into Ciern," Jonas said. "He delayed his visit to Thornstall but told me your father is waiting to discuss the treaty."

"Several things have transpired since my brother met with you last. Could we sit and discuss it together?" She knew there was no returning to the manor until they had suitable reinforcements.

One thing at a time.

"My lord, there was a clear itinerary put in place," Jonas's advisor said with a displeased glance aimed at Rosalie. "The Yorkes have already disrespected you by delaying the process several times. You ought to insist the original plan be kept."

"I don't expect people to keep strict appointments during wartime. I'm willing to get off my feet for a few hours," Jonas disagreed before turning back to Rosalie. "Is there somewhere we can sit and get a good meal?"

"One of the inns should be able to accommodate," Rosalie said. She was nervous, unsure if she could fare through a diplomatic meeting on her own—even without Durane soldiers crawling over her city. But since she was the only Yorke left in Ciern, she had no choice.

CHAPTER 50- THE CAPTAIN

Reis had expected to be out of his depth in the middle of a noble meeting, but he found it was similar to his life as a captain. Sometimes tact was preferred over violence. Negotiation was as much of an art as hand-to-hand combat was.

Rosalie had promised a place to rest, and she had delivered. Even though she'd had to bang on the inn's door until the owner timidly poked his head out. Reis presumed the sight of the Gunns' flag had spooked the older man into hunkering down. But at the sight of Yorke nobility on his doorstep, the innkeeper had ushered them inside. Reis slipped the man a few coins for a nice meal and a little extra for his discretion. Once the fire had been lit and the scent of a warm dinner wafted from the kitchen, the meeting began.

Rosalie sat across from Jonas. She kept her spine straight and wore a pleasant and welcoming expression.

Reis stifled a laugh. Her demeanor was very different from when they first met. He was proud to see her speak with such ease and uphold the measures of decorum. But he much preferred her feral side, yearning to see her pout and spark an argument that made her cheeks pink.

"Circumstances have endangered Ciern's security," Rosalie began in a measured voice, although there was panic behind her green eyes. "I'm afraid something has happened to my father. He has disappeared less than an hour ago. I believe the Duranes have planted spies in our city."

Jonas glanced to his advisor before meeting Rosalie's gaze again. "And where are your brothers?"

"They should be near Cross Row. Unfortunately, we were forced to split up due to unforeseen events." Rosalie spoke in a remarkably steady voice for everything she had been through. It was a far cry from the panicking young woman who'd flinched every time the *Deceit* fired a cannon.

Reis caught himself staring and averted his eyes. The men surrounding Jonas glared at him unforgivingly. Even worse, Jonas's military advisor watched the captain with heavy suspicion. Reis cleared his throat and feigned interest in the cobweb-covered rafters of the pub.

"I've heard a lot of strange rumors the past couple of weeks," Jonas said. "It seems the Duranes have grown bolder. Something has changed."

"They have," Rosalie agreed. "I know my family wants to negotiate a treaty, but I'm afraid we must ask more of you in our time of need."

Reis could see she was holding off on talking about Silence until she was certain they were in the company of allies and not enemies.

A sour look crossed the Northern advisor's face. "I knew it. My lord, they led you down here to speak to the youngest of the family so she could sweet-talk you. I would urge you to reconsider this treaty entirely. We are not at the service of the Yorkes and have made enough sacrifices for them. They have not returned the favor."

Reis gritted his teeth and fought the urge to defend Rosalie. Unlike with Rydlan, Reis couldn't punch this man—no matter how much he wanted to.

Jonas held up a hand to stop the advisor's venomous words. "In the Western Cliffs, the oldest son or daughter assumes the highest title. After her mother passed, Rosalie inherited the title of lady. Because of this, she is a step above her brothers in rank until one of them inherits the title of lord. Am I right, Lady Yorke?"

Reis noticed the slight bewilderment on her face, but she nodded. "Yes, that's true. I know every house grants titles differently, but that's how Yorkes have done it since the founding."

"It's similar to the way the Eastern Hills granted them. Titles were assigned by birth order, not gender. A female heir could rule alone if she so chose." Jonas looked upon Rosalie with a good deal of respect in his expression.

Reis leaned back in his chair, letting his tense muscles go slack. Maybe this would go smoother than they had expected.

Rosalie clasped her hands together on the table. "The Eastern Hills is why I'm here. I know why the tide of war has changed so drastically. The last Weller has been found, and the Duranes have captured her."

The only sounds were clanks from the kitchen. The Northerners stared at Rosalie.

Lord Gunn dared to broach the subject first. He tilted forward in intrigue. "The missing Weller? I've heard the rumors since I was a boy, but I never thought it was true."

"It's true. Silence has been my friend for a long time. But now the Duranes have her, and I don't know what their plans are. What I do know is that her power is significant and catastrophic. If the Duranes use her magic against us, I'm afraid our military will never recover. She is good. Silence would never hurt anyone on purpose. But her powers… without the talisman her magic can be unpredictable. I fear Eldon will try to use that vulnerability to his advantage. Unfortunately, Silence doesn't have the talisman in her possession." Her breath caught in her throat.

To console her, Reis gently tapped his knee against Rosalie's under the table. Her hand resting on her thigh relaxed. He yearned to entwine his fingers with hers.

Jonas paused. Reis had already seen others come to terms with the fact that Silence existed. Her life affected so many, and it was almost surreal to know how one person could change the course of an entire war. With a power like hers, it was possible she could end the bloodshed altogether. However, Reis wasn't sure who would come out on top.

"When my father died," Jonas said, "I was just a boy— completely unfit to rule. I feared my family would meet the same fate as the Wellers. Now I am comforted to know Eldon failed and she's still alive."

Rosalie nodded. "The odds are stacked against us, but I have hope. I know it's a lot to ask for you to risk your men. But Silence is much more than just my best friend; she could be Seity's saving grace. And without my father, I fear that what happened to the Wellers will happen to my family as well."

The lord drummed his fingers on the table in thought. "Two armies against one would have a better chance of survival. Do we have intel as to where the Duranes are keeping Lady Weller?"

Rosalie shook her head. "Not yet. Our first attempt to get into Belris was disastrous. I've narrowly escaped Eldon's sons more than once; I'd rather not risk another time until we're prepared."

The thought of Rydlan's betrayal spiked through Reis. Maybe there was a way to combine his revenge with a plan to save Silence. He sat forward to call attention to himself. "If I may interject, I might have a way to find Silence. I've done it once before; I'm sure I could do it again easily."

Jonas sized him up with a confused glance. "I apologize, but I don't believe we made introductions."

"Er, Captain Crowe of the *Deceit*," Reis answered. He knew he could've come up with a false backstory with no issue. But if he was going to have some involvement with nobility, he knew his lie would be found out soon enough.

Jonas's advisor slammed his fist down. "Your ship looted two of our sloops of all our guns not four months ago!"

Ah yes—the guns were still sitting on the *Deceit*.

Reis knew when a talk was souring, and he went for the flintlock pistol at his hip. But Rosalie's hand shot out and grabbed his wrist.

"Easy, easy." Jonas held out an arm to hold back his advisor from lunging over the table. "Let's not make this peaceful meeting go sideways."

"My lord, the Yorkes are openly conspiring with pirates!" the advisor protested. "This is unthinkable behavior, and we cannot indulge their treachery."

Reis crossed his arms to further resist the temptation to reach for a weapon. "I don't work for the Yorkes; I'm no privateer. But my ship has been loyal to the Weller family for two decades. I can lay down my differences to fight for a greater cause; I was almost certain Seity's nobility could do the same. Surely, a no-good pirate wouldn't have higher moral standards than nobility."

The advisor's face was turning bright red as he spluttered, "You dare talk ill of Lord Gunn in his presence?"

Jonas merely chuckled. "We can let bygones be bygones. If Captain Crowe has proved himself a suitable opponent, then we would be lucky to have him on our side rather than as an enemy."

Reis basked in the little chunk of flattery. "I'm lucky to have the best crew on the seas."

But the advisor wasn't done. "Sir, these two are hardly grown," he said. "You're trusting an action of this magnitude in the hands of children?"

Jonas clapped his advisor on the back. "You trusted me when I was no more than a boy." He turned to Reis. "Captain, what did you have in mind?"

CHAPTER 51- THE LADY

Rosalie watched the manor devolve into nothing but a speck on the horizon as they sailed away from port. Before, she had worried she would never find her way back to Ciern; now she worried she would have no home to go back to.

"You did good with Jonas," Reis said. "At least, it sounded good to me."

The two were in his cabin, avoiding the biting wind carrying them toward the southeast. Rosalie sat on his berth, her knees pulled to her chest. "It wasn't a complete disaster."

Reis was across the room, inspecting a loose button on his coat. "That advisor was out for blood, and you smoothed it all over."

"I think that was Jonas's doing."

He lowered the coat to find her gaze. "You shouldn't be so hard on yourself."

"Reis, I have no idea how to help Silence. She won't be able to destroy them without that card."

He took a tentative step toward her. "You've seen how strong she is. She could demolish half their army just by taking a single breath. That leaves just three men for us to handle."

"Three men who have terrorized this country."

He nodded. "But without an army, what are they? What could they possibly do?"

Rosalie let her head hang forward. She could be at risk of losing everything. Then, she felt a warm touch on her cheek.

Reis stood in front of her, gazing down at her. "Sometimes I think you could hold the entire world on your shoulders, and you'd still believe you weren't enough." Sheepishly, he dropped his hand away. "You act like everything is your fault until you accomplish something. Then it's not enough."

Her eyelids were heavy as she tried to conceal her tears. Her heart thudded, and she feared a fit was coming on. Rosalie took deep breaths, but the feeling didn't fade. Was it a fit? It was like her heart was pulling her forward.

She looked up at Reis, and he gave her a sympathetic smile. "Anything I can do?" he asked.

Rosalie's knees buckled as she stood. Without a word, she pressed herself close to him. Without a moment's hesitation, he wrapped his arms around her. They slipped into place as if they were molded for one another.

Tingles traveled down Rosalie's spine, and she cried harder. She'd never felt so comforted by someone's touch before. When he kissed her temple, she knotted her fingers in his hair and held on for dear life as she trembled.

"We're going to be alright," Reis said.

Rosalie had been worried it would be too hard to face the world. Blow after blow, she had felt another piece be taken from her. But there was still more to take, and she wasn't sure how much more she could handle.

"If I didn't think you were capable, I would've told you to stay on land. But you're strong." Reis tilted his head to the side. "Strong enough to make a pirate break."

She laughed weakly and looked up. "Break?"

He smiled. "Yes, you pestered me into liking you. That's impressive, don't you think?"

Her cheeks warmed, and she wanted to kiss him. But she lowered her eyes to the collar of his shirt. "Do you think you'll be able to find Rydlan? Couldn't he be anywhere by now?"

Reis shook his head. "He'll be in southern waters, close to Belris. Rydlan stays where the money is, and I imagine Eldon is a generous client. Besides, he'll think I'm dead. His guard will be low."

Danger was breathing down their necks, but for the moment they were safe. Rosalie rested her cheek against his chest and let her eyes close.

He let out a slow exhale. "He's not going to know what hit him."

Reis's need for revenge wasn't a surprise to Rosalie. It was the first thing she'd learned about him before she'd even seen his face. It was his thirst for retribution that had brought the two together. All she could do was hope that it would help them find Silence.

* * *

THE UNREAD PAGES in Constance's diary were running out. Rosalie knew how the story ended; each page brought her closer to Constance's final day. Her stomach twisted in dread as the entry dates ticked by. The diary served as another reminder that Rosalie couldn't help Silence. At least, not as well as she'd hoped. Whatever card Constance had referenced was gone. Maybe Silence never had it. Maybe it had been lost with Constance.

While Reis was busy talking to Kennedy, Rosalie climbed

up to the quarterdeck, where Upton stood at the helm. She gave the bosun a smile and sat down.

She skimmed through Constance's journal. Her eyes didn't land on any words; she just needed to keep her hands busy. Or maybe she wanted to torture herself with the persistent sense of failure. Reis could comfort her, but it was hard to scrub away the stain of guilt.

A good deal of the diary had been left blank after Constance's untimely death. As Rosalie flipped through the empty pages, she noticed an inconsistency. The back cover of the journal felt thicker than the front. A piece of extra parchment had been glued to the backing, yet it seemed out of place. She fiddled with the edge of a corner that had curled with age.

An eerie feeling came over Rosalie when she saw a piece of lined paper poking out. "Upton? Do you have a small blade?"

"Sure do." He pulled a dagger from his belt but withheld it for a moment. "I'll give it to ya if you promise not to curse the ship again."

She let out a bemused huff. "I'll try my best not to." She took it from him and carefully sliced the backing away so as not to ruin Silence's possession. When she'd made a big enough slit, she pulled out a twice-folded sheet of parchment.

Dear Constance,

I am troubled to hear about the stirrings in Cross Row. I should think my family can offer asylum to you and your parents. I worry an attack from the Duranes will result in war. My husband seems certain of it.

I would urge you to speak with your father again. I sympathize with his resiliency and adherence to the Weller tradition of nonviolence. But I believe if he does not defend himself, he could lose the Eastern Hills. The Duranes do not respect Taran's dedication to do no harm.

I will ask my husband about sending a squadron to help extract you and your family from Avorae. I know this goes against your determination to stay and protect your people, but I fear you will have no chance to protect them if Eldon targets your family first.

I will do my best to assist you in any way I can. Unfortunately, my mother passed away earlier this year, so I am the only one left with Cardin blood aside from my sons. However, in this instance, I don't know how much that will help you. Instead, I can offer military support should our advisors agree.

Please write back to me as soon as you can, I worry for your safety.
Your friend,
Emelia Yorke

Rosalie's hands trembled and tears brimmed in her eyes. She was holding a letter written by her mother's hand. She underlined Emelia's name with her index finger.

Rereading the letter once more and then again, Rosalie picked out the important bits. Her mother had been in contact with Constance before Eldon's siege. She was trying to save the Wellers before tragedy struck.

Cardin.

Rosalie recognized it as her mother's maiden name. Emelia Cardin. But what did she mean by Cardin blood?

"Upton?"

"Yeah, lass?"

She stood and handed the dagger back to him, hilt first so he didn't flinch. "How much do you know about Seity's history?"

"S'pose not much more than you do."

Rosalie doubted that. The old pirate had been around a long time, and rumors seemed to travel fast on the ocean. "Does the surname Cardin mean anything to you?"

Upton scratched the back of his neck, and his eyes narrowed in deep thought. "Cardin… Eh, there's an old myth 'bout the sea. Lass in the Cardin family—don't remember her first name. Don't matter, I s'pose. Had to do with the Wellers too. Now what was the name of the Weller lady…" He leaned over the railing behind the ship's wheel. "Kennedy, what's that myth 'bout the Cardins and Wellers?"

The quartermaster turned to look up as he was leaving the captain's cabin. "The Sea's Daughter? There was a Weller who could control water. Something about her father being mad with power. I don't really remember it."

"He wanted to make an alliance with the Ivory Kingdom, which would've sparked war in Seity," Reis piped up, following behind Kennedy. "His daughter flooded the entire northern part of the Eastern Hills to stop him, but she failed because Wellers can't use their powers against blood relatives."

Rosalie peered down at him. "What about the Cardins?"

"They were a family of advisors to the Wellers. They had a special power connected to the noble family," he explained.

"The Sea's Daughter discovered a Cardin's touch could enable her to use her power over her father."

Rosalie froze for a moment. The final piece slid into place.

"Don't hex me, lass." Upton shifted away from her, apparently spooked by her silence.

"Upton, hush," Reis said. "Rosie, what's wrong?"

Instead of answering, she lifted her mother's letter. She found the surname and used her thumb to cover the last two letters.

Card.

Rosalie hadn't failed at all. She'd had everything they needed from day one. "Then there's a way Silence can use her powers against the Duranes," she thought aloud.

Reis rested his hands on his hips with a doubtful look. "I don't see how. You'd need a Cardin, and I don't think anyone knows what happened to their bloodline. They fell out of relevancy decades ago."

"I know what happened to the bloodline. My mother's maiden name was Cardin."

A slow smile formed on Reis' face. "Well then. It seems fate really did bring you and Silence together."

* * *

DUSK FELL, and the *Deceit* sailed smoothly through calm waters. The moon hung low in the sky, encircled by blinking stars. Most of the crew was on the main deck, all the day's chores now completed. Upton was telling a riveting story about a ship crewed by a ghostly horde that haunted the waters of Aefen.

Rosalie hadn't thought pirates could be enthralled by anything. They lived such exciting lives. But Upton had the crew on the edge, rabid for the ghastly details. She would've joined the fun, but she needed quiet to think. She wandered to the quarterdeck, where she found Reis sitting alone.

"Are they being too loud for you?"

She shook her head and sat next to him. "No, I couldn't sleep."

Despite having had hours to process it, Rosalie couldn't wrap her head around her mother's letter. She didn't feel powerful, certainly not how Silence was. It sounded like a mad dream, but they wouldn't know if it was true until she found her way to Silence. All Rosalie had left was hope.

Then she noticed Reis gazing at her.

"We'll find Silence," he said. "The Duranes are outmatched this time."

"She deserves a better fate, something more peaceful. She never asked for this. Maybe if Edme took her out of Seity, then they'd be happy."

Rosalie thought about her friend, the quiet but kind woman who never wanted to hurt anyone. However, her identity was beyond her control. An identity that had set off a chaotic chain reaction.

Reis made a thoughtful noise. "It's nice to dream about what might've been. But this reality is the only one we have. Thinking about what's gone wrong and how we could have avoided it will only make us miserable. Life and loss come as a pair."

Rosalie went quiet, too burdened by thoughts to speak. She couldn't even allow herself to think about losing any of her loved ones.

"Want to hear a story?"

"Yes, please." Rosalie needed to huddle away from the world.

He rested an arm over her shoulders. "I don't remember much of my mother, but I do remember the story she used to tell me. An old one from when the Territories were still a monarchy. See that bright star there?" He pointed out a star and traced out a figure with his fingertip. "There's the head and arms."

As the picture was painted—connected by invisible lines—Rosalie could see the figure spanning across the sky.

"That's the moon's queen. The tale goes that there was a woman so beautiful that the moon fell in love with her. She would walk the beach to spend time with him. He would draw the ocean back and forth, changing the tides to capture her attention. But they were two worlds apart. One night, they spoke about how they could be together forever. The moon couldn't leave the sky, so she begged to join him among the stars."

Rosalie rested her head on Reis's shoulder, keeping her eyes on the constellation in the sky. "Did he let her?"

"He did. Sailors believe the moon still moves the tides to impress the love of his life. That's why the ocean is a sign of love."

Rosalie believed him. The ocean was where she felt free. Where she could release herself from the burden of becoming someone she would never be. And yet, she could still be like her mother. Her mother, who had tried so hard to save the Wellers. Her mother, who had given Rosalie the power to aid Silence.

She looked up at Reis. Her heart skipped a beat when she saw a stray strand of his black hair swept over his forehead. His gray eyes still looked up at the moon's queen. "Reis, whatever happens…"

"It's okay, love. I know."

She let her eyes close, content to remain in that moment for as long as time would allow her.

CHAPTER 52 - THE CAPTAIN

Even from a distance, it was sickening to see Rydlan's ship again. The wound of betrayal was still raw and deep. Reis knew of only one way to heal.

The ocean was his ally. It was a gray morning, but the waves were calm, and the wind was perfect. Though, even if they were hit by a hurricane, nothing was getting between Reis and Rydlan's comeuppance.

Reis shucked off his coat and tossed it aside. He rolled up his sleeves and caught Rosalie watching him. "I'll be okay," he prefaced.

"I know."

His eyebrow lifted when he watched her green eyes trail down his exposed arms. "Is there something else on your mind?"

Her cheeks reddened. "Huh? No."

The thrill of revenge made his blood run hot. The way she'd looked at him only stoked the flames. He stepped closer to her and grazed his thumb over her cheekbone.

Her lips parted as she was taken by a subtle shiver. "Reis…"

The sound of his name on her tongue drove him crazy. He tilted his head toward her but heard someone clear their throat.

"Captain, we're ready to fire when you are."

"Hold that thought," Reis said to Rosalie with a wink. He let his hand drop so he could face Kennedy. "Right—fire the warning shot."

The quartermaster nodded, but before he could convey the order, Reis stopped him.

"Hit the ship's figurehead. Make him understand I'm not here for a friendly chat."

"Will you allow him to surrender?" Rosalie asked.

Reis reached into his pocket and slipped on his eyepatch. "No. Today is his last."

He expected her to shy away from the brutal statement. Instead, she reached up to adjust the patch. "As long as you come back to me." Her hand cupped his cheek.

When his lips touched hers, the *Deceit* fired a warning shot. Rosalie didn't flinch. She only pressed deeper into the kiss.

* * *

RYDLAN'S CREW acted as if they'd been accosted by a ghost ship. In some respects, they had reason to believe it. The *Deceit* and her crew were meant to be rotting under the waves. Reis dropped onto Rydlan's deck and took a direct path to the captain's cabin as his crew dealt with the raiders.

Reis kicked open the door and lifted a pistol. Rydlan startled to his feet. The raider's face went pale at the sight of the man he had betrayed.

"Oh... Reis. My boy, I was just about to come and find you."

Reis fired a shot, grazing past Rydlan's ear and hitting a

window. The glass shattered, and Rydlan let out a terrified yelp.

"Walk," Reis ordered.

"N-Now, I can explain myself..." Rydlan took a few cautious steps as Reis swapped his pistol for his cutlass. "It was Eldon's idea."

"Eldon didn't know anything. You did. You sold me out. Now walk." He held Rydlan at the end of the blade as he forced him out to the deck.

The raiders had been subdued; they all cowered away from the *Deceit*'s crew. Upon a cursory glance, Reis noticed that Rydlan was traveling with a lighter crew than usual. Another big mistake.

"You've no idea what Eldon knows. You don't know where he's getting his information."

"I know he's getting information from you."

Rydlan turned around and let out a short laugh. It seemed he now believed the attack was just a scare tactic. "I'm not his only informant."

Reis didn't care for riddles. "I warned you if you double-crossed me, I'd kill you."

"You won't kill me," Rydlan said. The initial shock melted away, laying bare his arrogance. "You're still desperate for information. I know you don't know where the Weller is. But I do. Kill me now and you'll never know."

Reis adjusted his grip on the hilt. "What will make you talk?"

The corner of Rydlan's lips turned up. "I'm a fair man. But such information is not cheap."

"You betrayed me," Reis said through clenched teeth. "Let's consider us even."

"Lower your weapon, boy. There's no need to act tough in front of me."

Reis glared as he pointed his blade to the deck. "Talk."

"Avorae," Rydlan said, no doubt still thinking he was in control. Reis knew the man was already cooking up a new way to betray him. "They brought her to Avorae. Now, are you going to go marching inland with the Yorkes? A soldier now, are you?"

"You never double-crossed Braxton."

Rydlan gave a hoarse chuckle in response and his eyes darkened. "Because Braxton was a man. You're a child who thought he could order me around. I hope we've come to an understanding." He turned toward the *Deceit*'s crew intimidating his men. "Can we finish up this little show? I'm a very busy man."

Reis clamped a hand down on Rydlan's shoulder. "I warned you that I was going to kill you." He plunged his blade up between the man's ribs and leaned in to hiss, "Unlike you, I don't go back on my word."

Rydlan sputtered out a guttural moan before collapsing forward. His body went limp, and blood pooled on the deck beneath him. Even in death, he was a weak-spined coward.

The raider crew watched as their captain ceased moving. Like the coward that once led them, none of them moved to retaliate. A few even set down their weapons.

"Push him overboard," Reis ordered. "If any of his men even attempt to attack, they can join their captain on the ocean floor. Make quick work of this. We're headed east."

* * *

REIS FOUND Rosalie in his cabin. He was relieved she hadn't seen the violence. She stood and turned to him—her shoulders sagging in relief. "You're okay."

"Settling a score is good for the soul," he said, and removed his weapon belt. "I know where Silence is."

"You do?" She lit up.

"I wouldn't be so optimistic. We're being set up."

"Set up?"

"Rydlan gave up the location too easily. The Duranes fed him that information because they want to be found. They know we'll come to rescue Silence, but they have the advantage. They're using her as bait before they use her as a weapon," Reis predicted with a grim expression.

"But we have the talisman," Rosalie pointed out. "And with me there, Silence will be able to fight them."

"The Duranes already know she doesn't need the talisman to produce her power. It might be that you won't get to her before they use her magic to lay waste to everything."

Rosalie didn't look disheartened. "Well, I have no choice but to try. We need to get the information to my brothers and Jonas. We'll head to Avorae immediately."

Reis's stomach turned at the idea of Rosalie storming into a three-army battle, but there was no convincing her otherwise. Without the Cardin power Rosalie held, the Duranes were untouchable.

* * *

REIS FELT he was proving his usefulness, but it was exhausting being so obedient. He stood at the forecastle deck, his arms crossed tightly over his chest. "How is it that we waited days for a Yorke warship to show up and one never did? Now one shows up an hour after we need it?" he muttered to Kennedy.

They watched as the sloop's small boat rowed to the warship. The fast vessel had snuck up on them once dawn broke. Everything about the Western Cliffs felt off, but he couldn't put his finger on why.

"The ocean doesn't have a routine," Kennedy said. "Sometimes you're lucky, sometimes you're not."

Reis grunted in disagreement. "It's too convenient." He was happy the message about Silence's location could be disseminated quickly to the Western and Northern forces. But he couldn't shake the bad feeling.

"Captain, there are storm clouds on the horizon," Danny reported from a few feet away.

When Reis groaned, Kennedy just shrugged. "No routine," he reminded the captain.

"Right—rig the storm sails, we'll ride it out as best we can. No use in trying to force our way to Seity. It'll still be there in the morning." He turned away from the sloop. "At least, I hope it will be."

* * *

ONCE THE MILD STORM PASSED, the *Deceit* sailed through the night and into the afternoon of the following day. They were behind schedule, but Reis was grateful for it. Maybe once they got there, Rosalie's brothers would have a plan in place. But the hope didn't settle his nerves. The future was cloudier than the day before. Reis would prefer sailing an endless storm over whatever he was about to come across on land.

Under a clear sky, Reis took a moment to stand at the helm. He sighed and took in the sight of his beautiful ship as she sailed into the bay.

"Captain, we're preparing to drop anchor," Kennedy said at the top of the stairs. "Is everything alright?"

"Just giving her one last look," Reis said, surveying the main deck and rigs. "Can't believe I'm going back on land. Willingly too."

His quartermaster looked uneasy. "I know you want to make Braxton proud by upholding his loyalty. But even he knew when a battle wasn't winnable."

"It's not about the odds," Reis said. He was standing in

front of the unknown, staring it down in hopes he wouldn't appear afraid. But truthfully, he was terrified of losing everything, especially the ones he cared about most. To his dismay, the list of people had gotten longer in the past month.

"Do you think he'd go to Avorae to find Lady Weller?" Kennedy asked.

"I think Braxton would set this ship ablaze if it meant saving one of his allies. He died fighting for us, not for the ship."

"I know, but I'm afraid what is happening here is not aligned with Braxton's beliefs. Captain, the nobility are fighting for land," Kennedy reminded him.

"Maybe. Maybe it's more than that. Far be it from me to understand the goal of a lord or lady." He paused and side-eyed Kennedy. "You're still following me into battle, aren't you?"

"Aye, I suppose I am."

Reis stood square in front of his quartermaster. "But if I don't return, you lot will need a new captain."

"And who would you suggest?"

"I'd give her to you, but you'd never agree to that."

"I'm more suited for the position I have now," Kennedy said without a lick of hesitation.

Reis snorted, always amazed at how content the man was with the status quo. For a pirate, Kennedy was fond of a routine. "Then I say you put it to a vote. I think they'll be able to find the best man for the job."

Kennedy didn't appear amused. "I have a bad feeling that this isn't the last of Seity's troubles."

Reis watched Rosalie step back out of the cabin. "Aye, I don't think it is. If need be, tell the crew what I've said about a new captain." He ended the conversation before Kennedy could voice more of his concerns. "But I warn you, Kennedy, they're probably going to vote you into the position."

"Captain…"

"You think I wanted to be in charge? You remember how sick I was with panic." Reis shook his head and began downstairs. "A good leader doesn't want to be a leader, but the people usually insist upon it." He took a deep breath and rested his hand on the hilt of his cutlass, his fingers curled over Naomi's name.

He felt Braxton's presence next to him and imagined a proud smile peeking out through his bushy beard.

"Right!" Reis shouted to his crew. "Silence Weller is in danger. The Duranes intend to murder anyone who gets in their way just like they murdered Braxton. We owe it to our lost captain to avenge his death and protect the ones he swore loyalty to. If you have an issue with that, I suggest you jump ship now. From here on, we risk our lives to save Lady Weller, understood?" he barked. "It'll be dangerous, and it'll get ugly, but those aboard the *Deceit* don't back down from a fight."

"Aye, Captain!" they all responded.

"You'll be surrounded by soldiers and nobility, but you don't answer to them; you answer to me. That said, don't start any fights with these men or I'll tie a weight to your ankle and drop you in the ocean."

"Reis," Rosalie chided behind him.

He sighed. "Fine, but you'll clean this ship top to bottom. And I'll leave you with Lady Yorke so she can scold your ear off. That's probably a worse punishment."

"I heard that!"

Reis grinned. He was preparing for the fight for his life, but Rosalie would remain his most suitable adversary. Never before had he had a foe get under his skin the way she did. But that's where he wanted her to stay, nestled next to his heart.

CHAPTER 53- THE LADY

January 17ʰ, 1840

> *I woke up to hear Eldon talking. It was as if he was speaking in code. Silence needs to escape. I fear he found out about her. I do not know if Anselm will*

* * *

THE MOUNTAIN RANGE loomed over the cove by the time Rosalie had finished the abrupt end to Constance's diary. It saddened Rosalie to arrive at the place Constance had longed to return to.

The Eastern Hills.

Some of the mountain peaks reached far up into the sky until they were concealed by clouds. Like the ocean, the mountains made Rosalie feel small. How could someone so small go up against giants? She was no match for the men who stomped over Seity, destroying everything in their paths.

Still, she wasn't alone.

Reis held out a hand to help Rosalie step out of the dinghy they'd used to reach the shore.

"Are you acting like a gentleman for my sake or to impress my brothers?" she teased. Her stomach was in knots, and she was desperate for the distraction Reis had always provided her.

"Haven't I already proved myself to be courteous?" As if to poke fun at her, he offered his arm in a dramatic fashion.

"Courteous, maybe. Perhaps I'm finally rubbing off on you." She rested her hand on his arm, letting him escort her up the beach.

Up ahead, a large encampment was starting to grow. For the first time since the beginning of Seity's history, flags of the Northern Front and the Western Cliffs flew side by side.

It might've been a good omen. Or perhaps it was one final stand where the Yorkes and Gunns would be defeated together.

"Hmm," Reis said. "I'll rue the day I ever become an aristocrat. In fact, I think it's the opposite. You've taken well to the pirate life."

"Quite a sharp turn from what you believed when we met."

"First impressions are tough. Trust me, I know."

Rosalie snorted. "As if you haven't crafted your identity, Captain Crowe."

"And you, Rosalie Yorke, First of Her Name, Lady of the Western Cliffs?"

She rolled her eyes, about to return a quip, when a cavalry of men passed by on horses. It was a harsh reminder of where they were—on the cusp of succeeding or failing.

"Be honest, how likely do you think it is that we'll win?" she asked in a hushed voice.

"I'm not one to try to judge the odds before a battle.

There are a lot of different factors. But I won't let anything happen to you."

Her lips parted as she gazed up at him. "I can't believe it; you're admitting that you *like* having me around."

He snorted, but his expression remained affectionate. "Maybe I'm just worried your brothers will have my head if I let you get hurt."

"Interesting, Captain, you've seemed to change your tune entirely about me."

He tugged her closer to his side. "If I admit I like having you around, you'll never let me hear the end of it."

"Maybe, but that's the fun of it." Rosalie caught the smile he tried to hide from view.

* * *

To see both of Rosalie's brothers in the same place was a miracle. After all the close calls they'd had, it was a wonder the three of them were still alive.

"Why didn't you return on one of Father's ships?" Emerson looked over his sister's shoulder at the *Deceit* anchored in the bay. "And what is the pirate doing here?"

"I see you're starting to warm up to me," Reis said.

Emerson glared at him with scorn.

"Something happened to Father," Rosalie interjected.

Emery stepped forward in alarm, but their older brother maintained his composure. "Not out here," Emerson muttered, and gestured for her to follow. When Reis trailed after them, he scowled. "Not you, *pirate*."

Reis looked ready to dish out a retort, but Rosalie squeezed his arm. He let out a short huff and pursed his lips. She smiled and stepped away from him. Before she could, however, Reis took her hand. Like a gentleman, he bent his head to kiss her knuckles. As his lips brushed her skin, he looked up and winked at her.

Rosalie heard Emerson muttering something unpleasant, but she was too faint with adoration to care.

Just like that, Reis gently dropped her hand and headed back toward Kennedy and the others.

An uncomfortable pause lingered between the Yorke siblings until Emery blurted out, "What in the world did you do to make a pirate so amenable, Rose?"

"Enough," Emerson snapped, and gestured to them both. "Come with me."

Rosalie stayed between her two brothers, trying to hide her blush as they walked through the military encampment. Western soldiers stopped and bowed their heads as they passed. Northern soldiers stopped to let them by, but their bows were reserved for Jonas.

"What happened to Father? Was he there when you arrived?" Emerson asked. He led them to a large tent and held the flap open for Rosalie.

Inside was a round table with a detailed map of Seity laid out. Emery pulled out a chair for Rosalie, but she declined.

"I saw him when I arrived," she confirmed. "I don't know for sure what happened, but I think Southern spies have infiltrated the manor. Someone broke in and tried to attack me. After that, I went to find Father, but he was gone. Everyone was gone except for the men trying to find me."

"So, the West has fallen?" Emery whispered, his face going pale.

"No," Emerson said curtly. "Not while we're still alive. Wherever the Duranes are keeping Silence, Father is no doubt there too."

"They're in Avorae," Rosalie added.

"That's just north of here," Emerson replied. As an

obedient soldier, he did not complain when more weight was added to his burden.

"What's our plan?" Emery asked. "We've never fought in the East. The Duranes have; we're at a disadvantage."

Emerson shook his head and squared his shoulders. "I've done enough reading about Avorae to know some of the terrain. So, I have a few strategies in mind. A tunnel system runs under the city. It connects to the mining tunnels in the mountains. But for now, we have to unite our forces with the North's. That's our first obstacle." Without another word, he went to leave.

"Wait," Rosalie called after him. "Did either of you know about Mother?"

Emerson turned to face her. Emery furrowed his brow. "Mother?" the middle Yorke asked. "What about her?"

Rosalie took Emelia's letter out of her skirt pocket. "I found this."

Emerson took the paper from her hand and began to read. The further he got, the more hurt shone through his green eyes. His strength cracked and he swallowed. "What does this mean?"

All her life Rosalie had relied on her brothers and Silence for information. She hadn't known how hard it was to be the one with answers. "Reis told me that Cardins were once advisors to the Wellers ages ago. They possess a certain power...I can't say for sure how it works. All I know is, it's the only way Silence would be able to harm the Duranes. Constance wrote about it in her diary."

"Em, is that true?" Emery asked in disbelief. "We inherited some magical gift from Mother?"

"I don't know." Emerson's words lashed out as a tinge of fear disrupted his stoic expression. He swallowed and softened his voice. "I don't know. But I don't want to discuss this right now."

Rosalie went to protest, but her eldest brother had already slipped out of the tent. She looked to Emery, who just shrugged.

"I guess we won't know until we try," he answered her unsaid question.

"But that means I have to be the one to find Silence. You two will be busy leading our forces."

Her brother hesitated. "We'll talk about it more later."

"Yeah, it's always later," Rosalie mumbled as she followed him outside. She wondered when the men in her family were going to stop dismissing her.

* * *

ROSALIE RECALLED a time when she would have jumped at the chance to sit in on an important meeting to prove her usefulness. Yet after everything, the desire became stale. Sitting in a stuffy tent, staring at a map on the table, was making her itch. Maybe Reis had made more of an impact on her than she anticipated. Her heart urged her to storm Avorae, blade in hand, but she had to stay put for now.

Unfortunately, she was sitting at a table surrounded by men. She felt both uneasy and annoyed that she was the only woman in sight. But she was ready to show her peers just exactly who they were dealing with.

"I appreciate your willingness to be here," Emerson addressed Jonas Gunn. "It seems we've finally found common ground so long after our fathers entered this war. It's never too late to rekindle peace. I'd like to take the time to extend my condolences for any losses you suffered in the war."

The same Northern advisor Rosalie had met in Ciern sat next to Jonas. He bore a stony expression. "Your family has yet to apologize for the death of Lord Abram Gunn."

Rosalie tried not to sink in her seat. She was center stage at the head of the table with her brothers, and the scrutiny was making her sweat. The three of them faced Jonas Gunn on the opposite end of the table. To the right sat Reis and Kennedy—the unofficial pirate ambassadors. To the left was a mixture of high-ranking military officers from both the North and West.

"Again, I can offer my condolences, but we have no definitive answer to what happened to your father that day. My family will not take any blame for an unfortunate death we did not inflict," Emerson said.

The advisor scoffed. "You Yorkes are so proud even when you know you're in the wrong."

"No proof exists as to who the culprit was. All three armies were present at the battle in question." He looked at Jonas. "We were both boys when it happened. I think for both our sakes we can look past this."

Jonas looked at all three of the Yorke siblings. "It's true, we all inherited this war. I would like to see an end to it. But our families have been distrustful of each other for generations. Bad blood is hard to wash out."

Rosalie's attention was drawn to Reis, who rolled his eyes. She willed him not to speak, but it was too late—his mouth was already open. "Is this common with Seity folk?" The pirate tilted back in his chair, looking bored. "Dancing around your grudges? At least Lady Yorke has the decency to voice her opinions."

Emerson stared daggers at the pirate. "Our men have been at war for years; I would not call that dancing around our grudges."

Reis didn't look shaken by the confrontation. "You're all so happy to have your long meetings. Constance Weller was imprisoned for nearly two years before she was killed. And no one in your families attempted to rescue her. My former captain was there to witness the chaos. He saw the nightmare that Easterners faced in the aftermath. I've known plenty of refugees; they're still out there if you care. Your families were so eager to start a war, but why? Were your fathers truly heartbroken over the loss of the Wellers, or did they just want an excuse to shed blood?"

The table went quiet for a moment. Rosalie knew Basil had always touted that they were saviors of the war. The Yorkes protected the innocent and avenged the victims. But they had not helped the Wellers. The only aid the Easterners had gotten came from renegades like Braxton.

The Yorkes may not have started the war, but they had thrown gunpowder into the inferno.

To soften the discussion, Rosalie said, "Our mother attempted to help the Wellers before the attack, but it wasn't enough. Had it not been for Edme saving Silence, the Wellers would have been permanently eradicated and we would have no chance."

A hush fell over everyone. Scared she had ruined everything, Rosalie nervously looked at Reis. He gave her a reassuring nod.

Emerson took a deep breath. "Each family has made mistakes. The Duranes have clouded our vision as we've tried to keep our people safe. It has caused rifts and grave errors. But the only way we can mend the past is to ensure the future. My father did not act in time to save Constance. But we are in a position to save her daughter and the Weller bloodline." He touched Rosalie's shoulder as if trying to console her. "We just can't do it alone."

"Either we join forces and fight together, or we die alone," Jonas said. "You have my army's support."

"The *Deceit* will stand aside you as well," Reis added and snuck a small smile to Rosalie.

"Then we're all in agreement," Emerson said. "We leave at dawn."

CHAPTER 54 - THE LADY

By the second day of the journey toward Avorae, Rosalie's nerves got the best of her. Nevertheless, she maintained a calm outer appearance even when her insides felt like the turbulent sea. She tried to focus on the distance they traveled, sometimes even counting every step she took. Each step brought her closer. With every pace, Rosalie mentally spoke to Silence.

I'll be there soon.

They limited the times they stopped so there were fewer opportunities to be spotted. They had walked hours through the night, stopping only for a brief rest before dawn broke. Rosalie had much preferred life on the *Deceit* rather than sleeping in the open air. Every little noise kept her awake. She missed the ship's atmosphere, which had felt like a warm embrace.

"The lake is up ahead." Emerson pointed toward the horizon, where a large lake glittered in the morning sun. "We'll get there by the afternoon."

"Good, I'm in desperate need of a wash." Grime and sweat clung to Rosalie.

"The water will be cold, although I must say I'm impressed by your resiliency. Living on the ocean is tough; I can hardly stand it for more than a week. I would've thought you'd become too accustomed to life at the manor."

She picked at her nails as she dared to be honest. "I actually liked it."

Emerson's lips turned down. "I was afraid you would say that, given you were so keen to return to that ship."

"It was fortunate that Reis offered to help. It just made the most sense to go with him. The *Deceit* is very fast."

Her brother made a faint noise of disbelief. "I appreciate you lying to make me feel better." He gestured ahead of them. "It looks like Emery enjoys the pirate's company as much as you do."

Indeed, Emery appeared enraptured by a story Reis was telling with animated arms. "I wonder which tale he's telling," she said.

"He told me a crow pecked out his eye and that's how he got his nickname and eyepatch. Now I suspect he was spinning a yarn."

Rosalie smiled at the knowledge that Emerson had fallen for the same ploy. "I think he tells a different story to everyone. He has both of his eyes."

"Well, if your pirate captain ever tires of sailing, he could become a celebrated storyteller."

"I don't think he'll ever return to land. At least, not for very long."

The loyalty Reis had to his ship, his crew, and the ocean was something she admired. Loyalty during wartime was so fickle.

* * *

NONE of the maps Rosalie had ever seen did the lake justice. It lay halfway between Belris and Avorae and was so massive the naked eye couldn't see where it ended. Just like the ocean, it stretched on to where the sky met the world.

Reis seemed unimpressed as he sized up the body of water with scrutiny. "It's no ocean, but suppose it's alright."

"I don't know, I could be fooled into thinking it's the ocean."

"No salt." He shook his head. "Means there's no soul to it."

She laughed. "So protective of your beloved ocean."

"When you become accustomed to one thing, you have a hard time adjusting." The wind crossing the plains passed through his dark hair. The sunset cast a warm glow over his usually wintery eyes. He looked at peace, even if they were marching toward their possible demise.

Standing beside him, Rosalie also felt at peace.

Aside from the mountains in the distance, the surrounding land was flat. It was a far cry from the roads in Ciern that snaked up and down cliffsides. The group had charted a course through the emptiest part of the plains. It'd been days since Rosalie had seen any sign of life aside from the occasional burrowing animal and flock of birds.

"It'll be cold tonight. Avorae is almost parallel to the Northern Front." Reis shrugged off his coat and placed it over Rosalie's shoulders. It was heavy but a welcome warmth as the sun descended to hide behind the horizon.

She touched the navy wool and lifted her gaze to his. Everything she wanted to say was on the tip of her tongue.

"Lost in your thoughts?"

"I suppose," she said, and dug her hands into the coat's deep pockets. Her fingers brushed up against the compass that he kept on him. "I haven't sorted through it all yet. Everything has changed in such a short time."

"Tomorrow, it'll be a month exactly. You know, since we

met. Er, or since you left Seity for the first time. *Left* is… perhaps not the right word. But you know what I mean."

Her eyes widened. She hadn't been keeping track of the passing days because some of them had blurred together and others she'd wanted to forget. But she didn't know Reis *had* been keeping track.

He looked a bit sheepish at his admission. "I'm used to keeping track of the date for the ship's log and the moon cycles," he explained with a vague wave to the sky. "Helps anticipate the tides and… Why are you looking at me like that?"

"I'm not doing anything! I could listen to you talk about tides for hours."

He rolled his eyes and adjusted the collar of his shirt. "You're teasing me," he grumbled, and began to walk away from the lake.

"I'm not!" She giggled and stepped lightly to catch up to him. "I promise I'm not."

The two walked through the long grass that led from the lake's edge to the field where the squadron was setting up for a stop. The men chatted around the fire as it flickered to life.

The unusual group of people was something to witness. Pirates mixed with soldiers, and Westerners mixed with Northerners. It'd made for interesting conversation as the three groups attempted to find common ground.

"Which story were you telling Emery?" Rosalie asked. They ambled along, taking their time to return.

"I thought he'd be interested in hearing about a sea monster I saw."

She cocked a skeptical eyebrow. "A sea monster? Are you sure it wasn't just a large fish? Or a whale?"

"Should've seen the size of it, Rosie—you'd agree with me that it was more monster than fish."

"How do you define a monster?"

He shrugged. "Anything unnatural, I suppose. And that thing was a monster; never seen anything like it in my life."

"Are you talking about that sea monster, Captain?" Emery called out once they were close enough to the camp.

"Aye, your sister doesn't believe I saw one."

"I believe you saw something. I just think you're mistaken about what you saw." She lowered to the ground to warm up by the fire.

"Well, there are plenty of shanties about sea monsters. How could so many be fooled?" He posed the question as he settled next to her.

Emery appeared delighted by all the pirate talk. "You've yet to sing us a shanty, Captain."

Reis ran a hand through his hair, a tell he was nervous. "Don't think it's right to sing a shanty on dry land."

"Come now, there's no harm in it. I think it would lift everyone's mood a bit, don't you think?" the middleborn Yorke cajoled.

Rosalie could've argued that they were coping well given the grim circumstances. But she also wanted to hear Reis sing, so she just gave him a smile and a nod.

"Sing the one from Strohis," Upton added to the goading. "The one 'bout the lost sailor."

Reis's face lit up a bit at the mention of the song. "Haven't heard that one in a while. Right, I'll try my best." His eyes jumped from the fire to a few of his crew members, not once landing on Rosalie.

"When I left for the sea, she begged me to stay
My fair-haired maiden, the one from the bay
I told her I'd return a better man
And when I came back, I'd ask for her hand
She feared the only thing I'd find is death and not gold
And alone she'd have to grow old
Who do you fight for, for whom do you die?

If you leave me here, I'll never know why
If you never return, I'll beg and I'll cry
For the ocean to take me where it buried you."

Rosalie listened as he continued to sing. It was softer than when he spoke; the way the words drifted through the air sounded more like a lullaby. Eventually, her eyelids became heavy, and Reis' warmth lulled her to sleep. The words followed her into a dreamless rest.

Who do you fight for, for whom do you die?

* * *

DAYS LATER, Rosalie climbed a small grassy hill to stand next to Emerson. From the vantage point, she could see Avorae across the flat plains. The wall looked heavily damaged from Eldon's first attack decades ago. Now the area was crawling with soldiers wearing gold.

"Do civilians live there?" Rosalie asked.

"No, it's been abandoned since the war started." Emerson lowered his spyglass.

The wind blowing in from the mountains bit at Rosalie's arms. She glanced behind her at the men making camp. It would be their final stop before they attacked.

"Silence will be in the manor; I'm sure of it," Emerson said.

It was difficult to be so close to Silence yet still so far away. "How will I get in to find her?"

"One of the tunnels leads right into the interior of the manor. That will keep you away from the battle. If I had to guess, she's being held in the dungeons while the Duranes organize their troops."

Rosalie didn't want to face the Duranes alone, at least not until she located her father and Silence. The fear was so numbing, her thoughts drifted to another subject, although one that was not much easier to tolerate.

"Why didn't Father ever tell us about Mother?"

"I don't know." Although his voice was softer, his face was still hard to read. It seemed years of being a soldier had taught Emerson to resist the emotions forcing their way to the surface. No doubt it was a method of survival. Through it all, he remained restrained. "I'm sure he had a reason."

"Don't you think we would be better prepared if we knew everything?"

"I suppose in an ideal world it would be great if we had known everything from the start. If Silence had been honest…."

"Do not blame her," Rosalie warned in a fierce voice. "What else was she supposed to do?"

"I don't know, but look where it has landed us! If Father had known, then perhaps *he* would've been better prepared. I don't know why he didn't tell us about Mother. But it doesn't matter, because we know now."

Rosalie knew she didn't want her last conversation with her brother to be one of anger. If something happened to either of them, the guilt would be impossible to wash out. "I never got to meet Mother. You and Emery did. You have memories of what she looked like and how her voice sounded. And this one thing we have from her… how could we have not known?"

Emerson sighed and hugged her close. "I'm sorry. This isn't fair, and if I had the chance, I would bring her back for you. But whatever happens, she's watching over you. She always has been."

Rosalie swallowed her tears and clasped her hands over the talisman.

CHAPTER 55- THE CAPTAIN

"If you're going to get close to the Duranes, you're going to need more than just one blade," Reis said, handing her three small daggers, each of varying sizes. The hour was upon them, and the Western and Northern armies were moving into position. But before Reis went to join his crew alongside the military, he had one more job.

"Do you always have these on you?" Rosalie asked.

"I'd rather be carrying an overabundance of weapons than be caught without one."

She tucked the daggers in her belt next to her cutlass. "I suppose that's reasonable."

"I'm pretty sure Upton has about twenty of these on his person at all times." Reis smiled, but it was hard to keep up even a faux calm appearance. He wanted to pick Rosalie up and carry her as far away as possible from any danger. He didn't want her to be in the vicinity of the Duranes, especially not alone.

Less than an hour earlier, Reis had asked if Emerson or Emery could stand in her place to make the daring mission to find Silence. But Rosalie had told him that idea was already off the table. They'd gone back and forth, bickering with as much vigor as when they'd first met.

Finally, Reis had to admit defeat. Rosalie Yorke never backed down from a challenge.

"Alright." Emery approached the two. "Emerson said the tunnel entrance is a quarter of a mile west of the city. Think you can find it without a map?"

"My navigation skills are as finely tuned on land as they are on sea," Reis answered. "I'll find it."

"Rose, you're sure you want to do this?" Emery asked.

"There's no other way. I'm going to fight to rescue Silence. We'll get Father to safety, and then this will all be over." Her smile wavered, and Reis knew she was trying to stay optimistic for everyone else's sake.

Her brother hugged her close. "Stay safe; I hope the captain has taught you a few fighting moves."

"I'll be okay," she promised as they drew apart.

Emery nodded and nervously gave her a final look before returning to his post.

"You know, it's okay to be afraid," Reis murmured. "If there was ever a time to be afraid, it would be right now."

"I spent a lot of my life being afraid of everything. Yes, I might be afraid now, but I'm not going to let fear continue to stop me from doing what's right."

Reis knew, after everything Rosalie had seen in the outside world, she had every right to hold on to the fears she'd developed while isolated in her family's manor. Nevertheless, it only seemed to have made her stronger.

* * *

THE ENTRANCE WAS FARTHER from the wall than Reis had expected—or maybe time had slowed to grant him a few extra moments with Rosalie. The sounds of the armies grew fainter as they crossed the grassy plain. Eventually, they found a set of stairs dug into a slope in the ground. At the foot of the deteriorating stairs, a flat stone was propped upright against a tomb-like entrance.

Reis grunted as he shifted the stone away from the mouth of the tunnel. Rosalie held up a lantern, but there was no telling how far it went on.

"It looks like no one has been down here in decades," Reis said. The stone walls were covered in moss and cobwebs. "The Duranes must not know about it."

Rosalie stepped into the tunnel and kept the lantern out in front of her. The light could only travel so far into the dark abyss.

"I don't know if this is a good idea." Reis eyed the passage with suspicion. Anything could be lurking beneath the city.

"It's the only way around the battle," she reminded him. "Either I go through it or under it."

Reis's heart ached when her green eyes met his. He feared it would be the last time he ever saw her. It tore him up that their paths were diverging away from each other again. He could only hope they would cross once more. "You'll be careful?"

"Always." She smiled as if to ease his pain.

"I know I can't stop you from being reckless."

"I guess not."

He sighed and fought the urge to stay with her. The desire to whisk her back to the *Deceit* was strong. But he knew she would never leave Silence. And he knew it was his duty to fight until the end just as Braxton had done.

Rosalie touched his cheek and lifted onto her toes to kiss him. When she went to draw away, Reis wrapped his hand around her wrist. His forehead was wrinkled in pain as he looked down at her hand.

"I was so wrong about you," he whispered.

"I was wrong about you too."

He chuckled, never thinking he would admit to Rosalie Yorke that he'd been wrong.

She smiled and stepped away. "I'll see you soon, okay?"

Reis reluctantly let his fingers go limp, and she ventured into the tunnel. He watched the light of her lantern travel farther and farther. He closed his eyes for a second, and when he opened them, Rosalie's light had disappeared.

CHAPTER 56 - THE LADY

Only a small halo of light protected Rosalie in the tunnel. Every so often, water would drip from the ceilings; the echoing noise made her jump each time.

Emerson had warned her that the tunnel system under Avorae was a labyrinth. Soon enough the path forked in two directions. Rosalie pulled out one of the daggers Reis had given her and carved an X into the wall.

Taking a gamble, she chose to follow the left path first. Several times she had to retrace her steps when she reached dead ends, caved in paths, or doors that led back outside.

Rosalie thought about everyone she had left behind, all the ones risking their lives for the future of Seity. She thought about Silence and Constance. She thought about her mother doing everything she could to protect the Wellers.

Emerson's words echoed in her head. Emelia was somewhere out there watching over her sons and daughter. Rosalie wasn't alone, and she would continue fighting for what was right just like her mother had.

Rosalie didn't know how long it took her to traverse the maze of tunnels. Every second felt like an eternity. Her anxious thoughts crowded the space, making it seem less quiet belowground.

Eventually, she found a set of stairs at the end of a path. Some parts of the wood were rotting, so she had to be careful where she stepped. The wood bowed underneath her, and she held her breath while she continued to climb.

She reached the top and found a door with light filtering through the cracks. Holding her breath, she pressed her ear to the door. It was quiet on the other side. Slowly, she pushed it open and peeked through the small gap to see a stretch of red carpet. To her excitement, she found herself deep in the heart of the Weller manor. Inside, it was eerily still, but the sounds of battle could be faintly heard through the thick walls.

Rosalie had never felt so frightened by daylight. For once, she preferred darkness as she inched her way down the corridor. The manor felt like a crypt, housing the traces of the family who had once lived there. Splintered pieces of furniture were strewn about in the hall, the windows were broken, and dried blood stained the floor.

Silence and Rosalie's father could've been anywhere in the massive manor, and she had very little time before someone caught her sneaking around.

Her usual pain pricked all over, but she pressed on and found the main foyer at the end of the hallway.

The room must have been grand during the Wellers' rule. Its stained glass windows and high ceilings were scant traces of the manor's former glory. But it was dampened by the Duranes' destruction. On one wall hung the singed remnants of a burned tapestry. All that was left were the tines of a deer's antler.

The wide staircase had fallen into disrepair, and a mouse skittered out of one of the holes in the steps. Rosalie made herself small as she reached the second floor.

Several voices floated down the hallway. Stifling a gasp, Rosalie ducked into an open room. Leaving the door ajar, she listened and drew her blade.

"Lord Durane wants us to do another sweep of the first floor."

Rosalie peeked through the crack of the door to see flashes of gold uniforms passing by.

"They haven't gotten past our first line of defenses. Why should we even bother?" another soldier asked.

"Because that's what he has commanded!" the first one snapped. "The tower can remain unguarded for now if no one has breached the manor yet."

Rosalie perked up. Silence and Basil were in the tower then, not the dungeon. Adrenaline muted her anxious thoughts of self-doubt. All she had was tunnel vision, the single goal to get the talisman into Silence's hand.

She had done so much to get to this point. Nothing could stop her now, especially not her fears.

Once the coast was clear, Rosalie stepped back into the hallway. She searched for another set of stairs that might lead to the tower. In a cruel twist of fate, it felt like a game of hide-and-seek from her childhood. She remembered spending all afternoon trying to find Silence in the Yorkes' manor. How innocent they'd been back then, never thinking they would find themselves in the same game where the stakes were death.

"I told you there was no one down there."

Rosalie froze when she heard the same soldiers returning from the foyer. She had to keep them from the tower. She slipped into another room and picked up a broken piece of a chair leg. Holding her breath, she waited for the soldiers to pass by on their way back to the tower. Rosalie stood in the doorway and, with all her might, threw the object in the opposite direction. Ducking behind the door, she heard a window shatter.

"What was that?"

"The manor's been breached," the other one said. "Let's go!"

Footsteps thundered away from her. She exhaled and hurried out of the room. To her relief, she soon found a narrow door leading to a set of spiral stairs.

She pressed a hand against the stone wall, keeping her eyes on the steps. With every movement, she knew she was coming closer to Silence. But that meant she could be drawing closer to the Duranes as well.

The climb seemed endless, but eventually she saw an archway. It appeared to lead to a small library, although it was torn apart like the rest of the manor. What had been a large window on the east-facing wall was now a gaping hole. Only the frame and stray shards of glass were left. Wind from the mountains brushed through the room, ruffling water-stained pages of ruined books. One of the bookcases was sagging from rot, and two armchairs had been pushed over.

At the center of the ruined remnants of the Wellers' legacy stood the three Duranes, surrounded by soldiers lining the round room. Basil Yorke stood next to Eldon.

Silence was nowhere to be found.

"Lady Yorke, come in," Eldon beckoned.

Slowly, Rosalie stepped farther into the room, her eyes fixed on her father. Basil didn't look relieved to see his daughter. He was not looking to be saved. His hands were not bound—not like hers had been when the raiders had kidnapped her.

She had not found her kidnapped father. Her father had found her.

Her breathing became shallow. "Father."

Basil stepped toward her, extending a hand. Not to embrace her, but to receive something. "I know you have the talisman," he said in a cold voice. "Give it to me, and all this can end."

"Those weren't spies at the manor," Rosalie whispered. Unlike the usual tornado of thoughts she had when confronting the truth, her mind felt serene.

For weeks, the puzzle pieces had been scattered in a haze. Now it was all clear. Rosalie could step back and see the full picture in all its terrible detail.

"This is not a conversation." Basil took another step toward her. "Give it to me."

Rosalie tried to retreat to the stairs but ran into a soldier guarding the door. "Who tried to attack me? Who broke into my room while you fled?"

"I told you—"

"Tell me!"

"A loyal soldier," Basil said. His eyes were unforgiving as he glared at her. "Someone who knows his place and doesn't dare question me. Someone who knows what's best for his land and his people."

Rosalie's eyes shifted to Eldon and his sons, who watched on. Lowell had a wicked grin on his face.

"What did he promise you?" she asked.

"That doesn't concern you." Her father held his chin high as he glared down at her. "I am lord, and I make decisions for my people. Without me, the West is nothing."

"They have tried to destroy our home for decades, and you're going to let them?" Her knuckles tightened around the talisman.

"Enough; you sound manic. Give me the talisman." When she didn't budge, he moved closer. "You're defying me? After I took care of you? Be grateful I didn't abandon you. Without me, without my protection, where would you be, Rosalie?"

"I'd be free!" she cried. "You've done nothing but lock me in a box to keep me obedient. You manipulated me into believing my only place in life was trying to win your approval! I crossed this entire country to save my friend, and you want me to give in to *them*? You always told me Yorkes would never bow down to the Duranes!"

She had spent years disappointed in herself. She was never enough. Basil had told her who she was and how her life would end. Wasting away in a cold manor, quietly dying without notice. All she'd been to him was a disgraceful mistake. The girl who had taken his wife from him.

But Silence didn't think she was a mistake. Neither did Emerson or Emery. And Reis… he saw her in a way no one else ever had.

"I don't need you to see my worth," Rosalie said.

"Your worth?" He crowded into her space. Hatred gnarled his words into ugly sounds of spite and resentment. "You murdered my wife, and I still took care of you for eighteen years. You are *worthless*. You were supposed to die the day you were born, yet you refused to perish no matter what I did."

The tower went silent. Rosalie felt an odd sense of acceptance wash over her. It was obvious. No matter how hard it was to face, the truth had revealed itself and she was still standing.

"It was you. All of it. You knew who Silence was this entire time. You were willing to hand her over to Eldon, but you wanted me gone too." She didn't cry, and she didn't yell. "All to keep your power. That's all that ever mattered to you."

Basil was trembling with rage. A man beloved by his people, an infallible entity whose birthright was all the credibility he needed. When his truths were exposed, his anger was palpable.

"I should've seen the kind of man you are. You're only

devoted to yourself." No longer was Rosalie the child scrambling for any shred of attention she could get from him. The ocean current ran through her veins, giving her the strength to stand up to him. "I'm done showing respect to a man who never respected my life to begin with."

Without warning, Basil grabbed her by the throat. The world fell away, and everything faded to oblivion. She struggled to breathe—her vision clouding over—while his fingers crushed her windpipe. Rosalie's body went numb. She didn't feel the hilt of her cutlass in her hand and didn't feel the pressure as the blade dug into Basil's chest and pierced his heart.

CHAPTER 57- THE LADY

asil's hand went slack. Rosalie gasped for air as the world flooded back to her vision. When the spots cleared away, she found herself face-to-face with her father.

"Rosalie…" His eyes were wide with shock, and his face was ashen. With a groan, he fell to his knees.

When Rosalie saw blood blooming across his shirt, she screamed. Her knees buckled, and she staggered back. The cutlass pulled from Basil's chest and slipped from her grip. It sent flecks of blood flying as it clattered to the ground.

"I'm sorry," she sobbed. The words made her bruised throat ache.

Basil reached up as he collapsed. His eyes glazed over, and blood dripped from the corner of his mouth. Through his labored breathing, one word fell from his lips: "Emelia."

Rosalie's body was racked with tremors as Basil went still. No, she didn't want it to end like this.

As her ears stopped ringing, she heard Fineas Durane laughing. "One down, three to go."

Rosalie knelt to pick up her cutlass, but before she could,

a rifle was pointed at her head. Slowly, she straightened her spine, leaving the blade between her and Basil's body. Her hand tightened around the talisman.

"You turned my father against me," she said in a shaky voice.

Eldon didn't look the least bit concerned about Basil Yorke's death. "On the contrary, Lady Yorke, your father came to me. He knew he would never win this war, so he struck a deal. He could have power in that little city he loved so much in exchange for his loyalty. It was a small price to pay; my reward was far greater. He led me right to the missing Weller." He tilted his head to the side and gave Basil's lifeless body a simpering look. "Now it seems our deal is through. No matter, I got what I wanted."

Rosalie's jaw clenched. "You're a monster."

"Am I?" Eldon raised an eyebrow in amusement. "I didn't kill my father, Lady Yorke. Duranes do not kill their own."

Her body was hot with anger. "Where is Silence?"

"You'll see her soon enough, but don't expect a touching goodbye. Don't think I don't know who you are, Rosalie Yorke. I know Cardin blood runs through you. Do you think it was a coincidence that traitor midwife brought Silence to your family? Constance Weller directed her to find your mother. In doing so, she brought me right to the source of the last magic in Seity. So many mistakes." He clicked his tongue in disappointment.

"You won't win." Rosalie's voice wavered. Tears streamed down her cheeks, and she did everything in her power to forget what she'd just done.

"Friendship is a foolish venture, Lady Yorke," Eldon said. "This is not your fight. Your family and the Gunns are a dying breed, just like the Wellers were. Your father was smart enough to surrender. I'm afraid you and your brothers have not yet learned."

Rosalie held her ground even as she trembled. "When I was born, my father believed I would succumb before the sun rose. But I'm still here. You've been thwarted at every turn. You have failed time and time again. You will fail today too."

"I think you'll find that I've already won."

Rosalie could hear the battle outside getting louder. It was coming closer, and she knew time was running out. "You talk about building a country in your family's design. But all you do is destroy. Anselm might still be alive if not for your hunger for power."

"His death was because of that Weller," he spat. "Your friend is lucky she was born with such powerful magic. Had she possessed a lesser power, she would not be alive. She would've quietly been snuffed out in the night while she slept."

Anger pierced through Rosalie. But she felt helpless with the guns aimed at her.

"Don't look too upset, Lady Yorke. Be happy that I'll keep her alive to subdue anyone who would challenge me." He tilted his head with a patronizing sigh. "Though I can't say she'll be pleased. You talk about the destruction I caused? It will be nothing compared to the chaos she'll unleash. You might think Durane blood makes one a monster, but the world will see it's Weller blood that ruins. After she destroys this city and everyone nearby, she can reconsider her Eastern pride."

Rosalie desperately wanted to comfort Silence, wherever she was. Hope was fading quickly, and she again stared down the dark abyss of impending death. She had eluded it for so long, pulling out of its cold grasp time and time again.

But her luck had run out. There was no victory. The day had been lost. She hadn't found Silence.

Lowell Durane pulled a gun from his side and cocked it as he crossed the floor.

She had nowhere to run to. Trapped on all sides with no weapons on hand, she was helpless prey. She had come so far, but in the end, she wasn't strong enough.

Rosalie only wished she had seen Silence one more time. And Reis. A fresh wave of tears flooded her eyes. She wanted him to hold her just for one second more.

"Looks like you're on your own this time, Lady Yorke," Lowell mocked. "Where are your pirates now, hmm?"

Rosalie squeezed her eyes shut. She prayed Reis was safe and far away.

CHAPTER 58- THE CAPTAIN

Reis couldn't tell if he'd been stabbed or shot. From experience, he knew that being shot was so painful, the mind tricked the body into ignoring the worst of it. Whatever it was, it hadn't hit anything vital because he was still on his feet fighting. When he moved his arm to crack a soldier across the face, he felt a bullet lodged in his shoulder.

Ah, so he had been shot.

Reis had seen plenty of horrors on the ocean, but there was something so barbaric about the battles on land. Perhaps it was stepping over dead bodies or the lack of cannon fire drowning out the screams of the wounded. He wasn't a fan, but he kept fighting, pushing closer to the manor's walls.

Reis knew he'd made a mistake in letting Rosalie go on her own. He couldn't leave her to fend for herself. In his gut, he knew she was in trouble, and he had to get to her.

"Go, Captain! We'll hold them off!" Kennedy shouted when the crew of the *Deceit* charged the manor gate.

Reis gave his quartermaster a nod and ran for the manor. The first soldier he found had made the grave mistake of patrolling the foyer on his own. Reis pushed him into a corner, his cutlass pointed at the man's throat.

"Where are the Duranes?" he demanded. He pressed the point of the blade farther into the soldier's skin.

"The tower," the soldier wheezed. "Upstairs."

"Look at that," Reis snarled. "You'll die a hero." He drove the steel through the man's throat and let him drop to the floor. Taking what he'd learned from Braxton about stealth, Reis made his way upstairs. He couldn't move fast enough, hoping with every fiber of his being that he wasn't too late.

As he turned into a doorway, he heard voices from above. Creeping up the spiral stairs, he kept his cutlass drawn.

"Give me the talisman, and my son will grant you a painless death."

Reis had no time to wait for the perfect moment. He burst in through the door, blade drawn. But he was quickly subdued by two soldiers in his blind spot.

"Typical; I should've known the pirate would show up," Lowell scoffed. "Trying to save the day once again? You clearly haven't learned your lesson yet."

To Reis's horror, Lowell was holding a gun to Rosalie's head.

She looked back to Reis. Terror glazed over her green eyes. Her lips moved to speak his name, but no sound came.

Eldon held up a hand to silence his son. "We don't need her anymore. Kill her."

All the thoughts in Reis's head went mute, the way he often operated while in the middle of battle. He had no time for wasteful seconds thinking about consequences or rewards. He had to survive. And he couldn't survive without Rosalie.

Before he could act, Rosalie beat him to it. With a quick motion, she knocked Lowell's arm up. The gun fired wildly into the hole-ridden ceiling. Giving Lowell no chance to recover, Rosalie elbowed him in the sternum and swung around to punch him.

Reis grabbed one of the soldiers' wrists and twisted until it popped. He pushed the rifle away just as it shot a bullet into the floor, inches from his foot. The other soldier was quick to fall when Reis slashed through a tendon in his ankle.

He lunged to his feet and arced his cutlass. Lowell stumbled back, still wheezing from Rosalie's jab. The blade sliced down his thigh. When Reis had pushed the Durane far enough away, he grabbed Rosalie by the waist. He pulled her back, desperate to get her to safety. In the chaos, the talisman fell from her hand.

Fineas Durane sneered and kicked the talisman across the room. It skittered across the floor toward the shattered window. Rosalie pulled away from Reis and threw herself across the room to catch the object before it fell from the tower.

Reis saw Fineas draw his sword. He scrambled to defend Rosalie. Reis pointed his weapon at the Durane's chest, the steel dripping with Lowell's blood.

"Leave them!" Eldon barked at his sons. "We can't delay any longer."

Eldon rushed Fineas toward the door. Lowell limped after them, clutching his bleeding leg.

In the doorway, he turned to give Reis a deadly glare. "Looks like you got away again, pirate rat. But I'll end you one day," Lowell spat and went to follow his brother and father.

Rosalie rose to her feet. She opened her fingers to reveal the talisman in her palm.

That was when Reis noticed someone else was in the room with them, albeit someone who was dead. Someone who bore a striking resemblance to Emerson. "Is that your father?" he asked, still trying to catch his breath.

"Yes," she whispered.

"Did Eldon kill him?" He looked back and was alarmed to see a dark bruise forming above her collarbone. Her fingertips grazed the black-and-blue skin.

"No. I did."

Reis held out a hand to steady her. Out of the corner of his eye, he could see Rosalie's blade on the ground next to Basil, dripping with blood. "I suspect what you learned was bad." He picked up the weapon and wiped it off.

"He planned everything," she said in a distant voice. Tears stained her red cheeks, but she looked numb to the world. "He sold out Silence and had me kidnapped to dispose of me. He was going to cooperate with the Duranes."

It made sense; Reis had never trusted the man. But he didn't want to gloat about being right, nor did they have time to linger on the betrayal.

Rosalie had found her balance on her feet and moved past him, toward the stairs.

"Hey, wait. Rosie, what are you doing?" He tried to reach out to her, staggering a bit around the spiraled steps. But she broke ahead of him and reached the hallway first.

"I have to find Silence."

"Rosalie!" Reis shouted as she started to run.

At the end of the hall, right before the staircase, Rosalie stopped. Reis caught up to her and saw chaos in the foyer.

Silence was being pulled toward the front doors. "I won't surrender to you!" she yelled. "You can't use me!"

Reis remembered how Silence had looked on the Durane's ship before she unleashed her power. The panic in her brown eyes and the way her entire body had trembled, unable to hold back the strong force from within.

"Silence!" Rosalie cried.

Reis watched in horror as Rosalie tipped forward to descend the stairs. Her hand was outstretched toward her friend. He couldn't let Rosalie get any closer. He knew what was coming.

Silence dropped to her knees, and her shoulders hunched.

With his last burst of energy, Reis caught Rosalie by the waist and yanked her back.

Silence's mouth opened.

Reis dropped to the ground, covering Rosalie's body with his own.

The scream shattered every window in the foyer and hallway. Colorful glass shards and pieces of the ceiling rained down on them. A loud crack made Reis look up. The base of a pillar fractured and teetered. He pushed Rosalie to the side and rolled out of the way just in time. The heavy marble crashed into the floor.

The aftershocks subsided, and Reis sat up to see if anything else would fall. Silence and the Duranes had vanished in the chaos. "She's getting stronger."

"That was my last chance!"

He frowned. It was certainly a funny way to thank him for saving her life more than once in a matter of minutes. "She would've killed you if you got any closer."

"No, she wouldn't have!" Her voice was hoarse as she stumbled to her feet. "I have to go after them." She swayed on her feet and her face was pale.

"You need to sit down. Your heart can't take all of this." Reis reached for her, but she slapped his hand away.

"I can't let this all be for nothing," she sobbed. "I killed my father! I did everything to save her!"

The adrenaline was wearing off, and a shooting pain from the bullet pulsed through Reis's shoulder. Defeat started to settle in his bones. He heard the clash of steel and shouts of men outside. He prayed his crew was still okay.

"We did everything we could."

"No." Fresh tears brimmed in her eyes. "Don't you dare give up. I'm not giving up on her."

"You're about to faint; I'm bringing you back to camp. Where is the door to the tunnels?" he asked, and started to make his way to the stairs with her in tow. Silence's power had further destroyed the foyer. Rubble had fallen from the lofty ceiling, and spindly cracks covered the walls. Parts of the staircase had crumbled under the strength of her scream. The marble floor where she knelt was fractured by deep rifts. Reis carefully helped Rosalie down the steps, picking their way around any damaged areas.

Once downstairs, Reis craned his head around a hallway to find the doorway. "Was it down this hall? I'll bring you back to camp, and then I have to—" He glanced over his shoulder to catch a flash of Rosalie's blond hair dashing out the door. "Rosie!" He swore under his breath and ran after her even as his muscles ached in protest.

But when he reached the door, there was no sight of her. All he could see was death and carnage.

CHAPTER 59- THE LADY

Rosalie wedged herself into a small gap between two decaying buildings. She turned over her hands and inspected her limbs for any injuries. But the only thing she saw was her father's blood on her hands.

A breath rattled through her as she crouched down. She clutched her hands to her chest and let out an anguished sob. A fit loomed over her. Her lungs ached, and her vision swam.

Her life had been contorted and directed by an unseen force. All Rosalie could ever do was weather it. A father who had never loved her. An illness that had controlled her from her first breath. A friend torn away from her. And a man whom she feared she would never have.

What did it mean to survive? To breathe another breath? To see another sunrise? Or had she been kept alive for one day when she was needed?

Silence needed her. If Rosalie made it to her, what did tomorrow matter?

Every moment with Reis flooded through her like waves crashing onto a ship's deck before draining through the scuppers. Ebbing and flowing, punching another hole through her heart. She didn't want to give up tomorrow if there was a sliver of a chance she could spend it with him.

But unless the Duranes were stopped, tomorrow wouldn't be a promise.

With a wince, Rosalie stood up. She hunched over as her body screamed in pain. *Survive*—she had to keep surviving.

* * *

THE BATTLE HAD SPILLED out past the ruined walls of Avorae. Out on the flat plains, soldiers in gold attacked those in green and blue. Rosalie kept her gaze up so she didn't see the death scattered on the ground around her. She staggered toward the wall, clutching the talisman against her chest.

Taking cover from the fighting, Rosalie spotted Silence. Lowell and Fineas still had a hold of her as they directed her in the battlefield like a weapon. Silence dragged her feet, her face stricken with panic as the two Duranes had to force her along.

Picking her way over the stone rubble, Rosalie kept low. In her addled state, she felt a dark shadow trailing after her. She recognized it as Death. The relentless force that was bound to claim her one day. At one time, she'd been so scared of it. But as she stared across the battlefield, she was at ease.

Exhaling sharply, she stood tall. "You can take me to the other side when I'm done," she promised to Death, then began to run.

"Rosalie!" Emerson appeared out of the fray and grabbed her arm. His sword was drawn and blood was splattered across his face. "Go back to safety!"

"Cover me; I need to get to Silence!"

Her older brother looked conflicted but nodded. The siblings crossed the battlefield together. Emerson shielded her, fending off anyone who came near them.

Rosalie's knuckles were white around the talisman as if she were clinging to a cliff's edge.

"Call a retreat; Silence is going to use her power," she told her brother.

Before Emerson could say anything else, Rosalie pushed ahead. Silence stood atop a small knoll, restrained by the Durane heirs. There was no sight of Eldon.

From yards away, she saw Silence speak, but the words were drowned out by the roaring in Rosalie's ears. The ground rumbled under her feet with each blow the armies struck. But her feet kept moving, undeterred.

She didn't stop, even when Lowell spotted her. He grinned and drew his gun, aiming right at her.

Rosalie didn't hear the gun go off. She didn't see the bullet, but she felt it barely miss her stomach, scraping across her hip. The stinging heat seared her side, but it didn't slow her down; she was no stranger to pain.

"Silence!" she screamed.

It was now or never.

Silence elbowed Fineas in the gut and escaped his grip. She ran the thirty paces toward Rosalie, reaching out her hand.

With the last ounce of life Rosalie had, she lunged forward. She grabbed Silence and pressed the talisman into her palm.

Rosalie felt her friend's fingers close around her hand, and a pause of quiet took over.

Then, like an earthquake, the world shook as Silence screamed. Rosalie ducked her head, waiting for the fallout. But she only felt a light pressure passing by her as Silence's power exploded from all sides.

It was over in seconds. Everything settled, and Rosalie lifted her head. Blinking through the dust, she saw that they stood in a circle of razed earth. It spanned hundreds of yards around them. Everything had been shoved away; the crater was completely devoid of any life except for the two women. Beyond the smoke and dust, Rosalie thought she saw men regrouping, but she could not see any gold uniforms nearby.

Rosalie hesitated to let go of Silence's hand even as her knees buckled. "Sie…" She couldn't believe Silence was there.

Gently, Silence lowered Rosalie to the ground. "Easy. I've got you."

"Look, Sie." Rosalie slowly unfurled her fingers and revealed the wooden talisman.

"Rose… you found it. You found it an-and you came back for me." Silence pulled her close.

"Of course, I did." Rosalie was fading fast as the blood trickled down her side. She slumped in Silence's arms, too tired to keep herself upright. As exhaustion seized control, her heart battered against her ribs.

"Is it over?"

"I don't know." Silence seemed to spot something in the distance. Her lips turned into a deep frown, but she didn't move.

There wasn't enough time to say everything Rosalie wanted to. "Silence, you're not a weapon. You're not a villain; you're a hero."

Silence tucked a piece of Rosalie's hair behind her ear. "It's okay, you can rest. Take deep breaths."

It was getting harder to breathe as Rosalie clung to Silence's shoulders. "I couldn't let them take you again."

"You're here, I'm safe," Silence soothed. "Keep breathing."

Rosalie felt her arms slip away from Silence, and she sagged backward. "I still need to tell him something…"

"Tell who? Rose… Rosalie?"

CHAPTER 60- THE CAPTAIN

"*R*osalie!" Reis's voice was hoarse, and he'd lost all feeling in his arm. In the bloody mess, Reis found Kennedy plunging his blade into a soldier's side.

"Kennedy! Have you seen Rosalie?"

The quartermaster turned. Before he answered, he unsheathed a dagger and threw it. The small blade zipped past Reis's shoulder and lodged into a soldier about to attack from behind. "She went past the wall," he answered.

"Get the others and head back toward camp. This is coming to an end one way or another," Reis warned. He could thank Kennedy for saving his life later.

He fought his way toward the wall. But before he could go any farther, a scream erupted.

Soldiers were flung back like rag dolls, and the ground shuddered. Reis ducked when pieces of the wall began to crumble. His ears felt like they were blocked by cotton; the ringing was now familiar. Disoriented from the noise and blood loss, Reis lifted his head.

He knew where Rosalie was.

He pushed past confused soldiers and blindly moved through the cloud of dust kicked up by the scream.

When the dust settled, Reis found himself at the edge of a shallow crater. He spotted two figures huddled together in the center.

"Rosalie!" he shouted, and ran. His boots skidded across the rocky terrain of the uprooted land.

Silence was sitting up while holding Rosalie's head upright. Reis's heart dropped. Silence looked up when he came near. Her lips moved, but he couldn't tell if she wasn't speaking or if his hearing was still affected by the scream.

Reis dropped to his knees. He was relieved to see Rosalie was at least still breathing. He held her head in his lap, unable to do anything but watch as her body seized in uncontrollable spasms.

"Do something!" he begged Silence.

"She's having a fit." Silence's voice sounded far away. She kept her fingers pressed to the inside of Rosalie's wrist, monitoring her pulse. Her hand shook and tears spilled down her cheeks. "She'll get through it. She always does. She has to… She just has to."

Reis adjusted Rosalie's limp body so she was resting against his chest. "Come on, Rosie, come back to us. Please. Please come back."

CHAPTER 61- THE LADY

"*L*ook how far you've come."

Rosalie wasn't sure if her eyes were open or closed. The pain had vanished; her muscles were still and relaxed. The weight of life disconnected itself from her, freeing her from any feeling.

"When I held you, you were so tiny. Not even the size of a loaf of bread." The woman's laugh was like the sweetest melody. It swirled around, and Rosalie swore she could see the sound illuminated like fireflies. "I was so afraid you would follow me. But look at you. You've done more than just survive."

Rosalie waded through the darkness. She wasn't walking; she couldn't even feel her hands or legs. Maybe she was swimming or floating in the middle of the ocean.

Despite her confusion, one thing remained clear. She knew that voice. She didn't remember hearing it, but it existed in the depths of her heart, carefully kept safe.

"Mother?"

A faint glow neared, and a presence stepped out of the light. Emerson was right: Emelia didn't look so sad in person. She looked as she did when she passed, not much older than Emerson was now. Her pale green eyes were soft as she gazed at Rosalie. Her lips formed into a loving smile. "You did everything you set out to do."

"I know." Rosalie wanted to run and hug her mother, but she was frozen in place. She bobbed in the murky abyss.

"So, is it time for you to rest?"

Rosalie recalled the promise she made to Death before storming the battlefield. "I can't leave Silence. And Reis…" Her voice faded. "I still have more to do. I can't rest now."

"You have the heart of a Cardin. I'm so proud of you." Emelia's voice washed over Rosalie like a warm summer rain. "It's time for you to go back."

Rosalie's heart kicked to life in her chest. Feeling returned to her fingers and toes. Her eyelids fluttered. "Wait!" she cried. "Will I ever see you again?"

But the image of Emelia diminished with the glowing light. Someone grabbed Rosalie around the waist and drew her away from the misty darkness.

CHAPTER 62 - THE LADY

"Rosie?"

She let out a loud gasp and jerked forward. Her hands blindly reached out until she felt someone's arm. A warm hand cradled the back of her head.

"Rosalie, talk to me."

When she heard Reis's voice, she couldn't help the tears that formed in her eyes. Her vision cleared, and she saw both him and Silence hovering over her. Relief crashed into her like a tidal wave. Despite everything, she got to see them again.

"Sorry, I don't think I've ever run that fast before." She mustered a weak smile.

Silence sighed in relief, pressing a hand to her heart. "That was too close. Never do that to me again," she scolded but seemed happy Rosalie was well enough to joke.

Reis pulled Rosalie to his chest. "Thought my own heart was going to give out."

"You can't get rid of me that easily," she murmured.

When the two drew away, Rosalie saw Silence watching in disbelief. "I think I missed a lot. You two are friends now?"

Reis cleared his throat. "Friends? Er... what makes you say that?"

Silence lifted an eyebrow in amusement. It was a weak deflection when his arms were wrapped around Rosalie.

Rosalie could fill Silence in about everything that had happened later. More pressing matters were on hand. "Where did Lowell and Fineas go?"

"I don't know; I didn't see what happened," Reis said. "It was a mess out there."

"I saw them," Silence muttered regretfully. "They escaped, but... they were injured. I don't understand how. I thought I couldn't use my power against them."

"Rosalie has Cardin blood. She's able to block any protection they might have had," Reis explained.

"Rosalie?" Silence gaped in shock. "I didn't know that."

She shrugged wearily. "Neither did I. I found a letter my mother sent to Constance in the diary."

Silence smiled. "Then we really are quite the pair, just like everyone has always said."

"Causing trouble and ending trouble," Rosalie said.

"Pair of troublemakers," Reis agreed. "Right, we should get somewhere safe. I don't like being out in the open." He helped Rosalie up.

She pressed her hand to his shoulder to stay steady. But he hissed in pain. "What is..." When she withdrew her hand, it was coated in blood. "Reis!"

"Yes, thanks for reminding me. I have to get the bullet taken out of my shoulder." He offered a hand to Silence.

"You're hurt?" Rosalie gasped.

"Hurt? No, can't feel it right now. You gave me a good shock, so everything feels a bit numb. Besides, it's not the first time I've been shot, love. Won't kill me."

She huffed in frustration. "Stubborn even as you're bleeding. Honestly, Reis, sometimes I wonder."

He just laughed.

Silence paused and gave them a funny look. "Wait, what did you just call him?"

* * *

THE THREE VENTURED across the battlefield. The fiery wrath of war had been extinguished. An eerie quiet settled in its stead.

From the sky above them, Rosalie heard a bird of prey wailing out.

Tired soldiers slogged back to the camp around them. None of them had come out unharmed. Rosalie glanced over her shoulder and saw soldiers in gold vanishing on the horizon. "They retreated, then."

"Well, they don't stand a chance against Silence anymore," Reis said. "She has the talisman, so they'd be wise not to try again."

But Rosalie knew Duranes didn't fold easily.

When they reached the outskirts of the camp, Jonas was the first familiar face Rosalie spotted. She waved him down. "He needs help; he was shot in his shoulder. The bullet's still in there."

"Looks like you got him here just in time." Jonas ushered over another soldier as they propped Reis up against an artillery wagon. "Tend to Captain Crowe, please."

"Yes, my lord." The young man inspected the wound.

Jonas straightened up and laid eyes on Silence. "Lady Weller, I presume? Lord Gunn." He bowed his head in respect. "I can't tell you how relieved I am to see you safe."

Slightly out of breath, Silence pocketed the talisman. "You can call me Silence."

Lord Gunn looked a little out of sorts as he shook his

head in disbelief. "No, I'm afraid you are well deserving to be addressed by your full title."

Silence smiled slightly. "Well, I guess I have to thank you and the Yorkes for coming to find me."

"Captain!" Ori shouted as he came running over. "Captain, are you okay?"

"I'm alright," he assured the young boy. "How did the crew fare?"

"All accounted for," Ori reported. "Danny got it the worst. Upton carried him on his shoulders all the way back here. Thought we were going to lose him, but he woke up 'bout ten minutes ago."

Reis let out a sigh of relief and let his head fall back. "Best crew on the sea *and* land," he mumbled.

"Lady Yorke, could you apply pressure to the wound?" the soldier requested.

She nodded and knelt beside Reis. She pressed down on the cloth and tried to sort out her flurry of thoughts. They were safe, but it wasn't over. The Duranes had escaped with their lives.

"I'm sorry," Rosalie whispered to Reis.

"Why're you apologizing, love?" He winced as she stemmed the bleeding.

She swallowed and tried to wrangle her guilt before it sent her into another fit. "For bringing you into this awful mess. You wanted so badly to leave and wash your hands of this. And instead, you found yourself in a battle."

"It was an honor to fight," he said. His voice was woozy as the blood loss caught up to him. "But I wanted to make sure I found my way back to you. Glad I did. I'd never forgive myself if I hadn't."

She hushed him softly with a kiss to his forehead. "It's alright; you found me. You're going to be okay."

"Rosalie, you're bleeding!" Silence gasped.

"Huh?" She looked down at her side. "Oh, I think the bullet just grazed me." She untucked her blouse and examined the wound. "I'll just need a bandage."

"Stay here," Silence said, and flagged down another soldier.

"Don't think I've ever seen someone so brave," Reis mumbled with his eyes closed.

Rosalie smiled. "I know. I can't imagine how afraid she was being held by the Duranes this whole time."

"Well, yeah." Reis bobbed his head, and his eyes fluttered in exhaustion. "Silence has survived the Duranes more times than I think anyone else has. But I was talking 'bout you, love."

"Me? I just…" Her voice trailed off. "I just thought about what my mother would do. I felt her watching over me, and I knew I was doing the right thing." She looked down and saw that Reis had dozed off. "You taught me to be brave," she whispered.

* * *

THE AFTERNOON SUN was losing its strength by the time the Duranes' military had fully retreated. The soldier taking care of Reis had told Rosalie the bullet was deeper than expected. So, they would have to dig it out. Rosalie wanted to sit by his side, but the soldier had advised against it.

To her relief, Emerson and Emery returned from the frontlines. They'd been roughed up, and Emery had suffered a bullet wound to the leg. But they were alive, and that was all Rosalie could have hoped for.

Upon seeing them, Emerson had gathered Silence and Rosalie into his arms and hugged them for a long time.

Once the damage was assessed, Emerson and Jonas went to speak in private. Rosalie sat with Silence, telling her everything that happened since they'd been separated. It was difficult to recount the things Rosalie hadn't even fully processed yet. But there were a lot of unanswered questions that Silence needed to know.

"I thought you were going back to Ciern," Silence said, her brown eyes wide with disbelief. "I truly never thought I'd see you again. But some part of me knew that you hadn't given up on me."

Rosalie leaned forward to grab her friend's hands. "I would never give up on you. Silence, I wouldn't rest until I knew you were safe again."

Silence smiled and squeezed Rosalie's hands. "Well, now you can rest. We all can."

"I can't believe what I did," Rosalie said quietly. "I don't understand why my father would do that. I didn't want to kill him."

"I know. I have a hard time believing it myself. I think it's best we just let it be for now. You did what you had to do to protect yourself, and that's all that matters."

But Rosalie knew not everything was solved, even if they wanted to ignore it. "They're still out there."

Silence's eyes went downcast. "They are, but we've proven that they no longer have control. They saw the Western Cliffs and the Northern Front united. If they come after us again, we'll be prepared. I doubt they will make another attempt any time soon."

"I hope so." Rosalie knew the Duranes were frighteningly resilient. But against all odds, Silence had won the day. "Then what happens now?"

"Well, I suppose it's a matter of working out the future of coexistence."

Rosalie looked over her shoulder at Avorae. "You are the heir to this place, Sie."

"Yes, but I don't know what that means yet." Silence stood

up and faced the city with her hands on her hips. "I'd at least like to see more of it."

"Well, you don't need to ask permission."

"It doesn't feel like mine," Silence said. "I wasn't even born here."

"That doesn't change who you are." Rosalie stood up too, feeling a painful tug from the bandaged wound at her side. "Come on—let's see if someone will walk with us back to the manor."

* * *

KENNEDY and a few Western soldiers escorted Rosalie and Silence back to the manor. The group passed through the walls again and traveled down the roads of the city.

After decades of violence and neglect, the buildings were derelict. Some were nothing but piles of debris; others remained upright but showed signs of neglect. The wooden structures sagged from the tolls of nature. Plant life had reclaimed the space. Flowers sprouted from cracks in the road, and ivy wove in and out of windows.

Dead and injured soldiers were still being carried away. Blood stained the cobblestone roads, and abandoned weapons were strewn about.

Rosalie and Silence walked with their arms linked. Silence didn't say anything as she scanned the city her mother had once inhabited. Her hand fidgeted with the talisman, smoothing her thumb over the contours of the wood.

Silence had reclaimed her birthright. But the Eastern Hills was a shell of what it once was. What would she do with an empty city?

"Do you know how many Eastern refugees might still be out there?" Silence asked.

"Hard to tell," Kennedy said. "Most abandoned Seity altogether. Xavier, an old crewmate, was from here. He said a lot of Easterners took to the sea or the Koralia Islands. It's one of the safest places from the Duranes."

"I wonder how many would return now that it's safe," Rosalie mused. But she saw the doubt in Silence's eyes. She wasn't sure how to comfort her friend, even as they came to the manor's entrance.

Now that there was no imminent danger, Rosalie could get a better look at their surroundings. It seemed most of the Wellers' possessions had been ransacked a long time ago.

Silence's arm slipped away as she wandered ahead. She looked around the foyer at all the damage her power had caused. Following a few steps behind, Rosalie remained a little apprehensive. Perhaps it was the atmosphere of sadness that permeated everything.

The two made their way up the rickety stairs, and Silence turned down the hall. She appeared fixated on a door that was ajar at the end of the corridor. "I saw this when Eldon brought me up to the tower. I thought I heard him say something about Taran," she said as they approached.

Silence pushed the door open and gasped.

Rosalie trotted ahead, worried she had stumbled into a gruesome scene. But the room held an amazing secret. "Silence…" she whispered in awe.

Standing before them were the portraits of the last Wellers.

Taran Weller was a gentle-looking man with dark curls cut short and a forgiving gaze. On his arm was his wife, Gwendolyn. Her skin was a deep sable tone, and she had beautiful brown eyes that resembled Silence's. She held herself with confidence and her smile was genuine.

Constance had a separate portrait next to the one of her parents. She had the same color eyes as her mother. Her gaze was sharper, though, and her smile was more playful. She wore her braided hair in a similar style to Silence. Rosalie wondered if Edme had helped Silence recreate the hairstyle.

Slowly, Silence walked closer to the portraits. Her hand reached out to touch the gilded frames. "I always wondered what they looked like. I would have dreams about them, but I could never picture their faces."

"You look so much like your mother."

A few tears slipped down Silence's cheeks. "Could I have a moment?" she asked. "I just have a few things I want to say to them."

"Of course." Rosalie hugged her close before stepping out.

CHAPTER 63- THE CAPTAIN

When Reis came to, his head felt like it was full of fog. The kind that made traversing the ocean nearly impossible. He groaned and tried to rub his eyes, but a dull pain stopped him from lifting his hand.

He grimaced and opened his eyes to find there was still sunlight left in the sky. So, he hadn't been out that long. Unless he'd been unconscious all night.

"Easy, lad." Upton's voice was at his left, but the bosun was just a blob of colors as Reis's eyes were slow to adjust. "This one got you good, aye?" He placed something small in Reis's hand.

He blinked a few times to straighten out his vision. Reis's neck ached as he looked at his palm. Sitting in the center was a warped bullet with traces of blood still on it. He curled his fingers around it and let his head loll to the side. "Where's Rosalie?" he asked.

Ori was hovering behind Upton's shoulder. He looked relieved to see Reis awake again. "She went back to the manor with Silence," he answered.

"What?" Reis sat up in alarm.

"Easy, easy." Upton kept him from getting up too fast. "It's all been cleared; nothing to fuss 'bout. Kennedy went with them."

The wave of panic rippled through him until it ebbed. "Ori," he said in a raspy voice, "go on and round up the crew."

"Aye, Captain." The boy nodded and hurried off.

Reis pinched the bridge of his nose with his uninjured arm. "Upton, have you ever been in love?"

"Eh, only ever had one love. The ocean. She's a testy mistress, ain't she?" The bosun chortled.

"Yeah, I've heard you say that before," Reis muttered. He winced as he sat up and found his arm wrapped to his side in a makeshift sling. He sighed and knew life aboard the *Deceit* would be tough only working with his non-dominant hand.

"You love the Yorke lass, aye?"

"What?" Reis tried to at least look surprised. "That's not— I never said—" He sighed. He was too tired to pretend. "How did you know?" If it was that obvious to the bosun, then everyone around must've known.

"I've seen love in the eyes of others. Like Braxton whenever he went ashore to see his wife."

Reis frowned. "I didn't know you had met her." After six years, he'd thought he had Upton figured out, but it seemed the older bosun still had tricks up his sleeve.

"Aye, Braxton loved her more than life itself. More than the *Deceit* and more than the ocean."

"Then why did he leave her alone for so long?"

Upton shrugged and reached inside his coat pocket to pull out a flask. "Pirating was his life's work. If he was gonna be a pain in Eldon Durane's side, then he was going to be a big pain." He smiled and took a swig. "He didn't think Naomi was suited for the life. But he regretted it when he lost her."

Reis rested his head back and closed his eyes. It was driving him mad that he was so far from the coast. He couldn't even look to the horizon to see the ocean. But he heard it calling to him. "I don't belong here," he said.

"You've done your job here, haven't ya? I think you need a long rest in Ivona; what d'you say?"

He wanted to jump at the idea. He wanted some warmth and peace. So why did he feel so hollow? What was standing in his way?

Someone cleared their throat. Reis opened his eyes to see Emerson a few feet away. The eldest Yorke sported a few cuts and bruises. "Captain, if I could speak with you?" Rosalie's brother asked. "Alone?" He gave Upton a side glance.

Reis jerked his head to tell Upton to leave. The bosun pocketed his flask and stood up. He gave Emerson a half smile and a sloppy salute.

The Yorke eyed Upton as he hobbled away. "You have interesting characters on your crew, Captain," he said, and came closer.

"On the ocean, you get a bit of everything," Reis replied, and grunted as he got to his feet. "Used to be we didn't get any nobility on board, but that's certainly changed."

"It would seem that way." Emerson cleared his throat. "I came to thank you. I heard you kept my sister alive in the manor."

Reis shrugged but winced at the pain in his shoulder. "You know Rosalie—she's resilient beyond anything I've ever seen."

"She's fought every day of her life to survive. However, it seems she's only recognized that in your presence." Before Reis could comment, Emerson continued. "My men found my father's body in the tower. You wouldn't happen to know anything about that, would you?"

Reis's defenses went up. "Look, I didn't do it. But you can't blame Rosalie for it either. Didn't you see the bruise around her throat? Who do you think caused that?" Although it was the truth, he braced himself for Emerson to lash out.

But his face remained impossibly still. "I'm to believe the word of a pirate?"

"You don't have to believe a word I say," Reis said in a prickly voice. "But Rosalie told me that your father planned the whole thing."

"Planned what?"

Reis was still feeling weak from the bullet he took. But he knew the day wouldn't be done until everything was laid to rest. "The kidnapping. He made a deal with the Duranes."

The news didn't seem to surprise Emerson, which was a surprise to Reis. "And he tried to kill Rose?"

"Probably more than once. Can't tell you how many times Rosalie's survived death since our paths crossed. All those funny coincidences make more sense now."

Emerson didn't move a muscle for a long while. "It seems my father had his own agenda in this war."

Reis's defenses broke down piece by piece. It appeared he and Emerson had reached some understanding with each other. It had only taken a few threats of violence, but he was glad for the change.

"I thought all nobility were like him. But after meeting your sister and Silence, I've seen that there are still good people who want to help the innocent. People who aren't driven by greed or lust for power." He was afraid to gauge Emerson's expression but found there was no way to tell what the man was thinking behind such a stoic face. "You might not want advice from a pirate. But now that you're the lord of the Western Cliffs, I'd suggest you *not* follow in your father's footsteps." He cleared his throat. "I mean— I assume you're lord now. Frankly, I don't know how that all works."

Emerson sighed. "When Emery told me you refused the ransom money, I thought he was joking. Never in my life did

I think I'd hear about an honorable rogue. I can't tell if that makes you a good man or a terrible pirate."

"I'm still alive, and I still have my ship. Don't care what that makes me—just glad I have those two things."

Emerson shook his head in amusement. He went to turn away but paused. "I'm curious. Why is the ship named the *Deceit*?"

It was a question Reis was surprised Rosalie had never asked.

"Her original captain was a vice admiral for the Cross Row naval fleet. But Braxton saw the deceit of war. He saw how the lords orchestrated things to their benefit. Behind closed doors, men in power benefit from misery," Reis replied. "The *Deceit* was named so we all might remember that not everything is as it seems on the surface."

The lord of the Western Cliffs looked lost in thought. "Interesting." He gave Reis a respectful nod and turned to leave.

Reis knew it wasn't his place to worry about Seity in the aftermath of the battle. But he wasn't concerned about Emerson becoming mad with power. He'd seen men who were rabid to rule over the masses, and Rosalie's brother didn't seem like the type.

He hoped Emerson would tell Rosalie about the ship's name, because Reis wouldn't get the chance to.

Across the camp, his crew was congregating. They were talking with large gestures, no doubt exchanging battle stories. Danny was on his feet, but he was leaning against a makeshift crutch, and his clothes were drenched in blood. It was a wonder how the boy was alive.

Kennedy appeared next to Reis like a wisp of smoke. "You called for me?"

"We're heading out," Reis said. "See if you can scrounge

up clean clothes for Danny; he'll attract bears wearing that much blood."

"Rosalie is—"

"Where she needs to be," he interrupted. As much as he wanted to stay, Reis knew it was time to move on, and he couldn't muster up the strength to ask Rosalie to come with him. She was safe, and now it was time for him to get back to the only world he understood.

CHAPTER 64- THE LADY

The sunset shone through the broken windows behind Rosalie. Her stomach growled, and her eyes itched with sleep deprivation. Well, one more minute avoiding sleep wouldn't kill her.

She sat at the top of the staircase, waiting for Silence. But Emerson showed first. He passed through the foyer, his eyes looking in all directions. None of them had seen another family's manor before. They'd shared many firsts that day.

"Your pirate is going to be fine," Emerson said from halfway up the stairs. "He's awake; I just spoke to him."

"Good." Rosalie sagged in relief. Now she could sleep.

Emerson sighed as he sat next to her on the step. He clasped his hands between his knees. Part of his palm was wrapped in a bandage.

"I had a few men recover Father's body."

She didn't have enough strength to fight back tears. "Em, I'm sorry. I never wanted things to end that way."

"I know," he said. "I considered asking you for details, but I'm not sure I could stomach it."

"I didn't know what else to do."

Emerson wrapped an arm around her and pulled her close. "You had to protect yourself. You learned the first lesson of war."

"It doesn't make it right." Rosalie pressed her tearstained cheek against his arm.

"Death is seldom the right thing. I've had to kill for our land, but I never felt it was right. Some things are out of our control. I'd like to say Father had grown mad in recent months, but I'd be lying." He paused and cleared his throat.

Rosalie shifted to look up at him. His eyes shone with tears.

"I was there when Mother passed away."

Since Emelia's name was so closely guarded, she hadn't known Emerson was present that night. "I didn't know," she said in a small voice.

"After the midwife said you were breathing, I looked into your cradle." He swallowed as he recounted the story. "Father warned me not to get attached to you. He told me you wouldn't survive the night." A bittersweet smile finally cracked through the stoic expression on his face. "But you survived that night and then another and another. Of course, Emery and I got attached to you. You were a miracle to us— our baby sister who defied the odds." The smile dimmed. "But I could see Father didn't feel the same way. His resentment only grew along with you.

"I know I should've done something sooner, but truthfully, I was just as afraid of him as you and Emery were," he said. "Everyone was afraid of him. I don't know why, but I always believed he would change his mind about you."

She choked out a sob. "Why does it have to be this way?"

"I don't know. All I know is our family will continue on."

* * *

ROSALIE KEPT WAITING FOR SILENCE, but Emerson left. The new lord of the Western Cliffs had a lot to sort out.

As day slipped into night, Silence emerged from the room. Her eyes were red from crying, but she had since composed herself.

"Rose, look what I found." She held a red garment in her arms.

She gasped in surprise as Silence donned the shawl. Rosalie walked over to pat a few flecks of dust away from the crest. The embroidered deer's head was lifted to the sky. "You look just like your mother. The lady of the Eastern Hills."

"Just two ladies now, right?" Silence still seemed nervous about the role she had denied for so long. But she wore it well.

Unfortunately, Rosalie didn't feel the same about herself. After everything that had happened, she feared she would never have a place in her family again.

"You'll fit right in." Rosalie smiled to hide her self-doubt. "Emerson told me the plan. Emery is going to stay here with some of his soldiers to repair the manor. It'll take some work, but people are falling over themselves to help Lady Weller."

Silence's smile wobbled. "Rosalie, I don't know a thing about ruling. I never thought I'd be standing here. I don't know the first thing about anything a lady does."

"Neither do I." Rosalie shrugged. "But Emery will be here to support you in whatever you need. You outrank him, so you make the rules."

"I hope he doesn't expect me to boss him around."

Rosalie linked arms with her friend and strolled outside with her. The city streets were nearly cleared, with a few soldiers surveying the area. As they passed, they stopped to bow their heads to Silence.

"Lady Weller," they said with reverence in their voices.

Silence's eyes were a bit wide. She leaned over to whisper to Rosalie, "Does it ever get easier to be addressed like that?"

"Never." Rosalie reached over to tilt Silence's chin up. "But you must look regal while being addressed."

They both gave each other side glances and burst out laughing. All of Rosalie's hopes had been realized. She and Silence were safe in Seity again.

"And what about you?" Silence asked. "Will you go back to Ciern with Emerson?"

"Oh, I was actually thinking—"

"I hope you don't expect me to fix this place up single-handedly, Sie," Emery interrupted as he walked over to them.

Silence pretended to think, tapping her finger against her chin. "Well, is the lady supposed to roll up her sleeves?"

Emery grinned and jostled her. "She's Lady Weller for a few days and she's already drunk with power."

"For your information—" she batted his hands away, "—I've always been a lady. You just didn't know."

It felt like old times again, and it settled Rosalie's heart. Still, someone was missing. "Emery, did Kennedy go back to check on Reis?" she asked.

"Huh? No, he left with the rest of the crew."

The sudden news slapped the smile off Rosalie's face. "All of them? Where did they go?"

"Reis said they had to get back to the ship."

Silence squeezed Rosalie's arm. "Maybe he'll be back once he knows the *Deceit* is safe."

Rosalie shook her head. "No, I'm sure he wants to be back on the ocean." Her brave face started to slip. "I just wish I could've thanked him for his help."

"I'm sure you'll see him again."

"I'm exhausted," Rosalie said, avoiding the topic before

she let the grief consume her. "I'm going to go back to the camp to get some rest."

"Sie, why don't you show me around inside?" Emery suggested.

Silence gave Rosalie a lingering look. "I'll come find you in a bit," she promised.

"Okay." Rosalie turned to pass through the city. She hardly acknowledged the soldiers greeting her in respect.

Her feet dragged as she crossed the field trampled by the battle. She paused to look up at the night sky. The moon's queen appeared to wink at her as the stars twinkled.

Rosalie's heart ached to see the ocean again, but she knew sometimes it was best to let things go.

CHAPTER 65- THE LADY

The stone floor was unbearable in the morning once winter hit. Rosalie had made the mistake of leaving her slippers on the opposite end of the room. She braced herself as she slipped out of bed and touched her bare feet to the cold floor.

The Weller manor had become cozier in the months since she first moved in with Emery and Silence. But the mountain chill was a force to reckon with.

As Rosalie dressed, she smiled at her own griping. She'd been shot at mere months ago and now she was complaining of cold feet.

She'd found her routine helping Silence grow into her role as lady of the Eastern Hills.

While the city was being rebuilt, the two Yorkes and Silence worked on a plan to inhabit the Eastern Hills again. It was a slow process and a tedious one at that. They corresponded back and forth with Jonas and Emerson about coinciding plans of unification. There were many Eastern refugees in Seity, the Outer Territories, the Koralia Islands, and perhaps further beyond. But they remained in hiding.

Word spread across Seity and the outer lands that Silence Weller had reclaimed her rightful place in Avorae. It was too soon to know how the news would be received.

Rosalie yawned as she wrapped herself in her shawl. To her dismay, she noticed the crest needed mending again. Maybe her time aboard the *Deceit* had been tough on the fabric.

She scolded herself for even thinking about the ship. Those days were behind her.

The wind howled outside as Rosalie shuffled down the hall, still shaking off sleep. Luckily, she felt a warm fire emanating from what was once Taran Weller's study.

Inside, Silence and Emery were already hard at work. They always woke before her.

"Good morning." Rosalie made a beeline for the hearth, warming her hands and the back of her legs.

"I poured you some tea." Silence pointed behind her to the desk.

"It's probably cold now," Emery noted. "You've been asleep for ages."

Rosalie just patted her brother's shoulder as she passed by him. "I'm not sharp in the morning, so I wouldn't be much use anyway." She wrapped her hands around the teacup and inhaled the spiced scent.

"Well, I hope you're sharp now."

"Why? What's on the agenda today?"

Silence held up a couple of envelopes. "We have a new contact who may be able to connect us to Easterners living in the Islands. I've written missives to establish communication."

"Okay. When should we expect them to arrive?"

Emery checked his pocket watch. "Half an hour ago. They're in the foyer waiting."

She frowned. "If they've been waiting, why haven't either of you two gone to welcome them?"

"We were waiting for you to wake up, Your Majesty," Emery quipped.

"Me?" There was nothing Rosalie wouldn't do to help Silence. But talking politics was not her favorite thing to do, and discussing politics with a stranger was even worse. "Can I finish my tea first? I just woke up; it's too early for pleasantries and all that nonsense."

She caught Silence and Emery exchanging a look. But Rosalie couldn't quite tell what they were quietly communicating to each other.

"Go on—they're waiting," her brother prodded.

Rosalie huffed and gulped down the rest of her tea. She grabbed the letters and headed to the door, disgruntled to start her morning this way.

"Wait! Don't you want to fix your hair a bit?" Silence called after her.

Rosalie mindlessly flicked her loose hair over her shoulder. "I might be a lady, but nothing in the job description says I have to look presentable before nine in the morning," she replied and left the room.

Dragging her feet, Rosalie turned at the center of the hall to go downstairs. But before she could take a step, she saw who was waiting in the foyer.

"Thought you were going to sleep all morning," Reis said as he looked up at her.

Time came to a screeching halt. Rosalie blinked a few times, wondering if he was really there or if she was still asleep. "Well, I didn't know you were the one waiting. I didn't think I'd ever see you again."

Reis rubbed the back of his neck. His left arm was free of a sling or bandage, reassuring Rosalie that his injury had healed. "I know. I thought that it would be easier not to say goodbye. But it only made it worse."

She met his gaze and felt her chest tighten. Even after their time apart, he still had a hold on her. "Worse?" She lifted an eyebrow.

"Don't play coy. You have a way about you, Lady Yorke."

She bit her lip and wished she had listened to Silence about fixing her hair. "And what way would that be, Captain Crowe?"

"My crew says I can't get more than a few miles away. No matter what I'll end up back in front of you. But they've always known my penchant for trouble, so they can't be surprised." He stepped closer to the foot of the stairs.

"Trouble?" She feigned offense. "I can't say I've ever brought an ounce of trouble to you."

"Right, because meeting you didn't lead to fighting against the Duranes."

Rosalie walked down to the first landing of the stairs. "Aren't pirates so fond of free will? You could've said no."

He began climbing the steps toward her. "You know as well as I do, I can't say no to those eyes of yours."

Her cheeks flushed red. "Still, you manage to find trouble on your own. You never needed my help."

"That may be, but getting into trouble is far more fun with you." He stopped a few steps below her, so they were almost at eye level with one another.

Rosalie felt overwhelmed with peace to be in his presence again. "So, you've found trouble again."

"Well, thought I would travel down to the Islands. We were meant to go there, but I'll admit we didn't make it very far. I kept changing my mind. Kennedy said my crew would mutiny against me if I didn't go back and see you. They thought it might set my head straight so they can finally get to Ivona."

As if to keep him there for the moment, she interlaced her fingers with his. It seemed inevitable that Reis would slip away again. He was too good to be true, and she worried that good things were fleeting in her life. The pain of being torn apart again was unbearable, but Rosalie would gladly suffer the grief of waiting if it meant she'd see him again one day.

"Right, well, Silence asked if you would bring these to the Islands." She handed him the letters. "We'd be grateful for your help."

He tucked the papers inside his coat. "I'll make sure they arrive safe."

"And after you go to Ivona… will you be back?"

"You know me, love—pirates don't stay in one place for too long."

"Right." She tried to force a polite smile. "Well, now that you've come back for a proper goodbye, I can give you a proper thanks. What you did for Silence and Seity was valiant. Your mother was right to name you after a hero."

"No need to thank me, love. Happy to be of service. The *Deceit* is fond of noble ventures, it seems."

Rosalie knew that if she told him how she truly felt, it would make everything harder. He was right—goodbyes were tough.

"Then I wish you well, Captain," she said. "You're always welcome here. Lady Weller of the Eastern Hills has declared it."

He chuckled. "I wish her luck. Can't say I envy her. I'd never want to take on that responsibility."

She sucked her lower lip between her teeth in thought. Rosalie didn't want to take on the responsibility either.

Reis started to back down the stairs. He didn't turn, his gaze lingering as long as it could. "Take care, Rosie."

She swallowed and exhaled shakily. "You too, Reis." Giving him one last look, she returned to the second floor.

When she turned the corner, she found Silence waiting. "Sorry that took so long. He has the missives and will deliver them."

Her friend nodded toward the stairs. "Go," she urged.

"What?"

"Go with him," Silence said. "I know you don't want to be here; you want to be out there. You want to be with him."

"Don't be silly; I can't go anywhere." Rosalie shook off the suggestion. "I need to stay here with you. If anything happened, you'd need me to—"

Silence held up a finger to stop her. "We're fine here. This isn't forever; you'll be back. But I want you to go with him. Emery and I spoke about it; we'll be okay doing all the boring nobility work."

Rosalie's lower lip quivered, and she hugged her friend. "But I just found you again."

"And you're not losing me again," Silence replied gently, squeezing her tight. "If I need you back here, I'm sure Emerson has men who can find you and that pirate of yours."

Rosalie giggled and touched Silence's cheek. "I'll never be too far," she said. "I'll always come home the second you need me to."

"You're not fooling me," Silence chided. "Your home's out there. Now, go."

Feeling jolted with energy, Rosalie turned and ran down the stairs, skipping the last two steps. She crossed through the repaired foyer and out the manor gates. Outside, soldiers were patrolling Avorae's streets.

The sky clouded over, and snowflakes like wisps of cotton began to fall. Rosalie saw Reis walking down the street with his hands in his pockets. "Reis!" she called out to him.

He turned, and the confusion in his face only lasted a

moment. When she began to run to him, he opened his arms to her.

Overwhelmed with joy, Rosalie jumped into his embrace. She looped her arms around his neck and kissed him.

The snowflakes fluttered around them; the chill in the air was no match for the warmth between them. As Rosalie opened her eyes, she saw the snow catching in his dark hair. "Take me with you."

His eyes lit up and it was clear he was holding back a smile. "Is that an order?"

"Yes—you pirates need a lady to keep you all in line."

He chuckled and ran his fingers through her hair. "Ah, so it has nothing to do with me. You just want to seize my title as captain from me. You're going to stage a mutiny and take my ship."

She laughed. "No, it's because you can't stay away. You said it yourself; you can't get too far from me. And I'd like to ease your poor heartache."

"How kind of you." He wrapped an arm around her waist and continued walking with her. "But I hardly made it out of the city limits before you came running," he reminded her. "So, who can't stay away from whom?"

"Fine." She stuck her tongue out at him. "Let's just agree that we're both at fault here and we both like being with each other."

He grinned. "Agreed."

Rosalie looked back at Avorae and saw Silence up in one of the manor's windows. Her best friend smiled warmly and waved.

For ten years, Silence and Rosalie had done everything together. They were inseparable. Nothing could keep them apart, not even their fiercest enemies. But Rosalie knew their paths would diverge for a brief time. As Silence grew into the inherited role that she'd kept hidden, Rosalie would experience what it meant to be her own person. She could live the life she wanted, not the life she thought she had to live.

And Rosalie looked forward to the day when she and Silence could sit down. Silence would tell all the stories of how she was bringing the Eastern Hills back to its former glory. And Rosalie would tell of her adventures on the high seas.

She looked forward to every second of it.

EPILOGUE

Rosalie breathed in the salty air and felt at home. She watched Seity's coastline fade away. There was no plan to follow, no urgent matter, and no hidden plots. She was free.

Behind her, Reis cleared his throat. She turned and found him holding a dueling saber out to her.

He bowed at the waist. "My lady."

She grinned and took the blade. "At ease, Captain."

He peered up at her with a smirk before drawing his own weapon. "As per the new rules of the ship, the lady has the first move."

She scoffed and rolled her eyes. "You take away all the fun," she protested, but lunged forward.

Reis sidestepped and advanced from her left. In a fluid movement, he grabbed her wrist, spun her around, and looped an arm around her waist.

With her back pressed to his chest, Rosalie giggled. "That's a new strategy."

"Not one I usually use on my enemies. But it's effective. Sorry that I won that round so quickly, love."

"Don't speak too soon, *love*," she warned, and directed his attention to the dagger she held at his side.

He groaned. "I knew it was a mistake to give you more weapons." He released his hold on her.

"I win," she gloated, and pecked his cheek.

His smile softened, and he pressed a hand to the small of her back to pull her close again. He pressed his lips to hers, relinquishing all the hastiness from before when each kiss felt like their last.

When he drew away, Rosalie traced the scar on his cheek. She couldn't help the smile on her face. She wasn't sure when she had ever been so happy.

"Best two out of three, Lady Yorke?"

"Draw your sword, Captain Crowe."

THE ADVENTURE CONTINUES

The Silence of Vengeance, Book Two of The Deceit Trilogy

Coming 2026

ACKNOWLEDGMENTS

I began *The Silence of Deceit* in 2017, shortly after graduating high school. Without the encouragement of so many incredible people, this book never would have seen the light of day. The team that supported this book spans three continents and six countries.

To my mom—who was the first to read this story and who printed out pages to edit while sitting on the beach—thank you for everything you've done for me.

To Maggie—who helped me develop the fantasy elements even though fantasy isn't her thing—thank you for roughing it through my very early drafts and for being the best friend a girl could ask for.

To Karlein—my wonderful critique partner—your edits and support were crucial in helping me reach a place where I could publish.

Thank you to every teacher who encouraged my writing. A special thanks to Dr. Pope, who provided invaluable support throughout my college years. I'll never forget her telling me that a messy family makes for great writing fodder. Oh, how right she was.

A huge thank-you to my professional team: to Sarah, who helped me immensely with plot and character development; to Misha Kydd, who provided excellent copyediting, and to Clem Flanagan, who proofread with a sharp eye.

Thank you to Samantha Sanderson-Marshall for designing a beautiful cover and bringing my ideas to life. And thank you to KhaosBooks for the incredible map, chapter art, and crest graphics. Thank you both for being so precise and attentive to every little detail. I truly could not have pulled this off without these amazing people.

And finally, thank you to Silence Rising, my great-great-grandmother, whose name inspired me to write a story about a girl named Silence.

ABOUT THE AUTHOR

Jillian Eagan reads and writes by the ocean—her greatest source of inspiration. A lifelong Massachusetts resident, she graduated from Emmanuel College with a B.A. in Creative Writing. Her experience with chronic illness has shaped her storytelling and commitment to increasing representation of chronically ill and disabled characters in the Fantasy genre. *The Silence of Deceit* is her debut novel.

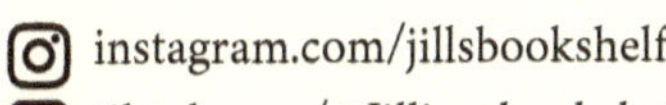

instagram.com/jillsbookshelf
tiktok.com/@Jilliansbookshelf

www.ingramcontent.com/pod-product-compliance
Lightning Source LLC
Chambersburg PA
CBHW050505110726
47899CB00005B/1330